The Woman in the Picture

Viki Wright

Viking

VIKING
Published by the Penguin Group
Viking Penguin Inc., 40 West 23rd Street,
New York, New York 10010, U.S.A.
Penguin Books Ltd, 27 Wrights Lane,
London W8 5TZ, England
Penguin Books Australia Ltd, Ringwood,
Victoria, Australia
Penguin Books Canada Ltd, 2801 John Street,
Markham, Ontario, Canada L3R 1B4
Penguin Books (N.Z.) Ltd, 182–190 Wairau Road,
Auckland 10, New Zealand

Penguin Books Ltd, Registered Offices:
Harmondsworth, Middlesex, England

First published in 1988 by Viking Penguin Inc.
Published simultaneously in Canada

LIBRARY OF CONGRESS CATALOGING IN PUBLICATION DATA
Wright, Viki.
The woman in the picture.
I. Title.
PR9619.3.W73W66 1988   823   87-40429
ISBN 0-670-82215-9

Printed in the United States of America by
Arcata Graphics, Fairfield, Pennsylvania
Set in Garamond No. 3

This is for Denis, Max, Jonathan, and Helen,
who are the most important reasons
in my world.

There is an unmapped and frequently hostile desert territory between the oasis of salaried journalism and the mirage of authorship. I may have dehydrated on the way without the loving encouragement—in different forms—of my friends and relatives, whom I thank with all my heart. For special reasons, known to them, I mention a few here—Werner Geisler, Annabel Frost, Shelley Neller, Jenny Fisher, Lisa Highton, Judith Curr, Louisa Woolley, Hilton Ambler, and Meg Ruley. And Lois Battle, who is Rosemary's godmother.

The Woman in the Picture

One

There were two long mirrors in the fitting room, to show the profiles and rear views of stripped shoppers. Rosemary Quilty was used to looking at her own reflection in ideal circumstances: full front, a faint lift to the eyebrow, an alert, kindly expression, and nothing much from the neck down. It was a look for reassurance, not reality. But here, half out of a tight pair of designer jeans, in the light that glared off the mustard curtains, bits which the rest of the world saw all the time but which were usually secret from herself were revealed without mercy.

She was horrified. The unexpected rear-view chunkiness made her think of grain-fed beef, of sturdy cows lined up at abattoirs. Her bum, which she'd always thought of as pear-shaped, was distinctly apple-ing at the hips. Apple-dumpling-ing, to be exact. Worse than that, the back of the tops of her thighs made her think of her Auntie Gwen, whose visits to Coogee Beach in her pink, black, and green lycra swimsuit would, in an earlier age, have had her arrested for exposure. Auntie Gwen oozed over the edges of deck chairs. She made a mockery of the slimming clinics' claim that inside every fat woman was a thin one trying to get out: there was enough of Auntie Gwen to contain at least one and a half average-sized women or two small ones.

Rosemary, who had always seen herself as thin, or better still, lean, was stricken by the revelation of her own potential.

The Pritikin diet, immediately! And tennis! she told herself. Outside of me there is a fat lady trying to get in!

The plot of her life, which had always seemed like a vivid, sometimes startling, but usually hopeful adventure suddenly, in that booth, seemed to take a sinister turn. She had a presentiment of herself old, waddling, wheezing, probably smelly in hot weather, with too many sweat-filled creases to clean out properly by arms hampered by piggy rolls. A farce her life would be—neither the dramatic, Dostoevskian ending she'd begun considering since accepting the idea of divorce nor the happy, TV-land one on which all her prior-to-separation plans had been based. Those fade-into-the sunset plans had starred herself and Daniel liking each other and not fighting at all, a vigorous, silver-haired couple with secure investments, dab hands at tennis and bridge, and frequent visitors to New York, Kashmir, Port Douglas—they would probably not even die. Now she'd glimpsed a sexless, divorced, shapeless old age, the sort in which death would be boarded with relief, like the last train out of a very small town. Oh, dear, she told herself, not tears again. It'll bugger the mascara, and the sunglasses are in the car.

The jeans were quite wrong. Rosemary had hoped they would make her look fit, a member of the ageless Levi's set, but they accentuated the fact that she was thirty-four. She had felt that thirty-four was quite young until the woman at the employment agency had said, checking the form Rosemary had filled in, "Of course, a woman is washed up at thirty-five. You'll have to knock off a few years to give yourself a chance." And then she'd smiled very brightly, as though she were visiting Rosemary's bedside, and what she had was terminal.

It was then that Rosemary noticed the dress which the previous occupant had abandoned on the fitting room's other hook and almost covered by the courtesy gown. The dress was red. Not the almost orangey-red of arterial blood but that richer colour of the warm, silky trickle which happens when a healthy thumb is cut. The fabric felt alive, its sheen a gleam of energy. "Try me," it said with its sly, knowing shine, and so she did, though it was entirely impractical for any sort of role she could imagine. When she slithered it on, it seemed to make a point of touching her skin on its way down to her hips. Like a miracle, or paint, it turned what she had just seen of her own rear into a smooth, sleek line. She tightened her pelvis as though respecting the dress's wishes.

Its folds, which originated from intricate pleating at the wide shoulders, fell into shapes that seemed designed by nature, like the patterns in petals or the swirls left by retreating flood tides. The front plunged to about the level of her navel. On most people it would not have come quite as close to the navel but with her, because she had fairly small breasts, there was a certain amount of slack in the material and her navel moved into range.

The dress was intended to be worn with nothing on underneath the top because otherwise it would have looked, through the slit, as though she had a bandage around her chest. The feel of it against her forget-me-not nipples, which were usually encased in a softly padded bra, made her remember sexual ecstasy and so she bought it without debate. It seemed like a talisman, a worker of magic, a mysterious symbol of the flowering of a woman who seeks, finds, and holds. Or at least that's what she told herself to justify paying seven hundred and ninety-five dollars for it.

Daniel, in remorse partly sparked by a letter from her solicitor, had sent her a cheque in February for three thousand dollars as a contribution towards the emptiness he had left inside her. She had hung on to the money all the way through the autumn and the winter and through all his increasingly strident hints and messages about the need for budgetary restraint. Like the government, she'd thought, who'd been lavish with promises while courting power but once in had immediately become mean. Daniel had never queried the bills when he was eating what the money bought. That three thousand dollars was hers, she'd decided. It had nothing to do with the children, the housekeeping, or anything else practical—it was there, elastic enough for any personal emergency: a trip, plastic surgery, a funeral. But nothing, until now, had seemed worth having so it was all there, with some fledgling interest.

Rosemary had decided to shop for jeans in response to a fashion spread in a recent weekend paper which had suggested that she—and everyone else for that matter—should add some new leisure gear to her working-woman image. Her working-woman image was still a faint pencil sketch, but there were clear signs that just ahead was the sort of work she'd have to have serious clothes for. So the jeans were intended as a gesture—a symbol of the time when leisure had seemed permissible. They would be something for weekends in her sophisticated future.

It was a sign of Rosemary Quilty's optimism that she could think of herself as a person with a sophisticated future. The more likely reality—and the suburbs were full of evidence of it—was that she would simply remain what Daniel had caused her to be: a discarded woman in a man-run world. For the next eight, ten years at the most—her son, Bobby, was, after all, nearly eleven—she'd have the role of single parent. But he was already showing tendencies to independence and sixteen-year-old Phyl, her daughter, hardly seemed to need her at all anymore. Technically, after Bobby left home, there would be the choice between growing bitter or growing eccentric. Or dull, of course. She'd have to fight like hell!

She sighed. She wished she were beautiful. Beauty was like a magic password to the steps on the ladders of life, in fact those who were beautiful usually started off on a better kind of ladder. She'd observed it often—beautiful women with hardly any brains or charm would be invited on yachts or weekend trips to Hawaii or offered jobs that led to glory. And they'd accept these as their right, and they'd flourish.

People like Rosemary who were merely attractive—and even she had occasionally seen that she was attractive—had no magic password. They had to save for the keys to things, or steal them, or borrow them. She would not have minded doing any of these things, but having started being a career woman about fifteen years later than most, she'd have to climb twice as fast from ground level to catch up. Or she would have to make some sort of aerialist, death-defying leap from the middle rungs of her present ladder-to-nowhere to near the middle of one more promising. Fortunately, she had the energy, and despite what the employment agency woman had said, she felt far from washed up. So she stood and admired the dress and—because of what it did to her—herself. And in that reassuring, three-dimensional reflection she did what she believed was an objective audit of a potential ladder-leaper.

Here was a strong-faced woman whose hair, by nature tentatively tending to the reddish end of brown, had been expensively encouraged to be more positive about it.

Just as she was not quite a redhead, neither did she have quite a redhead's complexion—that top-of-the-milk and ginger-biscuit-crumb-freckles combination with its perennially youthful connotations. Instead, she simply had pale skin. Neither strikingly good nor strikingly bad. Just pale.

She had a straight nose and a nice, roundish sort of chin, though her jaw was square, and there was a certain angularity about the part of it where it met with her ears which made her avoid family snapshots in profile. Her teeth caused her no embarrassment.

The best thing about her face was her eyes—large, grey, round, and serious. Her irises were printed in scribble patterns in dozens of shades of shining grey, with black, white, and yellow flecks in the mosaic. People often commented on them. And though her lashes were naturally pale, that was easily fixed.

The thing that had made Rosemary the most angry with the beauty fairy who had attended her birth was that her eyes were terribly short sighted. She had been a teenager with gingery hair, thick glasses, bands on her teeth, and no boobs, and the scars to her psyche still lingered, never having been banished, as her mother had promised they would be, by a sudden change from ugly ducking to swan. She had simply changed from ugly duckling to attractive, and that had involved a lot of hard work plus getting used to contact lenses.

So there she was. Rosemary Quilty, ladder-leaper-to-be. A person who believed that if things appeared to be right and good they probably were.

One thing that she liked about herself was her name, which suited her both in its Shakespearean and in its culinary sense. It also secretly made her think she was two people—Rose, an energetic, sexy person and Mary, who would have been more suited to conditions a hundred years ago. Mary spent a lot of time trying to keep Rose from saying and doing things that would get her into trouble. Fortunately, she didn't always win, so Rosemary's life was not dull. She had never told anyone, not even Lucy, her best friend, about this theory of her divided self. Quite enough people, Lucy included, had been looking at her oddly lately.

In her assessment, Rosemary added something else on the redeeming side, something that had surprised and pleased her a year ago, before the long, separated time in which there had been few signs of redemption.

A year ago the communications course she'd been doing at the Institute had had a Students' Work Assignment Display Day, and it was while standing with Daniel, Phyl, and Bobby, looking at herself on closed-circuit colour TV presenting a program that she'd written and devised—and got a credit mark for—that she realised how much of her attractiveness was due to the alert, chin up way she sat, as though prepared for anything: dancing, for example, or child-bearing, or tyre-changing, or fun. It was a definite plus. Bobby, who used to like her in those days before his father left her, had seen it, too.

"Some people's mothers look like sacks," he'd said, standing close enough for his shoulder to touch her arm.

Standing in her underwear in the boutique's yellow-curtained fitting room, surrounded by the limit of four pairs of jeans to try on, Rosemary felt tentative, as stiff and vulnerable as a hyacinth's pale shoot and just as full of promise. It was the first time in nine months that she'd felt this way. The coating of grief which, a few months ago, had seemed to settle permanently onto her life was now beginning to peel off like crisp skin. She checked on the last of the little scabs around her throat, chest, and underarms that a dermatologist had caused the previous week when, using an instrument whose red-hot wire made her think of torture, he'd burned off, one by one, an array of stringy moles that had emerged during the winter. It had been less painful than its sizzling sounds suggested, but the barbecue smell had made her fight not to throw up.

It's worth it, she'd encouraged herself. When I meet someone worthwhile I won't be anxious to have the lights off first.

Her skin looked smooth again. Only a blind friend or a very critical lover would have been able to detect the stumps of those first deposits of old age which, with luck, would not now reappear until she was ready—at, maybe, seventy-five.

She had bought the dress in Double Bay on the city's east side and so, to get home to her house in the northern suburbs, she'd had to go through the city and cross the Harbour Bridge—something she tended to avoid, having never been a bold driver. She had achieved motherhood before a driving licence and was still inclined to travel as though someone fragile was loosely confined in a carry-cot on the back seat. But she had been for a job interview at nearby Edgecliff and the opportunity of swanning around Knox, Cross and Bay Streets like a regular Double Bay shopper had been too good to miss. Besides she'd felt in need of a bit of pampering, considering the way the interview had gone.

Mr. Gillespie of Gillespie Computer and Business Services had kept her waiting twenty minutes while making a series of loud-enough calls from the next office. One was to someone called Derek about a freezer for his old man. It seemed that Derek wasn't in that line anymore but, far from deterring Mr. Gillespie, the obvious lack of enthusiasm at the other end of the phone line had made him more determined. To Rosemary the conversation was a series of increasingly shorter silences while Derek talked, punctuated by Mr. Gillespie saying "Yes, but, listen, mate, you owe me, right?" Finally he'd worn Derek down to some agreement.

Then, even though he knew Rosemary was waiting, he'd started another phone call and switched his line of repetitive stubborness to someone called Mack, who appeared to be his accountant and who appeared to be reluctant to agree to some deal involving a Saab Turbo that Mr. Gillespie thought would be a good tax-reduction scheme. This phone call had ended on a threatening note—the accountant was advised to pull his head in.

Then he'd spoken to someone called Honey Lamb, who'd also seemed reluctant to part with goods and services Mr. Gillespie felt were his due. With Honey Lamb he was less successful than with the other two, evidenced by the fact that he slammed the phone down.

The employment agency woman had made the job sound good, even glamorous. Rosemary would be her own boss in an air-conditioned office, parking no problem, though of course it was right on the train, doing word-processing and data processing functions for nearby offices and meeting interesting people. And the money was particularly good since it was a bit out of the city. But Mr. Gillespie's chats had given Rosemary enough time to look around the brown-and-orange reception cubby-hole with its two cane chairs and one cane table piled with copies of very old *Business Review Weekly* and computer magazines and a dying variegated philodendron and to decide that the extra money probably would not be worth it. So when Mr. Gillespie, a thin-haired man not much older than she, had finally brought his light-grey-suited, pale-green-shirted self in to interview her, she didn't mind the look of disappointment that he'd displayed as immodestly as a flasher.

"You're here for the job," he said, cleaning a nail on his left hand with a nail on his right. "They said you were a beginner."

"I am," said Rosemary with a curious surge of anger. "A beginner at computers but not at office routines. Or life."

"Yes, well," Mr. Gillespie said, switching to a different nail, "the job's taken." And then he'd walked away, too quickly for her to mention the Anti-Discrimination Board or the Equal Opportunities Tribunal, even if she'd thought of it.

Even though she hadn't wanted the job, she had felt depressed about not having been interviewed, never mind offered it. It would have been the first job interview of her life, and she'd been rehearsing for it. So she had driven to Double Bay for the solace of merchandise, and the red dress had been a miracle cure.

On the way home in the car, the dress in its froth of tissue on the seat beside her, she switched on the radio, hoping for some Vivaldi which would have matched her now-buoyant mood. But all she found was news on every station. All the announcers had in common the fact that they told what they told in cheerful, up-lilting voices, as though hinting at happy endings. But she knew, whipping past more new allegations of police corruption and large parcels of money handed over to senior officers and the lack of progress in investigations into a mysterious death, that there would be no happy endings on the news. She wished her tape deck was working.

Having negotiated the merging lanes onto the bridge, worked her way into the correct lane for her exit, and then managed that without incident, she began to relax in the familiar territory of the upper north shore—invariably described as "leafy" in the real estate brochures.

She had just stopped at a traffic light on the main arterial road nearest the expensive, tree-lined suburb where she lived and was humming, drumming her fingers on the wheel, when she saw a large cat, moving in a swift, low-crouching blur, arrive into the front of the nearest garden, with a large green-, blue-, and scarlet-feathered bird in its mouth. Instantly she flung the gear-shift into park and, with the engine still running, raced through the gate, across the garden and after the cat, to the sound of three indignantly wailing horns of the cars behind hers, now forced to miss the green light.

She could never have stopped the cat if a middle-aged woman had not emerged from the house at the same time, intent on the same purpose. When the cat saw itself outflanked it dropped the dead-looking bird and fled.

"I'll put poison down!" the woman said angrily. "It's the second this week! Takes them at my bird feeder in the back."

Rosemary was more concerned with the victim than the murderer. It lay like an exploded patch of rainbow on the lawn, the wrinkled blue membranes around its eyes piteously closed, like lids. But when she touched it with a gentle finger it fluttered to its feet, and, dragging an obviously injured wing, very quickly disappeared into the darkness under a Diosma bush.

The hooting of those cars still stuck behind hers made her start moving reluctantly back to the road.

"It'll die under there, surely?"

"No, dear, it'll be right. Tough, these lorikeets. I'll put some water out. But never you mind, its own kind will look after it. Those cats! Feral, from the Davidson Park." She pointed to the lush treetops which loomed over the house-tops a few streets away to the west. "Truly, I'll trap the blighter. I've got no compunction."

Pointedly ignoring the shaking fist of the old man whose progress home had been delayed by less than two minutes, Rosemary thought about what the woman had said—the lorikeet's own kind would help it. But how? How would its own kind even know it was there? And supposing there was a way for a lorikeet to communicate with its flock, what could they do? They might bring food in their beaks but they could hardly carry their injured companion away. The cat knew it was there; it merely had to bide its time and come back again. She hoped the woman knew what she was doing.

· · ·

The Quiltys' house was in one of the suburbs where each is a village whose boundaries are clear to the locals. In most, from just beyond the high-rise jungle of computer and advertising offices in North Sydney to the beginning, some eighteen miles away, of the bush at Hornsby, the kindergarten, primary, and high schools represent the core. Those with private schools have less clearly defined edges as they attract children and their supporters from other areas, some quite far away, depending on the brightness of the child and the ambition of the parents.

To have a house on a quarter, half, or even full acre block in St Ives, Lindfield, Pymble, Wahroonga, Killara, and others that flank the Pacific Highway on its way north is to publicly proclaim your worth and, in most cases, your right-of-centre political attitudes. Privately Rosemary and Daniel were inclined to cancel each other's votes, she having never relinquished a sense of tender sympathy for Labor, which had been the underdogs for most of her life. When the Labor Party had surged back to power under Bob Hawke at the last election, she'd had a celebration with Lucy, her friend and neighbour who worked in television, who was a single parent and referred to herself as a sociological anomaly in their street full of married couples.

The upper north shore is, as Daniel had described it when they were house hunting, the breeding ground for Sydney's genteel middle class. Both Rosemary and Daniel had grown up in somewhat lower middle class areas, so the house they had worked hard to buy was as much a proclamation as a shelter against the elements. They bought it when Bobby was six months old at a mortgagee sale. The suburb was new enough to have the confident-though-predictable stamp of a single developer's design team but old enough for the trees, the dogs, and some of the children to have reached adolescence.

Within two seasons the Quiltys had softened the house's contours with heavy plantings of scented jasmine and wisteria, selected despite a general neighbourhood preference for natives. In the summer the creepers had helped to keep the heat out, though Phyl usually grumbled that they had also helped to keep the spiders in. But in spring, when their lush pinkish-white and light purple blooms entangled with each other and filled the air with competing and equally delicious scents, everyone forgot the spiders.

Rosemary had never flown over Sydney, though it was one of her secret dreams. She liked to imagine herself in a large, red-and-yellow-striped balloon, drifting slowly over her suburb, spotting swimming pools—one in every back garden in some streets. From the air they would look like blots of light turquoise enamel paint covered in Glad wrap.

When Rosemary pulled into her drive, Lucy was hosing the petunias they'd both planted the previous weekend. Behind her the wisteria and jasmine, tangling up her house's walls as though in a sort of arboreal wrestling session, added the last of their mauve and pearly lustre to the late spring light and drove bees mad. The whole scene—pretty house, pretty flowers, pretty lady—made Rosemary think of a TV commercial for margarine, with herself in her bottle-green car arriving to be astonished at the lightness of the scones.

"Hi!" Lucy waved with the hose, sending a silver rope of water across the Volvo's path and Rosemary stopped sharply. "I've been on the lookout for an hour. Where did you go for your jeans? Wollongong?"

"Aladdin's cave. Fairy godmotherville. Bugger jeans—I bought the world's most beautiful, beautiful dress."

"Dress." Lucy's half-smile communicated pleasure as well as amusement—she'd been trying to encourage Rosemary to indulge herself and had been given plenty of stern lectures, in return, about the importance of preserving every penny when you're a person in a breaking-up marriage.

"An expensive dress, that I don't need. After the world's lousiest job interview."

"The first one's always rotten—it's Fate's test to see if you mean it. Let's see the consolation prize?" Lucy leaned into the car window with the confident air of a policeman at a road-block, girlish in the tight jeans Rosemary couldn't get away with, slim-legged enough to cross them at the knee as she stood, with one foot turned out, the other pointing, toe downward; a legacy of years of ballet lessons.

Lucy had long black hair which constantly divided itself into strips, responding to gravity in ways which required her to correct it, push it back, tuck it back, sweep it back in long-fingered ballet gestures. She had thick black eyebrows over very dark, rather small eyes, an effect that had made Phyl say she looked like a jungle cat. Rosemary thought she looked like a Gypsy doll made of fine china.

"Oh—to die for! The colour! Now you can't possibly say no to what I'm going to ask," Lucy said, stroking the silk with worshipful fingertips. "It's Malcolm's birthday tomorrow and he's doing the most enormous thing for me—we're taking Tom and Eve out to dinner to Kables. And you MUST come, too. You can christen it."

"Is it going to be like the last time, when Malcolm took your friends and neighbours out on a jolly treat to Kinselas?"

"No. It'll be wonderful."

The outing to Kinselas had been for a late-night show written by the assistant producer of Malcolm Henry's TV show where Lucy worked as a researcher. They'd gone for loyalty and taken Tom and Eve Everingham, who lived across the road, as a "thank you" treat: Eve, who earned her pin money by being a child-minder, occasionally looked after

Mattie, Lucy's eight-year-old daughter, when an urgent late story came up. But Eve refused to take any money from Lucy on the pretext that Mattie was a great help: she kept Ben, Eve's little boy, out of trouble. The real reason was that Lucy was a struggling sole parent and Eve was kind, in an awkward sort of way.

Before Malcolm arrived on the scene, Tom and Eve had often included Lucy and Rosemary in their barbecues, trips to the local movies, and parent-teacher nights. Tom, who moved with the deliberate air of heavy, short-legged men, behaved proudly, like a bantam cock. He would urge the three women to chairs and bring them cups of tea on trays improvised from empty cartons. His solicitousness, Rosemary often thought, disguised a question or two about why her and Lucy's husbands had felt compelled to abandon them.

Rosemary and Lucy knew that, with them in the group, Tom and Eve would flirt with each other and show off the public face of a happy marriage. But when they were alone together, as could be clearly seen through the thin white curtains of their front room, their faces slacked into TV-watching poses. But at least Tom and Eve belonged to each other and however much Rosemary and Lucy sneered, they knew their sneers were based on envy.

The outing Rosemary had hated had been in March, two months after Daniel's defection, when she had concluded that she was unloveable. Lucy had begged her to go, claiming that the show, a comedy, would cheer her up. So when it had turned out to be embarrassingly corny, Lucy had felt bad, but not very bad and not for long—she was too newly in love to stay solemn. She and Malcolm had been the only ones in an audience of fairly drunk friends and relatives who were able to make convincingly encouraging noises about their colleague's leaden play.

"It was a pretty dreadful evening, I admit. Boring—not Kinselas' usual. And you were pretty much out on a limb."

"Oh no, I wasn't entirely neglected in my broken-hearted state," said Rosemary. "Eve noticed me. I wish she wouldn't always look at me as though if she wasn't watching closely I might pounce on Tom and he'd then be mine, as though he was the last seat in a game of musical chairs."

"No. Not a chair. Chairs are hard, firm things. Eve treats Tom as though he's something quite little, with limited but specific value—like a medal she can pin to her bosom. It's her upbringing, Ro. Or bad experiences at school. Nothing personal, believe me. In her circle it might even be interpreted as a compliment."

"We're Eve's circle."

"Then at least she's got good taste in friends!"

"I shouldn't be lousy to Eve. She's OK. Nice with the kids. You'd be pleased to see how well she treats Mattie. Ben's so used to getting his own way, but when Mattie's playing with him Eve doesn't let him get away with anything more than a fair share."

"You mean she's using my child as an object lesson for her own brat?"

"Lucy! You know I don't mean that." But they laughed anyway, united in mild bitchiness, until Lucy's conscience bothered her.

"She is kind to Mattie. She's nice to all the kids. Maybe she should have more of her own. They're not exactly poor, are they? Tom's some sort of an executive, isn't he?"

"Middle management is what he calls it. Like something Hobbits might do."

"Of course! Tom as Bilbo, in a light blue suit!"

"It's not just the Everinghams. You and Malcolm stare at each other's eyes like student ophthalmologists cramming for exams."

"But you'll come anyway."

Yes! said the red dress.

"That's wonderful," said Lucy. "You're wonderful. You'll see—it'll be much more fun than last time. I really want you and Malcolm to like each other."

"You mean, I was a wimp."

"Come on, Ro."

"Say it!"

"Well, you were a bit low-key. But you're not now."

"Eve really won't be pleased if I'm there."

"Yeah. Well, I'm not Eve, and she's not paying. And you're not so bloody thin-skinned anymore. And, though I am sure you and Malcolm will like each other—and he might even be good for you to talk to, since you're looking for a job—I'm prepared to take the chance that my two favourite people will continue to prefer me to each other."

"We'd have to! Anyone who has the power to drag him away from his secret boat and his private farm and show him off in a public place is . . . is . . ."

"Irresistible? Actually, it wasn't me, it was Tom. He's hinted so often now about dinner out that Malcolm feels he can't put him off any longer. He says Tom may start to take it out on Mattie when she's there being looked after."

"So he's prepared to take the chance that a show-biz writer might be having a drink at one of the bars in the Regent when you walk in? You know what this means, don't you, Lucy? You've stopped being a secret.

I'll bet it's not Tom's idea at all—it's Malcolm's! He wants to show you off!"

For years gossip columnists had speculated about Malcolm Henry's romantic life but there had been no evidence that he had one. This was because he was wilier than Prince Charles had been in the pre–Lady Di days. Social page shots invariably showed him "squiring" someone rich, ugly, and old enough to be his mother: a formerly famous British actress, perhaps, or a successful Australian fashion entrepreneur. As a result, there had been hints that perhaps he preferred men to women. But now no one who saw Malcolm with Lucy could have any doubt: he was almost ridiculous. He frisked like a stallion, laughed, beamed, and touched her: surprising behaviour for a man who had spent about twenty years carefully cultivating an uncrackable shell.

"A few people at work know and there has been some gossip in the industry. But do you really believe he wants to show me off?"

"Of course!"

Pleased, graceful, Lucy dealt with a whole collection of slipped hair strands by ducking her head and then whipping it back.

"It's been how long? six . . . seven months? And I'm still in the 'pinch me' stage," she said. "God, its wonderful! So corny! Happy Ever After is bliss only to the immediate participants, isn't it? I just wish I could bottle it, share it around."

"Oh, but you do, you do, all the time. It seeps out from you like radioactivity—though it's probably only twice as dangerous. You're like a flag of hope to me and all your other dumped and undesired friends, Lucy!"

.   .   .

Nine months earlier, on a very hot summer night in the middle of January, Rosemary and Daniel had had a party.

Although they had lived in the house for more than ten years, they had never actually had a big party, despite the fact that renovations to the rumpus room, extensions to the back deck, and the insertion of a pool had been justified by the contribution they would make to entertaining. But in January, when they had been married for sixteen years, Rosemary had decided it would be a good idea to have a really big night where her new theatre group friends and a few nice people from her class at the communications course and the friendliest of Daniel's clients could come and meet each other and, she hoped, be drawn into the established core of neighbourhood friends they'd made together. At first Daniel had not been co-operative but Rosemary had been determined.

"Since I stopped working for Patchwork our lives have started taking different directions," she'd said. She was scrambling Daniel's eggs while he buttered his toast. He had looked at her steadily from under his thick, golden eyebrows. This had made her uneasy, so she'd filled the uneasiness with words. "I mean, we hardly see each other. We used to do all our real talking driving to work and home again. Now you're always at meetings or I'm at rehearsals or doing a communications project."

"I thought you liked doing those things."

"Oh, yes. Yes of course. It's just that I thought now we don't have the business as the main thing . . . shared interest . . . that you . . . that we should develop some new ones." She'd been aware that she sounded tentative, guilty even. It was because three times in the last fortnight she had had to leave Daniel's dinner on a white plate with instructions for microwaving it because he'd been working late and she had had to rush off to a class right after feeding the children.

He had eaten one of the three. The other two times, he'd told her, he had stayed in the office, sent out for a hamburger, and kept on working. He had not complained but she'd guessed that he had been put off by the prospect of a lonely, re-heated dinner. In the old days she would have been working at his side, or at least she would have eaten with him when he came wearily home.

Daniel had agreed, over his second cup of black coffee, to have the party—"Go ahead if you want to"—but he had baulked at inviting the more friendly of Patchwork PR's clients because, he said, he didn't mix business with pleasure and that anyway most of them were fuckwits and those who weren't would die rather than go to a suburban wedding anniversary party. She had told him he was being snobbish and un-friendly. He had told her she was a sentimental twit and that the trouble with her was she didn't know anything about business or, indeed, the real world. It had turned into one of the old-fashioned, air-clearing fights that she realised she'd been missing lately and she'd actually enjoyed it, especially when they'd made up by getting back into their unmade bed— which had been so good that Daniel didn't even make a fuss about cancelling his first three appointments.

Afterwards, lying limb-stretched like Leonardo da Vinci's anatomical man on the middle of the big bed, Daniel had said, "On the other hand it'll be a good way to celebrate the main-frame computer."

"Oh, Daniel! You've ordered it!"

"Yup," he'd said with the pretend-grim look she knew to be pride. "Took a while to reassure the suppliers about finance—the software and installation will cost almost as much as the thing itself. But it's under way now; it's ready to sail from Manhattan as soon as we've signed the bank papers."

"And it's really going to be worth it?"

"Oh, hell, Ro, you know it is! There'll probably be nothing else like it in Australia. I told you—it can do literally thousands of personalised letters in an hour, with no fuss and no clatter, because of the laser. We can design and illustrate books. God, Ro, the thing could pay for itself in typesetting alone if we decided to move into that area. No one would be able to touch us!"

Thirteen years earlier, when Daniel was twenty-three, he had been one of the first really bright journalists to give up the slow, complicated, but nevertheless visible route to somewhere up near middle management in a big Sydney newspaper organisation and start a public relations company. When he'd left the newspaper his colleagues had thought him reckless, possibly stupid; at the very least there was good, sure superannuation at the end of the line and, in between, there was the security of the almost invincible power of the Australian Journalists' Association to protect against a man's being fired, no matter how he might provoke. Not that Daniel, with his keen sense of news, his smiling approach to everything from layouts to staff politics, and his honest-looking face, was ever likely to need the safety net. Chief sub, news editor, an influential post on the back bench and, eventually, an editorship of his own were almost inevitable, provided he watched his step. But, despite twelve years of indoctrination by schools into the business of team spirit, Daniel had never been good at deference.

Although Phyl had just graduated from being a toddler at the time Daniel thought of starting the company, Rosemary had encouraged him, eager to help, and prepared to scrimp along on the proceeds of a little insurance policy her mother had bought at her birth and which had matured when she was twenty-one. Her faith in Daniel was like a shining rope which had connected her to him so firmly that she'd felt utterly safe, no matter how precarious the actual circumstances of their living had sometimes been in the beginning. Their occasional noisy, wordy fights were a tweaking, a testing of the connecting rope, and thrilling for Rosemary in a scary way. But the rope had always survived and then been reinforced in the fun and passion of making up afterwards. Daniel, of course, had usually won the fights, and that was the way she had wanted it to be. She was his pupil, his greatest fan, his child bride, his groupie. He was Superman, she was Lois Lane, and each needed the other to demonstrate the quality of their gifts.

When Daniel had started giving his former colleagues lucrative little writing jobs and opening doors for them into glamorous jobs in TV, they also began to admire his courage and his brilliance. As a result he was often in the news, almost as often as his products were, and this had done the business more and more good.

.   .   .

Despite the heat, which overwhelmed the capacity of the kitchen air-conditioner, Rosemary had enjoyed preparing for the party whose guest list had soon swelled to sixty.

"Only half'll turn up," Auntie Gwen had said reassuringly, up to the elbows in flour for cheese straws she believed no party could succeed without. "Give them plenty of watermelon and chuck them in the pool. People think they're eating real food when you give them watermelon and it cuts down on the grog so they don't all get plastered. You told them to bring their bathers?"

"Some will," Rosemary had answered politely, much more involved with the lists she was checking, cross-checking, and ticking for things bought, people phoned, and services ordered. "But they're not exactly teenagers, the people who're coming."

"Hnf," said Auntie Gwen, scrunching up a recent newspaper full of egg-shells, cheese rinds, and scraped-up flour. Rosemary caught a glimpse of a headline that said "The World Is on the Brink. Precious Little Time Is Left," and quickly turned away. "Give any human being a coupla drinks and they're teenagers. Two more drinks and they're infants. Crying to be picked up."

Auntie Gwen was really sorry that she couldn't come to the party, but it was her night to drive senior citizens to the bingo and she couldn't bring herself to bugger up the roster again because the secretary, who was ninety-two, got very mixed up.

"Where is that damn husband of yours anyway? He should be giving you a hand," Auntie Gwen said when the cheese straws had turned out perfect and she was preparing to leave.

"He's gone for the ice."

"To Alaska? Isn't it amazing how men always manage to wriggle out of the real work."

Apart from Auntie Gwen, and despite the random breath tests which had been introduced just in time to put a blight upon Christmas, every-one else came, including some of Daniel's more friendly clients. Taxis did a good trade that night.

Since Rosemary was the hostess she'd had to be constantly on the move, meeting people at the door, finding towels for those who, even though they hadn't brought their bathers, had decided to swim anyway, and passing dips around. (Auntie Gwen's cheese straws were a hit—most people had never tasted 1950s party food before). So Rosemary's impressions of the party were taken in small chunks, in passing.

She noticed, pleased, that Peter Eberhard of Glen Rossfield—the winery and one of Patchwork PR's most important clients—had found an old friend in Jim Begg, a local solicitor with whom Daniel sometimes played tennis. The two big men, having hit each other on the back and laughed violently, were now leaning on the railing around the high back deck, outreminiscing each other about school Rugby Union matches.

The party had started off well, with plenty of laughter and loud conversation. There was a lot of splashing and shrieking from the pool which, floodlit for the occasion, looked as though it were floating in space on its high terrace beyond the back deck.

She noticed, concerned, that her four friends from the drama course were stuck together in a little knot, and she suddenly realised that they were probably the only homosexuals there. There was huge Melissa whose body gave contradictory messages about her age; her strong, square, line-free face said thirty-five but her little, mottled, knobbly fingered hands said sixty. Rosemary, who knew how long she'd been part of the Sydney theatre scene, guessed she was close to fifty. There was Martha, whose body was a compulsive truth-teller; loads of make-up, shiny gold chains, a low-cut, clingy, pumpkin-coloured top, and a wig like an explosion of mahogany-coloured curls did nothing to disguise the fact that she was well into her sixties and a candidate for osteoporosis. There was slight, thin-boned Jeremy who nevertheless delivered a very powerful and resonant voice that was often heard on voice-overs in commercials; he still did the odd radio play, though not, he said, for the money. And there was Patrick—Martha's nephew—the newest member of the class group, a tall, well-built man of about forty who looked preoccupied, perhaps even sad, as he stood with his hands in his pockets and gazed beyond his friends' chirpy gossip.

Melissa was head of the drama school. Martha had joined six months earlier to do the books, some stage managing, some walk-ons, and a good deal of restoring of emotional harmony. In weeks she'd become the group mum, in a few more weeks she'd become Melissa's darling. Some of the younger students had thought it was very romantic, but Rosemary, who secretly believed that homosexuals were people who'd tragically got stuck in a developmental phase, thought it was rather sad.

A compromise—not the real thing. On her way to the kitchen for more food, Rosemary felt she should get them mixing.

She didn't have to bother. On her next round, bearing a tray of dolmades, taramasalata, and olives, she saw that Lucy had helped. Martha was now talking to a very pregnant young woman who was married to one of Daniel's computer clients. The girl's eyes were nearly as big as her stomach and Rosemary assumed Martha was engaged in one of her pet topics—the hideous complications hospitals can cause to the karmas of not-quite ready babies by inducing them to suit obstetricians' golf tournament dates. Martha was all for home deliveries, preferrably under warm water. Though she had never had one herself, she'd helped with a few.

Melissa was talking loudly to a group, which included Tom, of half-naked, beer-drinking husbands still wet from the pool. Her special subject was the sex lives of every TV and movie star in Australia, and she made it sound as though they all phoned her with bulletins every day. And Lucy was with Jeremy and Patrick, who, Rosemary noticed, was talking with meaningful hand gestures about the fact that good sense had prevailed in South West Tasmania when protests had stopped the building of the Franklin River Dam. "And I speak as a water man," she heard him say.

Rosemary laughed at lot. Between handing out food and drinks and introducing people with restless eyes to people who were already enjoying themselves, she dropped in on groups. To the talk about the Opera House turning ten or about Joan Sutherland, who was going to sing in *Die Fledermaus* at next week's free opera under the stars in the Domain, or about business and love and food and the rumour that the Federal government might be forced to call an early election, she contributed bright lies or scraps of gossip. She liked the look of approval in people's eyes, especially in men's eyes.

Women's high, shouted laughter broke like exclamation marks through the tinkle-clatter of glasses and voices. It's a good party, she thought.

. . .

Rosemary Quilty had been the last to know about her husband's love affair. Not that there was much time between her friends finding out and Rosemary herself finding out. If she had been in the living room when Angela, a little drunk, arrived in a taxi to gate-crash that sixteenth wedding anniversary party, she would have been among the first. But she was in the kitchen, getting more ice, and when she got back with the bucket full of lovely round silver balls from the automatic dispensing gadget on the double-door refrigerator she had the impression she'd stumbled into the wrong play.

The party had frozen, less beautifully than the ice. The only sound was persistently happy music. A female singer, backed by a dozen versions of her own voice, was singing "No more pain, no broken hearts for me again." Someone quickly stopped that.

Daniel had turned the colour of a manilla envelope and appeared to be dancing with a woman whose noticeably elegant legs jutted out at odd angles from their embrace. He was saying, "Not now, not tonight, please, Angie, please!"—or something like that.

In the instant of clarity that precedes severe shock, Rosemary registered the intimacy of Daniel's dealing. There was none of the reticence of strangers—this was a situation he'd handled before.

Rosemary let everyone down by not having a tantrum. It would have been a satisfying break to the tension which filled the room as rapidly as teargas if she had screamed or thrown something, if she'd lunged at Daniel, killed Angela and/or herself with the ham-slicing knife that glittered invitingly on the buffet, still surrounded by crumbs of pink meat, causing SCORNED WIFE SLAYS headlines in the next day's papers. But instead she quietly suggested that Daniel take Angela home, and he quietly did.

"I'm going to follow the bastard," Melissa had yelled. Though heavy and rather drunk, she was very strong. Daniel had provided new theatre by driving Angela away in his red BMW, and it had taken the combined strength of her three companions to restrain Melissa, whose black kaftan had floating panels. Forever after, the image of the night was encapsulated for Rosemary in the vision of Jeremy, Patrick, and Martha holding onto the roaring Melissa's clothes, which stretched like hawsers from a liner to its tugs.

"I'm going to find their tryst!" Melissa had projected. "I'm going to make sure they never have another peaceful screw! The swine! I knew the type! I should have warned you, Rosie, darling. Those quiet ones who smile a lot. Men! Fucking men!" And lots more.

Another persistent image was Bobby's white face as he stared and stared and stared and seemed to shrink, much smaller than his usual leggy ten. Like hers, his free flow of words had been stopped by shock.

The rest of the guests had lingered, supportive but uncertain. There were plenty of offers, most practical, some ridiculous, but all she'd wanted was for them to go away and for the whole night to prove to be a simple mistake.

Of course it wasn't simple, and now, after going through the pain-filled winter, the long and sometimes dangerous tunnel of grief, Rosemary had experimentally begun to suspect that perhaps it wasn't even a mistake.

Tomorrow night, she thought, glancing at the chair where the red dress lay, will be my debut into a new life.

Two

Rosemary had a lot to see to: hair, nails, painting a pair of strappy shoes the same colour as the dress—it was as much fun as a first dance. In fact, she reckoned, even if the evening was doomed, she'd had a good ration of pleasure for the day. Bobby pretended to be sickened by it all when he splashed in from the very cold swimming pool for food reinforcements.

"Yuk, Mom, what've you done to your hair? That's like the photos of you in Auntie Gwen's album being a debutante! Was that the fifties?"

"It was the late sixties, you dum-dum. And I think it makes me look like Madonna," she said and squirmed voluptuously with a hairbrush for a microphone.

"Spare me!" he said, rolling his eyes and clutching his stomach. But she could see that secretly he approved of the floating corona of red-gold curly hair teased, twisted, and fluffed out to look longer and more vigorous, more dangerous than its just-reached-the shoulder length. He was even more impressed when she put the red dress on; the glow was still there—its magic was not just in her imagination. As she walked, the hem of the deeply folded fabric trickled around her calves, an effect which reminded her, with each step, to straighten her knees, stretch her spine, and lift her chin.

She was interested by Malcolm's reaction. He was the last to arrive, and when she let him in he stared at her, then blinked, as though replacing a transparency in his mind's slide projector—out: Lucy's tear-rimmed neighbour whose husband had run off with a younger woman. In: sleek Rosemary Quilty, curly haired and high with energy. Tom, following Malcolm's focus, announced that Rosie had brushed up well.

"Don't you think Rosie's brushed up well?" he demanded of Eve, since no one else had responded.

Eve said, "You're lucky to be able to wear red," which, on a sliding scale of friendly remarks, Rosemary rated a six. She noticed Eve's eyes sliding around the details of the room. Looking for dust? she thought. Instantly she imagined a scene: Eve, in a happy house, points to a dark corner. "Look, a cobweb," she says. Rosemary, pretending surprise, says, "Oh, goodness, yes, you're right—and it's thick with dust. It must have been there at least three weeks! You can see Frank doesn't love me for my housekeeping." (Frank, John, Peter—for the scene any name would have done.) She thought this while laughing at the men's small talk and handing around tiny asparagus sandwiches to keep them all alive until the entrée.

Tom, who had rarely been given a greater cause for animation than Malcolm's arrival in Lucy's life and in his neighbourhood, had established the key in which he planned to play the evening: pawing and bouncing around the edges of Malcolm's and Lucy's mutual preoccupation with the ardour of a newish puppy. The middle-aged man version of pawing and bouncing took the form of plenty of pleased, usually inappropriate, laughter. But apart from Rosemary, only Eve had noticed—she'd thinned her lips.

Though Malcolm's real attention was on Lucy, Rosemary was pleased and amused to notice that a ration of it was for her. His face fascinated her because of the pattern media muscles had imposed on it. On television, his forehead lines were horizontal when he listened to interviewees or when his own comments were on general topics. But as soon as poverty, loneliness, or death were spelled out on the auto-cue—which was fairly often, given the wide-ranging nature of his program—vertical lines would appear. These muscular reactions he carried into his own life so that sometimes, in mixed groups when he was reacting to a variety of input, the vertical and horizontal lines would change rapidly enough to give the impression of a computerised chess-board. His face criss-crossed in fascination as Rosemary told them about the bird-in-the-manger kookaburra that arrived early each day to sit on the bird-feeding table in order to quark and shriek away the humbler, seed-eating birds for whom the food was intended.

"He's such an old chauvinist! He reminds me of my Uncle Henry who wouldn't let anyone get into the bathroom in the morning until he had been in there forever. I used to sneak out, in desperation, and go behind the garage where Gran couldn't see and be horrified by such unladylike behaviour."

"And how do you deal with the chauvinistic kookaburra? I'll bet you don't just let him get away with it!"

"No, you're wrong. *He* deals with *me*. He makes me do what he wants—like put strips of meat on the balcony rails. It's blackmail! It's the only way to get him to leave the other birds in peace. And it doesn't even always work. Sometimes, just to show who's boss, he'll grab the meat and take it back onto the seed table in order to bash it to death there. He scatters the sunflower seeds onto the lawn and laughs at all of us: me and the poor, dyspeptic lorikeets and mynahs."

Malcolm laughed, too—a sound, Rosmary thought, only slightly more tuneful than the kookaburra's. He laughed again when he heard her trade with Bobby the right to stay up until midnight in exchange for finishing his homework and changing the light bulb in the upstairs bathroom. The red dress had made her witty. It also made her worth helping: as soon as Lucy mentioned Rosemary was job hunting and would like to work in television, he put on his serious face and asked her questions.

.   .   .

There was enough of late October's warmth and light to encourage Malcolm to open the sun-roof. Rosemary, very conscious of the clean breeze which furled her new-styled curls in the way of a shampoo advertisement—curls which were going to require careful combing again when they got to the hotel—drifted in and out of the conversation by means of a few agreeable noises. She was enjoying the rare feeling of being beautiful.

"Look at the clouds," said Lucy. "Those fat, golden ones. They look better than smoked-salmon omelettes!"

"You're hungry," said Malcolm, his hand on her thigh, and as they looked at each other the big pale green car lurched out of its bumper-to-bumper lane.

"Don't let's die for love!" said Rosemary, trying not to sound alarmed, and Tom obligingly giggled.

"Sailor's delight," he said. "It's going to be a stinker tomorrow."

The pink-gold of the summer night had cast its rich glow equally on everything, giving a quality of stage-set magic to all the city buildings. Even the few quite ordinary ones that had so far managed to survive development were touched by fantasia. The taller towers bounced rose, silver, and amber highlights from their glazed walls, and the rows of terrace houses at the Quay and at Woolloomoollo, visible behind the Opera House, took on the colour and charm of doll's houses in children's book illustrations. Rosemary, inspired by the glamour of herself and of the evening, suppressed the urge to remark that the Opera House looked liked piled slices of melon on the golden plate of the harbour. Not only was it another food analogy, it also sounded like a pop song. Instead, she pointed to the huge, usually hideous blue water tank at Kirribilli and said, "Look what the light has done to even that! It looks like a fat opera singer, dressed in silk."

"Anyone you know?" Malcolm asked. Eve smiled, but politely, lips only. She didn't like the word fat. Fat was her enemy, against which she waged a ceaseless and, to her, interesting battle. She called it 'weight problem' with the same mixture of disgust and familiarity a prudish aunt might use to talk about sex.

"Kirribilli's a good place for units," Tom began, with the air of a man delivering a paper. "Trouble is, they've got a draft 2C zone application before Council, which'd mean nothing new higher than two storeys plus attic. Though, of course, if the site is already prejudiced by three or four storey units you could go that high again. If I had that sort of money I'd like to rip out some of those old cottages and put in town houses. Really good stuff, with security parking, the lot. It'd be paradise—people'd kill for them!"

Rosemary glanced at the cheerfully disorganised architecture of Kirribilli and wondered which of the flats contained Daniel and Angela. Bobby knew—he'd even spent a night there. Phyl knew, too, the result of one reluctant glance, and said it was like a Barbie doll's house: all white lace, polished silver, and pink candles. Being tactful, she hadn't mentioned the bed, though Rosemary guessed it would be brass.

The two men were still talking about money and property. Rosemary suspected that, to Malcolm, for so long insulated by fame, forays into Lucy's suburban environment were amusingly exotic. She imagined Tom working references to it into his daily conversations: "Actually, I was just saying to Malcolm Henry the other night—a few of us went to the Regent for a meal. Nice chap. I was just saying to him that, for a second car, you can't go wrong with the Civic."

She wondered how Malcolm, used to conversations about who was in and out of government, who was sleeping with whom in the highest places, so to speak, and which countries were enduring coups or copping it rich in heroin deals, really felt about Tom's line of conversational Muzak. He'd been nice to the point of eagerness about the kookaburra; now he was responding with what sounded like real enthusiasm to Tom's real estate lecture, mentioning things like the killing a bloke he knew had made in Balmain.

Rosemary reminded herself of an opinion she had long ago arrived at: Men are much nicer to other men, especially ugly or silly men, than they are to women—much more tolerant and much less demanding. The whole carload of intelligent people had lapsed into what Tom believed to be his due—a respectful and possibly even fascinated silence. For a moment Rosemary's mood touched on the despair she'd managed so well, recently, to surmount. Even though Daniel was more interesting than Tom, his treachery had filled her with a huge load of disgust. It was a flowing, khaki-and-charcoal-coloured load which had crept over all trust and all the bright, hope-filled things upon which relationships feed. It had left a thick, drab coating. She didn't want him back, tainted with the flesh and echoes of shared confidences of Angela.

But what was the alternative? Some decent, dull widower, another Tom whose Eve had dematerialised? Someone who would compete with the children for her attention and never really love them as much as they deserved? Or would she be alone, doomed, in this couples society, to miss out on dinner parties or settle for being number three, five, or seven in groups of friends? For a moment she understood Eve's suspicions: Tom was her passport to enjoyment in Sydney, the flagpole on which the banner of her life could flutter, and she was not about to let him get snatched away by someone thinner. Eve, Rosemary realised, would not even consider that Rosemary regarded Tom as a deadly bore. But even if she did, she probably wouldn't think it made any difference. He was a man, the right age, shape, and size, the right money bracket, and *hers,* and she intended to make sure he stayed that way.

    .   .   .

They arrived, sweeping grandly into the hotel's cramped half-circle drive as though it really were a carriageway. Then, after Rosemary had recombed her hair so that it looked more tastefully windblown than the reality, they headed for the restaurant. With a special look the maître d' simultaneously acknowledged Malcolm's star status and, because the table was in Lucy's name, granted him anonymity. Tom, fairly absent-mindedly, took Rosemary's arm instead of Eve's, which led to a quick, slightly embarrassed reshuffle. As she was shoved off to the side, Rosemary thought it probably would not have happened in France or Italy. Or even America. Men there were surely more sophisticated and women less possessive—in public anyway.

At the bar they arranged themselves, perhaps unconsciously, around Malcolm like disciples in a Renaissance painting. A very elegant group, Rosemary observed. There was Eve, her blonde hair piled and twisted like a glazed, plaited loaf, her buttery skin offset by an ice-blue dress cut low enough to present her breasts and shoulders in smooth, pale mounds which glistened like risen dough. Her face, often sulky in repose—the weight problem no doubt at work on her facial flesh—looked glorious that night, a sweet-faced fertility symbol with something charmingly childlike about the blue eyes. She looked like the highly coloured, soft-fleshed women whom Norman Lindsay had painted so worshipfully. Tom certainly worshipped her—his hands and eyes were drawn to her—awkward moths to an opalescent light.

Lucy wore black, not, she said, because she was mourning for Malcolm's advancing years but because it was clean. Shiny earrings—diamonds he'd given her for her birthday in July—drew attention to her dazzling, strong-toothed smile which, like the smiles of the others, was directed at Malcolm. The proximity of two such overtly sexual couples made Rosemary suddenly decide to go and check her contact lenses.

In the Ladies' mirror she half expected to see a lonely-looking, slightly anxious woman like the ones in "before" advertisements, but her twinge of jealousy had been too weak to affect the red dress's magic. It brought her pale skin to fruit-toned life and the mysterious folds over her chest bones were, she believed, more tantalising than the actuality of a pumped-out bosom. She decided that she looked highbrow, but also like a good lay, and she was pleased by this moment of mutuality. But she took the lenses out anyway: mascara, the possibility of cigarette smoke and maybe another touch of sadness here and there could lead to unattractive threads of red in her eyes' nice whites.

When she got back a strong-looking man was talking to Malcolm. They looked as though they were about to pull apart, the way people do when they meet unexpectedly in public places and each was hurrying to say the right things to the other in respect of their relationship. Rosemary was surprised to notice, as she got close enough to observe his body language, that Malcolm was subordinate in this one.

Rosemary, all her faculties in harmony, slowly walked up close to Malcolm. The slowness and closeness were partly because she was rendered somewhat blind without the lenses. Marilyn Monroe looked very sexy in *How to Marry a Millionaire,* bashing her way short-sightedly round a restaurant, and Rosemary was never really sorry that she did it that night —her life took interesting turns as a result.

"This is Rosemary Quilty," said Malcolm. Although he seemed as cool and controlled as usual, the fact that he did not mention the man's name indicated a certain well-hidden fluster. He obviously thought that she already knew. In fact, she was almost sure she did know but could not locate the mind-file in the time available—important things were happening quickly.

Before she'd said a word she knew she'd made an impression on the man because he stopped pulling away from Malcolm in a supple, simple sweep of behaviour and offered to buy them a drink. It was more like a command.

He took Rosemary's arm and led them to a newly vacated bar table with the air of a person who, if he didn't already own the place, could do so by making a phone call.

"Quilty. Aren't many of those about. You related to Daniel? Patchwork PR?" His style was brusque, slightly rude, in what she recognised, from years in public relations, was an acceptable way of indicating power.

"I'm—I used to be married to him. We're separated."

What an opening! she said to herself. The start of a lifetime's excuses and explanations: Why I'm Not Married, Though Living in Sydney. However, she was sure none of this showed through the expression she'd chosen—serene, confident, possibly a little mysterious.

He looked at her as closely as an examining doctor might, stopping just a split second before the scrutiny became uncomfortable.

"So what do you do with your life, ex–Mrs. Quilty?"

She had already collected the details: two children to look after, getting ready to find a job . . . when suddenly her tongue rushed in and took over.

"I'm an actor," she said. "I've been an actor most of my life."

The others, even Malcolm, looked surprised. Both Tom and Eve prepared to speak in a way that was certain to be reproving but Lucy instantly cut them off by asking loudly, firmly, how Ben, their little boy was doing in his remedial reading classes—an inspired bit of side-tracking neither could resist.

Rosemary had a flash of panic. Then, Shut up, she told both aspects of herself. We're committed now.

"Don't you mean actress?" the man asked. Oh, God, not a Women's Lib argument! she thought. So instead of answering, she laughed as though he'd been witty.

"What acting do you do?" He didn't look like an academic; with the same mixture of professional detachment and close interest, he looked more like a customs officer. It seemed safe to say, "Right now I'm thinking of teaching for a few years. Possibly at NIDA."

"You're not actually working, then?"

This was true, she agreed, though she needed to, as there were the children. Fortunately he didn't ask her their ages. (It had been thrilling, wonderful, and shocking at the time when she'd had Phyl—a more grown-up thing to do at eighteen than write the first year university exams which most of her former schoolmates were struggling with. But now, having a sixteen-year-old daughter could suggest that Rosemary was older than she was.)

"Done any television?" he asked, thereby revealing to her part of his mystery. And she realised she was about to be offered a job.

It was one of those comet-like moments in Rosemary's life, when she got a rare peep into the heart of a bright, flashing reality. Usually she was not quick enough to catch the comet by the tail, but that night, in the red dress, with all her faculties in order and all the elements of herself working as a team, she caught it.

"A little." She could tell he liked her voice. "Mostly in Canada."

"Commercials?" he asked, and there was the touch of a sneer. But she nodded anyway, as one as yet undiscovered.

"Who for?" he demanded.

Despite her best efforts, Rosemary's ability as a liar was only good in short bursts. This was because she was essentially moral and because her short-term memory was patchy, so she was forced to stick to small stuff she could handle without aid. She knew he wanted readily traceable details. She imagined him placing an intercontinental call or two to check. She realised that if she was not careful she'd bore him. So she leaned towards him slightly to draw attention to the white band of skin on her chest and said, "Du Pont."

It worked. He was not prepared to insist that he'd meant a TV production house or station, not a product. Instead, he said, "I see," looked round the table, glanced at a waiter who appeared to be waiting just for him, and ordered another round of drinks.

She still did not know who he was, but Tom, Eve, even Lucy (because of the strain), and Malcolm (because of a media man's fascination with lies) were looking like shocked rabbits. She knew they would tell her soon enough.

"I didn't know you acted professionally," said Eve, escaping at last from Lucy's net.

"Didn't you?" Rosemary asked, looking as amazed as possible.

"Aren't you doing those classes, with Melissa whatshername and Jeremy Clark?"

"Of course," she said sweetly. "Teaching programs."

The drinks came before Eve's puzzled "But . . ." could do more than make Rosemary wince.

The important man turned his attention to Eve, who, Rosemary observed, changed from looking like a startled rabbit to looking pleased but wary, like a new mother Persian cat whose kittens are being fed scraps of sardine by a stranger.

"I knew your wife at school," Eve offered. "Elaine, her cousin, was one of my best friends at Drakeswood." But he did not regard this as a suitable conversational opening and instead allowed bright-faced Tom to catch his ear.

"I've always admired the way you put the unions in their place," said Tom. "No man in your position can let the tail wag the dog."

The man's face stiffened slightly as he established a quick barrier between himself and this line of talk also. Malcolm looked uncomfortable like one about to be judged by his choice of friends; Rosemary could see him planning a diversion. However, it was not necessary.

"It's never easy to put people out of work," the man said, sounding reasonable, patient, hardly at all patronising. "Technology advances, people are superseded, they've got to go. But it's not a nice thing to have to do."

"Well, you'd get someone else to do the dirty work," Tom said merrily. "Someone like me. I had to give forty blokes their pink slips at our Nowra plant last year."

Tom was doing her a favour, Rosemary realised. By comparison, her own words and gestures were sophisticated. There'd be no curbing Tom next day when he told his mates at work whom he'd drunk with—his eyes showed that thoughts of future opportunities had begun to rumble across his mind.

"Have you ever thought of going into the food-processing business?" Tom asked.

"Lucy Barlow. You're one of our researchers, aren't you?" The warm beam of the dark man's attention focused on Lucy as though she was the most interesting and attractive person he had ever seen and Rosemary was surprised to feel, not jealous exactly, but something close. Something like, That's what I want. That should be for me! But she was fascinated at the same time: this was the way his boss was telling Malcolm that he knew about his love affair. Lucy smiled, shining and appealing as a girl in a Macleans commercial. She was flattered that he knew exactly where she fitted in.

"Heard some good things about you," he said, as though confirmation was needed.

And now it was Rosemary's turn. She was ready for him. She wanted him to see, by the cool way she looked right into his eyes, that it did not matter whether he offered her a job or not. He handed her a card.

"Phone this number at about ten-thirty tomorrow," he said. "Michael Stoner is directing a new series for us, and he might be able to use you."

"Is that the new, fabulous, travel game show we've been hearing rumours about?" asked Malcolm.

"Nope. It's the mini-series you're not supposed to have heard about yet. 'The Mount Victorians.' Mean anything?"

"Oh, sure. Of course. I thought that was all finished a while ago? When they were shooting at that old guest house in the mountains."

"Yes, there were some people who thought it was finished. Including the script editor and a producer and a director. But this particular mini-series won't lie down and have its loose ends tied up." Watching him closely, Rosemary was fascinated by the emotions which she was sure she could discern behind his benevolent executive mask. A quick flicker of irritation. Then humour. Then pain. Settle down, she told herself, noting that he'd handed her the card upside down. He's guessed that I don't know who he is. So Rosemary decided to keep playing. She reached for the pen, still in his hand, wrote her telephone number on the blank back, and handed it to him without turning it over.

"Perhaps it would be better if he called me," she said.

It was a dangerous moment. He stood up, which made the other two men do so, too. At that moment something not quite begun could have ended, and Rosemary suddenly realised how important it was to her to follow his invitation, wherever it may lead. So when he half turned to her, to say goodbye, she gazed up at him (straight up his nostrils, actually), and then smiled, deeply, warmly, willing him to imprint her on his mind.

It took a few moments. His dark-browed eyes and strong, square face filled her vision as though he were on a TV screen. She could see the thin spattering of old acne scars here and there between his cheeks and his neck, the dark freckles on his strong lips and something rather sensual, or perhaps sensitive, bracketed by the line between his nose and chin. Then his eyes sparkled, and when he smiled back she knew for sure what would happen. He would phone her late on the following day and invite her for a drink.

"Well. See you later, Mrs. Quilty," he said.

　　　　　·　　　　　·　　　　　·

"The thing that surprises me is that you didn't recognise Robert Talbot. He's in the papers all the time," Eve said as soon as his large, dark-suited figure was out of range. "And all that about being on TV!"

Rosemary hid her "Of course!" reaction and said smoothly, "I don't read the financial papers."

"No, I mean the front pages. And the social pages. His wife does a lot for charity. Terrific woman—I saw her, last week, in the lift when

I took Ben to the allergist in Macquarie Street. She's nice looking," she added.

"He's nice looking, too, if you like that about-to-growl expression and all that dark hair," said Lucy. "Perhaps he's just not photogenic."

Rosemary pretended not to be interested. She thought about Robert Talbot's face: a certain heaviness of feature accentuated by thick brows which cast shadows over the hollows of his eyes. A crooked nose, probably the result of a perfectly acceptable childhood accident, and broad, high shoulders that gave him the look of a fighting man. But his face, especially when he smiled, which he did every now and then, was really quite attractive. Yet she was surprised at herself for not having connected the man she'd just met with the glowering tycoon who, judging by his TV and newspaper appearances, spent a good deal of time in conflict or conference with unions and whichever government was in power and whose interests included tentacles into almost everything.

It was hard for Rosemary to sit still among her friends, chatting as though nothing had happened to her while her imagination was lighting little bushfires in the accumulated scrub of her libido.

"I just wish I had the knack," said Tom. "Man like that, how many hours a week do you think he puts in behind the desk? Forty? Fifty? Less, I'd say; a lot goes into racing, golf, sailing—all business, of course. But its not exactly sitting around getting piles. Secretaries do most of that. Say sixty. But even sixty hours is only fifty percent more than what I clock up, but I bet he takes home a bit more than fifty percent up on what I earn." (And believe me, that's not peanuts, his tone implied.) Malcolm, whose earnings were well known, via the afternoon newspapers, to be more into the macadamia than the peanut class, adopted the same tone, in propitiation.

"He shops at a different supermarket to us, mate. He's into the take-over bargain basement business—the high-class poker game. You make five million here, you drop two million there, you pick up another million somewhere else, and at the end of the year the Deputy Commissioner of Taxation comes around to shake your hand."

"Unless you've managed to hide your millions at the bottom of the harbour," said Lucy.

"Well, he's smart enough and I bet his accountants and his lawyers know a good trick or two. But hiding money isn't what he's into—he prefers using it. New businesses and new ventures and the odd, judicious take-over. He's a restless bugger. Of course, he burns his fingers every now and then."

"He must enjoy it, like a game," said Rosemary.

"Yeah. Or perhaps it's just a habit. Being filthy rich and getting richer."

"Well, it's a better habit than smoking," said Eve, and Tom glanced at her apologetically, as though she'd just diagnosed what it was that caused him not to be a billionaire.

While Malcolm detailed some of the recent take-overs, mergers, and other headline-creating ventures the big corporation had made, Rosemary listened for hints about its chief executive. Everything Malcolm said was admiring, though, as Lucy pointed out, a new arrival to Australia might not have realised this. He referred to Robert Talbot as "the stupid bastard" and "the sly bugger." As though glee were a pulled thread, Malcolm's face creases gathered themselves up more and more tightly while he described a venture that had flopped because of some tricky, possibly even illegal behaviour by a competitor.

"Gee, I'd have loved to have seen his face when he realised why the shares had gone through the roof," he said happily. "Some financial so-called whiz is looking for a new job now, I'll bet. Musta losta coupla thousand grand."

"It's a good thing he's gone into the film production business. Seems as though there's a job for you in this new soapie, Rosie," said Tom.

"Mini-series," said Malcolm. "I wonder what he wants you for? I can't imagine the producer and Stoner being too pleased if the boss starts dabbling in the casting. Anyway, you'd think they'd have tied that up by now—I mean, they're shooting already, by the sound of it. And with more than half of Sydney's actors driving taxis and washing dishes, they're not exactly scratching around for talent." Then, realising what he'd said, added, "With respect," and, without standing up, bowed at Rosemary.

Eve, who looked to Rosemary like a large conscience—as though anything she had to say would start with "But . . ."—prepared again to speak, but Lucy beat her to it.

"You were wonderful. Wasn't she wonderful? I didn't know you were such a good fibber. Television experience!"

"But it's true. It's all true! I did do commercials in Canada. Well, a commercial. Two years ago when we went to stay with Daniel's sister. She does it a lot, and she dragged me along on a day when a model about my size and age didn't show up—she'd run over someone's English sheepdog and then freaked out. I had to run down some snowy steps with a group of kids, first wearing winter clothes, then wearing long underwear. Afterwards, they alternated the images, so you had us flick-ing from dressed to undressed and back again, all smiling like mad. The

smiles were frozen into place by the last take, you'd better believe—
Edmonton is where Americans would send their political prisoners if
they'd annexed Canada in time. I'm sure the Gulag Archipelago can't
be so bleak, and yet perfectly nice Canadians live in Edmonton vol-
untarily!

"Anyway," Rosemary continued, preferring to distract everyone including herself from thinking about Robert Talbot. "We were supposed
to project energy and look as though it was the underwear that made
us so happy. It was Academy Award stuff, truly. I Method-ed myself
into that interlock!"

Malcolm, who had been listening with one knee up and his hands
around it—a pose more suitable for a panel interview than a restaurant—
let go and dropped his leg with a thump like applause.

"When Lucy told me you were looking for a job in TV I thought you
had in mind the research side, with her. I didn't know I was talking to
tomorrow's big discovery."

He is, Rosemary thought, behind an appropriately modest smile. And
it's about time, too.

.   .   .

Later, while undressing after an evening which had become deliciously
merry, she decided that when Robert Talbot phoned she would turn
down his offer of a drink because at six o'clock, with the bold sunlight
still streaming into the windows of every respectable drinking place, she
would not be able to look good enough to override the tiredness of his
mind at the end of a whole day's ruthlessness. He would be hungry, his
dinner already planned by his diary or his wife, and Rosemary would
have no alternative but to go home early, too, to feed the kids. She
decided she'd suggest lunch instead.

While transferring her contact lenses from the bit of tissue she'd
wrapped them in, into their container on the bathroom shelf, Rosemary
caught a blurred impression of herself looking serious, so she grinned.
"It's OK now," she whispered. "Not serious time anymore." Then, thinking about serious time, she put her glasses on—she hated them, but
there was no one else awake—and went to the kitchen for a late-night
cup of tea.

Serious time had started around March, long enough away from the
January party for Rosemary to believe, at first, that there was no connection, especially as the symptoms were physical. She had woken stiffly,
and late, one morning. Her skin had felt stretched and her muscles
ached a little as though flu was starting. When she got up she realised
she'd become clumsy, which was so out of character that it had occurred

to her, after the third stumbling lurch, that she might be having the start of a degenerative brain disease. She'd become aware of the taste of the inside of her mouth. These symptoms had gone on for days and weeks without getting better. Aspirins had not helped.

Next there had been the tears. It was as though there were a slow leak somewhere in her emotions which caused tears to form in a dam behind her eyes, backing up into her throat and lapping at the anti-Daniel walls she had had to keep reinforcing to keep them in. But her inner dam walls were defenceless against kittens, ginger-haired five-year-olds in school uniform, sad-eyed black teenagers starving on television, people in wheelchairs, and most of the things Bobby said. She went through a lot of tissues. Her nose was red most of the time, its tip chapped from being wiped, and her eyes were so irritated that the lenses became impossible, and for days she had to wear her glasses, which made her feel like a headmistress or even a headmaster.

"Howja feel today, love?" Auntie Gwen had asked on the phone one day.

"As though I've been dipped into a mixture of flour and water and left to dry in the corner."

"Get yourself a job, then."

"I can't. I really can't. I haven't got the time. Besides, what could I do?"

"As far as I remember, from what your mother told me—and that was long ago so you've had more experience since—you virtually ran that bloody man's company. Must be something worthwhile you could do to get you out of the house."

"Well, I drive a lot of kids around—school bus runs, the cubs and scouts when it's Bobby's night. And I do my theatre course."

"Yes, but that's just play-acting."

Lucy had been a constant visitor since the night Daniel left. In Lucy the inner heat of new love revealed itself in a glow that made Rosemary wonder if she would be visible in the dark. Her straight hair gleamed like Chinese lacquer, and the wattage of her greenish eyes was constantly set on high. There was a sheen to her, a light tan, gained from working on Malcolm's boat in all weekend weathers. Even without stockings her smooth skin made a faint, swishing sound when she crossed her legs; and her limbs, when she moved, seemed as pliable as plasticine. Every day gave nourishment to Lucy, like time does with those slow-release fertilising sticks you put in garden pots. And every day some of Rosemary's nutrients were leached out.

"We're on different trains, travelling in opposite directions," Rosemary said one night.

"Maybe the direction's the same. Maybe one of us is just taking the scenic tour."

"Give me the name of your travel agent, in that case. You've got the better trip!"

It was nice of Lucy to come, which she did almost every night that she got home before midnight, climbing over the crushed back part of the fence that divided their houses. Mattie was usually asleep on an improvised bed in the living room. She adored Bobby and he rather liked showing her how good he was at card tricks and singing his solos for her from *Joseph and His Amazing Technicolour Dreamcoat,* so whenever she could she wriggled out of the formal baby-sitting arrangement at Eve's.

Rosemary could hardly have borne the pressure of not being able to tell her daily accumulation of wrath to Lucy. And Lucy, at that stage still sworn to secrecy about her love affair with Malcolm, had needed to talk about the excitement of it, the danger and the miracle. Tactfully she'd played down the romance and passion despite Rosemary's assurance that she wanted to hear everything—"It reminds me that such things exist," she'd said.

Lucy had merely smiled and continued not to go much further than what the camera operator had said when, burdened with his folded tripod, he'd backed into a set and knocked it over onto Malcolm and Lucy who were standing there kissing. Or how she'd played dumb when a notoriously snoopy columnist from a morning paper had phoned and asked her outright if it was true that she was the researcher sleeping with Malcolm Henry.

Rosemary knew that Lucy had worried about the strange state she was in—she'd seen some signs of the clumsiness and plenty of evidence of the tears. Rosemary knew Lucy was watching but she had kept from her the suspicion that what she had was cancer or even insanity. Then, one night at a rehearsal, having learned Sister Woman's lines well enough not to be anxious about them anymore, Rosemary had listened carefully to the actress playing Maggie the Cat and suddenly realised, horrified, that what she had was sensory deprivation—sexual frustration, in fact— usually the fate of teenagers, the widowed, the crippled, the aged, and, presumably, nuns. Sexual frustration was not anything she'd been required to experience before. Once she knew she wasn't going to die she began to cheer up fairly quickly.

There had been no total solution to her sensory deprivation, but, aware of it, Rosemary had become more tactile. Bobby didn't like cuddling very much, though he sometimes let her brush his hair. When she and Phyl were watching television she sat so close that their arms touched, which was nice. She even thought seriously about getting a cat to stroke and then decided she preferred the bird table—the kookaburra, though not a friend, was certainly a loyal visitor, and the lorikeets and galahs were adorable.

One TV program she and Phyl never missed, when possible, was Malcolm Henry's show, which had Lucy's name on the rapidly rolling credits. Phyl thought he was fantastic. Tears would fill her eyes as she watched him talking in perfectly modulated sympathy to brave mothers of babies with rare diseases, or angry residents in areas where half-way houses for mental patients were being planned, or visiting junior royalty. Even Bobby had watched sometimes, though he was inclined to wander away as soon as politicians appeared. There had been an election in March, so Bobby had watched little TV for a couple of months.

What had helped Rosemary most was the acting classes. There were warm-up exercises first, in which the stretching and blowing and thumping left her feeling if not good then certainly better. And she could cuddle Jeremy, the director, who was very gay and very cuddly, and very hurt when the AIDS panic began and one or two people began to be fussy about which cup he'd used.

At all times she'd kept her mind away from visions of Daniel's golden-haired, naked body pressing itself into Angela's ivory flesh, though more than once she'd actually dug her nails right through the skin of her palm while trying not to see them together in a large, pastel-sheeted bed.

In about April, a surprising solution had presented itself, though she'd been shocked when it first happened. Her dreams became so vividly erotic and so delightfully satisfying that she could hardly wait to get to bed at night. Extraordinary, blissful, and sometimes distinctly unusual congress had taken place with the most unlikely people including Tom—knowing, witty, and slimmed down for the occasion. It had been such a thrilling encounter, so full of developments and procedures that Daniel had never thought about, that after that in Tom's company she found herself glancing at him, wondering nervously whether he could have picked up the knowledge of his knowledge of her through ESP.

Once it had been Lawrie, who had been married to Daniel's mother for a few years before she died, and so, even though he was youthful-looking and vigorous, had seemed part of the previous generation to Rosemary until he arrived, sprightly, in her dream, and made her come with him. They'd rolled in warm waves and licked the salt off each other's shining bodies until the salt had changed to taste like sea-food. Then they'd transferred sweet scallops to each other's lips, like feeding birds. And while they stood there, warm and cool in the waves, his hands, his virtuoso thumbs had described flowing, gentle pressure patterns around the electric edges of her body, smoothing and lengthening her pubic hair so that it grew and flowed, like milk, like silk, in long Aubrey Beardsley strands which cocooned them in the crooning, rolling waves.

Another time her lover had started off being a man and at some stage had become a middle-aged woman, generous, deft, and suprisingly able to do things Rosemary had always believed were the exclusive province of men.

This particular dream had made her feel guilty and confused, which had led to depression. She'd wondered who the woman was who knew her so well and to whom she had responded as though she'd practised lesbianism for twenty years instead of letting her eyes slide over the word when it was encountered on pages.

Then, by the sort of luck that happens this way and is undoubtedly what makes people who pray continue to do so, she'd happened to notice an article about dreams in a British magazine in the doctor's rooms. Matter-of-factly, the expert said, "There is evidence to support the theory that all the people in one's dreams are aspects of oneself."

The relief was wonderful! The notion of erotic egotism had appealed so greatly to Rosemary's sense of self-sufficiency that, instead of presenting a case for tranquillisers, which she had intended to do, she'd simply asked the doctor for a referral to the dermatologist, to have the little skin-strings burned off her neck. And she'd gone home feeling deeply amused, secretly pleased, and somewhat rejuvenated and put the doctor's referral letter in her Medibank file where it had stayed until she really needed it.

Since then Rosemary had enjoyed her dreams with no sense of guilt. She'd enjoyed the practical signs of their having been: of waking up to find herself flushed, panting, and suffused in the delicious sea-food aroma of her own sexual moisture. She and some figment had come again.

It was never easy to be self-sufficient, but at least in some ways it was possible, and once or twice she'd even begun to believe she'd never have to be troubled with real men again. But, Don't be silly, she told herself. Go on like this and it'll become a symptom of madness. Regard it as practise for the real thing.

Which was undoubtedly the next item on the program.

She rinsed her cup, still grinning about her winter fantasies and of the delicious spring which would surely feature the high-shouldered Mr. Talbot. Reality. That was what she craved now. It would stamp out serious time forever.

In bed, trying again for sleep, she could not stop thinking of Robert Talbot, the job, the tension between them, and the magical feeling of rightness about her own responses. This is the sort of man I should have married! she thought, with no conscience whatsoever about Daniel. I'd have been just the right wife: good at parties, diplomatic, full of the right advice . . . he's got such big hands. Briefly her fantasies became inarticulate. But it's not just sex, she thought firmly. Mine could have been the voice behind the throne.

It was a philosophical discussion, of course—nothing to do with realities like the wife in the Macquarie Street lift or her own beloved children who would have been different people if she hadn't married Daniel. But there were irresistible truths: a life with someone like Robert Talbot would have offered rewards.

Daniel had recently become fairly rich (which he would not have done without her help, as Auntie Gwen kept remarking), but he was still mean in the way of many men new to money, whereas the eminent Mr. Talbot would never have thought of rationing money for beautiful clothes, fresh oysters, foreign travel, fun. . . .

Rosemary was nearly asleep when she recognised the dark shape draped over her little grey armchair—the red dress. It was too important to lie there, dumped, so she got up, fumbled it onto a hanger, and hung it in the mirrored dressing room. And when its full hemline brushed across her face, she gathered the material in her cupped hands and kissed it.

Three

It was a mistake to have hung up the red dress, Rosemary decided shortly after she woke up. Had it still been there, that symbol of confidence glossily sprawled in the early morning light, it may have conferred another booster shot to her esteem. But the room was just as it had been since Daniel had gone—bleak, neat, with no sign of masculine occupation—and its bleakness matched the mood she'd woken up with, a mood left over from a night of troubling dreams.

Only one dream had left any visual image; from the others there was just the legacy of unease. Creature-people with small, ugly faces had mocked her. They had not been children's faces—they were too cynical and knowing for that—but imp faces, pinched and distorted like those malicious, muscular creatures who do strange things in Hieronymus Bosch paintings. She'd felt she knew some of them, that perhaps they were friends, dressed up and teasing her, that it was a game she'd soon understand and enjoy. But it was no game. There were no friendly faces as, casually, they had grouped and regrouped in order to cut off her lines of escape. Her growing sense of terror—which she was careful not to show—was of what they would do to her when they'd trapped her. There had been the sense that they could read her thoughts, so it had been impossible to outwit them. Her most cunning escape plans were known immediately, as though she'd said them aloud. They had surrounded her, moving easily, leering, and constantly watching her with hard eyes. There was no protector. They knew that. They knew she did not deserve to be protected.

She had shouted at them, hoping to scare them away, but they'd known the shout was a disguised cry of fear. But the muffled sounds of her dream-shouting had woken her as once they would have woken Daniel, who'd have comforted her back to sleep—though it was unlikely she'd ever have had that particular dream if Daniel was still with her.

The early light had already washed the last of night's monochrome with faint colour, and soon it would be dawn. Because her body was still damp with the sweat of anxiety, and because she was afraid to go back to sleep in case the demons were still there, she decided to have a shower. Then she dressed in a track suit and changed the sheets so there was no temptation to get back into bed.

The dream was connected, somehow, with the amazing sense of power and hope she'd had the previous night when she'd met Robert Talbot. What on earth did I say to that man? she asked herself, staring, out of focus without her glasses, at the tree outside her window. How arrogant! How could I play flirty games with someone so important? He must think I'm an absolute idiot.

The elm's delicate branches quivered suddenly and violently, blurring the pale green leaves like a rapidly tossed salad. She could barely make out the energy source, but she knew what it was—a grey blob now occupied one swaying branch. But the kookaburra didn't risk his break-fast to the chance that she might not have seen him; his loud yakkak-katakking would certainly have woken her if the dream gremlins had not done so first.

"There's no bacon. Why don't you go and frighten someone else for a change?" she asked but he yakkatakked again like one who knew his rights.

It was a Thursday. In an hour she'd have to start the slow, tense process of getting Bobby out of bed for school. Phyl was easier in the morning, but not much—they both dreaded the scramble and uproar of breakfast, lost compasses, lunch money, and lateness and so they postponed it. At a more rational time of the day, they would agree that getting up fifteen minutes earlier, would solve the problem but usually, next morning, it would happen again. Once she'd tried to trick them by setting their bedside radio clocks fifteen minutes earlier, but the an-nouncers had soon revealed the true time, which had made Phyl swoon gratefully back into her pillow and Bobby accuse Rosemary of cheating. She had finally concluded that snapping and snarling at each other and at her seemed to set her children up for survival and that her participation was a vital part of the anti-day game they played. And she was compelled to participate—to chivvy them, help them, and be the one to blame for lost things and for turning them out of where they'd prefer to be if it weren't for the law. Because if she didn't do all that they'd go so slowly that they'd miss their morning lift down the Wakehurst Parkway to

Mosman with Tom, who worked near there. Then Rosemary would have to get the Volvo out and fight the traffic.

It was ironic, she thought on the way to the kitchen on behalf of the kookaburra, that what the children wanted most—to stay at home doing nothing much—was what she wanted least. Yet this day she was compelled to do so in case the agency rang about another job interview with someone less sleazy than Mr. Gillespie. It would be a lonely, probably wasted day. She knew now, as surely as did the dream goblins, that no dazzling millionaire tycoon would phone to offer her a drink or a job in a film or any other such opportunity at a charmed life.

She crumbled a spoonful of cold minced beef off the solid block she had pulled from the freezer and zapped it for a few seconds in the microwave. The kookaburra didn't like mince; what he liked best was fillet steak which he could pretend was a lizard he'd skinned or a mouse achieved by skill and speed seconds before its hole. Rosemary, too, would have preferred fillet steak or even rump but lately the house-keeping budget had been the cause of unwelcome phone discussions with Shirley Coote, Daniel's secretary, who, since Rosemary no longer worked in the company, made out all the cheques.

Shirley's picky queries about household bills and store accounts in-furiated Rosemary, though she had managed to keep her anger under control during the inquisitions because, though Shirley obviously re-lished the role, Rosemary knew she was working under Daniel's instruc-tion. It was one of his ways of pretending not to inflict pain. It left Rosemary with the choice of enduring the queries—going into details about what she'd bought for whom—or of talking to Daniel himself, which was even worse, or of doing without. So she'd chosen to do without lots of things that, from the grey area between luxuries and necessities, she and Daniel together had regarded as necessities. Like theatre and concert tickets and little snacky things in case people came for drinks. And family dinners at Italian restaurants and occasional week-ends at mountain guest-houses and pâté and supermarket packs of frozen sliced salmon. And pistachio nuts.

"So," she said to the kookaburra who, having followed her progress from bedroom to kitchen, was now raucously perched on the patio railing where she usually fed it, "like Daniel Quilty's lawful wedded—but un-attended—wife, and his confused son and daughter, you will have to settle for mince. Or starve." It ate the mince as though it understood perfectly.

Perhaps it was the bright spring light, or the fact that the day was already well established for Rosemary and the split ends of her own early morning nerves had succumbed to the conditioning process of routine, but Phyl and Bobby were unusually friendly at breakfast.

"How was the dinner?" Phyl asked through a mouthful of multi-grain porridge and honey.

"Nice," said Rosemary. "Very nice. I had lobster."

Phyl gave her a look that said, "OK, so you don't want to talk about it," a challenge Rosemary was able to bypass by responding to Bobby, who'd said, "You looked pretty cool. Pretty zowie."

"Thanks, darling. Does that mean pretty?"

"Yeah. That, too," he said, and actually smiled, which was rare for Bobby who was practising being tough.

"I'll be late today. Got a rehearsal," he said, preparing for the sprint across the road and two houses down where Tom could already be seen raising the double door of his garage.

"Oh, Lord, that isn't the dress rehearsal is it?"

"No, dumbo, that's on Saturday, and then the first show is that night, that you and Phyl and Dad are coming to. Don't you remember they had to change the dress rehearsal because we couldn't get the full orchestra today or tomorrow?" He started to dash off, but Rosemary, who was confused by his machine-gun rattle of words, grabbed his T-shirt. He stopped as though shot and turned to give her a look which mingled impatience with condescension—a look he'd learned from Daniel.

"Exactly when is the dress rehearsal, Bobby? I would like to know," she asked, delivering her irritation in speech so deliberate that it could have been an elocution lesson.

Bobby recognised the challenge and answered in an even speedier blur. "I said. Sa'ry arvo."

"Saturday afternoon!" she said, and jerked his T-shirt.

" 'Swot I said."

She stared at him, preparing a parental lecture about slang, manners, and related subjects and then suddenly let go, so that he lurched slightly. It was not his fault that he sometimes looked so much like Daniel.

"Was it really nice last night?" Phyl said, following more slowly.

"Really nice," Rosemary said, in control again. "Interesting. I'll tell you about it when there's time. When you come home."

"I'll also be late," Phyl said. "There's that special maths coach coming that I signed up for."

"Ah, yes. Hell, your lunch won't be enough, not for either of you. Just a sec." And Rosemary dashed into the hall stand—old oak she'd stripped herself—to where a small emergency hoard of petty cash was hidden in the drawer under a pile of old bills.

"Take this," she said, putting four dollars in Phyl's hand. "Two each for something with protein in it. Love you."

"Love you, too," Phyl said, smiling like royalty as she stepped into Tom's Commodore which he'd driven up with a hurry-up flourish. Like an ideal parent, Rosemary stood on the front driveway and waved until they were out of sight. Then the ideal parent smile came off, and she took her self-doubts back inside, determined to do some cleaning to keep her blood going and her mind off the telephone.

She dragged the vacuum cleaner, polish, and rags into the living room, planning to pull all the books and magazines out and suck up every fluff ball and speck of wood ash so that even though she didn't feel very bright, her favourite room would. She'd drag every household mite and every secret moth egg out into the open where it could do no stealthy harm. She'd burnish every potential rust spot and chlorinate anything that looked like a mould spore.

The room was the product of hard work, good taste, and quite a lot more money than either she or Daniel had bargained for at the time. Its dark woodwork—unusual in a modern Australian house—had taken a slow-working perfectionist Italian cabinet-maker seven weeks longer to install than his painfully written quote had promised. Sheet-draped, higgledy-piggledy furniture and crates of unpacked books had overfilled the living and dining rooms for the whole of their first winter there while Mr. Menotti slowly laboured, and the family had been forced to live and eat in the children's play room—now called the rumpus room— surrounded by the daily chaos Bobby made with his toys, biscuits, and leaking nappies. And they'd been burgled, just as Rosemary had feared they would be, when Mr. Menotti was unable to thoroughly secure one of the half-framed windows. Now, ten years later, Mr. Menotti's wood- work was generally regarded as a tribute worth having lost the television for, a monument to the dying age of craftsmanship.

There were wide cedar sills to the big windows which, in most di- rections, framed scenes of bird-filled bush and in one provided a section of Middle Harbour, a blue strip variously described as "ocean views" and "harbour glimpses" in the hand-outs the real estate people had provided at the auction. The skirting boards, the heavy doors, and the huge, almost wall-sized panelled bookcase were mitred at the edges and wooden-pegged wherever screws were not essential. Their surfaces were immaculately grooved and then polished to a dark-reddish glow which dully refracted the light from the room's white, rough-plastered walls. Rosemary had furnished it in soft grey and tan colours, so that the brilliant yellow sofa, large, soft, and right in the middle of the room opposite the fireplace, was the focal point. It established a strong, tonal connection with the big Dobell portrait which hung in the recess left of the fireplace.

This was Rosemary's most valuable possession—a softly painted, angular portrait of a middle-aged barrister, a second cousin of Auntie Gwen's who'd left it to her in his will for some strange reason. And she had given it to Rosemary: "Don't like the thing myself. Bugger looks like a spaceman," she'd said, though Rosemary suspected the gruffness was intended to ensure that the Quiltys would accept it as a gift and not as a hint that they buy it.

Rosemary had bought quite a lot of paintings in the past decade, often from first exhibitions, small galleries, or sale rooms. She had chosen them because they'd appealed in different ways and not because she necessarily believed they would appreciate in value. But one of Daniel's clients, who'd visited a year ago, was a man with an interest in a major gallery, and he had been impressed by most of her choices.

A stiff, white-whiskered retired brigadier, whose bearing still revealed years of standing at attention, he'd actually become boring after a few ports, repeating, "Watch this space, Daniel Quilty. Watch this space, ho, ho, ho. Got a little gold mine here in the making." In Daniel's opinion, which he'd voiced every time she'd bought a new one, Rosemary's acquisition of pictures had been irresponsible if not malicious— a tourniquet on the company's cash flow.

The brigadier had done more than make Daniel look at Rosemary with new respect—he'd made her feel clever and feminine in that nice, old-fashioned, finger-fluttering way of Garbo movies. She'd asked him about one of her favourite pictures, the one she called "The Sad-eyed Lady."

One special day, when she and Daniel were on the way back from a trip to Katoomba in the Blue Mountains, she had bought it at a little "old wares" shop at Lawson. It was a bargain because the artist's name was too faintly painted for the shop owner or Rosemary to read, and because it was a portrait.

The woman in the picture had dark brown, shining hair parted in the middle and covering her ears in a sleek style like a dark cap. She was sitting, half turned, in a straight-backed chair, with one arm over the back. One slim-wristed, long-fingered hand lightly covered the other, which was visible from the wrist. She was not conventionally pretty— her nose was much too big for that, and her uncompromising hair-style revealed a thickish neck. But her face was fine-boned and there was a deep dimple in her chin that proclaimed a sensuousness her prim style could not conceal. She was looking beyond the frame at some point at floor level, with an expression of wistful yearning and deep sadness, as though only recently resigned to some dreadful loss, perhaps of a lover or a child. What could be seen of her dress was black. Her dark, slightly uneven eyes were partly hidden by shadow and by her brown-pencilled brows.

The serious plainness of the woman's face was softened by a touch of beauty—her red, soft mouth— which turned up at the corners as though more used to laughter than sadness. It was a strong face; someone Rosemary felt she would have liked if they had met.

"Very competent. Very competent," the brigadier had said after examining the little picture under three different strengths of light.

"I guessed it was done in the thirties, because of the hair-style," Rosemary had offered, like a bright child.

"Ah, yes. Yes indeed. Early thirties. Nice colour. Lovely work on the hands—she's been looking at a lot of Giotto."

"She?"

"Oh, I'd say it was a woman. Could even be a self-portrait, don't you think? Let's see that signature again? Looks like C. Lawland? Lawford? Sawford? No. Doesn't ring any bells. But even a good work by an unknown is worth something. Forgive me, my dear Rosemary, for presuming to lecture you—you know what you're doing." It surprised her that anyone could say that, even as a gallantry, since she'd seldom known what she was doing. But she didn't show her surprise; instead she'd said grandly as she led her guest back to the decanter, "The value doesn't matter. I'd never sell it."

Today, the sad-eyed lady matched Rosemary's Mrs. Mop mood. Beauty has bypassed us both, she seemed to say, apparently staring at the last of a huge pile of books on the floor which, one by one, Rosemary had been brushing before returning to a now-clean shelf. Perhaps love has passed us by, too, as well as adventure.

Having done the walls, light fittings, and picture frames, the books' load of brushings was the last to join the invisible rain of ashy dust that had clogged Rosemary's nostrils before settling on the carpet. No one ever talked about the disadvantages of an open fire when it was crackling in the grate, but spring cleaning was undoubtedly a less-black process in electrically warmed houses. The prospect of sucking all the muck up and getting rid of it for good was what had spurred Rosemary on through the cleaning frenzy, but as she switched the vacuum cleaner on it made a fairly loud popping sound, a whizz of electricity, and a little smokey sigh.

It was not a simple matter of a too-full bag (both Bobby and Phyl being inclined to pretend they'd emptied it when they hadn't) a strong smell of burning indicated that this time it was critical, if not terminal. When she rushed to switch it off at the wall the power point was hot.

"Shit!" she said, and kicked it. Long before he'd left, Daniel had known they needed another vacuum cleaner, but he'd kept fiddling with screwdrivers and poking knitting needles into its pipes to keep it going far beyond the point of its planned obsolescence. As it had taken eleven years to get a decent refrigerator, Rosemary had had little hope of a second new appliance in the same year, even though, she now thought crossly, it would have cost no more than two cases of wine or a three-hour business lunch.

"I've *got* to get a job!" she told the sad-eyed lady, who simply gazed reproachfully at the dusty floor.

In due course, Rosemary would have to have another stiff-lipped negotiation with Shirley Coote about a new vacuum cleaner. But for the time being she cleaned up the worst of the dust with a brush and pan, put the old vacuum cleaner in the corner of the garage where junk was kept between council clean-up days, and made herself a cup of tea and a buttered Ryvita biscuit. Later she'd borrow Lucy's Hoover, but in the meantime she had to think of other things to do to fill the time between now and when the phone might not even ring.

There had to be something to fill the nothingness, because sipping her tea in the lonely kitchen, she felt the first vibrations of panic. Sure there was more surface wiping to do—ultimately all housework can be reduced to wiping surfaces—but far from being an aid to blocking the memory, cleaning seemed to stimulate it.

All the potentially explosive things she'd disciplined herself not to think about since Daniel had left were held together inside by something as frail as webbing and camouflaged by the blur of energy she learned to create by moving briskly through lots and lots of things to do. This was how she'd managed to make a barrier which, nearly all the time, had kept Daniel out and her courage in. Now there was nothing to shield her from what was hidden within—Daniel would swamp her mind when the webbing broke. He would take over, the way "Jingle Bells" and other simple Muzak tunes do in shops at Christmas time.

.   .   .

On the January night that Angela had crashed the party and Daniel had left, Lucy was the one guest who succeeded in refusing to go. She'd made herself look as tall as possible, and stern.

"I'm not leaving you like this. I'm going to give you a glass of brandy and see that you get into bed."

"No, go," Rosemary had said, fearful that she'd have to talk about what she'd not even thought about yet. But Lucy would not listen.

Time, and the room she was in, even the air, had seemed to swim and shimmer around Rosemary. She remembered putting Bobby to bed, firmly, as though he were three, because he refused to go on his own. He should not have been there anyway: the deal had been that all the small and middling kids were to sleep in Tom and Eve's rumpus room after a feast of chips, Coke, and horror movies. But they'd heard Melissa shouting in the street and come out to relish the scene.

"I hate him!" Bobby had sobbed from his pillow. "I hate you!" Rosemary had bowed her head, agreeing on both points: too hateful, too hated, to be any use to him.

She had sat in her corner of the yellow sofa, aware of Lucy's cat-like watchfulness, and waited for the pain—or whatever—to come through the nothingness. Numb. She was numb. Her feelings had disconnected. Her mind had observed, anxiously, that there must be something unnatural about this state. Her emotions were covered by some sort of cushion and were unavailable.

What came through the nothingness first was a totally inappropriate giggle, closely followed by a trickle of fear. Next was intuition, dreadful as thunder: there would be more of the same—more nothingness, more silliness, more fear—whichever way she looked or thought from now on.

"I don't believe it," she said.

"Well, it happened. But you know, it's probably not important."

"It is to her."

Lucy had not argued with this.

"She's got confident legs," said Rosemary. "Like a window shop model."

"She looks altogether like a David Jones dummy, but only half as bright. Here are some more tissues and I'm going to make us some strong coffee to go with the brandy."

"The kitchen's in a mess."

"And that's important?"

Rosemary had to agree that gathering beer cans full of cigarette butts, damp paper plates full of chicken bones, and watermelon peels full of little ants was probably not as important a matter, right now, as dealing with the fact that her husband had left her. So she sat twisting tissues while loyal Lucy crashed around in the kitchen.

What had stung Rosemary, apart from the message of Angela's legs, was Angela's words: she'd called her a frigid bitch. Although Rosemary was known to have good legs (when their tops weren't too heavy), Angela's were in a different class. They were beautiful, like all the rest of her. And beauty, as Rosemary had observed before, gave great power to those blessed with it, like being dealt nearly all the spades in bridge.

Angela was about twenty-five with short-cut, pale hair around a face whose smooth planes and hollows suggested that the bones were moulded of something fine, strong, and fragile like porcelain, but warmer. The lines and curves from chin to temple, the look of silk about her skin— so delicate, so right—gave an effect that seemed more like a reflection of her will and her taste than a fortuitous accident of bone and tissue. There was something about her that made Rosemary think about pearls or ivory, an unused quality that could almost be measured and valued for insurance.

Her eyes were like those of a young, soft animal: wide, brown, richly belashed, and shining with what looked like innocence. Her neck was long and creamy. It was little comfort to know that in time it would go scrawny and she wouldn't be able to hide it, the way Marlene Dietrich couldn't.

Biting her fingers, damping and crumpling a series of tissues, much of Rosemary's energy had gone into disgust and humiliation about the fact that secretly, and who knows for how long, Daniel had been making comparisons. And about the fact that she'd ignored the warning signals which, looking back, he'd made so often and so clearly that he probably thought she'd given permission.

Maybe, she thought, I did.

Angela must have learned a lot about her. She had spent at least six months working closely at the more exciting side of Daniel.

"I've got a new girl," Daniel had said. "She's had some PR experience as well as being a pretty good secretary. I'll pay her a bit of overtime, and she can hand out the name-tags and the olives and work the video machine so you won't have to bother about seminars and cocktail parties anymore."

It had sounded like a pat on the back, an acknowledgement of her exhausting schedule. Now Rosemary suffered the irony. A new girl! And who paid whom what for the overtime?

"Where's Rosemary?" Angela had said, waving her ivory arms like a dry-land swimmer. Actually, she'd shouted—a little slurred but not enough to muddy the tones of her clear, confident, Eastern-suburbs-private-school voice. "Which of these suburban queen bees is Rosemary? The blood sucker? The frigid bitch with the legal document?"

"He must have given her the impression that I . . . that we

don't . . . that . . ." said Rosemary to Lucy, who had returned like an old-fashioned nurse with a tray full of comforting things, from which Rosemary had selected only the brandy. The sight of stuffed eggs and French pastries had made her nauseous, and she realised she'd probably never eat again.

She'd cried a little, then thought how ridiculous she looked, crying for her lost man, and stopped. Then, without consultation, she'd suddenly cried a whole lot more.

"Jesus! Frigid! He's crazy!" she said, gulping and snorting, not caring about the sound and sight of herself. "That's really the only bloody thing we had in common, apart from the kids. Who were caused by it!"

Lucy had not heard much of this, disguised and disjointed as it was by sobs. "Get it all out, get it all out," she soothed, like a mantra. But they both knew it was impossible to squeeze that much pain out in only one night's crying.

.   .   .

The day after the party, Rosemary had had Daniel's clothes, golf bag, trophies, and filing cabinet (from which she'd removed the file called "Birth Certs. Etc.") delivered to his office by taxi truck, collect. She'd kept on the move all day, rushing, without a script, from unrehearsed scene to unrehearsed scene. Among them were getting her hair cut in a new and, unfortunately, unsuitable way. Another was to drink a whole bottle of wine, which made her feel fuzzy and stupid about dealing with what had happened without actually blurring the pain. Three times she had started dialling Daniel's direct line.

Through the wine on that first scriptless day, Rosemary had gone up and down a piano key-board of reactions to her betrayal, from sharp rage to flat despair. She'd cleaned up the party's mess as though running on automatic pilot—calmly, efficiently, tirelessly, though in a blur—until everything was done. Even the records were cleaned of ash and fingerprints and put back in their plastic vests.

After half a day of it, she'd felt mildly concerned about this zombie state; she suspected that her emotions had died and that she'd spend the rest of her life like a slightly warm computer. But then, suddenly, she'd frightened herself in the serene, yellow-gold light of her usually ordered living room by exploding inside. It had come out in yelling "Swine swine swine swine bastard swine!" loudly enough to crack a larynx. Then she'd observed herself throwing things—his huge, largely unread pile of *Time* magazines, his rack of tapes and film clips of successful PR presentations, his pewter beer mug. This last item had smashed the amber glass of one of the wall light fittings, littering a pale silk-covered chair with shards like dangerous confetti. Then she'd sobbed, tissue-less, so that trails of snot, saliva, and glass festooned the yellow cushion.

At one stage she looked at the time and noticed, relieved, that there was a whole hour in which to recover from rage that bordered on insanity and tidy up before the kids came back from school, when she would have to properly start being a single parent.

She'd whimpered about what the hairdresser had done and what she had been too self-absorbed to notice until the fatal slice was taken: the last thing Phyl and Bobby needed was a new-look single parent with an aggressively jutting jawline and a hint of mannishness around the ears. The removal of her soft, though nondescript, curls had left her features with nothing to hide behind and there she was, all truths exposed, like a landscape after a bushfire.

But when the children came home the blurry bits of herself were all fairly neatly pulled together, and she was able to smile at them with real love. Phyl had heard the news from Bobby on the way home. Rosemary would have preferred to have told her herself, but there had been no other solution. Phyl had spent the party night with a friend in Paddington because the French teacher had succumbed without notice and organised a class visit to a restaurant with *crevettes, volaille, au vin,* and other useful vocabulary on the menu.

At first, when she came home, Phyl had seemed more amused than shocked and this had upset Rosemary until she'd realised that Phyl was trying to cheer her up by looking on the bright side of abandonment. That first day was like a trailer played on fast forward of what was to come. Some of the days thereafter were not so bad, others were much worse. There was a week or so when each day, as soon as the kids had gone, Rosemary went upstairs, got back into bed, and wept until two-thirty. Then she got up, fixed her hair, and made up her face carefully so that there was no trace when they came home. When her friends phoned she had put them off in such a reassuring way that most of them wondered if what they'd witnessed or heard about Daniel leaving was true.

These were the days she could not help remembering while drinking tea alone in her wood-finished kitchen, despite desperate months of successful forgetting.

.   .   .

"Did Daniel phone?" Lucy had asked two nights after the party.

"No. But when he does, I won't say anything to him. I'll be out."

"That's crazy—you've got to talk."

"No. I've got a new theory about anger. I've decided to hang on to it and see if it will turn into something better than just a big blast. I'm sure it can."

"You mean you want him back? You're going to pretend nothing's happened?"

"*No!* Not at all—just the opposite. I mean I'm not going to end it in a big, nasty fight. It can wither gracefully, like an autumn leaf, and I'll preserve the juice that would have gone into it."

"He won't know about the juice—he'll think you're just being a good Mummy, waiting for the naughty boy to come home and say he's sorry."

"How disgusting!"

"Well, unless you tell him your theory, what else can he think? If you're not cross with him for sleeping with whatshername he'll think you're waiting for the glow to fade. He'll probably want to come back soon, you know."

"No."

"How can you be so definite? You'll miss him. You'll forgive him."

"No."

"There's no point in talking about it now. There's nothing like hurt feelings to make people go deaf."

"No, you're wrong. I've got hurt feelings, sure, but I've got logic, too, so I've set aside the feelings for the moment and thought it out. I've thought about nothing else since he left, actually, and whichever way I look at it, it's over. I really don't want him anymore. I'll miss him. I already do—that's ridiculous, isn't it? I keep wanting to phone him up and say 'Something terrible happened to me last night,' and have him say 'Really? Poor Ro! Wasn't that awful.' You know, like when you give up smoking, and you keep thinking that what you need as a reward for being so strong is a cigarette. I'm not making sense."

"Yes, yes," said Lucy.

"I entrusted myself to him, believing he'd realise how fragile and potentially bright I was. Like a light bulb, with him to supply the current. But now I can see that it was like leaving a light bulb on the floor in a kindergarten—he's misused me, and probably hurt himself on the broken edges."

"You mean you married a man who can't tell the difference between a light bulb and a football?"

Rosemary didn't think that was funny. Then she realised that her sense of humour was another on the long list of things lost because of Daniel.

·   ·   ·

Rosemary's life with Daniel had been a circus trick, a balancing, juggling act: difficult, made to look easy, and in which timing was the essence.

She'd learned to be all the Rosemarys necessary for the smooth running of his and the children's lives and of the house and the business.

The trouble is that time, unlike money, cannot be handled objectively—not budgeted in advance nor invested to earn interest, nor can it be used as an asset to borrow more on. As the family's tacit assumption had been that she belonged to them—an assumption she had never thought of denying—there had been many frantic phone calls, cancelled lectures, and take-away meals; and the refrigerator had bristled inside with the components of quick meals and outside with green frog magnets holding urgent messages.

In order to fit in some want-to's among the have-to's, Rosemary had had to learn to run faster, to do more in less time, and to try not to let the family suffer from stress fall-out. At the time, because of both extreme busy-ness and long habit, she had not asked herself questions about the quality of her marriage—not often, anyway. If she had asked, her answers would have been cloaked in the lubrication of sentiment.

Having never been anyone else's wife or even lover, Rosemary had accepted that her marriage to Daniel was perfectly fine, even though their interests were essentially so different and their points of view were often lost in the mess of words—more and more words that each would pour forth in reinforcement of a communication gone wrong. Often the air between them would be an invisible battlefield so full of word-soldiers jostling for position, ducking, darting away, finessing and shooting at random that the sides would get mixed up and they would hurt themselves as well as each other. The casualties would be immense. It would seem as though there could never be any possibility of tenderness or tolerance or truce. Then one would touch the other, and all the lies of words would begin to dissolve and all the wounds would be healed in the pleasure of apologising in the only truthful language they both knew.

She and Daniel had been good in bed for nearly seventeen years and this had served to disguise, or at least lubricate, the truth that they were unlike in most respects. They had also been good in the bath room, the dining room, his car, her car, the hammock next to the swimming pool, and anywhere else they happened to be when the thought struck them and the kids were not around. Due to technical difficulties, the thought had only once struck them in the hammock. If asked, Rosemary would have said that all marriages were variations on the theme of sexual diplomacy.

She'd done the things good wives were supposed to do. She had made herself interested in Daniel's other passions: the business, fixing old cars, sailing, and providing the children with advantages. She had not asked him for more than that. It was the role of women, she believed, to do that difficult balancing, juggling act. But on the night Daniel left she had dropped the lot.

But not, she found to her surprise, forever. The children were still there and, in due course, hungry. The house was still there. Even she was still there, although there had been a time at the worst of it when she was almost surprised to see a reflection in her mirror.

Gradually, ball by ball, she'd picked most of the juggling balls up again despite the fact that it had sometimes seemed impossible or pointless. Now, as she reluctantly looked back, those first months seemed like a montage in sepia from a foreign movie full of scenes of herself as a haggard, weeping, wild-haired woman clutching her children, fearing the future and mistrusting the past.

.   .   .

It had taken nearly a week after the party for Daniel to phone. Every cell in every bone had been listening for his call from the first day. A loaded muzzle of feelings, diffuse and multiple as bird shot, was at the ready for him—but with its safety catch on in accordance with Rosemary's plan not to wham him.

Each time the phone had rung, she'd felt a confusion of relief and disappointment that it was someone else. But when it was actually him on the phone, she was in the shower, washing—again—the horrible new hair-style, and its ring had insinuated into the sound of the water in a way that suggested it had been going on for some time.

Thinking that it was Phyl from a call box near the ferry, in some trouble perhaps (a rush of menstrual blood, a lost bus pass—both had happened before), she had flung a towel around herself, raced for it, and reached it just as it stopped. But it had rung again almost immediately.

"Ro? Where were you?" Daniel said.

"Oh, it's you, darling," she said, then almost writhed with anger at herself. Darling! The word had long ago lost its lover meaning and become a handle, a nickname. But now, in changed circumstances, it made her sound pathetic, like one who wanted to pretend nothing had happened.

Daniel, who had undoubtedly been prepared for at least the bird shot, was relieved to hear Rosemary sound so friendly. "Yes, it's me, darling," he said in a bright, happy voice. "I want to come around and talk to you about all this. And I want to pick up a few things." Spasms of rage, like nausea, had rippled through Rosemary's body. She could not talk. Daniel had plunged on. "We've got to make arrangements about the kids and so on. And money," he'd said, talking intelligently, efficiently, as though this were a video seminar he intended to plan with her.

Her voice had been too small to reflect all the ripples of her anger, her loss, her deep, deep wound.

"Don't!" she'd said.

"What? Darling, speak up. I can't hear you."

She'd hung the phone up and leaned against the wall, knowing it would ring again. This time, more prepared, she'd said, "I don't want to speak to you. Not now. Maybe not ever. The kids do. Phone them in the morning before school. And you've got all your things apart from two more pairs of shoes, the stuff that was in the wash, and another box of the things you used to keep in the living room. These I'll send."

"Now listen, Ro," he'd said, "be reasonable. You can't . . ." But she did, and this time he did not phone back, which was a good thing, because Rosemary would have sobbed into the phone.

She was still leaning against the wall near the phone when Phyl had come home.

"Mom!" she yelled, and, dropping her school-bag, she acquired the instant, focussed efficiency of a paramedic. Her arms around Rosemary, she stumbled her to the bedroom.

"Was that Dad? What did he say?"

Rosemary had shaken her head. Phyl sat with her, trembling with concern and hurt, holding her hand and muttering "Bastard! Bastard!"—her own copy of Rosemary's refrain.

Later that night, Rosemary had heard Phyl sobbing in her room. The door was closed, and the sound was muffled through a pillow—Rosemary was not supposed to hear. Phyl had tried to pretend she'd been sleeping when she heard the door open. She's protecting me from her unhappiness, Rosemary thought. Daniel had done this! Daniel had caused this fifteen-year-old child to feel the wounds and guilt of betrayed love years before it was time for her to know any of love's rewards.

"It's going to be OK," she'd said, knowing it was a lie.

Phyl had fallen asleep holding her slim-boned, long-fingered hand across her hot forehead as though to retain the comfort through her sleep.

.   .   .

Shortly after two, when Rosemary had given up trying to fight the process of remembering, the phone rang and shocked her into the present. I'll need vitamin B complex for these nerves, she thought, reaching for the receiver. It was the employment agency with two secretarial jobs, one in a legal office and the other in the personnel department of a department store. Both jobs offered lower salaries than the minimum amount Rosemary had agreed to when she signed up and she said so. She reminded the woman of her experience in office management and public relations, but even to herself she sounded unconvincing and perhaps dishonest. Had she really done all those things? The day of nightmares, dust, and reminiscence had had the same effect on her self-esteem that a heavy hand would have if pressed on the thin-piped trellis-work of an iced cake.

"I haven't had legal experience," she said, trying not to sound too crumbled and fragile.

"Yes, that's why the starting salary's a little lower."

"It's a hundred and fifty dollars a week lower than the minimum Mrs. Pearson and I talked about."

"Well, as you know, the job market is very tight at the moment. I'd go and see Mr. Roberts if I were you." (No, you wouldn't, thought Rosemary. You probably drive a Ferrari.) "He might be negotiable. He said he doesn't mind older people."

Knowing that if she thought about that for even a second she'd feel both ancient and compromised, Rosemary said, "And the other one pays even less."

"Ah yes, but you get staff discounts on all your purchases. Except groceries, of course." At that salary there won't be any purchases, was what she wanted to say. Instead, numbly accepting this new turn in her destiny, Rosemary agreed to an interview at ten-thirty the next day with the department store, but she drew the line at the negotiable Mr. Roberts whose line of work was so far removed from her vision of herself as a creative person that she knew for sure she'd never do his law firm justice, even though she was an older person.

Idiot, she told herself when the call was over. Robert Talbot invited me to phone that film producer about a job. If I'd kept his card last night instead of showing off I might have had a really interesting interview lined up now—the first step into the way my life should be. But there was no use in brooding. She'd played her feeble hand boldly and lost.

She moved into the garden for a return bout in the unwinnable war against snails and caterpillars and to cut back the scraggy bits of jasmine that had finished blooming. There was evidence that hyacinths and Dutch irises had poked their pale shoots through the earth, but they'd all been levelled by snails, which made Rosemary shiver, remembering her evil dream. She was faced with a grim choice of preoccupations: the future, which seemed to hold no hope, and the past, which seemed to offer no advantage. Earlier in the year, despite Lucy's warnings, Rosemary had vowed never to let Daniel into her head again.

"Unexpressed rage makes you uptight," Lucy had said. "I know, I went through a bit of that when Jack left."

"I'll take the risk," Rosemary had said bravely, seeing herself as a symbol of one alone against the world. Now, rather than think about the job she didn't want and about the way she'd certainly ruined her chances of help from Robert Talbot, it was almost comforting to remember.

.   .   .

On the Saturday in January, two days after Daniel had rung and she'd twice hung up on him, he had arrived early and unexpected, to come knocking, banging, ringing, and shouting at the door. He'd tried his key but, since he'd left, Rosemary had got into the habit of putting the chain on.

When she heard the ruckus, Rosemary had locked herself in the bedroom. "I'm not going to talk to him now, Phyl," she said through the door, believing herself to sound reasonable. "We'd both get upset and say things that would be bad for later."

"But he's upset already."

So he should be, she'd been tempted to reply, but still reasonably she said, "So am I. And I'm trying very hard not to be. I can't afford to get upset." On the deepish level of female-to-female communication, Phyl had understood that what her mother was saying was, "If he gets upset there's someone to comfort him. I am alone."

"We're here, Bobby and me. We'll look after you. Dad just wants to talk about things. Us. Like when we're going to visit and so on."

Rosemary had been fairly sure that Daniel had made no mention of visits. One of the reasons she was most angry with him was that he had behaved as badly to the children as he had with her; the withdrawal of his love in one, large emotional moneybag had included the special love he'd had for his children. Even though she'd known the real reason was trivial and probably temporary—a man with grown, hurt children might find it hard to maintain a sexually dazzling image—much of her anguish was due to what he'd done to the kids by removing himself.

Her through-the-door debate with Phyl had been cut short when Daniel arrived at it himself, tried the handle, and said, "Rosemary, please open this door. We've got to talk."

He'd sounded so safe, so genuine, so much like Daniel that she'd actually half arisen to go to the door. But she'd been prompted to test his calm. "I don't see why I should," she said, forcing her voice into a smoothness that contradicted the fear-filled clenching within. "It must be quite obvious that, right now, I don't feel like talking to you."

Her instinct had been right, and Rosemary had shuddered with relief as Daniel had begun to shout outside the door—she'd never have been able to hold her tears and rage in, faced with that. He'd rattled the handle and shaken the door and shouted, and over his noise she'd heard Bobby's clear, shrill soprano voice:

"Please, Mom, let Dad in!"

Roaring with guilt and danger: "OPEN THIS DOOR! OPEN THIS DOOR!" Daniel had tried to kick in its panels. But it was custom-made of solid timber, no match for a man who exercised his mind more often than his body. So he had gone away after firing messages: "Tell your bloody mother to phone me. Tell her we've got to work out about the house. And bills. Don't stare at me like that. Yes of course I bloody well love you!"

After he'd gone, Bobby had looked at Rosemary as though she were a traitor. "He just wanted to talk to you," he said. She had tried to hug him as she explained that Daniel was much too cross right now but Bobby had wriggled away.

"He'll get crosser," he said. "You'll see."

Four

It was late afternoon by the time Rosemary finished chopping up all the garden trimmings and disposing of the junk, including the corpses of about fifty snails she'd drowned in a bucket. She wished she could destroy every snail in the world except, perhaps, in France, where people were apparently eager to eat them despite their resemblance to withered genitals. Snails did not seem to contribute anything beneficial to the ecology. In fact, in her suburb, they were winning a guerilla war, their target being nearly all newly planted annuals, except lobelia, and quite a lot of established ones, particularly marigolds. They were causing an imbalance of nature.

Two days earlier in the boutique's fitting room, Rosemary had felt like a tentative shoot verging on a deserved spring, but now she felt chewed to ground level. It was hard to recapture that elation, that post-struggle confidence which had made her feel as though the nine months of coping alone with the children without Daniel had been a tough learning course that she'd passed with distinction. Now, scratched, muddy, and alone with the trial balance of her memory, she realised the truth: this time, this way of life, was not just a learning course, a short-term preparation for something guaranteed to be better—this was it. A year from now she could still be right here, killing the descendants of the snails, who always managed to hide a thousand or so eggs before execution.

No matter how vigorously Rosemary chopped and clipped and dug, she could not shake off the mood of being trapped into ordinariness. She brought the radio outside to help put nice things into her head, but all that did was give the illusion, from time to time through the Haydn, that the phone was ringing. And every hour there was news about deaths in Iraq and Soweto or about children drowned in floods in places that sounded familiar or about men in Sydney suburbs who had murdered their wives.

．　　　．　　　．

In the beginning, after Daniel left and despite her resolution, Rosemary had not blocked him out. Her mind, in those first weeks, was so crowded with memories of her life with him that she could hardly think. Aspects of her memory had competed for occupancy of her attention, each insisting on having its pain dealt with at once so that it had seemed that her mind was the site of a terrible accident. Most of the memories, particularly the happy ones, would pop into her focus complete, like pictures in a slide show. They were images of Daniel in his slightly crouched, hands-free pose that gave the impression that under his clothes there were the rope-like muscles of a martial arts expert. It was, in fact, a false impression: family albums showed that Daniel had always stood like a hero, even when he was a flossy-haired toddler.

Unexpected, irresistible, he would pop into her head in an aura of colour, sunlight, and peace and then be gone again, leaving after-images of himself bending tenderly over Phyl to help her with something, or roaring and rushing along the beach with Bobby, spraying sand like beige rainbows behind his sliding feet, or looking deeply into Rosemary's own wide eyes as he traced the outline of her lips with one long, big-knuckled finger.

And then the images would bleach and leave her weak with a sense of loss that was almost a physical pain.

Auntie Gwen, surprised not to have heard anything about the party and whether people had liked her cheese straws, had phoned two days after Daniel's defection. Though strain had made her throat too dry to talk easily, Rosemary had explained.

"He'll be back," said Auntie Gwen. "Then you give him hell. That's what he's asking for."

Rosemary had tried to say that she did not believe this was a temporary matter which, after appropriate penalty and re-negotiation, would take its place among the other little scars left by the progress of marriage. She said she believed that she recognised in Daniel's departure a finality as unarguable as the end of a Beethoven symphony. Then she had annoyed herself by crying into the phone.

"Darn," Auntie Gwen said. "Me car's up the spout." It had not been a non sequitur. "You're a stupid girl, Rosemary," she'd continued not very much later, having arrived uninvited on numerous forms of transport from what Daniel used to call her eyrie in Bankstown. "Look at what you two have built up together. Don't you think that's worth something? I never had much time for that boy in the beginning—he had an eye, I could see that. But he turned out to be a good husband to you, even though he hasn't changed his spots. But you're talking of chucking all this?" She'd swept her chubby, freckled arm in the direction of the swimming pool, a view flanked by the garage which contained Rosemary's green Volvo.

Rosemary had not even thought of things like that, but she found herself defending what sounded like a clear idea: "Auntie Gwen, we live here, the kids and I. It's our home. Daniel chose to leave it, not I. You don't stay married to someone because of a house!"

"No? You've got a lot to learn, my girl. I wish your mother was still with us. She'd sort you out. She knew the value of security, believe you me."

Auntie Gwen had offered to stay and take over the cooking, but Rosemary had insisted, almost rudely eventually, that she go.

It was different with Lucy. When she came "just checking," she was always welcome. Mattie was there as often as she could negotiate to be, teasing Bobby into playing rummy with her or painting messily on butcher's paper at the kitchen table while he did his homework. Mattie, who went to a progressive school, didn't have homework. She had what Rosemary regarded as the burden of compulsory self-expression. For some children, writing poems about gumnuts and banksia trees and painting their feelings in thickened scarlet and shades of green would undoubtedly tap wells of talent a more usual school would concrete over. But Mattie had the opposite problem: no wells of talent, just little pools of it which soon evaporated in the brightness of over-exposure. Since her school teachers were adamantly opposed to the idea of competition, Mattie's work was usually highly rewarded with stars and loving comments in red felt pen and this, Rosemary thought, was not helpful. She believed it made Mattie regard the world as being soft on judgement, with herself as a star from whom no great effort would ever be required.

Rosemary had tried to talk to Lucy about this, but Lucy's eyes had narrowed and she'd changed the subject. Rosemary knew that Lucy felt that the schools that Bobby and Phyl went to were dedicated to the production of high marks, not fully rounded people.

Most of the nights that Lucy was late the potentially fully rounded Mattie—whom Rosemary regarded as egocentric and humourless—slept on a row of sofa cushions in a dark corner of the living room, covered with a beach towel until the autumn nights justified an old pink-and-blue knitted patchwork blanket that had come to be regarded as hers.

Lucy's romance had really started the day after Daniel left, when nothing seemed real to Rosemary. Lucy had arrived late, ostensibly to comfort Rosemary, but as Rosemary was behaving in an artifically cheerful way that night, comfort was not called for. Lucy had not sat down, despite having claimed to be tired; she had prowled around, her black eyebrows in a straight worry line, until Rosemary had asked her why she was carrying on like a puzzled panther.

"Oh, God. I think I'm going mad, that's why."

"Malcolm?"

Lucy had nodded. "It's . . . not just an ordinary thing. And what worries me is that maybe it is not a thing at all. I mean, for instance, it feels different from when I fell for Jack—more thrilling but, in a way, less real. Maybe it's just me. Just a . . . a delayed childhood crush."

"You mean he hasn't made a pass at you yet?"

"Yes, I suppose that is what I mean." Lucy had sat down, her shoulders drooped, her hands between her knees.

"How long has it been since you met? Three weeks! And during that time, how many times have you been alone together? Once. If he'd jumped right at you he'd run the risk of being reported for sexual harassment. I mean, he is your boss!"

"Yes, I suppose you're right. Though it was twice actually—he took me for a drink tonight which became dinner. He drove me home. I've left my car at the studio. *But*," she'd added, in response to Rosemary's expression, "we talked about the program."

"The whole time?"

"Just about. I told him about Jack, and he was much more interested in the fact that he is a banned white South African than that he's my . . . separatee? What's the word?"

"Estranged."

"Estranged husband. He kept saying that it would be interesting to do a program on people who live there and resist the regime. 'The silent protesters' or something like that."

"Foreign features! Wouldn't that be a bit heavy for his program?"

Lucy laughed. "You don't think much of it, do you?"

"It's not that." Rosemary had talked cautiously, trying to be tactful. "There's a slot, a—a format . . ." She'd drawn pictures in the air. "Interviews with movie stars and aerobics experts and politicians with Ken doll hair-styles—that's what he usually does, not foreign political rebels. I think that talking about Jack is his way of finding out more about you—about how you feel."

"He wouldn't have found out much because I don't really know myself how I feel; I'm so mixed up. Mattie and I have been here five years—

she hardly even remembers Jack." Lucy nibbled worriedly at the skin on the edge of a finger-nail. "I can see now that what I was doing was trying to explain to Malcolm, without actually saying it, that Jack has been more in love with politics than with me for years. Danger of arrest is part of the daily routine to him—it's a greater turn-on than I am, that's for sure. So, I wanted Malcolm to know that I was free, though married. He wanted me to talk about the fact that my estranged husband is in chains."

"Oh, very nice," said Rosemary, pouring port into two small glasses. "You should take up poetry. Or thoughts-of-the-day!"

      .   .   .

During the first months after Daniel left, Lucy's excitement about Malcolm and about Rosemary's despair became more apparent. Lucy, the good listener, had continued to glow through the cracks in her sympathetic expression. Rosemary believed that romance insulated Lucy from Rosemary's pain.

"Bloody Daniel. He's like a book I've read over and over again," Rosemary said one night.

"And never got the point of."

"I believed," Rosemary's voice was hoarse, "that he needed me, as confidante, partner, and co-planner—all that. Even though it was often such a strain—twelve-hour days, sixteen-hour days, as you know—rushing home for the kids and then back again, over that bloody bridge, to be there in time for a seminar or something, I had to believe it mattered, especially as I didn't get paid for it. Well, not a salary. Not anything for me, personally," she added in response to the way Lucy exaggeratedly looked around the house. "I'm so mad at him . . . I feel like a hand grenade with the pin pulled out!" Rosemary was striding around, twisting a tissue to shreds.

"Be careful where you throw yourself, in that case."

"It's sexual jealousy—I know that. But it's more than that too: betrayal. That's much worse. I feel as though I've discovered termites chewing away underneath at the building of my life."

Until the moment when Angela had brought her proprietary sense into their living room, and even though Rosemary and Daniel had often misunderstood each other or engaged in those loud, silly, circular arguments which contained more talk than listening, Rosemary had felt Daniel was her friend. It wasn't as though passion didn't figure in their lives, even in the weeks, the months before the end. In fact, she said, marvelling at the implication, it was no wonder Daniel had been looking tired—sexual embezzlement must be exhausting! Daniel was nearly thirty-seven. People of thirty-seven dropped dead jogging. People of thirty-seven—well, men of thirty-seven—could not possibly maintain a state of sexual frenzy. In retrospect this explained a certain lack of application, if not frequency.

Rosemary remembered that Lucy had sat perfectly still most of the time on those long, listening nights, sometimes with her slim, tanned hands between her knees and sometimes with knitting needles twitching at full speed and a lap filled with dozens of small, brightly coloured balls of silk or wool. Lucy was good at knitting complicated picture jumpers—acanthus leaves, political slogans, Blinky Bill, a vintage Holden car and an imitation Modigliani were some of the things she'd done, having first drawn them on graph paper and coloured them with Mattie's crayons. Although most of them were for Mattie or for herself or friends, she'd even taken orders from time to time. She said it kept her head balanced and that it was better for her than smoking.

It was Lucy's stillness and devotion to Rosemary's confusions that had made her attention so clearly a gift.

.   .   .

Rosemary felt that what Daniel had been to her was what the pip is to the avocado: the firm centre nourished by her rich flesh, their marriage a neatly packaged symbiosis. Without him she felt barren, purposeless, and as though if not used soon, she'd go bad. This she had tried to explain to Lucy, though words had seemed inadequate.

Daniel had been her sculptor (though for some time before he left, and very impatiently, he'd tried to reshape her in areas where she felt change was not needed. And he'd been inclined to ignore other areas which, she knew, badly needed remodelling). She had felt she'd been his project until quite suddenly he'd lost interest in moulding her life, or lost sight of his original vision of how she should develop. So, when he left her, she felt like a half-made sculpture, casually abandoned.

The fact that he'd left her to gather dust, so to speak, had frightening implications. Either she had had to accept his judgement that she wasn't worth any more of his creative attention and settle for withering or she'd have to do something quite extraordinary: consider finishing the sculpting herself.

"Nothing to it," Lucy had said. She'd spent the past few minutes untwisting about twenty shades of red, pink, apricot, and grey wool—the mess that had created itself on the back of a huge, carefully shaded chrysanthemum that was destined to cover a bit of her arm, all of one breast, and part of the other. It would be beautiful, but just looking at the necessary mess had made Rosemary's temples throb.

The first time Rosemary had dared to think about herself as the sculptor of her own life, an image from *Don Giovanni* had superimposed itself: the huge statue that comes to life and pours power and terror onto the world around it. But Commendatore is macho and impervious, and once he begins roaring and crashing around he gives every sign of enjoying himself. To Rosemary, visions of herself as powerful seemed like doom—she was sure that no man would love her unless he could be in charge. And, she suspected that if she took up the power of remoulding her own life, it would never be possible to relinquish it again.

"What it amounts to," she said, "is that Daniel has doomed me to shrivel into dust or doomed me to keep going nowhere, for the sake of the kids. And both of those are terrible."

"Good heavens, Rosemary! It's time you got drunk. Because sober, your perspective is completely warped!"

"No, you're wrong! I'm seeing things clearly for the very first time."

Lucy's brows had formed a serious line across her face. She'd got up and poured two whiskies, rather more in Rosemary's glass than in her own.

"Here," she said, ignoring Rosemary's reluctance. "Regard it as medicine. My mother told me that after Dad left and after she'd got over being hurt, she started feeling like a patch of lawn someone had taken a brick off, and it will be like that for you—you'll start to grow and go all springy again."

"Yeah. And green," Rosemary had answered grimly, then laughed at herself, but not for long. The thought occurred to her that she was egocentric and humourless, but she quickly dismissed that. Glittering with the energy she was using to keep herself from crying, she went on.

"I saw myself as part of a 'we' that I thought Daniel was the other part of. But all that time his ego was clicking away, unimpaired, separate, looking for opportunities that had nothing to do with me. OH! I could kill him! And do you know what's so awful is that this isn't new—you read about it all the time. I have this terrible feeling that the worst thing that's ever happened to me is just another twentieth-century cliché. It's just ingredients for a soap opera."

"You know very well that soap operas are actually based on the things that happen. In fact, the things that happen to people in real life are often too corny, too far-fetched, and too coincidental for soap opera; no-one would believe them. You're mad with Daniel, so tell him. Have it out. You'll rip yourself up inside if you keep swallowing your anger—people get cancer from that."

"No, no. A bit of judicious swallowing is good politics—you know it's there, you express it when it's safe to do so, and hold it back when it's not. The ones who get cancer don't even know they're angry—they've repressed it. I'm not doing that. I take it out and give it frequent airings—like now, telling it to you."

"Great. Then I'll get cancer," said Lucy and then looked surprised when Rosemary took her seriously and insisted on being reassured.

"I'll turn anger into—into useful fuel," Rosemary said as soon as she was quite sure it had been one of Lucy's little jokes. "And burn a bit of it whenever I need warming. But I'll just make sure I keep it from the person who caused it, the bastard! He knows it's there! Let him dangle, waiting for the bomb that may never come!"

"That's dangerous though, Ro. People are like countries—they erect terribly strong defences if they think someone is aiming bombs in their direction."

"Well, he's had a little bomb, indirectly. From Jim Begg. Perhaps he'll think that's the lot."

.   .   .

Later, after Lucy had lugged her sleepy child over the fence, Rosemary had lain in the bath and thought about that hot January Saturday morning when Daniel had come knocking on her bedroom door. After he'd gone, she had realised that she'd reached a limit, and, since she did not want war, it had been necessary to provide a peace-preserving treaty.

She had managed to persuade Jim Begg, Daniel's former tennis partner and the only local solicitor she knew, to delay his start in a tennis round-robin and see her for fifteen minutes. Jim had claimed he didn't mind—that it gave him a good excuse for a pre-lunch beer. In fact, she'd guessed that he, like everyone else in the neighbourhood who had been at the party, was agog.

She'd said goodbye to her children, who were lounging on inflatable plastic air mattresses in the pool and talking as though they were friends, which was good. As she'd left the cool, quiet house, Rosemary had glanced in the oak-framed hall mirror and grinned at herself, a little embarrassed. Her reflection was of a serious, almost regal person. There'd been no hint of the boiling inside.

Looking down on that day, which had started bright and glassy and threatened to reach a record-breaking temperature at noon, a passing balloonist would have noticed that the streets and gardens where Rosemary walked were full of healthy, tanned children, playing heat-engen-dering games. Some of their BMX bicycles still gleamed with the unmistakable stamp of Christmas. The children shouted bossily or hap-pily and ran around a lot in the shimmering heat, most dressed in nothing more than swimming gear and generous blobs of pink, blue, or white zinc. Nearly all the pools in the street were available to all the kids so it had been surprising to Rosemary that they weren't sensibly swimming. She'd wished she'd come in her air-conditioned car. She'd wished she could float away from all this in a brightly striped balloon which would let the high, cool breeze take it somewhere lovely. But what do you bet they don't allow balloons over suburbs, she'd thought gloomily.

To Jim Begg, Rosemary must have presented a controlled, intelligent though heat-flushed—picture. She had asked questions about divorce, she realised now, in the way of a person being interviewed for a job.

"What's the hurry?" he'd asked, a can of Tooheys all but hidden in his large, red-brown hand. Jim was generally regarded as a great guy. Jim and Ef, whose real name was Frances, were generally regarded as a great couple. Ef had gone ahead with the kids to broil at the tennis courts.

Jim had massive legs which more than filled his vivid white tennis shorts and his pale green, cotton mesh T-shirt was heavily ringed with damp stains, as though he'd already played a vigorous set or two. Sweat appeared, a continuous supply of small sequins on his ample forehead. The small sequins became big sequins, then merged, tipping into drops which slithered into his immense black eyebrows and down the sides into his beard. Every now and then he mopped up the overload on a greyish handkerchief.

Rosemary and Jim had sat under a grape-vine-covered pergola, the last of the fruit turning into raisins in the sun and driving a few bees and blowflies crazy. Obviously there had been quite a crop, from which birds and insects had mainly benefitted: the smell of fermentation arose from dark patches which had been swept under the bordering hydrangea and canna clumps, and there were navy splash stains on the brick tiles. Jim had reached his second can of Tooheys Lite before Rosemary started the tomato juice she'd agreed to.

"Dan's only been gone a few days. He's been on longer business trips than that! And he probably wouldn't have gone at all, if you hadn't kicked him out."

"Jim, don't be ridiculous! You make it sound as though he were a tenant I've evicted. He has gone away with another woman. The marriage is over."

"It's not a simple thing, Rosie. Marriage is a project, not an impulse. How long have you been together? Seventeen, eighteen years?" She didn't deny it. Details like dates would come later. "You're part of today's world, girl. You know people have affairs. Nearly all people do, but it doesn't necessarily break up their marriages. If they're found out, and most of them aren't—you and Dan were unlucky there—they have a row. They kiss and make up. He buys her a mink or they go to Hawaii, depending on the age and the money bracket. What I mean is, there are economic and social issues at stake here. You two might have got married for romantic reasons but these reasons have become subverted into business. You've got a child-rearing business. You've got a property-owning business. You've even got a commercial business. You are involved in Patchwork PR, aren't you?"

This had annoyed her. It was so much like what she'd said to Lucy, with different emphasis.

"I'm not involved anymore. Not really. Well, yes, technically. I'm a director. I signed the last lot of annual returns and things; they sent them to me. I worked a lot though, especially in the beginning when we couldn't afford staff."

"But you're still a director of the company?"

"Yes. Technically," she'd said, trying not to sound impatient. "It all has nothing to do with my feelings. I can't go on being married to Daniel, no matter what the financial entanglements are. As for the kids, he doesn't seem to care much about them anymore."

He'd glanced critically at her serene expression, having, perhaps, caught a hint of emotion, but no refreshing tears had followed; she had made sure to present an image of perfect, adult control.

"Listen, Rosie," he boomed, reaching for another beer. "You've got to do some thinking. You're not really going to throw all those years away, break up your family because Daniel got the hots for some secretary?"

Her marriage, her involvement in the business, her very life, she told him, had been based on trust. Now that the trust was broken she could see no way the marriage could stand up. That was it. It was a pity about the wasted years, but both Daniel and she would simply have to do their best, separately, to make new patterns for their lives.

"What you mean," Jim said, "is that you've met someone else, too." She had been furious.

"You're outrageous! Are all men so damned cynical? Or is it single-minded?"

"No, no, no, no, no," he said, and grabbed her arm. "Sit down. Sit down. I was just trying to understand your position and, honestly, from where I sit, you look like a woman who is too smart to throw away half a lifetime's investment for a romantic notion. And you don't look like a cold fish, though, God knows, Rosie, you sound like one!"

Stunned, Rosemary had needed all her resources to beat away a sudden spring of misunderstood tears.

"Dan's a great guy, Rosie. Really great. Why don't you two just talk to each other, you know? Come to terms. He's probably worn out by that girl already. He'd be pleased to come back to some home cooking, see his kids. See you," he'd added, trying not to make it sound like an afterthought. "You're a great girl, Rosie. Good wife. Nice looking. Great kids."

She'd wished he would not call her Rosie. She'd wished he'd stop staring at her as though she were a blue-tongued lizard that had turned up in this garden, requiring him to deal in ways beyond his experience. She'd wished she were strong enough to break his nose. Later, she'd wished she'd thought of saying, "Look, Jim, you're talking about quantity marriage. I'm talking about quality marriage. It's not the same thing." It would have sounded less petulant than, "I came here to ask you to start doing whatever it is to get a divorce. If you want to act for me, that is. If not, I'll have to find someone else."

He'd looked at her then as though he'd caught a hint of what it was that had driven Daniel away. But, like her, he was good at dealing with surprise.

"Yer. Well, Rosie, when the time comes I'll start things rolling for you. But you've got to be separated for at least twelve months first, you know, before you can be divorced. Then there's counselling. Nowadays they virtually insist on counselling."

"Counselling?"

"Marriage guidance."

"But what's the point? What could a marriage guidance counsellor do?"

The tears had rushed back again, and this time she had not won the battle, to her own annoyance and Jim's apparent relief. It had taken a few seconds before she could talk again.

"You're supposed to be on my side," she said. "I didn't expect to be cross-examined. I feel as though I've died and you're St. Peter at the gate!"

"Rosie, Rosie, Rosie," he said, the whole of his huge frame providing a sincere backup to the litany. "I *am* on your side, for God's sake. That's why I don't want you to make any mistakes."

"They've already been made," she'd said bleakly. "It's too late, Jim. I really don't want to be married to him anymore. There must be things that have to be done now. Like a letter giving the date he went. Otherwise who's to say the separation was twelve months?"

"Half the neighbourhood, Rosie."

"What about things like money, child visits, and that sort of thing? Surely there is something that should be written down?"

He'd sighed and stood up.

"OK. I'll write to him. You draft something, in general terms. What you think would be a fair thing. I'll drop Dan a line for you."

The next time she'd seen Jim Begg, in his cool office in a suit, he'd been a lot more like a lawyer than a bloke in the pub. For instance, he'd demurred at most of the mild, civilised suggestions she had put in her draft letter to Daniel.

"You've got to ask for a reasonable maintenance for yourself as well as the children. You'll still be looking after them, won't you?"

"Of course. He can't take *them* away from me, too. But they're fairly big now; Phyl, especially. I'm not needed all day except in the holidays. And I'll find a job—part-time, perhaps. Enough to support myself. If Daniel's paying the school fees and for the kids' food, holidays, and medical things, that's enough."

"Well, ask for a settlement then. The house, if you don't want to go for cash. Does he pay you a director's fee, by the way?"

"Well, he has never actually handed me a cheque and said, 'This is your fee, Director.' I've got credit cards, department store cards: one for David Jones, one for Grace Brothers. And I've got the car. And grocery money. And I send the bills to his secretary for the usual stuff like phones and car insurance. . . ." She'd have gone on, even though she knew this sounded like a defence of Daniel. But Jim had interrupted.

"Leave it to me. We'll sort out a few things."

•   •   •

One night in the middle of February, Lucy had come late, tearful, and very, very tired. Malcolm Henry's program had made a special about the unstoppable bushfires that had ripped through parts of South Australia and Victoria, devastating the countryside more thoroughly than a bombing and leaving whole suburbs smouldering like giant ashtrays. Thirty people had been killed. Malcolm's program had concentrated on some of those who had barely escaped, and Lucy had spent much of the previous two days picking through the ash to persuade people to appear on the program: people in states of disbelief, who'd lost virtually everything except their lives. Lucy had never been away from the studio for a job before, but since most of the researchers were more deeply and expertly involved in the pre-election television frenzy, she'd been the one to go.

"I felt so—meaningless!" Lucy said, wiping her eyes. It was Rosemary's turn to administer medicinal whisky. "One group of mothers and children were in a school building, watching the flames come—like a tidal wave, one lady said. Just whooshing towards them. They were expecting to die, they couldn't possibly have escaped. But at the last moment the wind turned and the fire bypassed them. You watched the program?"

"Of course. It just seems unbelievable, doesn't it? I couldn't bear to watch, but I also couldn't walk away."

"To me," Lucy said, "the image that will stay in my mind forever is the man in South Australia whose whole, huge property and all the animals were burnt in a few minutes. Remember him? Standing there smiling with the only thing he saved? A painting of his mother."

"The week before, none of those people would have had the slightest idea that their lives were going to change like that, would they?" Rosemary sighed. "There's really no protection."

Rosemary had been making two lists: one of what had been right and one of what had been wrong with her marriage, and the "wrong" list was already three times longer than the "right." When Lucy had had some wine and some cold chicken and salad, she wanted to see the lists, since they had been her idea. She studied them while sipping coffee, and occasionally smiled.

Rosemary found this hard to bear since she had made a huge effort to be honest, objective, and fair. What had made fairness so difficult was the fact that everything on the "wrong" list had flowed from her Biro as though the blue ink were unimpeded flood water or dark blue blood driven hard by anger. She had examined the anger minutely from every angle, and it appeared to be nothing but righteous. She had ground her teeth while writing "Holidays: either none at all or just a week to somewhere cheap and nearby so Daniel could phone Patchwork every day and drive back if he was worried. Never my choice." She had punched the desk with her left fist while writing "Money: he would never discuss it, only fight. He got cross about all bills. I never had any money of my own, and if I asked he'd say, 'But you've got the credit cards.' He'd always know exactly what I'd spent, but I didn't know what he did." Angela had probably had lobster dinners while she, Rosemary, felt extravagant if she took the children to McDonalds!

But items on the "right" list had grown slowly, like faint scratchings with a soft finger-nail, and some, once they were written, were then decisively crossed out. "He loved the children" was one of these. He loved the children? she'd snorted. He hardly saw them! Pretending to be earning their living while for months he'd been getting home hours after they were both asleep!

There had been a few moments on the "right" list when the pen had trembled in her hand as she remembered his usual, his frequent, and his now missed "Guess what?" on the phone. It was always a prelude to telling her some juicy gossip or something funny that had happened at a launching or something wonderful that Patchwork was going to do to promote a new product. "Daniel shared the best part of his days with me," she'd written, then vigorously scratched it out as she thought of Angela. "We had similar tastes in food and clothes," she put instead.

She wished Lucy would say something, but she simply went on sipping, half smiling, and occasionally glancing up over the top of the lists.

"I think the worst thing is that there was never any time for me," Rosemary said when she couldn't stand it anymore.

"Don't you count the college course and the drama school?"

"Yes. Of course. But they weren't things for me that the family—that Daniel—made a space for. They were things I snatched time for, or tagged on to the end of everything else. Crumbs from the marriage table."

"Oh, Ro. You've forgotten! You're not being fair, to him or to yourself."

"Fair!" said Rosemary, indignant as a stepped-on snake. "Fair! Hell, let me tell you about fair!"

But Lucy's eyes flickered with tiredness, and Rosemary suddenly had a warning glimpse of herself as obsessed—one of those heavily lined, self-involved women who corners people at parties in order to parade their much-practised indignation about the things people have done to them to ruin their lives.

"Do you know what you should do right now, before you can't move?" Rosemary asked gently. "Go home and get into bed. Come, I'll bring Mattie." And Lucy nodded like a grateful, feeble child and headed off up the steep back path.

·   ·   ·

Rosemary had begun the communications course as soon as she and Daniel had got back from Canada, from the trip that had actually, looking back, contained the last really happy moments of their marriage. Of course it had also foreshadowed some of the most unhappy, but Rosemary had not realised at the time that Daniel's kind insistence that she stop working full-time in the company to "do her own thing" would soon mean her doing her own thing on her own.

When he'd suggested it at a little coffee shop on Prince Edward Island overlooking the Gulf of St. Lawrence, the gulf Anne of Green Gables had so loved to gaze at, Rosemary had had no idea what her own thing might be, having devoted the previous fifteen years to Daniel's thing. In fact, she'd felt rather hurt, being summarily dismissed after years of sterling service, and was hardly comforted by knowing that it would take two people to replace her.

"I'm a director, too. Shouldn't you have consulted me before making this decision? Had a directors' meeting and taken notes for the minute book?"

Daniel had responded first to Rosemary's words in a quick, rude "Don't be bloody ridiculous. You're a paper director!" which had made two elderly, hatted ladies at the next table stop their cups halfway to their lips. Then he'd seen Rosemary's hurt expression. "I didn't mean that. Honest. Patchwork would have been nothing without you," he said, and had kept saying soothing, propitiatory things until she was prepared to look at him again without tears in her eyes. Then he'd held her hand and looked at her with the sincere, deeply intimate, almost consuming stare that had made her fall in love with him in the first place. It was a look which was always able to transfix her like a rabbit in a torch beam, even though she'd seen how often he'd used it on clients, creditors, and pretty women at parties.

"You were the one who knew how important it was for me to have my own company—my own successful company. You helped me—I don't think I could have done it without you," he said, and it was closer than he usually came to thanking her. He whispered over the coffee froth that she might like to have another baby, "One you can really enjoy instead of fitting it in between A and C in the filing system."

So she'd felt comforted, like one honourably superannuated rather than one dismissed. On the boat back to Nova Scotia they had clung together so tightly, so tense with desire that the same hatted ladies had glanced at them and one had shrugged and mouthed, "Honeymooners!"

Daniel and Rosemary had hardly been able to wait to get back to their hotel room where they had spent hours and hours in blissful passion as though they were indeed honeymooners. It was quite a long time later that she realised it was good luck she hadn't become pregnant, since travel had disrupted her pill routine.

Soon after that Daniel had left Rosemary at his sister's place in Edmonton and gone to New York to a computer trade fair. Computers, no matter how clever, had not interested her.

The day Rosemary had spent making the television commercial had been like the first meeting with someone she'd known she would fall in love with, though at the time she could not imagine how this love would ever be consummated.

Back home, she'd been lucky to get into the communications course, which was abundantly applied for by each year's new crop of high school graduates, but someone had dropped out mid-term and she'd managed to convince a course co-ordinator (and former colleague of Daniel's) that she could catch up if they let her enrol.

At first it had seemed ridiculous: too hard on the one hand, when things she knew nothing about were speedily assimilated by the rest of the class, and too easy on the other, when things she'd been doing for years seemed to stump everyone else and hold back the flow. And there had been the age gap, of course: at least ten years separated her from the next most senior student. So it had been tempting to accept the co-ordinators' invitations to have tea or drinks with them instead, but she'd usually resisted—she was too much of an outsider already to successfully survive being regarded as the teachers' pet.

This had left her socially isolated, which, at first, had seemed like a punishment—just the opposite of the warm, involving fun she'd wanted. But after a hard and lonely six weeks, the work itself—the business of scripts and editing and sound and lights and writing things precisely to deadline and presenting them well—had begun to enthral her and she'd begun to do well and to find that the barriers of age were not insuperable.

A few months later she'd seen the advertisement for Melissa's drama course and decided she could handle that, too. Daniel had been dubious. "You're already charging around too much during the day. Now it will be night-time, too."

"Yes, but that's because I haven't really retired from Patchwork. I was in three times this week and four times last week."

"What the hell for?"

"Daniel, you *knew* I was there. Every time they hit a snag or have to do something new they call me. I had to sort out the invitation list, for one thing. Half the journalists on it have been promoted or moved sideways or fired in the past six months and Marie didn't have the faintest idea how to go about updating it. Then who do you think did the backroom planning for the Glen Rossfield presentation? Or did you really think that all I did was swan up on the night in my best black to charm all the old directors? And that those caviar toasts and rare roast beef slices and the Waterford crystal got there by magic?"

"Maria is supposed to do all that."

"She would have, given another eight hours in each day. She's steady but very slow Daniel, you must have seen that. She doesn't know what a deadline means. And she's much too polite to suppliers and people's secretaries—she gets messed around."

"Well, I don't see what's so bad about you giving a hand from time to time. Training the girls . . ."

"Uh uh," Rosemary had interrupted, firmly shaking her head. "Patchwork has been pulling me in more and more, and I can see which way it's going; soon I'll be there twenty and then thirty hours a week. Except I won't officially be there, since, in your mind, I've left. So I'll have the drudgery and my time used up but none of the decision making or the status. Or the fun."

"Fun? That's all you're interested in, isn't it?"

"Yes," she said quickly, since, even though it was not entirely true, it was a way of preventing an argument. And so Rosemary had crowded her own life to the limit by joining the drama class where, as well as putting into practice some of the techniques she'd been learning about in the communications course, she hoped she'd meet people closer to her own age than her other classmates or the members of Bobby's Cub Scout group, who were inclined to treat her as though she were a dim-witted chauffeur.

Daniel had replaced Maria with the person he had called "a bright girl with some PR experience," whom Rosemary had not met until she crashed the wedding anniversary party and took Daniel away.

Five

In February, Rosemary had found Daniel's new home phone number on a little slip of paper in a shirt pocket of Bobby's in the laundry. Possession of this telephone number meant Bobby had been talking to Daniel behind her back, and this betrayal had left her feeling angry and vulnerable.

At first her anger had been at Bobby, with whom she'd had a lot of clashes since the night of the party because he had instinctively moved towards the power position his father had abandoned, only to find she believed she'd got there first.

But Bobby was only ten and his father was his hero, his golden god. Daniel knows this, she'd thought. He's deliberately trying to get at me through the child! So late one lonely night towards the end of the month, after weeping alone in bed, Rosemary had embarrassed both Daniel and herself by phoning him at the Kirribilli flat where he lived with Angela.

When she'd dialled, a chunk of anger had made the call seem justified. But it had soon turned into a sodden ramble to which he'd listened with reluctance. "I'll call you in the morning," he'd whispered.

"Fuck the morning!"

"Are Phyl and Bobby . . . all right?" His imagination had been stirred by her uncharacteristic coarseness; Rosemary had felt that he was bracing himself for the news that she had cut their heads off and was now preparing to crunch a cyanide tablet. So she said, "How should I know?" and let him suffer for twenty seconds before adding, "Should I wake them up and ask?"

Feeling ashamed, and in case she was ever tempted to do it again, she burnt the scrap of paper with the matches and in the ashtray she kept for guests who smoked, then flushed the ashes down the toilet. But Daniel had arrived very early next morning, leading with his shoulders and they had confronted the distorting mirrors of hurt, guilt, fear, and anger which had made them both ugly. And something had happened that could have led to a really terrible fight involving Rosemary's whole arsenal of accumulated emotional hand grenades with their pins pulled out. The children had been there, and Rosemary had felt it was unforgivable that Daniel should accuse her of being a lousy, selfish bitch of a mother with them listening.

"She's not, Dad! She's not!" Phyl cried, grabbing Daniel's arm to make him hear.

"What's this? A bloody consipiracy?" he asked, shaking himself free as though her hand had been a shackle. "I can see you turning out just the same, and God help the poor bastard who marries you!"

Phyl's deepest fear was that no man would ever love her, and Rosemary could see in her white, clenched face that this remark had been a mortal wound.

"Daniel! How dare you? How dare you attack Phyl? She's your child!"

"Oh, yeah?" he said, thrashing in deep water. "How do I know that for sure?"

Phyl had burst into tears, and Rosemary had grabbed a heavy glass vase from behind her and swung her arm around to give it the force of a cricketer's bowl. If Daniel had not ducked, it would have smashed his face. Instead it glanced off a hi-fi stereo speaker cabinet and exploded in three large chunks, one of which bit into Bobby's arm. Bobby screamed as his blood welled into the cut.

"Jesus!" said Daniel, getting in the way so that Rosemary couldn't hug Bobby or see if it was a scratch or something worse that needed stitching. "You're a bloody madwoman! You're not competent to look after your own children!"

"Get out!" she screamed. "Get out! Get out! Just get out!" She'd hit at Daniel, desperately eager to scratch him, cut him, bruise him, and leave him wounded the way the children were, but he had backed away with one arm up, just out of her reach. However, he'd backed to the door and as soon as he was half-way out of it, Rosemary, still screaming, had tried to slam it on him. But he was heavier than she, so although it was not easy for him to sound dignified while pushing against eviction, he said to Bobby in a fairly normal voice, "Just give me a ring, kiddo, if you need help. You want to come sailing on Saturday?"

"Yes, Dad," Bobby replied through his tears. "Can't I come with you now? Can't I come and live with you?"

Daniel must have ducked away then because Rosemary managed to slam the door and run the bolt, so his pretend-reasonable voice was muffled through the heavy timber: "Not right away, kiddo. But we'll work something out, OK? I'll pick you up at eight on Saturday morning, OK?"

The lines were clearly drawn after that. Although Bobby had allowed Rosemary to put Mercurochrome and a Band-Aid on what was, after all, a very light scratch, he had done it with the stoic loathing of a soldier taken captive.

"You hate Dad," he said in response to all Rosemary's attempts at apology and her gentle strokes.

. . .

That was the day Rosemary decided to never again give Daniel the moral advantage. She would keep her dignity showing and her feelings concealed. She knew that only the iceberg tip of her tightly packed rage showed. She knew that what was there, held in, held down with all her strength, was anger so vast that, released, it would change her in an elemental way over which she would have no control. It would change her as a stroke, the loss of a limb, or blindness would have changed her. Her self of the previous month, even the previous week, had been erupted and its molecules and values rearranged.

She worked hard to cover all the cruel words—hers as well as Daniel's— with shovelsful of time and good thoughts, but their ghost still haunted her and from time to time she was forced to exorcise it. She would visualise him standing in front of her, and she would rage at him terribly, running perfect scenarios through her brain as though they were films in which she was simultaneously the scriptwriter, the director, and the star. He didn't stand a chance.

. . .

The tempo of Rosemary's life had speeded up almost without her realising it. Everything had changed, even, or perhaps especially, parenthood. Before, the process of being Phyl and Bobby's mother had had no particular shape—she had simply fed them, driven them, listened and talked to them, liked them, loved them, and felt sure they were aware of it. Now it was as though the three of them were involved in a difficult new language course, one at which she was not much good.

For the first few weeks after Daniel left, Phyl and Bobby had been alternately frightened and comforted by Rosemary's behaviour, which had included being dazzlingly nice to them. For instance, one night over lasagne (everybody's favourite), she had decided that it would be a good idea to buy a caravan and leave Sydney almost immediately for an indeterminate trip around Australia.

"We'll take a nice schoolteacher," she said. "Then you won't have to

repeat when—or if—we come back. A man, I think. Strong enough to
change tyres. Someone who's good at fixing things." And then, because
of the *et tu, Brute* look Phyl had given her, added quickly, "An oldish
man. Homosexual, perhaps." At which Bobby had looked alarmed. "Not
one that likes *little* boys, though."

Bobby, who was ten, had been so thrilled about the idea that he'd
told his teacher, as a result of which she'd given another boy the part
of Joseph in *Joseph and His Amazing Technicolour Dreamcoat* and had told
him how sorry she was that he, the best singer and actor in the school,
was leaving.

He also told all his friends, one of whose father had arrived at Rosemary's door with a practical offer: "I know a bloke who's got a really
good Viscount going quite cheap. His wife and him used to live in it
before they got the unit," he'd said, and offered to drive her to Parramatta to look at it and perhaps bring it back again since he had a tow-
ball on his car.

There had been phone calls of the Are you *sure*-you're-all right-you're-
not-planning-anything-silly? sort.

When, a few days later, Bobby had learned that they were not going
around Australia in a caravan and that the only changes in his life were
the fact that his adored father had left him and that his chance at the
dream role of Joseph was gone, he went wild with no attempt at control.
He had come home from school and headed straight for the main bathroom where Rosemary was placing clean towels on the navy blue shelves.

"I'm going," he said at the door.

"Where, darling?" she asked, not recognising the dangerous note in
his voice.

"I'm leaving this fucking house. I'm moving out."

She had responded to the words first: "Don't be vulgar. And of course
you're not leaving." Then she had turned to look at him.

His white face was bent and wet with rage, his freckles incongruously
vivid on such an adult expression of hatred. He had struggled to hit
her, which had surprised her, as physical violence was not a feature of
their relationship, and because he was so strong.

"You made him go, you horrible thing!" he shouted, sobbed, splut-
tered. "He went because you were never here! You were always at
college or that acting class with those weirdos! He hates you! Everybody
hates you!" He had vomited—milk shake, tomato sandwich—and had
fiercely tried to shake off Rosemary's hands as she supported his heaving
head. As a result, vomit had splashed all over the bathroom and onto
both of them, which had made Rosemary's gorge rise, too.

His anger had been so fierce, so undeniable, that she had believed him: it must have been her attempts at self-improvement that had driven Daniel away. That and the fact that, obviously, she was unlovable.

Bobby had calmed down enough to allow her to wash his face. But still sobbing, he said, "I'm never going back to that school. They're all dags, and just so full of themselves, everybody. I hate them. I'm going to live with Dad."

What can I say? she wondered, trying, without confidence, to hold him. She had not realised that he hated her, but now, of course, she could see that she deserved it. She had not been, after all, a success as a wife and mother. She'd blindly gone ahead doing the things she'd believed were right, unaware that her husband and child—perhaps both children—were being neglected to the point of crisis.

It was a shock to discover that she had failed her son as well as her husband. All the things she'd done for them were obviously the wrong things. Perhaps they had been imploring her, in a language she didn't understand, to give them the emotional equivalent of water while all the time she'd been offering more and more bread. What she'd thought was her best had not been nearly enough.

Then suddenly her temper took over. "If you want to go, too, you can bloody well go," she shouted. "I've had enough of people criticising me and telling me I'm not good enough. If I'm not up to some sort of Quilty scratch, you and your father can have each other!"

And with her there had been no control either. She'd sat on the edge of the bath and sobbed, making rough, gulping noises and talking between the sounds. "Go on, go," she said. "Why don't you all go?"

Terrified, Bobby had run to find Phyl who hadn't heard the shouting because she was doing her homework in the rumpus room, wearing a Walkman and tapping her foot in time to the rock beat.

Rosemary had got through the worst of it by the time Phyl ran into the bathroom yelling, "What's the matter, Mom? Are you OK, Mom?" and was blowing her nose on toilet paper.

"It's OK." Rosemary said. "It's OK."

It had taken a while for the three of them to calm down. An air of hurt and hostility had persisted between Bobby and Rosemary while they cleaned up themselves and the bathroom. Phyl had made tea and opened a packet of lemon chiffon biscuits and this they ate in the middle of the downy cream ruffles on Rosemary's big bed.

"I'm leaving," Bobby said, though with less conviction than in the bathroom. "Mom says I can go."

"Go? Where will you go?"

"To Dad," he said firmly. "And . . . Angela."

"You're the one who's crazy," Phyl said matter-of-factly. "You'd probably starve to death. I'll bet that isn't a lady who can cook."

Rosemary had been impressed by her daughter's right-on-target shot: of all his vulnerabilities, food was Bobby's greatest. His mouth was too full of lemon chiffon biscuit to even try to protest.

"Anyway," Phyl went on, "I know why you're saying that. It's because Mrs. McWilliam gave Joseph to Guy Anderson."

Although this was news to Rosemary the effect it had had on Bobby confirmed its truth.

"Why?" she asked. "You're the best singer. She told you at the end of last term that you would be Joseph. That other boy isn't any good at all!"

He looked so miserable, angry, and sheepish that Rosemary guessed— "You told her we were going around Australia?"

He nodded, tears dripping down the gullies between his cheeks and his nose.

"What a stupid woman!"

Then it was easy. With a common enemy—two actually, because they rapidly included Angela—they were able to unite with the sort of loyalty that binds people in casualty.

"I don't want you to go. I need you," Rosemary told Bobby, hugging him. "I didn't mean it when I said you should go."

"Mum was a bit jealous," Phyl explained kindly.

"And I'll fix something up with Mrs. McWilliam. It'll be OK," Rosemary said, as though she hadn't heard what Phyl said.

There had been nothing on which to base this promise, but it turned out to be true in a way that was fortunate for everyone except Guy Anderson; for him a lingering cold had turned out to be glandular fever. Everyone else, especially Mrs. McWilliam, was immensely pleased to hear that Bobby would not be leaving after all. However, the truce had not bridged Bobby's vast sense of loss, for which he continued to blame Rosemary. But although the fights with Bobby were uncomfortable, at least they were clean. She wished she knew what the more stoic Phyl felt about the failure of her parents to love until death them did part, but Phyl refused to be a burden.

.   .   .

"What's going to be the hardest," Rosemary had said to Lucy, "is to resist the lust for revenge. It's so tempting! There is so much I could do to hurt Daniel now. I know all his business secrets."

"But what would you gain from that? I know that to you, right now, Daniel's more rotten and less desirable than a cow corpse in a stream. But don't talk crap about destroying him."

"No, no, don't misunderstand. I won't. I couldn't. I just *wish* I could. Honestly, I feel as though I could explode. Fermenting grapes do. But then they settle down and if they don't turn into vinegar, they become good wine. It's a process I wish—I hope—I can control. Right now I'm aware that I run the risk of turning into vinegar. But I hope that after, well, after something—after getting used to it, after not being so wounded anymore, after, I don't know, finding something to do with my life that matters to me—it'll be good wine. Or even vintage port; something to sustain me into lonely old age."

"You lonely? You'll be having dashing old men trying to sip from your port barrel when you're ninety-five!"

"Don't tease, Lucy. I could end up alone. Not too many men fancy marrying second-hand women with expensive, half-grown kids. They prefer getting brand-new ones they can push around and who will give them pink little babies of their very own. I'm used goods on this market."

Lucy winced but said nothing, and Rosemary had a flash of conscience about revealing the entrails of a quartered marriage to a friend so newly in love.

"It's different with you," she said earnestly. "You're beautiful. And you've gone back to being single again—you don't look as though your spirit's bleeding where it's been torn away from the body."

"You mean I've reacquired my virginity?" Lucy's laughing eyes belied the irony of her tone.

"I mean, Malcolm loves you. You're still desirable," said Rosemary firmly.

"Oh, Ro, don't be so hard on yourself. You're gorgeous! Just give yourself some time, for heaven's sake. You're still in pain . . ."

"No, no. This isn't a bid for sympathy, just objective truth in this so-called liberated society," Rosemary said, keeping her voice light, calm, humorous. "The maddening thing is that Daniel, who really was such an arrogant, ill-formed jerk when we met—though of course I couldn't see him as anything apart from perfect—is now really a fulfilled, successful, sophisticated man. As a commodity on the marriage market he's now worth a lot, like a vintage car in good condition. While I'm just the old crate it came in."

"Some old crate!" said Lucy. "You should see yourself. You look like a portrait, in that pool of light I'm no good at painting, but if I was, I'd do you now—long-boned, strong, supple. You worry about getting fat, but you should see yourself: even when you relax, you look as though you're holding your stomach in."

Rosemary laughed. "You're a good friend, Luce. My mother said something nice like that to me once. She said, 'On you, Woolworth's chains look like gold. You'll never have any trouble with bank managers.'"

"Which has no doubt turned out to be true."

"So far!"

            .   .   .

Lucy had brought Rosemary books by nice, life-enhancing psychologists who said it was OK to feel angry. But books were too slow for Rosemary in this mood, and besides, she felt Lucy was a little obsessed with the subject of unexpressed anger. What was happening to her, Rosemary explained again, was something she had to feel her way through carefully, and anger had nothing to do with it.

Lucy believed in books. "There aren't any rules for what you're going through, but there should be," she said. "Ro, seriously, it would be a best seller: *How To Stay Sane, Though Separated.* No? *The Delights of Divorce?* NO! But I'll get it. I'll think of something," and she started making notes in the small, spiral-bound notebook she always carried in her shoulder bag, ready at any time to jot down flashes of insight.

Malcolm had suggested that Lucy should write a book. Being spellbound by love, she had immediately made writing a high priority—higher than everything except time with Malcolm or, to a lesser extent, with Mattie or Rosemary, or work. Almost everything else—the washing, the business of food, sleeping—Lucy regarded as infuriating postponements of the day the best-seller business would begin.

"What will you say?" Rosemary asked. "What would the rules be?"

"I'd say," Lucy said slowly enough to write down her ideas as she spoke them, "that there's a fairly standard pattern. First it's all hell and internal chaos: shock and blame—all that. Betrayal. Then there's a plateau period when you go mad in your own way: drinking, for some, crying for others," she glanced at Rosemary. "Big spending for others. That's what Carla did—my ex-boss' ex-wife. She went on a credit card binge—all in his name. Harry nearly had a fit when thousands of dollars worth of bills came in," she grinned. "She took his gold credit card to Hong Kong, stayed in a great hotel, and bought at least two years' supply of Lancôme. Then she came back and bought a Renault Fuego. And Harry used to complain about going to her mother's in Tamworth for a holiday—said the petrol cost too much!"

"I could never do that," Rosemary said primly, though her imagination briefly ranged through the shops in Double Bay, where she'd seen some wonderful shoes and a blue leather suit that would make her look like someone of value. Ridiculous! she told herself.

"A good sign that you've graduated from heart-break is when you can talk for more than twenty minutes to the person who left you without either of you getting cross."

"Twenty minutes? I don't think Daniel and I ever talked that long, even when we liked each other," said Rosemary, who was enjoying this.

"Come on! You were good friends," said Lucy. But she was more interested in her project than in Rosemary's exaggerations. "Then there comes what's about to hit you now," Lucy went on, still writing. "The promiscuity phase. The length varies. Some women actually get stuck in that for years, sleeping around and getting free tickets to Paris or to soccer matches, depending on the guy. And then, when you get fed up with that, you either start fairly earnestly looking for a new husband or you settle for one, perhaps two lovers and a career. . . ."

"Is that all? It's not much for a whole book."

"I'll pad it out," said Lucy.

But Lucy did not always have all the answers. "Ro," she'd asked one night after a long, frowning silence, "do you think Malcolm's a poofter? Most interesting men are, nowadays, aren't they?"

"Stop it!" Rosemary had said, laughing at her. "You've given him the wrong signals, that's all. Perhaps he thinks *you're* gay."

Lucy sighed. "Maybe cupid missed."

"In that case, stick around. Isn't he supposed to be blindfolded? You can't plan these things, Luce." No, you can't plan anything, Rosemary had repeated to herself. She'd had no clear vision of her life. Yet after a while, without looking for them, she had perceived that in the rubble made from the broken boundaries of her feelings, a few lights of self still flickered.

After the first three months, though there had been occasions when the pain of Rosemary's loss of Daniel had seemed unbearable, it had begun to settle into something more like a bewilderment and sometimes even an irritation.

.   .   .

One night, a few weeks before the March election which had turned Lucy's working life into a double dose of frenzy, she'd come to visit late, exhausted, but elated by the fact that the prime minister and the new leader of the opposition had agreed independently to appear on

Malcolm Henry's show; and coincidentally, working with two different researchers, they had both picked the same night and time.

"Of course we had to sort it out. There isn't going to be any Great Debate, though they're both pretending it'd be a good idea. But what a coup it would have been!"

Lucy had been full of news, gossip, and speculation about the election, and Rosemary had loved to hear about the candidates behind their public masks: the flirty ones, the boorish ones, the arrogant, swearing ones, the ones who were smarter than they looked, and the ones who were dumber than they looked.

While Rosemary's connection with Daniel had parted, strand by strand, like slowly torn silk, Lucy's connection to Malcolm had strengthened by the day like a loomed tapestry under busy hands. On the night of the election when the nation was thrilled—or at least moved—to see strong Malcolm Fraser cry as he admitted that Bob Hawke had won, Malcolm Henry had proved to Lucy's satisfaction that he was not homosexual.

"It was bliss," she whispered, since Mattie was in the next room. "Oh, Ro, we just melted into each other!" After that, Mattie had frequently stayed with Rosemary the whole night. Rosemary and she had both lost Lucy to Malcolm, but they were no compensation for each other.

· · ·

When Rosemary finished cutting and trimming, the late spring twilight was well advanced. She had moved her gardening operations from the front of the house to the back where uninhibited clumps of Kikuyu grass threatened to spread over and start matting the pool unless eradicated. She wiped her sweaty forehead with a dirt-stained hand before considering the consequences—now, no doubt, she looked like a grumpy chimney-sweep. She was tired, the result, she suddenly realised, of having had virtually nothing to eat all day. It was time for a reviving chicken sandwich and the start of a re-heatable dinner for the children who would undoubtedly arrive at separate times, starving.

The phone actually did ring while she was in the shower, but she reached it too late. "Bugger!" she said to it after waiting damply for it to ring again, which it did not do until she was back in the bathroom.

"*Darling* love! Tell me everything. You haven't forgotten about Sunday? Martha—you know what she's like, never a kind word—said, 'You know what Rosie darling's memory's like.' "

"Oh, Melissa, how could I forget?" asked Rosemary, who had.

"Then you'll have remembered that it's going to be at Palm Beach?

Not that there's much point in schlepping everybody out there any-more—the old bastard tricked me. Knew I wouldn't invite him if I had it at the studio. So what did he do? He phoned me up, all thoughtful father, and offered me the house. Said he'd be away for the whole week on a model railway conference or something equally lower-middle class. And now that everyone's invited and its the eleventh hour and so forth, guess what, the old shit claims he got his dates wrong. And I *know* he planned it. I mean, you should see him—up to his baggy ears playing party-party. I've just been told he's hired a pig man, so now its B.Y.O.Pig. Oh, darling, it'll be terribly ghastly—you've got to come and help me control him."

"The pig man?"

"No. Father. You could fix him with that look. I guess you could fix the pig man, too."

"Your father is a darling, Melissa. Don't you harm a hair on him. And as for the pig man, I think that's a wonderful idea. He'll bring it along all nice and clean and dead and spit roast it, and you won't have to do a thing except salad. It says so in the *Herald*."

"Can you see why I need you there?"

"No," and Rosemary laughed, as she was expected to. "But I'm look-ing forward to it," she lied, as she was expected to.

Then, in a clean tracksuit, she made spaghetti bolognese. By six o'-clock, the sauce and the grated Parmesan were ready, the salad needed only to be dressed, and the noodles dropped into the big pot that had already boiled and would now take a mere minute or two to bubble up again.

Rosemary went to the bent-down part of the fence that separated her house from the one next door where Lucy and Mattie lived in the garden flat at the back but Lucy was obviously not home yet. Rosemary, having thought about Lucy so much during the day, wanted to say hello. There had been no time for a post-mortem about the night out with Tom and Eve—the night the red dress had tempted her into indiscretion. There was also the matter of the vacuum cleaner, which Rosemary would have liked to have borrowed from Lucy rather than have her lonely, pre-dinner whisky in the still dusty-carpeted living room. Rosemary stood on the crushed part of the fence near where the giant black bean tree bent, *tai chi* fashion, to lean its branches low enough for her, Lucy, and their children to use it as a support when they climbed over to visit, out of sight of the Hermanns. The Hermanns were Lucy's chilly, formal neighbours, who rented the main house to which her flat was attached and who were inclined to watch the neighborhood from behind half-closed curtains. But there was no sign of Lucy or her car, which normally lived under the carport at this end of the long drive.

$$\cdot \qquad \cdot \qquad \cdot$$

Through the autumn and the long, damp winter, there had been the sort of headlines for which there was not type large enough to convey the shock. Canberra had seemed to be full of Russian spies. Sydney had seemed to be full of magistrates, lawyers, judges, and politicians influencing each other into letting crooks out of jail. Large sums of money, it was said, were passed around. Even the premier of the State of New South Wales was implicated in the innuendo and grimly stepped aside for what seemed to Rosemary like the hundredth in a long line of judicial enquiries. Newspapers grew fat from it all, and television and radio found their time slots simply weren't long enough.

These problems bombarded Rosemary from banners and over the airwaves and in conversations as though they were seeking her out and demanding that she be shocked. If they could have been weighed and measured against her own, she may have laughed to see how ludicrously tiny and personal her problems were by comparison, but such is the nature of suffering that all of it simply provided an eerie continuo to Rosemary's solo plight.

There had been problems that husbands usually deal with and with these Rosemary had coped alone or invoked Tom's help if he was home, even though the Hermanns were in earshot of a scream. There had been a dogfight in her front garden for instance, in which Derek, a kelpie from down the road was torn almost to death by a pink-eyed bull-terrier no one had ever seen before. Other things were a broken fan belt and the theft of her lawn-mower (which Bobby had forgotten to put away). And there had been the mother possum and her adolescent child who had managed to find a way inside the house—a loose tile? a cracked barge-board? witchcraft?—nearly every night to sample the apples from the fruit bowl.

This Rosemary would not have minded so much if the possums had not been inclined to take one bite out of each apple and then throw it on the carpet, as though they were professional tasters reviewing for an agricultural show. But neither Phyl nor Bobby would touch an apple after a possum had tested it, no matter how carefully Rosemary removed the area around the teeth marks, and the price of fruit was going up. Besides, she was scared of them. They looked so knowing. They did not run when she flapped cloths at them but stared curiously, as though waiting for her to sing and dance as well. She believed they had terrible claws.

But it had been impossible not to involve the Hermanns in the pool crisis in May.

The Quiltys' pool, only one season old, had cracked. It was on the high slope behind their house and the Hermanns' house, next door, was directly in line of the water which had steadily leaked out, undermining the rocks, swamping both gardens, seeping under the hedge, and heading towards the Hermanns' house's foundations.

Because the Applesons, who owned the Hermanns' house, were away, all remedial negotiations had been conducted embarrassingly slowly through house-agents, insurance agents, and Shirley Coote, who, in response to the ninth or tenth and increasingly anguished call from Rosemary, had said, "Do you really want to know what Daniel says about it? He says if it were any other family than that damn frozen lot of slope-heads—those were his words—he'd come around and fix it himself. But that they can get stuffed. Something about a car." She pretended to sound apologetic, but there was glee in her voice.

Furious, Rosemary had imagined Daniel surrounded by his staff— her former staff—leaning against a filing cabinet and laughing. He'd have forgotten Lucy lived there, too. He'd have forgotten that it was his friend Dick Appleson's house's foundations that were being threatened with undermining by a suburban tidal wave. He'd have been enjoying himself too much to think of the cost.

Oh, yes, the car. Daniel loved cars. There must have been a time, Rosemary believed, about when his first pubic hair emerged, when he put away officially childish things and fell in love with old cars. When they bought the house it was because Rosemary had liked the light, air, space, and potential, and Daniel had liked the three-car garage. But even with three garages there had not always been room for all his bargains, so there had been times when roofless, rust-riddled Rileys or two-wheeled Jaguars were propped on bricks in front of their house. Well, more or less in front. Their house, being on a sharp curve, had a very small frontage, so it is true to say that the precious hulks sometimes overlapped onto the Hermanns' side, and this, for reasons Daniel refused to take seriously, was the only thing that had ever prompted Mr. Hermann to speak to them.

Once, while Daniel was still living at home and being a husband, the two men had happened to put the dustbins out at the same time. Mr. Hermann had pointed to the current shrouded treasure—at least forty-five percent of an E-Type Jaguar—and said, "How long will this rubbish stay here?"

Daniel had been so stunned at meeting a man who could call an old Jaguar rubbish that he'd immediately concluded his neighbour was insane and therefore not worthy of serious attention. His reply, hardly what one would have expected from a professional public relations man, even off duty, was something like, "Stuff you, mate. The street belongs to everyone who owns property in it! Tell the Applesons to let me know if they want me to move the car away from there! No one else minds!" This, as Daniel well knew, had not been strictly true—plenty of other people had grumbled about the visual pollution caused by Daniel's hobby, but they had told this to each other rather than to him since no one had wanted bad blood. Mr. Hermann, by speaking directly without the preliminaries of friendship and possibly a few beers, had acted in such an un-Australian way that Daniel was able to pretend he had not acted at all.

A week later, Rosemary had arrived home just in time to see a tow-truck crew attaching chains to the end of the car that had the fewest working wheels. They overran her attempts to stop them by showing her a copy of an official form which authorised its removal as an unlicensed, unregistered, abandoned vehicle. She'd phoned Daniel immediately, but even the way he drove was not fast enough to get there in time. Eventually he'd had to pay quite a few hundred to get his treasure back and have it trundled to MacMasters Beach where Lawrie lived in a cottage the Quiltys owned. Though Lawrie was technically Daniel's stepfather, since he'd been married for a few years to his mother before she died, he was really more like an older brother. He and Daniel had fixed old cars together before Daniel became too busy. So Lawrie had cheerfully made room in the overcrowded garage for the Jaguar's hulk.

Finally Rosemary had had to speak to Daniel herself about the pool. What had made her so furious was that she knew he knew she'd have to. Until this point she'd been in the position to maintain her secret anger, but now, through no choice of her own—except the choice to be responsible or reckless about her neighbours' house, of course—she'd had to reverse the decision not to speak.

Just as she'd known he would be, he was offhand, rude, pretending not to be interested. Daniel was always a better loser than winner.

"You fix it. Get onto the insurance. I don't even live there anymore."

"That was your choice, not mine."

"Are you inviting me to come back now that you need something done around the house? That's a joke!"

"No! No! Of course not! I just . . ."

"Why don't you just get your spanner out and fix it yourself?"

"The insurance policies—like just about everything else—are in the company's name," she had said, trying to deliver the information as impartially as computer-speak. "So the claim has to come from you. You already know that. Roy Carlton, remember Roy? From the corner house? The engineer? He says that the pool water has softened the Herm . . . the Applesons' soil so much that we only need a few more days of rain like this for their whole front garden to landslide into the street. Then it will cost a fortune to fix. And it has started undermining their foundations, so it is just possible that their house will follow their garden into the middle of the road."

"What the hell could I do about it now anyway? It's too late!"

"Sue the pool people. They'll quickly think of something. They've got insurance. Or call in a rain god to make it stop! It's just wasted here, when all the farmers' cattle are dying of thirst!"

"I find a rain god in the *Yellow Pages,* I suppose? Under *R* or under *G?*"

"You're the one with all the answers."

"Listen, Ro, while I've got you on the phone, there are things we must talk about. I think . . ."

"Please fix the pool, Daniel. OK? About anything else, Jim Begg's acting for me," she said and rung off quickly.

The rain did stop in time without intervention. And in due course, as a result of pressure on the pool company exerted mainly by Shirley Coote and occasionally by Daniel, the pool had been fixed by a team of men who had driven a big concrete-spitting machine up the Hermanns' drive. They'd broken some of a row of fully blooming azaleas, squashed the climbable fence even further, and left a legacy of lumps of rapidly drying concrete all over both gardens.

Despite Rosemary's, Lucy's, and the children's attempts at restoring everything, Mrs. Hermann had reacted as though there had been a bombing when she came home and grimly, in a grey silk dress and high heels, had begun bandaging azalea branches. Rosemary apologised, explained, but the woman had stiffly waved a hand at her and said, "Enough!"

.   .   .

The swimming pool, now thoroughly watertight, gleamed greenly in the twilight. Rosemary hadn't wanted to fill it until the weather was warmer, but the man from the pool repair company had recommended that she did so. He had talked a lot about contraction and expansion, but secretly Rosemary believed he just wanted to make sure his workers had actually fixed the leak properly. So for five months it had been full of very cold water and quite a lot of leaves that the children deeply resented having to scoop out since there was no immediate benefit. But now it was nearly summer. Already Bobby had been in.

It was lovely and peaceful, alone under the black bean tree. She wished she'd brought her whisky up with her—the thought of the un-vacuumed living room was depressing. She wondered, as she started down the steps she and Daniel had made from old wooden railway-line sleepers, whether her cleaning, chopping, surface-wiping day was the start of an old-maidish obsession for order and cleanliness. And that's when she really did hear the phone ring. Then she nearly slipped on the newly watered wood on her way to reach it in time. The "beep beep beep beep" signal, as she answered, proclaimed it to be an out-of-town call.

"This is Kim Haymes, assistant producer on 'The Mount Victorians.' Just confirming about tomorrow."

"Confirming what?" Rosemary asked, trying not to sound too thrilled or too naive.

"You are Rosemary Quilty, aren't you?"

"Yes I am, but I don't . . ."

"Your screen test, here in Lithgow. Is it OK for eleven A.M.?"

"Yes. Oh, yes. Where do I go?"

"Bloody hell. Hasn't the office been in touch?"

"No."

"Blast. There must be some mix-up. Sorry about that. Look, just get yourself here tomorrow, OK? We're running a tight schedule anyway and Fridays always stink."

"That's all right. Where do I go?"

"Eskbank House. Not far from town. Anyone'll point the way—it's next to the dog racing track."

"Must I bring anything? Prepare anything? I've recently done *Cat on a Hot Tin Roof* . . ."

"No, no, nothing like that. You'll be given a short script, not much to learn. Anyway, you know the routine. And wardrobe'll fix you up for the right gear. You a ten?"

"Either that or a twelve."

"No problem. I may not be here, so just ask for Michael Stoner, OK?"

"OK," she replied, trembling with pleasure.

All the monochrome clouds that had gloomed through the day instantly dissolved into limpid rainbows and after the phone call Rosemary whirled around her kitchen in a spontaneous dance of delight. The red dress had worked its magic after all.

Rosemary wanted to make it true by telling someone, but when the children eventually came home they were both exhausted and involved in problems. Phyl had discovered that a girl called Jeanette whom she'd regarded as a close friend had invited nearly every other girl in their group, plus their boy-friends, to a Chinese dinner for her seventeenth birthday. And Bobby, two nights before his opening, had suddenly got stage fright so badly that he claimed he wasn't going to do the show.

Rosemary had first tried teasing Phyl: "Do you think it might be your breath?"

"Mum! Be serious."

"I can't. You've used up all the week's ration of serious. I can see that you think Jeanette didn't invite you because you haven't got the right accessory—a boy-friend. But, you know, her father might have put her on a head-count budget and she's had to make some choices. You didn't make the list this time. That's all."

"So why did she invite Kate Rafferty? She always says she hates Kate Rafferty, but Kate's been going out with Terry Peterson for months and Jeanette's been trying to get his brother, Peter."

"You've answered your own question."

"But that's disgusting! They're not even friends!"

"It's sexual politics, which sometimes has a way of making itself seem more important than friendship. Those girls are playing a game you haven't started yet, but you will. You will."

"Mum, I know what you're going to say: 'Somewhere out there there's a wonderful guy just looking for a person like you and one day you'll meet.' You always say it!" Phyl was in tears at this stage. Bobby was in the shower; soon it would be his turn to have his ego dressed and mended.

He had taken longer to recover from his self-doubt, but eventually it had turned into anger which he'd diffused by yelling at Rosemary.

.   .   .

The sense of glorious excitement that had seemed to burst out of her during the phone call from Lithgow had shrunk to pea size by the time the children were ready for bed. To both of them Rosemary mentioned that she was going to Lithgow next day, leaving early, and that they'd have to be on the ball in the morning because she wouldn't be able to help much with the scramble for nourishment and lost property.

Bobby, wearing his Neglected Only Son expression had said, "Typical!" Phyl, looking wary and irritated, had said, "Why?"

"There may be a job for me. On a mini-series."

"That's mad," she'd answered, on her way to her bedroom. "You can't commute to Lithgow—it's about three hours if there's traffic!" Then she added, "Anyway, who cares if I never have a boy-friend?" before slamming her door for the last time.

Rosemary went up the railway sleeper steps again, to the black bean tree to have another look for Lucy, who would have been thrilled and full of good advice about the best route through the Blue Mountains at that time of day and about what to wear and so on. But the flat was dark.

Six

Having planned to leave no later than eight, Rosemary woke at six that Friday morning, so there was plenty of time for such morale-boosting engagements as washing and setting her hair in a modified-for-daytime version of the bouncing curls she'd worn with the red dress, and buffing her nails with fine powder, the way Victorian ladies did. She'd decided to wear a pale blue denim pants suit, a yellow T-shirt, and a rather cute blue-and-yellow-checked cloth hat—although it was still October, the day was going to be hot. (From now on she'd have to wear high-protection sun-screen and one from her arsenal of sun-hats virtually every day until next April.)

Even though she knew no one would see her legs, since she'd be wearing long skirts for the screen test, she'd carefully shaved them. But having not been exposed to the sun for more than half a year, they had the dead-looking whiteness of steamed chicken breasts. It was a battle, being so fair skinned.

Rosemary remembered a small sample of leg make-up she'd been handed some months ago near the cosmetic counters in David Jones's by an exquisite young woman in yellow hot-pants, whose golden brown legs looked as though they'd been lovingly treated by a craftsman in French polishing. She found it, rubbed it on, and was pleased by the instant gleam of health and vitality it bestowed.

Despite a steady stream of minor grumbles, Phyl and Bobby coped well enough, but until the phone rang, they still showed no interest in Rosemary's trip to stardom.

It rang shortly before eight, when, having finished her grooming—her actor's version of a sportsman's psyching up by a coach—Rosemary was looking through a pile of old maps and working at calming her anxiety about the trip.

"Get that, somebody, please. Say I'm out if it's Auntie Gwen—I'm running late."

Phyl answered, then, so excited that she sounded alarmed, yelled, "Mum! Mum! Quick!"

It was Robert Talbot's secretary. "I hope you don't mind me phoning so early, Mrs. Quilty."

"No, no. That's fine," she said in a tone she hoped suggested that early phone calls from tycoons were usual.

"I tried a number of times yesterday but you must have been out, so this is very short notice I'm afraid, but Mr. Talbot is driving to Lithgow this morning and would like to know if it's possible for you to go with him." Rosemary sat down. "Mr. Talbot wants you to meet Michael Stoner, the director, and watch some of the shooting and possibly do a screen test for a part in 'The Mount Victorians.' "

Rosemary tried not to squeak as she said that would be fine.

"A driver will pick you up if that's convenient, Mrs. Quilty. If you'll just give me your address." It was more than convenient—it was almost miraculous, though terrifying. She hoped Robert Talbot's secretary would not tell him how monosyllabically unimpressive Rosemary had been on the phone.

"Robert Talbot!" said Phyl. "Is that to do with the job at Lithgow?"

Rosemary nodded, smiling tight-lipped as though to contain an explosion of amazement.

"You didn't tell me you were going there with him!" Phyl was sitting on the bottom step of the stairs, too awed to concentrate on tying her laces.

"It's . . . it's just a lift. To a possible job. To save me driving," Rosemary said as ordinarily as she could, though obviously not ordinarily enough. Phyl's biscuit-coloured curls shrouded her face, but there were other signs that she was not fooled.

"I'll bet Robert Talbot's great!" Phyl said. "I saw a thing on TV— that night you were out—about his yacht. They interviewed the old bloke in charge of restoring it. It's big and old, and it's being fixed up to make it safe to go around the world or something. And I think he's even got his own helicopter."

General Studies was one of Phyl's Year Eleven options, which meant that she was required to watch current affairs programs—though Rosemary was pretty sure that, like Daniel, Phyl would have known what was going on in the world even if she lived in a phoneless, TV-less, radioless hole underground. People like Daniel and Phyl had an instinct for topical reality, a love of facts. Just as Rosemary derived most of her sense of self from dealing with feelings and motivations, so they, her daughter and her husband, were enhanced by information. Their conversations had often astounded her; when Phyl was as little as five she had been able to argue with Daniel—and sometimes even win—about such things as the number of months it took for a baby elephant to be born after its parents had mated or how many passengers a Boeing 707 could carry.

"I might be home late tonight, darling," Rosemary said, glad Phyl's interest had moved away from the man to his helicopter. "I'll phone you anyway; you may have to cook because I've got no idea when it will finish. Just don't talk about . . . anything until I tell you."

She knew she hadn't phrased that well when Phyl glanced up at her from her crouched position, then stood up quickly, one smooth, precise movement, and walked knowingly away.

The casual, outdoor-girl look Rosemary had chosen to present to a Robert Talbot-less film set would never do for a tête-à-tête two-and-a-half-hour drive and whatever might follow from it. It would take the car at least thirty minutes from the city so there was time to iron her soft, light green voile dress, to be worn with spiky sandals. Dior sunglasses would help defy the daylight and a lacy straw hat would give her star quality—albeit of the old-fashioned kind—and interesting shadows.

When they kissed her goodbye, Bobby said, "Are you going to the races?" and Phyl said, "Good luck with . . . anything!"

.   .   .

The big black limousine looked as though it belonged in a funeral cortège, and even in Rosemary's acquisitive street it was opulent enough to draw neighbours' glances. Its owner's initials were on the licence plate.

As they pulled away, Rosemary saw Lucy hurry down the long drive from her flat, stop as she recognised the car, then run towards it, waving importantly and smiling. But it was too late now for a chat about hopes and dreams, certainly not in the hearing of the hope-and-dream object's driver, so Rosemary waved back, pretending not to understand Lucy's stop signals.

The driver was a pallid man with a cap, a repaired harelip, and an apparent feeling of both obligation and strain about small talk, much of which she could not hear because she'd opened the window. They didn't click. Even before the expressway he felt he'd discharged his social duty and switched on the radio, leaving Rosemary to enjoy, for the second time in less than two days, the view of the bridge and the harbour from the vantage point of luxury.

It was a day clear as mineral water through which the strong colours—
Prussian blue sea, cobalt sky, sienna-and-vermilion-roofed houses—looked
like splashes from a starter paintbox. Even if it had been drizzly it would
not have detracted from her high-tuned, pre-surprise mood, but the
setting was a bonus on perfection: the sort of day Sydney people get
nostalgic about in grey, wet cities like London and grey, smoggy ones
like Tokyo.

The harbour scene looked to her like the toys of a giant's child: the
Opera House a neatly draining tea-set, the water a film of cellophane
with little white paper yachts and painted wooden ferries poking through.
Behind the intrusion of the expressway, shaped like an adult's shoulder,
the city's buildings loomed like Lego towers, and the bridge itself was
like a child's attempt to build a rainbow from Meccano. It looked like
the place for fun—only the clowns, balloons, streamers, and the children
themselves were missing. Instead, there were cars, trucks, motor bikes,
and buses efficiently whipping in and out of lanes, their drivers so busy
surviving that Rosemary believed no one but herself was taking advantage of the free look at the multi-billion-dollar view.

How nice to be a passenger. How nice to be driven to the start of a
romance!

The driver picked up his car phone and, through crackles of static,
spoke to someone called Doris.

"Tell him we'll be there in five, luv. Yeah, he said he'd come down
when we get there. Said he'd prob'ly drive himself, yeah. Suits me—I
was out last night and don't wanna be late for the club t'night. The wife
scored second in the ladies' darts last Fridy and now she's set on the
champ'nship."

When Doris replied, Rosemary could not make much sense of it
through the crackle, but the driver understood.

"Geez, Doris luv, that's a bit of bugger. Yeah, I gotcha. So we—er—
just proceed straight to Lithgow? Mr. Stoner, yeah, right, gotcha. Yeah,
me missus'll go crook, but. Give her a tingle will ya, luv? Nice day for
a trip but," then, replacing the phone, he turned to Rosemary and said
slightly more formally, "Boss can't make it yet. Says we're to go straight
on and he'll prob'ly meet ya there later. Says to phone his sec'ry later,
when ya get there."

Rosemary was simultaneously disappointed and relieved. It was as
though a count-down had been interrupted; one which, if it had reached
zero, would have had her sky-rocketing at great speed into unknown
territory. She could have got burned on the way, or crashed, but on the
other hand, it could have been the vehicle out of her bleak-futured

existence. Leaping ladders would be easy if Robert Talbot was holding her hand, and she'd got a very strong sense, in the restaurant, that he wanted to do at least that. But it would, nevertheless, have been a strain, starting up a relationship in the traffic with seat-belts on and no eye contact. At least now she could concentrate on the immediate matter of the film test and the possibility of a job. A job!

"Oooh wuh!" she said, loudly enough to startle the driver. "I have to make an urgent phone call. Can you stop somewhere, please?"

"You can use this one, I suppose."

"No, no. Just a public phone. I'll be quick," said Rosemary, who had noted the grudging tone in the driver's voice. Besides, her unreliability was none of his business.

"It's difficult round here. All the traffic," he grumbled, but he squeezed into a loading zone outside a fish shop. "Post office phone's just round the side there. But make it quick please, lady—don't wanna get booked for parking."

The employment agency woman was just as irritated. "Your appointment's in just over an hour, Mrs. Quilty. Don't you think it's a little late to cancel now? I mean, I've got plenty of ladies who'd like that job, but I made a special point of offering it to you first, with your experience."

Humbly, charmingly—after all she may need the agency again—Rosemary apologised, though she did privately wonder again how her experience in running the office of a public relations company could be valuable in the personnel office of a department store.

When she got back into the limousine, the previous morning's self-doubt seemed to be waiting for her on the big, back seat. What the hell do you think you're doing? she asked herself. You've been in one play in a drama course for adults—what did Daniel call it? geriatric play school. And here you are, perfumed, smooth as a tart, going off to try for a job in a profession overstocked with real, experienced actors. The employment agency woman could obviously see, better than she herself could, the humble slot in which society would permit her to belong. Not even trying to hide her anxiety, she leaned forward and tapped the driver on his shoulder. He half turned with a "What is it now?" expression.

"Excuse me. Look, I've changed my mind about going to Lithgow. I wonder if you could drop me somewhere here, near a taxi?"

His startled face was reflected in his mirror. The matter was so serious that he turned off the radio, cutting Dolly Parton off in the middle of "lerve."

"Whaddya say?"

She knew he was stalling.

"I dunno. Ya know, Mr. Talbot, he's going out there to meet ya. I think ya'd havta tell him if ya not going." He picked up the car phone and started summoning up Doris. But Rosemary, imagining the horror of an explanation—a cop-out—over the air waves, quickly decided to leave things as they were.

"Suit yaself," said the driver, indicating that it is a woman's right to change her mind. "Here." He handed her a *Herald* and turned on the radio, signalling that there would be no further discourse on how much nicer Sydney generally is than Melbourne and how the farmers still needed rain. But she couldn't read in the moving car. Somehow she'd bluff her way through the embarrassing day, and on Monday go back to the agency for a job within her scope. Patchwork PR had been within her scope. How sad that she'd had to lose it first, to see that.

Yesterday the housework had not been enough of a distraction, so knowledge of Daniel had poured through. Before that, because she was determinedly living in a Daniel-less here and now, Rosemary had made sure there was always plenty to overcrowd her thinking, to keep him out. The drama course had been a help.

The drama course had been on Tuesday and Thursday nights, with bits of Saturday and even Sunday when they were deep into rehearsal. But it had finished just over a week ago with the presentation of *Cat on a Hot Tin Roof,* an exciting and dramatic finale for the year's last semester and a great improvement on the play that ended the first semester.

Remembering, Rosemary grinned and shuddered at the same time. *Mother Love* was a play written by a thin young man called Terry Scott whom Melissa had "discovered." It was about a transvestite who wants to fulfil himself by having a baby. Rosemary remembered telling Lucy about it after she'd first read the script.

"It was really hard work persuading Terry to cut out the scene where the parent-to-be walks around with a saucer full of ova and sperm talking about the meaning of life. It was supposed to be moral—full of dilemmas like What Does the Post–Women's Lib Man Do? and Whose Child Is It Anyway?" Lucy had rolled around on her armchair, laughing. "It isn't supposed to be a comedy," Rosemary had said, trying to be solemn. "The actors tried a few times to ham it up, and when they did it was hilarious. But Terry has this bikey boy-friend who stands around sharpening his nails with a stiletto."

"Sharpening?"

"Perhaps trimming. I don't go close enough to be sure. I think Jeremy—the director—you met him here, remember? Nice little bloke with glasses and leather sleeve patches. I think he's too scared to do much, though he says he's giving them space for artistic expression. So it's a free-for-all, partly directed by the playwright, partly by the actors, and with input from me when I'm prepared to risk the bikey. He particularly hates suburban mothers, he told me. Jeremy makes the tea and says it will be all right on the night."

"What the hell are you doing it for? You'll kill yourself—driving your kids all over the place, making Bobby's costume, rehearsing for one play, stage-mothering the other. You don't even have a cleaning lady anymore. You've got to slow down!"

"I'm not rehearsing yet—that's next semester. I'm only learning lines now."

But *Mother Love* would probably never have opened if it had not been for Rosemary, and secretly, she realised that. Jeremy was a man who liked to encourage, he said, not command. Rosemary often felt this was a cop-out for indecisiveness. Many rehearsals would have ended in tantrums or walk-outs if she had not shooed, shushed, reinterpreted, fed, listened to, and occasionally even yelled at people. It was exhausting, particularly as familiarity with the play did not make her like it any more than she had at first reading. But it was a process akin to burrowing through a tunnel—the only way to survive was to keep going to the end.

The next semester had been even busier for Rosemary because, although her stage-managing of *Mother Love* had ended with the production in July, she had then done a computer word-processing course as well as starting rehearsing *Cat on a Hot Tin Roof* in earnest. Jeremy was the director, and Rosemary had been cast as Sister Woman, mother of the no-neck monsters. But, although every minute had been budgeted with miserly skill and although her already over-stacked schedule had had constant delays and interruptions which had put her stress level on a permanent state of red alert, the play had been wonderful: exhausting but fun in a way she'd never known before.

Patrick Price had been in it, too, and he had surprised her. Her first impression of the tall, quiet man was that he was part of Melissa's gay crowd. He'd stood with Jeremy, Martha, and Melissa at the party—that damned party—looking friendly, hopeful, shy, and defensive, the way some only children do as they observe groups of others having fun. But, with his lean body padded with cushions and a new, deeper, booming note to his voice, he had been astonishingly good as Big Daddy. Jeremy, the first one to have perceived enormous potential for power under Patrick's neat persona, was prouder than Svengali when he'd stolen the show.

The theatre course had been as buffeting and immersing as a naked ride through rapids. It had also been exhilarating because Rosemary had mastered the dangerous cross-currents, survived, and even triumphed in a little way. But now it was over; metaphorically she was dumped— vulnerable to all the troubling things her busy-ness had excluded. Ah well, she thought, to cheer herself up. I'll see them all at Melissa's party on Sunday. But in her present low mood, the prospect seemed more like a wake than fun.

There was nothing in the car to distract her but Radio 2KY, so Daniel kept slipping back into Rosemary's mind. Daniel. Those nights . . . She tried to bring her memory back to where Daniel was the villain, not the lover.

There had been times, especially after Bobby was born, when Rosemary and Daniel were working together so hard that there were no boundaries between day and night or office and home or being on or off duty. Bobby and his bottles and nappies had gone to the office, too, whenever the things Rosemary had had to do required equipment or face-to-face meetings.

For her and Daniel, finding time to be alone together had been the constant challenge; their ongoing game had been to spend every possible moment making love. There was a couch in Daniel's office—where the board of directors of Patchwork PR would sometimes meet at lunch- times—the door locked, the typist gone to lunch, the phone off the hook.

There were hints of power in Daniel's face, something to do with his fine-boned, high-arched nose and the way he closed his lips over large teeth that a weaker mouth might have relaxed around. When he stood up and talked to people with a slight but convincing frown, he looked, to Rosemary, like a hero—as though there was nothing he could not solve if the problem were presented to him. But when he was lying down and focussing on her he looked entirely different—almost vul- nerable—and then she had been almost fearful of her capacity for love.

There had been times when, because of the moon or hormones or magic, they had stumbled onto a level of communication that tran- scended passionate intercourse. It might have been at a dinner party or in a crowded shop or during a meeting when it began. Daniel would look at her and the look would be like a charge of something more subtle, more pure than electricity. It would knock her off her tune, as though the needle had been knocked off a disc, and the irresistible rhythm of lust would blot out all the other inner voices.

At those times there would be no time for the familiar tender preparation—Rosemary's body would lurch itself into a state of readiness as though an alarm bell had sounded for an emergency drill. Her womb would seem to hollow itself and her knees would try to let her down as though there were a bed just there, and whatever time it took between the appointment made by that electric message and the first strong, naked touch would be almost unendurable, passed in a dream of duty, accompanied by the sense of her own pulse which seemed to say, through everything, Yes, Yes, Yes. Now, Now, Now. And if the wait was long, as it sometimes had to be at client meetings or presentations, her own pulsing would gradually drive her into such an anger that she'd scream with relief when at last the passion was free to flow. She'd known how addicts felt.

.   .   .

"Shit!" said the driver, lurching the car out of reach of a small, wild blue van. " 'Scuse me. Didya see that bastard? Bloody Asians. Driving on a forged bloody licence, I bet."

Lewisham. Croydon. Haberfield. Burwood. Strathfield. The name boards of the suburbs they drove through were a litany from her childhood, stations on her way home from shopping trips to Farmers or the early show at Hoyts with a group of friends. Now they impinged just enough on Rosemary's reminiscences for her to peer, every now and then, along side-streets in the hope of familiar territory. But the suburbs were well camouflaged by the car-yard-encrusted edges of the Great Western Highway where new and old car prices and other virtues were displayed in Day-Glo colours on windows, banners, flags, and neon signs.

Those cars in the steeper yards looked as though they might at any time break off in a cluster, spill into the traffic-choked lanes of the highway, and get swept along, a dangerous clot borne into the heart of Parramatta. It is hard to imagine that anything as beautiful as the Blue Mountains—well, most of it is beautiful—can lie not too far ahead of this.

Time and the circumstance of Daniel's choices had put Rosemary so far away from her childhood that now, crawling through Strathfield in the limousine, it seemed part of someone else's life. For a moment she experienced an insecurity, a fear which expressed in words would have been something like, Now that he's gone, maybe I'll have to come back.

Nonsense, she thought. I've got the house. Anyway, it's too far.

Having stop-started for three blocks behind a car carrier full of new

Datsuns, the limousine finally escaped into the start of the stretch of expressway that bypasses Parramatta and reaches Emu Plains and the start of the long freeway to the foothills.

.   .   .

Daniel and Rosemary had started Patchwork PR when Phyl was four, with nothing apart from the proceeds of a small insurance policy Rosemary's mother, Jean, had bought for her first birthday and which had matured when she was twenty-one. Jean had intended it to be the start of home ownership, or, if her plans for her daughter's life had proceeded in a more orderly way, for a honeymoon in Europe or Japan. Instead, it had provided one of the first smallish computers capable of merging a list of addresses with multiple copies of a single letter.

Rosemary had soon learned to design the lay outs for the material Daniel wrote. She could change fonts, clear log-jams of paper, and even de-bug some of the machine's simple programs; and so the flow of beguiling direct-mail letters and clever press releases had begun, and they in turn had inspired a steady trickle of money into the company's bank account. Daniel and Rosemary had paid themselves very little— it was a time of lamb neck stews, clever things with eggs and lentils, and infinite variations on a couple pounds of mince—but the company's balance sheets showed tentative signs of health from the start. They all worked hard, even tiny Phyl, who had been perfectly capable of stuffing letters into envelopes, looking solemn, and holding her fingers just so with one pinky in the air.

Daniel had written all the copy, of course, and he was also the front man who charmed clients, both new and old, over drinks or lunches or late, long meetings, and who seemed to never get tired or lose his smile or stop having good, saleable ideas.

When she'd left the company, Rosemary had not looked back. It had seemed at the time like a release. But now, dodging through the Parramatta Road traffic, she suddenly found herself grieving for the way it had been in the beginning. The struggle, particularly in the early days, had actually been the main cement of her relationship with Daniel, though neither had realised it in the flurry of sex.

Despite the long, often tedious hours—she'd claimed to have personally stuffed and posted three hundred thousand direct-mail letters, for instance—it had been fun. There were nights when they'd sat up for hours planning new campaigns, their huge double bed covered with drafts, re-drafts, scribbled notes, and sketch plans. And out of that had come wonderfully attention-grabbing campaigns that had given their clients hundreds of precious centimetres of newspaper columns and dozens of bright, sometimes-controversial moments on TV and radio. Like the time they'd launched Indulgence, a new line of pre-cooked dinners, by persuading the manufacturers to donate enough—in the five different flavours—to feed a line of two hundred unemployed people every night for a week. They were people whose meals were usually supplied by religious charity groups.

After each meal some of the eaters were asked for their comments, as though they were wine tasters at a show. Many of them loved the TV cameras, especially the old people, who were no longer ashamed of eating at soup kitchens.

"Better 'n soup!" one impish old man had said, grinning toothless and twinkle-eyed. So they had put his picture on the packaging and given him a thousand dollars. There had been some strong public re-action—some people said the poor were being exploited and used like guinea pigs—but many said it was a good thing and that more big food manufacturers should help the charities.

"Tell them to keep going, once, twice, a week," Rosemary had sug-gested. "What will four hundred meals a week cost them? Nothing! And the good will is tremendous!"

Daniel had agreed and persuaded the manufacturers. Because of this and other generally favourable publicity, and because the meals were pretty good anyway, Indulgence dinners had become associated in the public mind with fun and generosity, and they quickly became best sellers.

Rosemary had mattered in Daniel's company. It was something to hang onto.

Despite a deep aversion to the big IBM type-setter, Rosemary had taught herself to type so she could key in Daniel's letters, and this had saved them having to hire a casual secretary every time there was a big job. And for the first six months, Jean had done the books. Then, when Phyl was four and a half, careful, safe-driving Jean had been killed by a drugged youth who had lost control of the car he'd stolen—borrowed, his family's lawyer later insisted, trying to lighten his client's load—and crossed the concrete barrier down the centre of the road and hit her Volkswagen head on.

If they had lived in a medieval village instead of an apparently civilised city, Rosemary's mother's supporters would have avenged her death. As it was, the youth, who had been a prefect at his famous private school and whose family was in the stockbroking line, was treated so leniently by the judge that anyone at the hearing would have got the impression he'd been the victim of the accident, not its cause. This, anyway, had been Rosemary's impression, and no amount of explanation about the processes of law changed her view that the judge must have been the boy's uncle, or in his father's pay. Her opinion, which had been cast in the heat of her loss, had set hard into a form of stubbornness most people would have said was uncharacteristic.

The happy part of her mother's life—freedom from responsibility and worries about money—had been just about to start after years of self-deprivation; the youth, with plenty of time ahead, had been trying to wipe himself out in an excess of self-indulgence. He was big enough to drive, big enough to kill. He was a killer, she'd said, ignoring people's winces.

Daniel had sued the youth's family—or started to. The boy had been unlicensed and therefore uninsured, so it could have become the sort of newspaper story his family was eager to avoid. But instead of a public, legal fight with them, it had turned into a really major private battle between Rosemary and Daniel when she'd adamantly refused to sue.

"You're not going to capitalise on my mother's death," she said.

"She'd have wanted it!" Daniel had raged. Auntie Gwen, though still too racked to talk much, had agreed. Rosemary had thought it was too cynical to even bother to counter, but with both of them glaring at her— Auntie Gwen through her tears—she'd had to explain again. In her opinion, since the boy had been allowed to survive, he should have been made to work weekends in rehabilitative hospitals until he'd learned the value of other people's lives. Money paid by his rich father would be nothing but blood money—it wouldn't help him with his ethics, his morals, and his guilt.

"Bugger him! What a bloody right-wing notion! You've lost your mother. The company has lost a valued staff member. And we need the money—look how we're struggling now. Think of it as compensation, Rosemary!"

"Put a price on my mother? Be bought off? Daniel, do be serious," she'd said, and walked away, into the bedroom, where she'd closed the door. Then she'd opened it again and said, "I'll do the books. I know how—she taught me."

Rosemary hadn't cried at first when Jean died. She hadn't even felt stunned, merely unconnected, as though she were watching some urgent, painful news on television with the sound switched off. Dr. Saxon had given her sleeping pills which she'd refused to take, having missed a period the previous month.

When she did cry, it was because the two month foetus, an oddly shaped dark blob, had disconnected itself from its life-source inside her after some hours of pain. And then it was as though she'd never stop.

"Take her away for a couple of weeks. The south coast somewhere—my shack in Mollymook. I'll come and help with the cooking and keep Phylly entertained," Auntie Gwen had said, but Daniel, white with guilt and overwork, had refused at first. "How can I leave now?" he'd asked, tears glittering in his eyes. "I've just got this business on its feet. I've got deadlines, regular newsletters . . ." But after a jibe about the crematorium being full of indispensable people, Daniel did delegate a few weeks of work to a former colleague newly returned from America and not yet in the mainstream of journalism, and in March, three months after the accident and the worst Christmas Rosemary would ever remember, the two of them had gone to a cottage at Avoca, north of Sydney, on the beach, and there among other pleasant experiences they had conceived Bobby. Which, they agreed later, they might not have done had Auntie Gwen been around insisting on late-night games of Scrabble instead of moving into their little flat to look after Phyl.

Daniel. It was hard to distract herself from thinking about him, now that she'd begun.

Jean had left them her house plus some savings in various little investment accounts, all of which yielded a total which astonished Rosemary and gratified Daniel. It was enough to properly capitalise the company after all.

"Next year, when the baby's about ready for its first Christmas, we'll buy a house. You'll see," Daniel had promised. In fact, it had taken considerably more struggling than either of them had anticipated, and six months longer.

Rosemary had kept on working throughout her second pregnancy—Phyl had started school—and after Bobby was born she'd run Patchwork's office from the middle of piles of nappies and squeaky toys, first in their little flat in Drummoyne and later in the new house.

There had never been time to think about whether this was what she really wanted to do with her life. It had to be done—all of it—and she was the one available. There were days when she'd almost got angry with Bobby because he stuck to his own feeding schedule, one devised without consultation. He would lie asleep, his curled, pink hands beside his ears, his knees splayed, beautiful and unreachable through the slack time before nine A.M. After that, she knew, the phone would start ringing.

She had often been tempted to wake him up at eight and play with him, feed him, be peaceful with him so that he could know her as someone to have fun with, but waking him had never worked: his heavy

Quilty lids would slide down over his slightly crossed, clear blue eyes, first one lid and then the other in a series of expressions that made him look like an old drunk rather than a young baby. "Go away. You bore me," he seemed to say. Then, when he did wake, his need was desperate, immediate, with no compromise, even though she might be reading a press release to a newspaper in Brisbane.

The whole of Bobby's babyhood seemed to have been taken up in this way: their timing was always askew. He would have loved some three A.M. or even midnight company, but by then her time belonged to sleep or to Daniel.

Phyl, she'd felt, was already partly lost to the school system: the once day-dreaming toddler had turned into a fairly formidable organiser almost from day one. She was always a school monitor or library assistant or class captain; a person who had stepped into efficiency as though it were a waiting, tailored garment.

It was different for Rosemary, whose attitude to organisation had always been much more ragged and patchy. For her the job of pulling the rags together and producing a reliable, uniform behaviour pattern had been so hard to do that it had consumed most of her nervous energy for the first ten years of her marriage. But no one else realised this, especially not Daniel, for whom the effort had been mainly intended.

.   .   .

Rosemary's ears popped and creaked and she forced a yawn to clear them. They had climbed up the winding foothills through Lapstone and Glenbrook, and now, near Springwood, they were in the mountains proper.

Between the tightly clustered shops and houses of each small village up the mountain, beyond the dirty black railway line and past the comparatively few gum trees that survived the great levelling into suburban building blocks, are surprising snatches of the endless view. Nearby, the mountains are soft green with skin-coloured sandstone or black-grey, weather-sculpted basalt rock faces. The green-green foreground gives way to green-grey, green-blue, and in the farthest distance, bluer than the sky, bluer than opal, tending almost to purple at the edges, are the taller peaks and ranges of the mountains. The blue is a trick of the light, Rosemary's mother had told her. Volatile oils from the gum trees fill the air with particles which absorb blue light and reflect all the other colours away. (Or was it the other way around?)

Close up, gum-tree leaves are more grey than green, and they are almost invariably chewed, or distorted by egg-containing lumps—the work of the multiplicity of insects who live among them. But in their thousands, their millions, the leaves combine to provide every chromatic possibility of green from lettuce heart to khaki and of blue from slate to Siamese kitten's eye. Being spring, the fugue in green and blue was accented by splashes of new-chick yellow; the wattle trees, comprising masses of fluff balls made almost entirely of pollen, were abundantly in bloom. They were, as Jean the pharmacist had pointed out, a boon to sales as well as to the eye: people had literally queued up with prescriptions for antihistamines and then gone home still sneezing, laden with new boxes of Kleenex and pricey nasal sprays. But Rosemary was not allergic to pollen. I could live here, she thought. If it were not so far. And so cold. When I'm old, perhaps. I'll grow azaleas and roses and get up late. Or have central heating.

.   .   .

Rosemary did not see Daniel at all after the time of the truncated fight in February until one day late in winter after the swimming pool was fixed, when he'd arrived and strolled into the house jangling his keys as though nothing had changed.

"What about some tea?" he said, standing in a stream of sunlight that illuminated him as though he were on stage. He was wearing, Rosemary had noticed, a pale grey linen shirt, French or Italian, and hooked over one index finger was a white, fine wool cable-knit sweater. Phyl, the traitor, hardly looking surprised, had eagerly leapt to the kitchen, pulling a new packet of biscuits from Rosemary's latest ultra-secret hiding-place. Rosemary's fury had been cold and ugly, like a toad.

"You can't just walk in here uninvited," she said as soon as her tongue worked properly.

"Yeah? And who pays for it?" he asked, sweeping his tanned, golden-haired arm around to encompass everything, including Rosemary, Phyl, and Bobby.

"We have separate lives now. I wouldn't walk in on you and your . . ."

"That's because it's her unit," he answered, as patiently as though correcting her on a point of etiquette. "This happens to be my house."

"No. It's *ours*. And as I worked for the company, unpaid, from the start, and as I'm bringing up our children in it, and as you have abandoned it, I expect that it is now rightly mine." She said it without stuttering, without shouting—in fact it had probably sounded quite bland.

"Ahh, don't come with that 'It's mine' business. God, it's our main asset! You've refused to have any sort of rational discussion about money, living here like Queen Victoria."

"What do you mean 'like Queen Victoria?' Suddenly, after you're not personally living in it, a surburban house becomes a palace too grand for your family?"

"Have you listened to a single word Shirley has been trying to tell you? About the way you spend money, Rosemary? Of course not! You don't know what the word budget means."

"It may interest you to know that I refuse to discuss my—our—domestic economy with a stuck-up secretary."

"Well, if you won't speak to Shirley Coote, and you won't speak to me about it, what the hell can I do to get you to understand that things have changed? Patchwork isn't rich anymore, Rosemary. We've lost some clients, and there have been other things that have held us back." Rosemary noticed that Phyl looked impressed, concerned. Maybe I'd have looked like that a year ago, she thought.

"I was banking on that direct-mail computer system," Daniel said. "But we're . . . well, organising the payment's not exactly easy right now since the Oz dollar's been devalued—the whole bloody thing's in U.S. dollars. The price has gone through the roof!"

"Oh, Daddy! Does that mean Patchwork's in trouble?" Phyl nibbled her lower lip, the way she did in sad movies.

"Well, no. No, of course not," said Daniel. "We'll sort something out, never you worry. And the day the new system's up and running is the day the business takes off. You've got no idea what it can do! Patchwork will hit the big time!"

Rosemary had always believed Daniel when he'd talked in this confident way, like a golden-haired prophet, so it had seemed almost like heresy when she heard herself say, "Patchwork's been going to hit the big time for so many years now that it's like an electric drill without a power cord. That big, fancy machine is probably going to cause more problems than it solves when you first get it—they always do, you know that. And you want us to starve to pay for your new toy!"

"Listen," Daniel said, clicking his keys as though they were teeth he was gnashing, "you've seen the balance sheets. You've read the report. You know we're down on last year. God, we're even down on the year before!"

She had not looked at the balance sheets when the courier brought them, having been too busy for routine things that no longer concerned her directly. But Daniel's bluster did not bother her; it was normal for him to talk as though the bailiff was due at any moment, often while he was poring through a BMW catalogue or pondering the purchase of an ocean-going yacht.

In the early days, before she could predict it, Daniel's easy ferocity had excited her and made her feel secure. If she had ever expressed it to him it would have been something like, "If you can fight with me and win, then, when I am otherwise occupied, I can feel sure that you'll deal at least as well as I could with my enemies." It had given her a sense of safety, during her pregnancies, to feel that her hero, Daniel, her warrior man, was standing at the entrance to their metaphysical cave, ready to fight off bears, kidnappers, and those who might insult her. But now his ranting seemed childish and hysterical, like the behaviour of those male magpies whose protective paranoia during the mating season makes them bombard passers-by and peck their heads. In spring, when the children were tiny, they had had to wear plastic ice-cream cartons, sticky-taped under the chin, to keep themselves from being lacerated by a swift, clicking beak. She was glad, now, that Daniel had never taken his tantrums to war on her behalf.

"Jim Begg's been in touch with you," she said. "I'd rather do the financial sorting out through him, Daniel, because quite frankly I can't bear this, I really can't. There should be rules of conduct for when people split up. An umpire . . ."

"A referee, more likely. But I didn't come here to fight. Listen, you've got to understand that I can't just go on carrying this can. It's a huge responsibility, running the company on my own, supporting two households. . . ." Rosemary had been so outraged by his self-pity that she'd burst out laughing, which had made him angry. "I'm serious," said Daniel. "Do you know what's happened to interest rates? You don't, do you? Every piece of equipment, every bit of cash is costing a fortune, and salaries are so ridiculous that I'll probably have to put off that nice little chap who helps Shirley."

What Rosemary had felt like saying was Why not fire Angela? but since this was not supposed to be a fight she said, "Okay. What do you want me to do about it?"

"I'm putting you on notice to get yourself onto a reasonable budget and stick to it, Rosemary, because I can't go on like this anymore. School bills, grocery bills . . . that last David Jones account was a joke! What the hell did you need three hundred and fifty dollars worth of—what was it?" He'd taken a crumpled bill out of his pocket. "Moderate sportswear. What the hell is moderate sportswear?"

This was like an exam for which Rosemary had not studied, but Phyl had had the answer. "Do you think it's my winter gear, Mum? My black pants, the jumpers and those shirts? And the tracksuit?"

Phyl was pale, biting her lips again, and this suddenly made Rosemary's fury hiss out like the chill smoke that rises from splashed dry ice. Speaking very steadily she said, "Never mind drinking that tea, Daniel. You've said your piece, now please leave. I will certainly submit a budget for your inspection—and stick to it. I've done that before—for the company as well—which is probably *why* it was rich when I was there and poor now that I've gone. You live your new life, Daniel. Spend up on fancy gear for yourself, Daniel. And Phyl and Bobby and I will learn to darn, recycle, and perhaps even beg for cast-offs here and there. And don't worry too much about our diet—I've still got my mincemeat recipes."

Daniel, equally furious, had slammed his cup on the table next to him where, unnoticed by anyone but Phyl, it had broken and spread its contents all over the books and magazines. But he hadn't moved. "Blast you, Rosemary! I came here to have a reasonable, civilised conversation—a business discussion. And here you are carrying on like someone in an Ibsen play. You're so bloody smug! So self-righteous! Lazy—and jealous. Yes, you are. You're jealous because . . ."

"No!" And the cold anger had turned hot after all. "You go, darling," she'd said to Phyl. "Don't get mixed up in this."

When Phyl had gone, obviously both reluctant and relieved, Rosemary had yelled, furious that the conversation had picked up traces of spite, like pure water inevitably contaminated by running through polluted soil. In a minute they were both talking and not listening, presenting inappropriate symbols that overlaid and replaced reality, and all the time, under it, Rosemary had been able to hear the small, scrambled voice which had wanted to remind Daniel of the way it used to be.

"You're being mean, Daniel. And rude: on the one hand you demand that I become independent. On the other, you give me no rights."

"Rights?" He sounded bewildered.

"Yes. Rights. For instance, what if I had someone visiting me here, some man, and you just—arrived? If I were anyone else, you'd phone first!"

Far from seeing this as a reasonable request, Daniel had become nasty in an even more absurd and melodramatic way—the way in which Rosemary felt Bobby took after him, and when he finally left, it was after having loudly, on the front path, threatened to fight for custody of the children, whose lives, he said, were being ruined by Rosemary's immoral example. The neighbours weren't even bothering to peek through their curtains—they were standing, worried, on their front verandah.

"What the fuck are you looking at?" Daniel had asked them—and anyone else in the street who'd happened to be listening.

Actually, the fight had done Rosemary more good than harm. Her public rightness had been immediately enhanced by at least thirty percent; any neighbour who, until then, might have had a sneaking suspicion that the broken marriage was her fault was, after that, with her all the way.

.   .   .

That feeling of public rightness had contributed to a small flowering of confidence which had led Rosemary, later that month, to do an inexpensive though not very thorough course in word-processing. She'd soon discovered that her years of the trial-and-error method of learning office routines had qualified her at least as well as the people who ran the course. And her self-taught skills on Patchwork's type-setting machine had paved the way for word processing, though at first she had not enjoyed the little desk-top computers. Although theirs was the sort of nit-picking logic that made the Mary side of her nature feel safe—a clear yes or no for everything with no shades of grey—the Rose side, which hated making mistakes, was deeply resentful of the reprovingly bleeping machines and had often wished to chuck the whole thing in.

But at the end of the fortnight, Rosemary had surprised herself by winning the speed test and had begun to get glimmers of a future in which computers might play a part.

.   .   .

The car was travelling through Lawson when Rosemary next became aware of the scenery. Lawson was where she and Daniel had found the little "old wares" shop just down beside the railway line that had sold them the small cedar table that now stood under the high window in the yellow room, and a dozen old, pretty blue and green bottles to fill the shelves on the bathroom window. There they had bought the portrait of the sad-eyed lady with elegant hands.

Even before the brigadier had surprised her and Daniel by endorsing Rosemary's picture-buying skills, she had thought of her occasional hobby as an investment—her own little hedge against inflation. "Hedge against inflation" was the term Daniel had used to justify his purchase of the hulks of expensive old cars which he had always intended to fix. But their exposed and trendy house with its high, rocky backyard was not the place to do it, even if he hadn't been working fifty or sixty hours a week. Usually, after taking up much more than a fair share of garage space while supposedly waiting for vital parts to be shipped or air-freighted from Germany or the U.K., each car in turn would end up not much different from the way it had been in the first place, and some younger man with more time and the same shining-eyed lust would buy it for hardly more than Daniel had paid for it.

Rolling along the curves of the Great Western Highway in the back of a big black limousine, it suddenly occurred to Rosemary that maybe she *was* better at money than Daniel was. She wished she felt more confident about her abilities as a parent.

·   ·   ·

The radio, which had provided a jingle-riddled commercial and country-and-western music and violent and tragic news counterpoint to Rosemary's excursion, was suddenly switched off. The driver peered at her in the mirror.

"Next town's Katoomba. Gotta stop fer a drink. Like anything? I could take ya to a petrol station," he said tactfully.

"Thanks, that's a great idea," she said, smiling at his reflection. Reminiscing was hard on the bladder.

Seven

The driver had hummed to the radio's songs and made the occasional rude comment about other drivers but otherwise had not impinged upon Rosemary's introspection, as a result of which she suddenly felt quite friendly and offered to buy him a Pepsi.

"Nah thanks, luv. Never touch the stuff meself. Got a bit of the sugar, ya know, and that diabetic lolly water—ergh! Druther drink milk and that's the truth."

"Some fruit then? Cherries?"

"Oh, a cherry or two would go down well, ta."

Katoomba. She'd never really seen it until Daniel saw it for the first time. To her it had always signified fun, in a rather stiff way. Auntie Gwen, not so fat before she retired, had had a little guest-house there so long before they were fashionable that it sometimes happened that no one booked at all. Then, if Auntie Gwen was feeling lonely, or if she had responded to the jagged, exhausted, single-parent note in Rosemary's mother's voice on the phone, the two of them would catch the slow train from Strathfield up the mountains to Katoomba station.

They would go in Auntie Gwen's battered station-wagon to The Three Sisters at Leura: dizzying views of the opal-coloured mountains from which the three strangely formed rocks protruded. Like old scabs, Rosemary had thought the first time she saw them. Healing crusts at the edge of the scar tissue of the mountains which, despite their soft, multi-shaded green coating, looked as though the trauma of eruptions was not forgotten.

Dinosaur dung, Jean, her mother, had called them, or troglodytes. Jean, who'd had few opportunities for making people laugh while selling them stuff for their sinuses, used to enjoy amusing Auntie Gwen. The two women, giggling, gossiping about people they had known before

Rosemary was born, and other topics that entertained grown women, had made her feel partly excluded and partly secure. Katoomba had been a place for being bored and reassured at the same time.

Sometimes they had climbed down the fairly easy bits at Blackheath into the heart of the view, where tall fern trees and waratahs grew from gaps between the rocks and tiny flowering mosses and vines trailed wherever they were likely to avoid being trampled. Once they'd gone on the zigzag railway at Lithgow—a high, cold, dizzy, though disappointingly short ride along the mountain tracks that used to carry the coal up from the first important mines.

Once they went to the Jenolan Caves, which Rosemary had fearfully hoped would be as dangerous and romantic as the ones Tom Sawyer and Becky Thatcher got lost in. But they had turned out to have lights, rails, steps, and ordered lines of unawed people who followed the guide as he recited the joke names of the caverns. He'd hardly mentioned bats.

Katoomba meant two sausages, one egg, and a fried tomato for dinner— Auntie Gwen being, in those days, better at breakfasts than anything else. In those days they had called dinner "tea." Katoomba meant deep, long, snuggly sleep under an eiderdown, safe in the sound of the two women's voices as they laughed, drank red wine, and occasionally argued in the next room. Sometimes on wet or especially foggy mornings no good for sightseeing it had meant a walk past the old, white, black-trimmed Carrington Hotel with its sweeping drive, colonnaded porch and tall, dark smoke-stack. Auntie Gwen, who had a brown photo of it in a box of old things, used to sniff at its "modernisation," which had been done in stages about seventy years before: the top storey had been boxed in and the side wings covered with tiles. When it was new and fashionable in the 1880s, it had had beautiful iron lace-work arches on the verandah with matching rails and cornices on the first floor. Little square dormer windows, eager as eyes, had blinked out of the iron roof.

Rosemary the child used to walk past the Carrington to the Paragon Café and sometimes stop at the hotel gate to stare at the entrance and imagine what it must have been like to arrive in a carriage along the famous curved drive. She'd seen old, brown pictures of smiling ladies with huge hats, parasols, and bustled skirts posing next to the entrance on the arms of mustachioed men. They would have come there for balls, weekend parties full of charades, card games, piano duets, and respectable honeymoons, and sent sentimental postcards to their relatives in Sydney.

The Paragon Café had been there nearly as long, comfortably living on its reputation for making the finest chocolates in Australia. Rosemary would buy a mixed brown-paper bag full of these—some with bits of ginger for her mother, some with nuts for Auntie Gwen, and plenty, light and dark, with almonds, which they all liked. Then the three of them would sit near the fire, playing cards and eating until they felt sick.

One hot weekend there had been real fun in an utterly exhausting way when a bus load of science teachers had turned up for a booking Auntie Gwen swore had not been confirmed. But there was nowhere else they could go—their coach had already trundled off.

"You two will have to pitch in and give me a hand," Auntie Gwen had said.

Rosemary had been about eleven, but because they needed her they'd talked to her like a grown-up, delegating the bed making, the carrot peeling, the urn filling and the flowers to her. They hadn't even argued when she'd taken a pound from Auntie Gwen's salt box and spent seven-and-six on forget-me-nots and white daisies for tiny table decorations and another five shillings on pink carnations and fern for the big vase on the sideboard. Auntie Gwen would have used fallen camellias and a nice bit of Christmas bush had she had the time to fiddle about herself.

Before Daniel judged Katoomba, Rosemary had simply accepted it for the sensory rewards it offered. Later, looking back at that day, she had felt his critical judging of the beloved but messy town had extended to her. Because on that judging day, that judgement day, her life had stopped being blurry and vaguely scary and had snapped sharply into focus. It was the day her adult life began.

Rosemary and Daniel had met six months before they visited Katoomba, when she was seventeen and half-way through avoiding a secretarial course her mother had insisted on in the deal they had made when Rosemary left school. Daniel was twenty and had recently finished his cadetship and become a graded junior journalist on *The Sydney Morning Herald.*

Katoomba. Rosemary had breathed it, felt it, smelt it, and believed she loved it. She had persuaded Daniel to drive her there as soon as his driver's licence was a month or two old—old enough to swing the balance in Lawrie's mind in favour of believing he'd bring the car back home safely again. Lawrie was not cut out to be a stepfather, as he'd often said while he and Daniel were fixing cars together or bush walking or catching fish. But since he'd married Daniel's somewhat older mother and then been widowed, he was all there was and he'd have to do. Sometimes the dozen years between them melted away, but at other times, to Daniel's fury, Lawrie would do what he called "pull rank" and behave the way he thought a father should. Lawrie had been very high-handed about the car, which because he had helped restore it from dubiously rusty-looking parts into a smooth-running, nicely finished triumph, Daniel believed was at least partly his. So he had started the trip to Katoomba in a temper.

"God in heaven! It's atrocious!" Daniel had said when they arrived, bumping, appalled, across the black-pylon-framed crossing where the main east-west railway from Sydney, the harbour, and the world runs right across the major road route in the same direction. A panoply of warning lights, barriers, and loudspeakers for the sirens were components of a driver's first view of the place. "If you were flying over it you'd think it was the crossed bones on a danger sign."

He'd pointed to the black-grimed, liver-coloured brick buildings near the track. "Look at that. You know what style of architecture that is? That's the leave-it-to-me-I've-got-a-mate-in-the-council style. Very popular after the war."

They had driven down the main street without bumping into anything, though Rosemary had been considerably alarmed by the fact that Daniel had kept leaning out the window, pointing with such viciousness that his finger looked like a weapon.

"How could they let them do that?" he'd demanded, glaring at a cluster of three shop frontages, one gabled, one modified Art Deco, and one rectangular concrete. "It looks as though cards from several packs have been shuffled together and the dealer hopes no one will notice."

Rosemary had felt first ashamed then defensive. "They're not really different from some of the ones in Parramatta."

"You think that's an excuse? Parramatta should be bombed! Anyway, this is supposed to be a beauty spot. Where's the beauty?"

"Over the next rise," she said, and there it was, the clear, endless vista of green and blue, surprising as a lovely eye in an acned face.

"They should save six, maybe seven, of these buildings and get rid of the rest," Daniel had decided. He had done art history in the single semester at university which had held his attention before journalism took over. After Rosemary had found and recognised Auntie Gwen's guest-house, she sadly agreed. It had looked smaller, and the new owners had painted it mustard brown through which the original white was already peeping. Of course, they had taken down the signboard that had said "Bed and Breakfast. Comfortable Rooms and All Facilities." But they'd also changed the garden completely: not even one of the giant camellias was there, and certainly none of the delicate Christmas bushes she'd helped put hessian over in the winter to save them from death by frost.

Rosemary and Daniel had spent at least an hour driving around arguing about which houses they would save. There were a few things they'd agreed on; their plan had been to tunnel the railway line or even abandon it for a few kilometers, offering an attractive alternative of buses from Leura to Medlow Bath. Daniel felt sure people would readily agree to this extra ten minutes of travelling time when presented with the aesthetic advantages. Rosemary had murmured about wheat and coal trains, but Daniel had found firm-sounding arguments for those, too.

"The thing is," he said, his serious, long-nosed, pointy-jawed face quite beautiful in his passionate earnestness, "for nearly two centuries we Australians have made a cruel joke of this magnificent country." Already she had known him well enough to tell that this was the way his next feature story would start. "The first thing the settlers did was reef out the trees, burn out the bush, and replace everything they possibly could with galvanised iron."

Daniel's passion for ecology was one of the things she'd most loved about him. It had also been one of the things about which he'd been consistent: he never billed any bona fide wilderness organisations for work he did for them, and as recently as the month he'd left Rosemary he'd seriously considered going to South West Tasmania to join the protest against the Franklin River Dam.

.   .   .

For a moment, cruising down Katoomba's main street in search of somewhere legal and long enough to park the limo, Rosemary wondered what would have happened if Daniel *had* gone there in his boots and rain gear to get wet and arrested with David Bellamy—the famous British ecologist who had come to lend his stature and profile—and all the other less-known heroes, and if, as a result of his being away, there had been no party. Would they still be together, maintaining the illusion of their marriage, unaware that what connected them was as insubstantial as paper and string? Would secret Angela perhaps by now be fading in the background? Would it have been better that way? She felt sure she was being objective about it. Well, almost objective.

The driver had parked the limousine and agreed to meet her back at it in ten minutes—long enough for her to buy some Paragon chocolates as well as two pounds of cherries.

.   .   .

On that decisive, long-ago visit to Katoomba, Daniel had decided that they would bury all Katoomba's power and telephone cables and, with the exception of the Carrington and one or two nicely kept other buildings, burn down every building in the main street. Looking now at the multifarious and in many cases definitely tacky facades, she could still see his point. But what Daniel had not been able to see was the patina of comfortable charm that ugliness—even architectural ugliness—develops in time.

Daniel had also wanted to burn down all the houses built between 1940 and 1960, but Rosemary, arguing on behalf of the householders and their children, had persuaded him to pull them down gradually, one by one, as soon as their occupants had been rehoused in imaginatively designed new ones that looked as though they were part of the environment and not like attempts to blot it out. The final list of buildings they had considered worth saving was a lot longer than seven—though the residents of Katoomba might have been interested to know that Rosemary's first serious fight with Daniel had been on their behalf. She'd dug in her heels about quite a lot of houses which, though imperfect examples of the Federation style, she'd believed even then were redeemed by character.

"You've got no bloody taste!" he said.

"You're absolutely right," she replied, red-faced and provoked beyond manners. Both had been only children and at that stage were not expert at fighting. "That's why I picked you!"

"Picked me? Threw yourself at me!"

It had been intended simply as a riposte but she'd paled into shock so profound that Daniel had noticed and stopped the car. "Leave me alone. Leave me alone," she said, trying not to cry while Daniel beginning to realise that there was more to this than an aesthetic disagreement, had clumsily tried to grab her and hold her. And so it was, that struggling, crying, shouting a little, and ultimately hugging each other, Daniel and Rosemary had faced the fact that she was pregnant.

The wedding anniversary party Angela had crashed had been their sixteenth, but as Phyl would turn sixteen only five months later, Rosemary and Daniel, who had turned out to be even more respectable than Jean, her mother, would have hoped, were inclined to gloss over the dates if anyone asked.

It had been a thrilling start to a marriage in which shocking factors like morning sickness and Rosemary's mother's reaction to the news had blended with exciting events like choosing rings, the wedding dress, and a broad-minded minister. Wearing pale blue and looking thin and slightly ill, Rosemary had been a bride divided by shame and romance four months before her eighteenth birthday. She'd insisted on the wedding despite the fact that her mother had spoken to their kind old doctor, who had made Rosemary an embarrassed offer of a quick, painless little procedure—one which could have cost him his licence.

Rosemary had been inclined to gloss over the wedding, too; it was full of memories of big Auntie Gwen weeping and, worse still, her mother's white, strained, silent face.

"You silly little bugger," Auntie Gwen had said. "What good are you going to be to a baby, let alone a husband? You haven't got enough common sense to fill a fountain pen!"

.   .   .

There had been no time for breakfast in the morning's leg-shaving flurry, so Rosemary bought some early apricots as well as the lustrous black-red cherries, pumped so full of sweet juice that a few had split their perfect skins. And a fairly big mixed bag of chocolates.

The driver was grateful for the cherries—he took the whole bag and began working through it systematically as soon as the car was back on the highway and he could free one hand. She watched his routine: hand up to mouth, insertion of cherry. Hand on steering wheel. Hand to console, where a rapidly filling white Kleenex lay. Kleenex to mouth to collect another cherry pip. Hand on steering wheel. He did it all as quickly and efficiently as a dance routine or an assembly line process and talked throughout, fruit notwithstanding, now that they were friends.

"That's chocolate you're eating there? Poison to me. Pure poison. Don't even like the look of the stuff anymore, though time was I'd lift a slab off Woolworths. Kids are awful stupid ya know—me poor mum had a time. Ah, diabetes! You get used to it," he added, as though she'd been solicitous, which prompted her to be so. He told her quite a lot about his diet and would have added even more if she hadn't managed to change the subject.

"Do you know anything about this movie they're making?"

" 'The Mount Victorians'? Well, you hear what the script fellows and the producer blokes talk about when you drive. Can't help it. Historical. Bit of a stop-start affair, actually. They did a pilot about a year ago—pilot means, ya know, one sort of movie-length episode shown on the one night. Then old Talbot, 'e liked that well enough and gave them the go-ahead to do it into a six-part, or was it eight-part? series. That was a fair run around for a coupla months but mainly in Sydney—old place at Redfern they had for a studio, so it wasn't such long drives at first. Then they moved the location up here in the mountains, mainly at Mount Victoria.

"It was supposed to be finished after that, Producer said, 'Thank God that's the end of that.' Supposed to go to air last May in the ratings season. But that Robert Talbot, I dunno. 'E gets a bee 'bout something, and—watch out! You know what those TV and advertising blokes are like—everyone's got an opinion and everyone's right. A poorer man than Talbot would have made a few enemies, I'd say. But he got his way—everything started up again. It's not a mini-series anymore—s'pose you could call it a maxi-series!" he added, chuckling at his own joke.

Rosemary was astonished by this spate of conversation punctuated by regular insertions of cherries. She'd thought him morose!

"Been a bit of strife, but," he continued, daintily adding another pip to the already overflowing Kleenex. "The script-writer—nice feller, big, heavy chap—'e's pretty crook. Poor bugger, pardon me, I had to take him to Westmead Hospital in a hurry coupla weeks ago—quicker than the bleedin' ambulance, prob'ly. He got a terrific pain on the set and they thought he was for it. Lump in the kidney, big as a cricket ball."

"A cricket ball!"

"Well, you know. But the thing is they're a bit stuck now. Dunno what they'll do. It's a real mess, believe me, carting people here, there." He sighed. "But. When Robert Talbot wants something, no one argues. Know what I mean? He wants it, he gets it or yer out."

As though the cherries had been a social link with Rosemary, the driver stopped talking as soon as he had eaten the last one. The couple she'd had before he'd commandeered the entire bag had been dazzlingly sweet—perhaps he was going into a coma here on the bendy mountain road? Perhaps she should have listened more carefully to his diet details and saved both their lives? But then he switched the radio on again—2WS this time, since the reception was better—and began to hum along healthily with Dusty Springfield, so she relaxed.

.   .   .

No, I wouldn't have wanted it to go on the way it was.

The words appeared in Rosemary's head suddenly, as though an internal committee had been working on her earlier questions and were now presenting its report. Startled, she waited for more.

I've outgrown him.

No, no, she wanted to answer. That's not fair or true.

It is true. Perhaps lots of marriages survive one person outgrowing the other, but this one hasn't. I was junior partner, child bride, beatable sparrer, and geisha, and that's all Daniel wants from the person he's married to. It's not enough for me. If we'd stayed together I might not have realised it was not enough until it was too late for me to change.

But, she wanted to argue with herself, even though realisation was beginning to change doubt into a wonderful combination of strength and confidence, But what about love?

Love continues to exist, the answer came. It does not have to be fed every day. That Daniel and that Rosemary, that young couple who married nearly seventeen years ago, they loved each other enough to change their lives' direction. Like pruned trees, they have continued to grow in those love-made shapes. The branches abandoned at the time can never be re-grown. We shaped each other's lives permanently.

But, I am still me, in this Danielised shape, she thought, suddenly exultant. I can be free! I can let go of him!

.   .   .

In her heightened state of realisation, Rosemary suddenly remembered something that had happened in June and left her in doubt about her confidence, if not her sanity. Now it no longer seemed like a symptom of madness—it had merely been a misunderstanding about the perennial nature of love. One day, before the swimming pool leaked, Rosemary and Lucy had cleaned up Rosemary's garden. Then, having suffered prickles, twigs, and blisters while pruning dead branches off all the trees in Rosemary's back garden, they had piled everything big enough to bother with in or near the living room fireplace to feed a wonderfully caveman-like blaze. Everybody had had soup and sandwiches in front of the beautiful fire. Then, after the children had gone to bed, they had stayed talking in their favourite spots, sipping tea or, from time to time, port, Lucy knitting and Rosemary ironing on the board she'd adjusted to lap level near her sofa.

"The wife can always get the husband back," Lucy had assured her. "If she really wants to." And that night, in the cosy winter but too-feminine scene, Rosemary had really wanted to. She had watched the children's faces as they sang some of Elton John's songs with Phyl while she played the guitar, and her eyes had filled with tears as she thought about how much Daniel was missing of the life he'd helped create. She had had a vision of him, relaxed, golden, genial, approving, perhaps even singing along. In fact, Daniel had seldom been part of any domestic tableau. Sitting still was not in his genes.

"It's just tragic, tragic, that he and I never got to like each other more," Rosemary said.

"I know what you mean," said Lucy. "I had the same thing with Jack—wonderful in the bedroom and a stranger in every other room of the house." But that wasn't quite what Rosemary meant. Solemnly she continued, aware that what she was saying would sound funny to an observer.

"We could never be real allies, the way I wanted to be. He was always uncomfortable unless he was way, way on top or ahead of me. I mean, he'd even cheat a little to keep me in the dark about things I was actually working on for him—like information I needed for press releases. Isn't that ridiculous? It had nothing to do with logic, it was just so he could be the one who knew the most. I'd get mad with him for being so silly, but it never made any difference: a few days later he'd do it again."

"They're like that, men. Competitive."

"The thing is, I wasn't competing," Rosemary said. "Just trying to share. I think Daniel is terribly clever—he's built that business up from nothing more than his talent and the fact that people like him. He's got guts, as I used to tell him. But he didn't even want to hear *that* from me. All he wanted was . . . was . . . I don't know. Pleased, surprised, happy smiles. He wanted me to be a geisha, perhaps. He wanted me to be thrilled by the magic of everything he did, even though we both knew perfectly well that I was his assistant—the one who fed the bloody rabbits that he pulled out of the hats!"

"Had you been a good Edwardian lady, your Mama would have taught you to maintain pleased, surprised smiles as part of the economic policy of marriage."

"So hypocritical! It must have driven them mad, those women!"

"Maybe not. Maybe they saw ego stroking as the little gift they could make in exchange for being adored."

"Ha! But I wanted much more than adoration. That's . . . distant. I wanted—I want—partnership. Equality. Sharing. To hell with adoration. Intimacy! That's what I want!"

"But that's what sex is for, Rosemary, can't you see? It is symbolic intimacy, a bridge across what is probably an unbridgeable chasm. For Daniel to have become your chum, your personal intimate, he'd have had to change not only the way he's always thought, he'd probably have to change his genes! Much easier just to strip them off—the Levi sort— and have a bit of *vive la difference*."

"That's ridiculous! I've read about fabulous marriages, where they're really tuned into each other's ideas and where each expands the other's life. That's what I want. I don't want to baby someone or sit around saying 'My my you're so clever' *all* the time!"

"Did he know? Did you ever tell him? Say, 'Listen Daniel, this marriage's constitution is superseded? It worked fine when we were barely out of our teens but it's too tight and old-fashioned and unaccommodating now. We need a new constitution.'"

"No, but . . ."

"Well, that's what you need to do. Go out with him if he asks, and try some real talking." said Lucy. "In any case, it's a good way of checking whether you've graduated from feeling married. Maybe you haven't, and who knows? Maybe the affair with whatshername has cooled off."

It had seemed like a wonderful idea. Rosemary had had visions of herself and Daniel on a second honeymoon, forgiving, explaining, re-planning their lives, talking about all the topics that they'd never dis-cussed before. Becoming friends for life, so that years later, they would both look on his dalliance with Angela as the catalyst for their mature happiness. "A Japanese restaurant," Rosemary had planned, clasping her hands in romantic enthusiasm and ignoring the ironing. "One that'll make us leave our shoes at the door and sit humbly with our feet in a pit. Don't you think that'll be the thing? A place where the waitresses carry on like geishas because they're paid to!"

So the next day, when after one of his weekend visits Bobby had said, "Dad wants to take you to lunch," Rosemary was thrilled by the coincidence, which had seemed like an omen. He's reached the same conclusion! she thought. It's marvellous! And she had gone around feeling in love for the first time in years, and tentative, almost bridal. It was a state she'd maintained for most of the next few days until Daniel phoned.

"Hi," she'd breathed, conscious of herself leaning sinuously against the hall wall. "How are you, Dan?" But then he'd spoiled everything by launching into a query about extras on Phyl's school fees bill and the conversation after that had followed the familiar course from query to querulous.

"Are you going to sit there like a parasite forever?" he'd demanded when the fight had become nasty. "Or are you too busy with your damn play school full of stage-struck geriatrics to even consider getting your-self a job!"

"Oops, there's someone at the door," she'd said. "Got to go now."

She had put down the phone, breathing hard because of all the feel-ings: disappointment, anger with him, anger at herself for so easily being seduced by her own fantasies, and hurt. Daniel hadn't changed. Daniel wouldn't change for her. He liked the way he was.

And the truth was, she would not change either. Not now that she too was beginning to like the way she was.

. . .

Now, four months after that week of romantic arousal, it felt safe to think about the things she'd loved about Daniel. In the big, black car, travelling towards her own future, she was safe from the consequences of nostalgia—no longer would she confuse it with hope. It was also safe to think about the things she didn't like about him. Instead of running the risk of being sucked into anger or despair, it was simply like licking at a formerly aching tooth after the dentist has fixed it. She felt quite distant from him, as though he was a sometimes-friendly relative to whom she could tell items of news. For instance, she would love to have been able to tell him about her truth-is-stranger-than-fiction meeting with Robert Talbot, which had happened at just the right time—less than a week after the end of the drama course. She would especially have loved telling him about the offer of a job in a TV film—Daniel had often said she should have been an actress.

So she sat back against the leather seat and enjoyed imagining the telling: Daniel's shoulders would have hunched with attention and his often deliberately impassive face would have registered a string of re-actions—excitement, campaign management, pleasure, and good ideas. He'd have told her what to say and what to do, and then changed those instructions for better ones. And she'd have sat and laughed, pleased by the attention, picking out the best of his advice and feeling good.

Actually she was not at all sure he'd have reacted that way, but sitting in the comfortable car on her way to a future she now felt confident about again, she enjoyed the sense that Daniel might have been proud of her.

·   ·   ·

There had been surprising similarities in Rosemary's and Daniel's child-hood situations. Both their fathers had fought in the war, survived it, and died later, while still comparatively young. Both their mothers had brought them up with the help of a friend who later became a surrogate parent. In Rosemary's case the friend was Auntie Gwen and in Daniel's it was Lawrie.

Lawrie had had quite a lot to do with Daniel's emergence from ado-lescence, since his mother had died when he was eighteen from what was recorded as heart failure after a stroke (though privately both Lawrie and Daniel believed she'd taken something).

The normal desire young couples have to buy a house as soon as possible had probably been exaggerated for both Rosemary and Daniel by a sense of deprivation. She had grown up in the flat over her mother's chemist shop which, until Rosemary was in the last years of primary school, had been rented. Jean, always clever with money, had managed in addition to saving for Rosemary's school fees, to scrape together enough for a ten per cent deposit on the whole little building: the shop premises and the flat. This outlay on stability had given her a lot of worrying payments, both fixed and fluctuating, throughout Rosemary's school career, and to her the place had seemed more like a millstone than a home.

Daniel's early childhood had been spent in officers' quarters wherever his father, the colonel, was posted. Of all the places they had lived in, Daniel had remembered Orange most clearly because that was where Lawrie, an American, had started cheering his mother up and where they had all stayed for some years after his father died.

Rosemary had never been sure whether Lawrie had started cheering Daniel's mother up before or after his father was killed at Singelton on a military training exercise. The point had never concerned Daniel much— to him Lawrie was the accessible, youthful Dad his older, dyspeptic father had never been.

Daniel's mother, who used to refer to herself as "the reverse war bride," was also an American, who had been a secretary on General MacArthur's staff. She had been widowed early in the war, and the posting first to the Philippines and then to Australia had helped distract her from her loss. She had met Daniel's father in the course of duty. Daniel, his mother's first and only child, was born when she was twenty-seven and his father was fifty-three.

As soon as Rosemary and Daniel had bought, refurbished, and furnished their house, they had looked around for another one, intending to buy a string of rental properties to enrich their old age. But for various reasons, mainly the company's insatiable appetite for capital, they had never got any further than the acquisition of a three-bedroom timber holiday house on a nice block of land near MacMasters Beach, about two hours drive north of Sydney. And that they'd given to Lawrie because, Daniel reasoned, it had been a timely loan from him two years earlier that had helped move Patchwork from a nice little man-and-wife concern into an efficiently staffed company capable of dealing on a lot of levels with a better range of clients.

"If we pay back the loan in dribs and drabs he'll just spend it on beer and weapons and still be broke. This way he gets interest, plus capital appreciation. He loves it there, as you know," Daniel had persuaded. So the temporary house-borrowing arrangement Lawrie had made with them in order to finish his fishing book had become permanent.

"Don' be crazy," Lawrie had said. Because he had not yet recovered from the surprise of their unannounced visit, the second surprise of the gift of the house had embarrassed him into abruptness. "You might be making a good profit now, but what about later?"

Daniel had punched him lightly on his arm. "We're OK, Lawrie, believe me. Did you think about later when you paid my school fees? Go on, you silly bugger. Just be glad."

Lawrie had blown his nose, glared at them as they stood on the wooden verandah with their backs to the beach, and then he'd said, "OK. I live in it. You can even put it in my name if you really want. But it'll always belong to you two." And, stomping past them on the way to his fishing boat, he had caught Phyl's hair in one hand, Bobby's in the other, and pulled them off balance. He hadn't looked back as they rearranged themselves.

"Charming!" Rosemary stroked Phyl's hair back into place and smiled comfortingly at Bobby, whose face was still angry and shocked. "He should get himself a job as Santa, don't you think? At the local store? Little kiddies would really warm to our Lawrie."

"He's all right," Daniel said, grinning. "I think he moulds himself on Ernest Hemingway."

"Well, he won't be much good at it until he learns to tell the difference between a family and a bullfight," Rosemary said indignantly, now cuddling Bobby, too, since comfort by smiling had been too remote.

"Don't know what you two are so sulky about. Didn't you hear what Lawrie said? This house will belong to you!"

"When he dies?" Bobby asked, clearly hoping it would be soon.

Later, Lawrie had come back with five whiting, already cleaned somewhere out on the rocks where the sea-gulls could benefit from the innards. He had cooked them in butter, refusing Rosemary's help, and they'd eaten them sitting on the cushions off his armchairs, which he'd brought onto the verandah so they could benefit from the full, golden moon which was rising over the sea. They had eaten the tender fish with thick buttered slices of the heavy bread Lawrie baked in his fry-pan—bread full of sunflower seeds and other surprises.

"Multitude special," he called the meal, twinkling at the children who hadn't understood until Rosemary nudged them.

Lawrie had drunk four cans of beer and then launched into a performance none of them had ever forgotten. He stood with his back to the moon, a dark-faced man whose strong, graceful movements made him look no older than Daniel. His khaki shirt and pants were lumpy with pockets full of knives, fishing gear, notes, and pens. For the next two hours he had recited Walt Whitman, Emily Dickinson, and large tracts of Mark Twain's travel stories, in an accent more pronouncedly American than his usual Aussie-coated style. Even Bobby, then only eight, had stayed awake to the end and clapped longer and harder than any of them. Lawrie had moved, in his heart, from villain to hero in a matter of hours.

"You look like Wild Bill Hickok, standing there like that, Gra . . . Lawrie," Phyl said, and quickly, to cover her gaffe about his name, added, "Without the hat." Rosemary would have liked the children to call him "Grandpa" or even "Uncle" as a respectful term, but when the subject was mentioned, Lawrie had been firm to the point of indignation. "Grandpa!" he'd snorted. "I haven't even gotten around to being anyone's dad yet!"

Lawrie ruffled Phyl's hair, much more gently this time.

"Guess I am some sort of frontiersman if you scratch the surface. I was born in the wrong century for my inclinations. By the time I'd gotten big enough there weren't no more frontiers in the U.S."

"So that's why you're here? At MacMasters Beach?" Bobby asked seriously, making everyone laugh.

"Well, yes. The fishing is wild, the locals are friendly. I'm learning the language. . . ."

Until Daniel left, they had visited Lawrie at least once a month after that, spreading sleeping bags on air beds in the spare bedroom whose walls were covered with harpoons, assegais, boomerangs, muskets, and daggers—a personal war museum collected over a lifetime of travelling.

· · ·

Being orphaned young adults with a keen eye for property and a mutual business interest had not been enough, between bouts of passion. Daniel had had his old cars, of course, and in the early days before he became a workaholic he, Lawrie, and two other friends had spent oily hours at weekends getting them going and refurbishing them to showroom condition. Rosemary's part of the enterprise had been to keep the beer and hamburger supply steady and to do things like travel to awkward-to-find little shops in narrow Surry Hills lanes to pick up small cans of paint in special colours. More than once she'd had to travel for half a day, beyond Gosford or Sutherland or Mittagong, to where a backyard engineer would have appropriately modified a crankshaft or skimmed a warped cylinder head which she would then bring home wrapped in sacking.

She had usually been allowed to drive a lap or two of honour in the finished products, to admire the rosewood dashboards and leather seats, the hot-knife-through-butter action of the gears, and the expensive quietness of the British or German or Italian engine. And then the cars would be sold. Twice she had had to propitiate the new owners, one a

Harris-tweed-jacketed, pink-cheeked doctor from Darling Point, the other a balding young adman from Neutral Bay, when they'd phoned a week after purchase to complain about oil leaks or the brakes.

When Daniel had graduated from fixing cars to merely buying them, he'd become more interested instead in tennis, then golf, and then boating. Of these Rosemary had tried boating, too, and enjoyed it when the weather was sparkling and the sea smooth, but not when there were wet ropes and shouting and people hanging over the side. Anyway, for at least fourteen and a half of her sixteen years of marriage, she had really been too busy to contemplate a hobby.

Then she'd started the drama course in August, and from the first night it had claimed her like nothing else had ever done, apart from Daniel and the children. Even now it was hard to decide whether that thrilling immersion of herself had been a cause or an effect of the breakup of her marriage. But it was no longer a debate of real significance, since the drama course had challenged her, made outrageous demands on her, and made her happier than she'd felt for years.

With the communications course it was different. It had been helpful in that she had learned some technical skills, particularly about video and audio, and it had also sometimes been fun. But the bulk of the course focussed on things she'd already taught herself at Patchwork PR. So it was one of the few juggling balls she'd decided not to pick up again after Daniel left and she'd dropped the lot. But dropping the college course had revived an old guilt—she had always felt she should have gone on and learned to do something useful instead of just filling in the gaps in her marriage between sensuousness and fights. However, it could not be helped. When the term had started she simply did not have the energy.

She had felt the same way about the theatre course; even though she'd loved it so much in her first semester, which had ended shortly before last Christmas, and even though it had seemed to have so little to do with Daniel's approval or otherwise, she had not had enough life force to pick it up again after he'd gone. But when the new year's first semester had started in February, Martha, Melissa, Patrick, and Jeremy had refused to let her drop out. They had been at the party. There was nothing much she could hide from them.

Melissa had phoned first. "If it's the money, darling, let me tell you right here that no one will ever accuse Melissa Scott-James of penny-pinching. I mean, this is a business. It's my fucking livelihood for God's sake. But, darling, you're *special*! And if there's trouble with the bill, then I'll just *invent* you a scholarship or something."

"No, no, no," Rosemary had said, firmly and often, hoping to be heard. "It's nothing to do with the money, really,"

"And if the scholarship idea doesn't grab you," Melissa had continued, as though Rosemary's voice was a mosquito's buzz in the background, "you could always do some assistant stage-managing. I usually pay for ASM-ing so we could work something out."

"Well, I'd intended to do the stage managing part of the course this year anyway but . . ."

"So that's settled then. You'll be here tomorrow when we start!"

"I don't think so," Rosemary had told the phone, but Melissa had put her end down already.

Jeremy hadn't phoned, he'd simply arrived in a cab, pretending such an unusual, unheralded jaunt was "just popping in." "I brought you a little French pastry, darling," he said. "Couldn't wait for my yummy one so I ate it in the taxi."

She said she didn't feel up to rejoining.

"But you must. I need you. You've done the basics now—you can fall and scream and cry like a pro and remember your lines, which is more than most."

That was when she'd first heard about *Mother Love*. Licking his fingers after absent-mindedly eating the cake he'd brought her, he told Rosemary about it while refraining from an opinion. "Melissa says she wants you to 'help with stage-managing it'."

"I know. She said."

"Which is a way of saying you'll do the whole job. And, darling Rosie Posy, you must admit its a nonpareil way to learn." When he'd hinted that later in the year he wanted to cast her in *Cat on a Hot Tin Roof*, Rosemary had burst into tears.

"Why are you both being so nice to me?" she asked through a nose now so accomplished at reddening and swelling that it had taken just seconds to do so again.

"Why not?" Jeremy had asked, swinging one crossed leg. "You're fun."

"Fun?" she droned.

"Well, maybe not now, since Daniel's only just done the dirty. But it's part of your nature. You'll be shedding the old metaphysical black sooner than you think. Did I ever tell you about what happened on *Virginia Woolf?*"

From the deep, drab emptiness into which all her feelings had fallen, she had obliged Jeremy by dredging up a laugh or two at his story of the night a stage-hand had got drunk during a touring performance of

Who's Afraid of Virginia Woolf? and had started loudly joining in the argument with "Slug the bitch" and other bits of gratuitous advice. The actors had struggled on as though nothing was happening while someone had tried to muffle the stage-hand, then to drag him away, but all this had been clearly heard by the audience. "They shrieked! They died!" Then the stage-hand had thrown a punch which had sent his fist through the back set—a living-room wall full of painted-on shelves of books through which his hand had burst, then got stuck.

"Oh, I wish you'd seen it!" Jeremy gasped, wiping his eyes because, as he said, the story never failed to break him up. "We offered them their money back but no one took it because they'd had such a good time."

Rosemary had humbly promised to come despite having no vision of herself ever being fun again. As an indication of her ability to face the world she'd got the car out and driven him home to Cremorne, and on the way he had distracted her with jokes and libellous gossip. On the way back, she'd had to make do with the radio which had helped until, passing near enough to Kirribilli to be sharply reminded of Daniel and Angela, she'd started to cry again. Then she'd cried so much that her lenses had threatened to slide out, and she'd had to pull the car into a side-street at Crows Nest and wait until she could see again.

The news on the radio hadn't helped to cheer her up. It was obvious that for some time deft, number-counting moves had been practised behind the political scene, because the sheer energy of ambition and innuendo had been breaking out, like acne, into public notice. Now, observing the world as through the bottom of an aquarium, Rosemary heard that Bob Hawke had become the new Leader of the Opposition, dramatically replacing Bill Hayden. And Hayden, hurt and tight-lipped, had been forced to accept that, in the opinion of those who mattered the most to him, his best had not been good enough. So she had cried for him, too. There had been no Vivaldi on any channel.

Half an hour after she got home, Martha had phoned to say that she and Patrick would pick Rosemary up "on the way" the next night.

"I'm not on your way at all, Martha."

"Oh, yes, you are. I'm staying at Patrick's, you see. Lending a hand. It'll be on our way."

"Where does he live?

"Hunter's Hill."

"But that's miles!"

"Now, no arguing, Rosemary dear," she said. "We'll see you at six-thirty."

"Is it that they're desperate for pupils or is it that you have more talent than you thought?" Lucy asked that night when Rosemary told her about it.

"Desperate," Rosemary replied promptly, though she'd enjoyed the compliment.

.   .   .

The next night Patrick had come alone to pick her up, Martha having announced that she could not make it.

"She's sitting with Geoff. He wasn't feeling well tonight," Patrick said, so matter-of-factly that she presumed she must know, and have forgotten, who Geoff was. She'd been silent, unable to summon up the energy to entertain the tall, watchful man. "I wish there was something I could say to cheer you up. There isn't though, is there?" he said.

"I don't need cheering, thanks. I probably need to crawl into a hole, like a wounded wombat. You're all very kind to pull me out and make me part of it again, but I'm more of a liability than an asset right now. Can't help it." Self-disgusted tears reached the brim again, and she squeezed her eyes angrily to shake them off. She was aware that he was making an effort to be kind. People are kind to the newly bereaved, she thought, and it puts an extra burden on them: they are forced to respond, and in itself response is a positive which jars with the negative of despair. But Patrick did not seem to mind her silence. His calmness was almost comforting.

"You probably won't be sorry you came," he said when they reached the hall, but she had been. As the course had a half-year intake, there were six new people to replace those who had graduated in December. In her doleful state Rosemary yearned for the ones who'd gone and decided she didn't like the looks of any of the new ones, who seemed too young or too old, too confident or too timid, and not at all promising as actors.

Most of the evening, after the intial confusion of enrolment, had been taken up with exercises and with listening to Melissa saying things everyone except the new arrivals already knew, and on the way back home Rosemary had privately decided to pull out after all. But they had refused to let her. They took it in turns to drive over and fetch her when she'd tried to make excuses not to come. Sometimes it was especially hard. Once Melissa had had to tug her out of bed and start dressing her like a child.

Another time, Patrick and Martha had arrived together to find Rosemary and Bobby trembling like angry cats, having just crossed the peak of a fight which clearly still had some way to go. Daniel had taken Bobby out in accordance with arrangements made through the medium of solicitors' letters, and Bobby had come home full of news of his father's new expertise on a sail board. He'd tossed his soggy kit-bag on the yellow couch and then said, "Ah, shit, Mom! *You* move it if it bothers you! Why must this place always be so bloody neat?"

At dinner he'd said, "Oh yuk! Not chicken again! Why can't we sometimes have T-bones?" Rosemary had picked up the breadboard to hurl at him and stopped just in time.

As Rosemary, Patrick, and Martha drove away they had heard Bobby yell, "You're always damn well going out and leaving us here!" and had heard Phyl respond even more loudly, "Bobby, if you say another word I'm going to kill you!" and Rosemary had sobbed. Martha, who had friends with grandchildren, had told her it was very healthy behaviour.

About a month later Bobby had given his very healthy behaviour another airing. "Why do we *always* have to have chocolate ice cream?" he asked one night when she was already running late. (Lucy had offered to drop her at the class on her way to the city while Phyl minded Mattie.)

"Daniel said he wants to talk to you. He says he wants to take you to lunch," Phyl said quickly, hoping to avert the row, but it simply contributed to Rosemary's rush of mixed emotions which had felt like hot soup full of discernible lumps. When had Phyl decided to call her father Daniel? And surely he knew, now, that she wasn't going to see him?

Bobby had shoved the dish away with such a jerk that the ice cream had sloshed out onto his woven-grass table-mat. Rosemary watched the gooey stuff settle into the fibres. "I buy it because you like it," she said politely and then, as though a starting pistol had fired, anger, like a racing swimmer, dived into her mind's forced calm. She thumped her fist on the table. "I can see a pattern emerging here!" she said.

Phyl, noticing her mother's dangerous change of mood, had nudged Bobby, who ignored her. "Like it! I hate the yukky stuff! It's like baby food, and it's made from whale blubber," he said.

"It certainly is not made of whale blubber. Or baby seal blubber or dolphin blubber or Franklin River blubber, for that matter, Bobby darling," Rosemary said, pronouncing each word clearly and slowly. Phyl put down her spoon, alert as a lion tamer. "It's made from . . . it's made of . . ." Rosemary picked up the carton. "Here you are, in two-point type, it reveals that this ice cream is made of milk solids, artificial flavouring and colouring, emulsifier, and some other things. I must say the other things look very like the ingredients in my hair conditioner. Phyl, do you like chocolate ice cream?"

"Not anymore!" Phyl said, laughing a little excessively.

"Right. That's it then. Bobby has grown out of hair-conditioner choc-olate ice cream, so we'll never have it again. Now, Bobby . . . Rob-ert? . . . Rob? Which one? Which name suits the bossy new you? I want you to give me a precise list of the foods you no longer like. Because"—and her voice increased to an Olympic crowd roar and she thumped the table again, a terrific crash, with shock waves that jangled the knives—"because this is the absolute last time you make any comments about the food at this table. Do you hear me? I'm not having any more of your bad-mannered tantrums. Now take that mat to the kitchen, run it under the tap until there's nothing left to feed the smallest ant. Then dry it, put it on the window sill. And I mean it—I want a written list of what you no longer eat, and another of what you now do eat, and I promise to refer to it when shopping, in future, and to be guided by it as well as the budget and the rules of nutrition allow." Red-faced, Rose-mary stopped talking in order to breathe.

"Geez, Mum," Bobby said solemnly, then burst out laughing. After a moment, so had Phyl and Rosemary, still breathing hard, had looked at her laughing children and joined in, too.

It was at about that time that they had started switching to a diet that was mainly vegetarian and health-food, but even on egg salad nights Bobby kept his protests to a murmur.

Their bad fights had been mainly at the beginning of the year. Bobby adjusted to the fact that his parenting was now compartmentalised, the tension had begun to ease a a bit. Phyl had determindely refused to have anything to do with Angela, so her meetings with her father were usually at the car door when he picked up or dropped Bobby.

Phyl had seemed to cope quite well with her broken home; she'd become more studious and had taken to spending a lot of time alone writing on lined pads in thick, loose-leaf folders. But since she smiled a lot, ate all her meals, had friends to visit, and was invited out quite often, Rosemary had not been as concerned about Phyl.

In the drama course's second semester, there had been a bonus in Rosemary's relationship with Bobby. As his much more slowly paced school production gradually approached its climax, plays became what they had in common. She'd borrowed Auntie Gwen's Elna and some technical advice and made his costume—an absolutely wonderful dream-coat of overlapping patches in every possible shade of red and pink, interleaved and trimmed with silver and gold. It was made of velvet, satin, brocade, and lamé bought from the remnant trays of a dozen fabric shops, and it flowed, glittered, and fluttered as Bobby walked, creating a powerful aura that perfectly suited him.

She'd gone to some of his rehearsals, and he to some of hers, and she'd been surprised by his observations. One, which helped her considerably, was: "You should feel greedy inside when you're talking about money. Otherwise you look like a rich lady who doesn't care what Big Daddy does with it so long as he doesn't give it to Maggie. You've got to bluff that you're being nice but be a real, horrible person underneath."

.   .   .

The limo was passing the Hydro Majestic, the extraordinary line of apricot-painted, linked, voluptuously styled buildings which successfully block out from the road the finest view of all. In its heyday in the 1920s, Sydney people came here for dirty weekends though the turnover from the honeymoon trade was steady, too. Her own Gran, whom she dimly remembered, had been here in her pointed shoes, puffed hair, and ankle-length going-away dress with a man in First World War uniform and a big, waxed moustache. Grandfather. He'd never come back from the Dardanelles.

Rosemary was the third in a succession of women who'd lost their husbands and had had to bring their daughters up alone. Except she had Bobby, too. And both Gran and Rosemary's mother had been widowed. She still had Daniel to torment her by being alive but not available. On the other hand, both Gran and her daughter, Rosemary's mother, Jean, had had to struggle very hard financially; Rosemary was spared that.

The driver had been whistling—more assertive than humming and quite a feat through his lip scar, Rosemary thought. Every now and then he broke off to point out a sight.

"Mount Victoria. See that old guest-house, the green one? That's where they stayed while they were filming last time. Full bed and board for the whole crew. Cost a fortune, this maxi-series."

Rosemary peered around, impressed by the pretty town which, apart from some modern sign-writing here and there, gave the general impression of having been unchanged for a century.

.   .   .

"Now here we go," the driver said. "Down the pass and into beautiful downtown Lithgow. Ya been there?"

"Not for ages." Rosemary cleared her throat, which had suddenly tightened up with nervousness, and said it again, "Not for ages." The sudden panic which had earlier made her try to cancel the whole thing had struck again, much harder. She could hear the driver's voice as he continued his jaunty monologue: "Don't like it, I tell ya. Freezing cold for ten months of the year, nothing to breathe but coal dust and smog. Nothing doin' after five-thirty weekdays when the shops close. Pubs are full, but . . ." It did nothing to quell the tension.

I'm going to make a fool of myself. I'm mad to have come here! Who do I think I am, playing at being an actress? she asked herself. She'd tensed up so hard that her wedding ring was pinching her tightly fisted ring finger and her jaw was aching from the strain of clenched teeth. I can't do it! I can't! she thought.

The little town emerged between two peaks of the roadside rock, looking compact and posed like a postcard photograph. From a slight distance its grey-stained air and nineteenth-century design gave it the look of an English town but closer, breathing the smog rather than looking through it, the place was distinctly Colonial. And they were approaching it at the same, steady, unarguable speed at which the whole, strange adventure had begun. There was no way out.

So, OK, she thought. I've got myself into this. I'll do the best I can not to disgrace the family. There was not much comfort in that sentiment, but it was the best she could do at the time.

The main street's busiest intersection was quiet, comparatively traffic-free despite the fact that it was nearly lunch-time on a Friday. Soon they were through it. They passed the entrance to the greyhound racing track and then turned off into an ungraded road that seemed to lead to a transport depot. But just before the end the driver turned through a gateway into a parking lot full of cars, near a cluster of temporary sheds and huge film trucks. Behind them Rosemary could see a beautiful, low-built, colonial-style house set in a large, old fashioned garden. And with a quick fillip her mood changed from fear to excitement. What the hell! she thought. It could even be fun!

"Here we are," said the driver. "Eskbank House. Office's over there."

Eight

The office was on wheels. It was parked across the ends of two parallel film trucks, one marked MAKE-UP. A temporary building, put together from shining aluminium sheets, stood nearby. RUSHES said its signboard.

There were curiously few people about as Rosemary picked her way from the area where two or three dozen cars were parked. Those who were there looked intense: busy on a tight schedule. A young man in a T-shirt that said "Boom Operators Always Keep It Up" ran past her with a clipboard in his hand shouting, "Where the fuck's Charlie?"

In the office a man with a round, multi-rolled face, a fringe of ginger around his freckled baldness and a little finger up his nose, was leaning back on a swivel chair saying "Yeah, yeah, I know. I know. *But.* You know the situation here, Sid: it's show-must-go-on time and we're in the shit. The Voice has spoken." He sounded not exactly bored but as though some original strong urgency had become watered down by repetition.

The two men sitting on the opposite benches eating sandwiches looked bored, and Rosemary was surprised to realise that one of them was a star she'd often seen in big-budget movies, shrunken, in this off-screen environment, to the dimensions of any hungry man. She presumed the other man was also an actor.

"Yeah?" said the ginger-haired man, placing his hand over the receiver. "Help you?"

"I'm Rosemary Quilty. I'll wait—finish your call." He frowned, puzzled, but did as she said. Neither the tone nor content of the conversation changed very much, though he took his finger out of his nostril and pretended to scratch his jeans with it.

"Listen, mate, gotta go. Someone here to see me. But please, Sid, this is really, really top priority. OK?" Then, to Rosemary, "What can I do for you?"

"I'm supposed to see Kim Haymes. Mr. Talbot sent me." One of his eyebrows went up and the two actors looked up from their egg-and-mayonnaise-on-whole-grain.

"Kim's flat out today, doing the producer's job," he said. "Producer didn't show, so things aren't good around here today."

"Well, Michael Stoner then, please,"

"Michael's on set, directing," he said, with the air of finality with which an airline company clerk might say, "Michael's piloting the Jumbo to Auckland" or a nurse might say, "Michael's performing open-heart surgery."

"What do I do?" she asked.

He shrugged. "You can wait. What did you say the name was again? We can get him a note between takes. Though they should break in the next hour, anyway, for lunch. I'm Jim Hacket, by the way. Assistant producer for the day. And you know these blokes." The actors nodded, not particularly interested in whether they knew her or not, though Jim's offhand manner indicated, to Rosemary, that he regarded her as an actor, which was a shot of strength to her confidence.

"One thing I'm supposed to do—phone Mr. Talbot's office."

"Oh, yah. Sure. Of course. Here, I'll do it—I know the direct line." He dialled and gave her the phone, not, she was relieved to notice, with the hand that had been nose-picking.

"Oh Mrs. Quilty. Hello," said the secretary. "I'm sorry about the mix-up this morning. Did you have a good trip? Obviously you found the place! Have you seen Mr. Stoner yet?"

"Not yet. I've just arrived. And they're shooting now, anyway—I'll have to wait until they break for lunch."

"Of course. I always forget how long it takes to get there. Well now, where's that message for you? I wrote it down here somewhere . . . oh, here we are. You're to . . . When you meet Mr. Stoner, please mention to him that Mr. Talbot was thinking of you in terms of the governess. That's what he said. And he said he'd probably see you later this afternoon—he has a short lunch meeting at Katoomba."

The actors had finished their sandwiches and the famous one squeezed past her on his way out of the caravan. Brushing hips with a star she and Phyl had swooned over was just another thrill.

"Coffee?" he asked. "Orange juice?" Jim Hacket nodded vigorously without specifying which—he was deeply immersed in a rerun of the conversation he'd had before, this time with someone called Monty. Rosemary stood smiling under her white straw hat, so happy that no one who saw her would have doubted that she was someone special.

"Sit down," said the actor she was supposed to know, talking quietly in order not to disturb Jim Hacket's pleadings. "I'm Tony, by the way."

"Thanks," she said, squeezing in. "Hi. Rosemary."

"And you've come to try for the governess?"

"Apparently."

"Three days ago there wasn't a governess. It's not exactly a tight script."

"What's it about? I mean, this part of the story?"

"Good question," said Jim Hacket, at that moment between calls. "The whole series is a bit of an 'Upstairs/Downstairs' thing, really, with added kookaburras."

The famous actor walked in with four styrofoam mugs of coffee, flat sticks for spoons, on a tray made from a small carton. One was for Rosemary, and, though it had been sugared, she was touched.

"That's what happens," said Jim, taking the coffee from the star. "One day you're the lover, next day the lover's dad. Same time you get busted down to canteen duty." Then he giggled, ducked, and spilled some coffee as the actor pretended to punch him.

"The driver told me you lost the script editor," said Rosemary.

"Yeah, Ed Blackwell, poor bugger. We lost him at a critical stage, though not so critical for us as for him—he's on the kidney transplant list now." He sighed and fondled the rolls around his chin as though they were warm, soft worry beads. "This part of the series has had so much going against it that you'd think they'd call it quits now. But Talbot put the money up, see, and he's developed a Cecil B. De Mille complex."

The phone rang, so he could not respond to Rosemary's puzzled look. Tony, who had a footballer's physique and a slight scar on the edge of his muscular-looking lower lip, took over. His voice was surprisingly smooth—a contrast to his he-man appearance that was instantly attractive. But he was at least ten years younger than Rosemary.

"The first part of the story ends somewhere in the 1860s—the pilot and three episodes that were finished, oh, months ago. It had already been tentatively scheduled, then Talbot decided to do a few more episodes, and a few more. For some reason he wants the whole series in the can before showing any of it. No one knows how long it will be; they just keep on revising the budget. And what a budget! Weeks of location shooting. Bloody ridiculous!"

"Sensible guy would run what he's got," said the famous actor. "At least there'd be some advertising revenue in the meantime, but this way all the costs are up front. I mean, it's all right for us. The money's good and most of us—our contracts keep extending. Though I'll be in trouble if it drags on more than another couple of weeks." He didn't look as though this worried him much.

"Do you like 'The Mount Victorians?' I mean, is it good?" Rosemary asked.

"Ah, yeah, for what it is. Better than most, I'd say. What about you, Tone?"

"Yeah, I guess so. Liked the first part of it, anyway. This part is a bit harder to get the feel of because they keep changing it—scrapping it and starting over."

"Gives you the shits," the star said moodily, making syrupy ropes on the tip of the stirring stick with the sugary dregs of his coffee.

"You're just saying that because you were the young spunk in the first part, now you're the spunk's dad," said Tony.

"Just watch it, son!" he growled. Then, to Rosemary he said, "The part we're working on now starts in 1895."

"Why is it being done here? I mean, don't they usually film in studios?"

"Yes. And they usually film when they've made up their foolish minds what to film and who is going to be in it," said the star. "They usually work to a budget and a schedule. Usually blokes like Jim here know exactly what's going to cause their ulcers. This is a disaster, a bloody disaster."

For a moment the three men settled into a state of reproachful gloom. Then Jim sighed and dialled again, and a girl who looked to Rosemary to be about Phyl's age leaned in at the door.

"Oh there you are, you two. They are going to reshoot the horse bit after all, so it's wigs and whiskers time."

"Jesus! See what I mean? Pure instinct made me get that sandwich, pure instinct! I'm now going to spend the whole lunch break in make-up." The actor was showing off for her, Rosemary realised, flattered.

"It wasn't instinct, it was a good fairy," said Tony and flapped his wrist and winked at Rosemary before jumping out of the caravan.

The girl stuck her head in again. "Stoner was on about some screen test. The governess. Know anything about it?"

Rosemary stood up quickly, which is dangerous in a low-topped vehicle: she bumped her head. Jim looked guilty.

"Oh, yes. Of course. This is er . . ."

"Rosemary Quilty," she said, readjusting the hat.

"Oh. Well, we'd better do you, too," the girl said, not looking very pleased, and vanished.

.   .   .

A delicious curry smell filled the air outside the office and all around the U-shape formed by the three big vehicles were trestle tables and folding chairs which had been placed there since Rosemary arrived. Large striped umbrellas had been set up to shield some of them from the midday sun. A lively group of people, some in late Victorian costume, most in jeans and T-shirts, wrangled and laughed as they waited to be served from a very grand-looking version of a field kitchen at the back of the unmarked film truck. Nearby was a bar doing a brisk trade in jugs of orange juice, tea, and coffee. A fat man was teasing the caterer's assistant.

"Come on, love, you know I'd kill for beer. We all know you've got it hidden in there somewhere. Gimme the key," and he pawed at the pockets of her shirt, making her giggle and slap him, quite hard.

The atmosphere in the make-up truck was subdued by comparison. The two actors she'd met and three others—another man, a girl who looked about ten, and a middle-aged woman—were leaning back in old-fashioned barber's chairs, draped to the neck in white cloths. Tony and the star were waiting in turn, the little girl was having her own long hair curled into ringlets; her face already looked like a china doll's. The woman's head was being pushed into an iron-grey wig with a bun at the back, and the man was having sideburns and a beard glued, wisp by wisp, onto skin made tan-coloured from tubes rather than the sun. Rosemary would have loved to watch, but the girl who had fetched the actors looked up distractedly, a bunch of grey curls in each hand and a comb in her mouth and said through it, "This'll take a while. Forgot we had to do the kid, too. Why don't you get yourself some lunch?" Exasperated, she took the comb out. "You'll have to push into the line but don't take any notice of anybody who gives you a hard time."

"Where do I pay?"

"You don't pay. Tell anyone who hassles you I sent you. Be back here by . . ." she looked at her watch, "one-fifteen sharp."

"I don't know your name." The girl looked astonished, as though Rosemary had said, "I don't know your gender." "Carol," she said firmly. Then she went back to applying glue and whiskers at greater speed than before.

The food queue had temporarily shrunk to three people. One of them, a pleasant-looking man of about her age, said, "Want some?" as he scooped avocado slices onto his own plate, and then obligingly plonked a spoonful on hers. "Let me do that," he said, as she struggled to juggle her handbag, plate, knife, fork, and napkin in order to take a bread-and-butter plate, and then, "Where are you sitting?"

"I don't know yet, that's why I'm encumbered by this bag."

"Well, come and join us. What're you drinking? Orange juice? Mineral water? I think they even have milk from a bottle with a teat if people ask nicely." It was difficult to know whether he was serious as his face was constructed along the lines of a Basset pup's, with deep, down-curving folds, so all he had to do to look solemn was relax. The table he led her to was one under an umbrella, she was pleased to see. The day was very hot, a fact the air-conditioned car and other vehicles had disguised from her before. Two serious men, one old and rather hunched, one about twenty, were playing chess.

"This is Gabor and this is Pete," he said. "I'm Walter. We're part of the camera crew."

"I'm Rosemary," she said, and Gabor, the old man, struggled up from his folding chair, nearly upsetting the chess-board in the process. She could tell by the reproving way Pete grabbed it that he didn't think much of old-fashioned manners.

"So you're here for . . . ?" said Walter, between mouthfuls of chicken curry.

"A screen test. A governess, I believe."

Pete rolled his eyes. "Christ, it's going to be one of those late Fridays again, I can see."

"Take no notice of him," said Gabor, then, "Hef you read the script?" It was obviously an in-joke.

"What he means," said Walter kindly, "is that he wonders if your part's been written yet."

"Oh, come on. It's not as bad as that," Pete said. "The way you all carry on about the script you'd think you'd never worked on current affairs TV."

"Yeah, but you've got to admit the Malcolm Henry Show was superbly organised from the top, Pete."

"Uh!" said Rosemary, thrilled by the coincidence. Pete didn't notice.

"The only chaos was on the floor and that was creative chaos, not this crap. At least we knew what we were supposed to be doing. Here one day it's a soapie, one day its a doco."

"To me," said Gabor in his sonorous mid-to-eastern-European accent, "that describes Australian history perfectly."

"Did you all work on the Malcolm Henry Show?" Rosemary asked as soon as she could.

"No, just Pete and me, until three weeks ago," said Walter. "Then Stoner made us an offer we couldn't refuse, didn't he Pete?"

Pete murmured something that sounded like "Shit."

"Before Malcolm Henry I was on news for seven years. Then one day I got sick of being a salaried voyeur—I'd filmed the last child burned to death in a council flat."

"Ah, you don't know what you're missing, mate," Pete said in the angry, ironic way which he believed was funny. It was obvious that he and Walter were used to telling this story in tandem. "Scrambled eggs and triple pile-up for breakfast. Hamburger and suicide for lunch. Just before you knock off you film a judge's house that some aggrieved litigant has blasted. Great for the digestion!"

"Malcolm Henry's program was like going into the loony bin after a stint in hell," said Walter. "They called it creative chaos. But it was pretty good—you got a laugh. Great guests—people like Peter Ustinov, Clive James, Robert Morley, talking and carrying on. Oh, I could tell you some things. There's that absolutely ancient American movie star, what's her name? Silent movies? Came here a couple of years back?" No one knew. "I've never seen anything like it in my life. Her face— well, her face, draped like an old brown theatre curtain. Like old dogs' balls, you know? Only the eyes alive. And I watched her, we all did— nothing private about it—stick thin film tapes all around the edges of her face"—Walter demonstrated— "and then she grabbed the tapes and tied them in a knot at the top of her skull." With one hand he pushed his own dewlaps up, trying to achieve the same effect. "When it was tied tight she slapped a candy-floss wig on and said—and her face was all stretched tight, so she talked like this"—he bared his teeth—" 'Darling, just don't get my left, please! I've already asked Malcolm to let me sit where he usually does—he's a dear boy. But no roving cameras and only one close-up just at the end. I'll tell you when—I'll look right at you, give a little wave, and then flicker my nails like this, and kiss them, like this . . .' "

"Lying bastard," said Pete respectfully.

"This Walter is on the wrong side of the camera," said Gabor.

"If you were on the Malcolm Henry Show you must know Lucy Barlow," said Rosemary.

"Lucy? Oh, yeah, of course. The gorgeous researcher." Pete and Walter glanced at each other, tactfully trying to ascertain how much more could be said but gained no comfort from each other's silence. Gabor began to look bored, fiddling with a chess piece.

"Want to have another go at beating me?" Pete asked him, and in the same tone, "How do you know Lucy, anyway?"

"She lives next door. We've been friends for ages."

"Have you ever met Malcolm Henry?" he asked, so casually that Rosemary laughed.

"Yes. A group of us went out to dinner on Wednesday night, actually."

Pete pretended to yawn, which she interpreted as "Don't think you'll impress me by name-dropping." So she bridged the gap by saying, "Lucy said that only the people she worked with and I knew about the big romance."

So Pete stopped being defensive, which was good—Rosemary was hoping for another opinion about Malcolm, since Lucy's happiness depended on him. Walter leaned forward eagerly, questions poised, and Gabor's hands dropped resignedly to his lap. But before she even had to think of ways of avoiding saying too much Carol yelled, "Mrs. . . . er . . . Whatever. You in the hat. Make-up!" and she had to go.

"See you on set," said Walter. "Let's have a real drink afterwards."

"Love to," she said, and wondered if she sounded like a real TV person.

.   .   .

"What size are you?" a thin-boned boy with a modified punk haircut asked Rosemary, who was having her turn in the barber's chair. Carol was slapping very pink-toned make-up base around her lips so she had to talk like a ventriloquist.

"Ten if it's jeans."

"They didn't go in much for jeans in 1895," he said, and everyone laughed in such an immediate and familiar way that it was obvious he was a renowned wit, so renowned, in fact, that he hardly had to be funny anymore.

"Yesterday's person needed to be told that she needed Palmolive Gold," he said, sniffing at the underarms of a demure, light grey, black-trimmed gown he was carrying. "Oh, you're in luck. This is the eight, which means the ten's clean. God knows how I'm supposed to keep things cleaned in a remote bush outpost like this. You know what they said last time I took costumes in to the local cleaners? 'Do you want them back by Friday, love?' Friday! It happened to be Tuesday and we were shooting next day. 'No, this afternoon I said,' and I swear the woman reached for the phone to call the cops. We had to send the bloody stuff to Penrith by taxi. Here you are. Try this one."

She liked the fuss despite the almost offhand speed in which Carol, having made-up her face, whipped her hair back and flattened it around her head like bandages and covered it in a dark wig with pinned up braids, and despite the disinterested though familiar way in which the dresser remoulded her breasts under the dress's lacy bib and then made no bones about the struggle he was having buttoning it up.

"Hurry up, hurry up," said Carol as Rosemary paused to look at the governess in the mirror, a woman in a bottle-green dress who looked back startled by recognition. She hurried up, hoisting her skirts over such incongruous obstructions as a ghetto-blaster playing reggae, an electric coffee machine, and, once down the steps, the rear end of a bright blue Porsche which partly blocked the doorway.

"Where do I go?"

"There, to the house." Carol flapped her hand impatiently and then relented. "You start cleaning up," she called over her shoulder to one of the other make-up people. "Come on. Knowing this place, you probably haven't even met Stoner yet.

"You're absolutely right," said Rosemary, trying to hurry in the tight dress while keeping cool at the same time. Sweat, she realised, was an occupational hazard.

In sight of the house's front verandah, Carol suddenly stopped as though she'd encountered an invisible fence and Rosemary nearly collided with her. "Shh," she said, and flapped her hand again. Then, in answer to Rosemary's bewildered look, murmured. "We could be in sight. And sound: they're shooting."

There were people all over the ground-level, covered verandah. An area of brightness much stronger than the sun was full of their backs as they formed a semicircle around something impossible to see somewhere near the house's doorway. Huge cameras on dollies were pointed into the heart of the light, as were large overhead microphones covered in what looked like grey leg warmers. There was an air of tension, a murmur of voices, some stiff movement.

Contrasted with the action, right in front, on a clean gravelled stretch of driveway over which masses of black power cables curved and coiled, stood a small, closed carriage whose horse was boredly chewing alyssum and begonias from a nearby bed.

"Bloody horse," whispered Carol. "They'll have to dig out all those plants and shove in new ones for the next scene: they've already shown that bit of garden."

Suddenly the backs relaxed. People began to talk and move normally and some of the lights went out.

"Quick," said Carol, and ran across the lawn. She had already shooed the horse and called a bored-looking youth in stable-boy's clothes to watch out for it by the time Rosemary arrived.

"Where's Michael?" she asked one of the backs, who turned out to be Walter.

"Called inside for a between-takes chat with His Nibs. Nobody's ever seen him before this week. Now, suddenly, he's everywhere. You'd think he was an extra on the set. He's making Stoner really jumpy!" Then, "Wow, look at our governess!"

"Do you think I'll do?" Rosemary flirted, frisking her long skirt about.

"Do I think you'll do what?" he replied and waggled his eyebrows.

"You'd better wait here," Carol said and glanced at her watch. Rosemary did the same and was surprised to find it was three-thirty—it still felt like lunch-time. "Do you know your part yet?"

Rosemary felt a lurch of guilt or fear. A part! Of course! Gabor had mentioned it but no one else had. She'd been playing around like a tourist or a kid at an end-of-term concert yet this was serious, her career—perhaps the children's livelihood. Carol looked furious but not, Rosemary soon realised, with her.

"This fucking place! What do you bet we've done you all up for nothing? Look, go and ask that stupid Jim Hacket for your part. Bloody hell! At least you could have been reading it while you were getting ready!"

At least, Rosemary agreed nervously, starting off. But Carol exploded again.

"No. Better still. You go," she said to the stable-boy, who glanced at her in terror and set off at speed.

"The governess bit," Carol shouted at him. "The bit they're using for testing. Not the interior but the verandah shot. Christ, you'd think I was producer!"

"Seize the moment," said Walter. "It's a job that's up for grabs by the look of things."

But Carol gave no sign that she'd heard as she rushed through the group on the verandah and into the house's dim interior. "Michael! Michael!" They could hear her yelling.

Apart from Walter, Pete, and Gabor, there were other people Rosemary recognised—the woman with the steel-grey wig, smoking a filter-tipped cigarette, and the little girl, who, she could now see by the hip-thrusting way she stood and by the way her make-up had dribbled a bit at the edges, was at least sixteen, not ten at all. The man with the glued-on whiskers was sitting with his back propped up against the house, gazing boredly across the garden.

Carol came out of the house just as fast as she'd gone in, her face grim. Rosemary was fascinated by her, having never seen anyone this young so positive and confident.

"Can't get near him," she said. "It's a behind-doors scene in there. Charlie's waiting, too, and having a fit—doesn't even know if there's another take of this scene or whether he should start setting up the horse." This was for the benefit of the actors and crew, who, though they swore a bit, didn't seem surprised. To Rosemary Carol added, "Just stick around, read your script, and catch him when they come out, that's the best idea."

Rosemary suddenly felt tired. At the side of the house, bright and newly painted, was a wooden slatted garden bench almost out of sight of the group. The young boy, still running, came hurtling towards her with a clutch of papers in his hands, and as soon as she had them she went and sat down, relieved.

It was not a full script, just a scene in which the governess, the mine manager, and the housekeeper argued about the little girl's behaviour. The child's father and the older woman were fairly keen on punishing her for having done something or other: it was not quite clear whether she'd absent-mindedly let the chickens out or the cows in while reading, but both of them had had enough of her vague ways to advocate the strap, on one hand, and bread and dripping on the other.

Both the father and the housekeeper were agreed that deprivation of reading material was the most important first step, and it was the governess, new to the job, aware of the rich, handsome boss's single status as well as her own desperate need—she having obviously fallen upon hard times due to circumstances beyond her control—who had to plead with just the right degree of diplomacy and wit to spare the child's books, if not her skin and digestive system.

The script was not as good as Tennessee Williams. This Rosemary found encouraging since she had been able to cope well with the part of Sister Woman in *Cat on a Hot Tin Roof*—that, anyway, was what the local suburban paper's theatre critic had said in his review. Though not particularly memorable, the governess's speeches didn't seem too hard, and for a few minutes she worked at them quite seriously. But the conversation in the room behind her gradually ceased to be white noise and became distinguishable as words, some said with more passion than the script would ever justify. Two men were arguing. She began to pay attention.

"Look," said one of them loudly, firmly. "You hired me to do this job because you knew I was best for it. You can't—you can't—you mustn't interfere."

The other one spoke more softly, but with heavy menace. "I hired you to do the job because you were available. You may be the director, but this is my project, and don't ever forget it."

"But, be reasonable. My contract specifies . . ."

"Bugger your contract. As far as I'm concerned, you can quit today."

"Look, you just can't do that, mate, I . . ."

"I just have," said Talbot coldly.

A door slammed. A man hurried out of the door and silently through the group of crew and actors. Rosemary was just in time to see him— Michael Stoner, obviously—stride angrily towards the cars. And then to see Robert Talbot, the man she had been waiting for all day, emerge, scowling, through the door.

Unintentionally surrounded by his employees he glanced around uncomfortably as though looking for bodyguards or, at least, senior henchmen, to do the talking.

He could have ignored the gauntlet of puzzled and in some cases supplicating looks of the people he had to walk through. Instead he said gruffly, "Looks like the project's off for the moment—your director has got the huff. Don't worry about your money: you'll all get what's due plus four weeks if you're not on contract. If you are, you're free to release yourselves, of course, but I'd advise you not to sign up for anything else for a few weeks—we've got a few problems to sort out, then we'll be in business again."

Rosemary was standing right in his path as he strode towards the film-trucks, but he obviously did not recognise her. For both their sakes she was glad of this; despite his suave and masterful delivery it had not exactly been a winner's speech. As for herself, she had no doubt that a visible pool of sweat had begun to form around the edges of the wig.

Unlike the rest of them, who had exploded into expletives and suppositions, Rosemary did not have a job to lose, so she was no worse off than before. So she was calm as she watched Robert Talbot stride away towards the metal building marked RUSHES. What are you going to do with me now? she wondered.

Everyone around her was still muttering and speculating and slowly the loop of their dismay hooked her in, too. Walter and Gabor were talking nearby so she joined them.

"I'm really sorry."

"Well, I'm not," said Walter. "I switched from one job to another

without a break and I could do with one. A few weeks off right now,
with the house quiet, the kids at school, will suit me very well. We're
only twenty minutes from Tamarama Beach and I'll virtually have it to
myself. I'll nick one of my boys' surfboards for an hour or two a day."

"Johanna will be glad to have you back in Sydney," Gabor said to
Walter. "I get the feeling those twins of yours keep her on her toes."

"Her toes? Climbing the wall, sometimes." Walter laughed proudly.

"And my wife will be glad to have me back, too," said Gabor. "She
tried staying in a motel here for a short while but"—and cut his throat
with his hand. "Terrible. Nearly drove the woman mad. The food! So,
Rosemary-Governess, Walter is OK, I am OK. But what about you?
You have not yet done your test? A day for nothing!"

I wish he hadn't said that, she thought, then rose above it. "I suppose
I'd better go and give them their costume back."

"OK. Nice meeting you. Might see you at the pub later?"

"I don't know—it depends on the driver, I suppose. Which pub?"

"Which driver?" asked Walter and both men looked a little concerned.
"Do you mean Olly, in Talbot's big black car? I think he's gone. Someone
said he'd been throwing up." He climbed onto the carriage and peered
at the parking area.

Bloody cherries! thought Rosemary. Greedy bugger!

"Not a sign. You'd better check with Jim Hacket—he'll get someone
else to give you a lift. Sorry we can't offer but we'll have to take some
of the stuff back now, by the look of it, and the truck's chocka."

"You'll be OK," Gabor added. "Plenty of people going back tonight.
And just about everyone will go to the pub first—it's the one near the
station."

                    .   .   .

The dresser with the reputation for being a wit was having hysterics in
the make-up truck. Carol was trying to calm him.

"Don't touch me, you filthy bitch!" he screamed, and crossed his
skinny arms over his head as though shielding his eyes from an atomic
blast.

Jim Hacket had not been in the production truck. Clive, the boy
whose T-shirt extolled the potency of boom operators, told her that he
was in the rushes room, summoned by Robert Talbot.

"Shouldn't be too long. Just clearing up, making arrangements like,"
he said. He wasn't able to promise he'd give Jim a message: "For today
I'm the gofer. May not see him. Best is, you keep checking him out."

"Darryl, come on Darryl baby. It's OK, OK," Carol soothed the
dresser, but she was too wary to get close to his jerking, angry arms.

"Gin and Valium, if not more," Anne, the other make-up girl, explained. It took a lot of coaxing and grabbing before Carol was able to feed him some strong coffee. "Probably clash with what he's on and poison the poor bugger," she said mildly. She held a bucket near his chin just in case. It took even longer before they got him into a bed they had improvised from the barber's chair cushions.

"You idiots don't even know who's behind all this!" Darryl shouted. His eyes could not settle on anything for more than a second. "You think this is all legit. I tell you what, there's bikie gangs, there's children, little kids, nine, ten, available at almost any price. All they have to do is ask. You can get it on Bankcard!"

"He's usually a pain, but not often as bad as this," Anne said, coldcreaming Rosemary's face. "His friend walked out on him last week, now his job, so he's got two excuses. He's good at his job, but one day people are going to start thinking he isn't worth the hassle."

With the wig off, her face unmade and greasy, Rosemary felt better and looked worse—her Madonna curls had darkened into lank slabs. In a corner, obviously knocked off its hanger in the struggle with Darryl, was her voile dress, crushed like a rag. A tide of tiredness flooded over her. What on earth am I doing here? she asked herself.

"There's a bathroom in the main house," said Anne. "In the back part, where the caretaker usually lives. You go and have a shower and I'll iron your dress. We've got dryers, hot rollers—you'll be OK."

She lent Rosemary an old camel dressing gown and two striped towels that didn't smell as good as they could have done but she was very grateful. "If you see Jim, could you please tell him I've been looking for him? I need a lift back to Sydney."

"Oh, sure. Don't worry. There are plenty of people going back tonight."

This was reassuring because she noticed as soon as she stepped outside that most of the cars had gone. The blue Porsche was still there though.

It was still there, glowing in the first orangy rays of the sunset when she came back again, clean. But, when at 6:30, curled, newly made-up, crisp, and relaxed, she stepped out again, it had gone. So, she soon discovered, had Jim Hacket, and probably everyone else apart from Carol, Anne, herself, and the supine Darryl. Even the horse and carriage had vanished.

"Bloody hell!" said Carol. "Typical! You'd think someone would check to see if we were OK. You can be sure Jim knew we'd landed Darryl again. I 'spose they've all buggered off to the pub."

"It's not far to town," said Anne. "You could easily walk there. And actually, if you hurry, you could catch the express train, the XPT—it leaves at about seven, I think."

"Yeah. Seven-fourteen, actually," said Carol beginning to feel relieved of half her responsibility. She drew a quick map.

"It's easy: past the dogs, left at the first big street, right at the next one, and the station is a couple blocks down. But you'll have to hurry!"

"What about you two?"

"We're okay," said Carol. "You hurry."

But Rosemary was reluctant to leave them without food and with the possibly still volatile Darryl.

"It's really OK. My boyfriend's coming to pick me up soon," said Anne. "We live in Lithgow, see. And if Jim or someone hasn't come back for Carol by then we'll look after her. Worst comes to the worst you can sleep on the sofa bed, Cal."

"Yeah, thanks. That's great. Meanwhile"—and Carol waved a little bottle of gin she'd just unpacked from a make-up box—"meanwhile . . ."

So Rosemary left, carrying her hat, hurrying in her spiky heels along the rough dirt roadside. Very soon little bindii thorns started working their way in between the straps, and as she bent to pick them out, sometimes lurching a little, the carloads of men who pulled up at the greyhound racing track stared curiously, whistled, or made offers she could easily refuse.

She began to give herself a reproving speech in which the sin of vanity featured prominently. Then she told herself to shut up. Just before she reached the first main street the blue Porsche came hurtling towards her from the town.

Oh, thank God, she thought. He hadn't left.

She stopped, smiling, waiting for him to stop for her but the car kept going, fast, past her. Which was when she saw that the person in it was not Robert Talbot at all, but Clive the gofer, obviously on the errand of mercy Carol was banking on.

It was 7:13 when, out of breath and sore-footed, she reached the station. The station-master, flag and whistle ready, was poised next to the sleek silver train, and she realised she'd have to run down the steps to catch it in time.

"Just a minute," said a ticket collector at the top of the stairs, and he put his hand out.

"I'll buy one on the train," she said, trying to push past him. But he was strong, firm.

"Sorry lady, you can't buy a ticket on the XPT—they're pre-booked seats."

"I'll stand, then, I don't mind," she said, desperate, trying to duck past him, but he was large and resolute and the train quietly began to slide away, half full of virtuous people in their booked, prepaid seats.

"I'll report you!" said Rosemary, too angry to cry, though that was obviously next on the list.

"Suit yerself," said the man. "I'm only doing me job."

Pinching back tears of rage, tiredness, confusion, Rosemary wished she was back in the make-up truck with Carol and Anne and the gin, confident of rescue. More still she wished she were home, and for the first time all day she had a rush of conscience about the children.

"What's happened?" Phyl asked, her excitement travelling just as clearly as her words along the telephone wire. Rosemary wished she didn't have such dreary news to report.

"I've missed my train," she began

"Train? You went in a car."

"Yes. Look, darling, it's very complicated. I'll explain the whole thing to you tomorrow—I'll have to stay here tonight. I just wanted to make sure you and Bobby are all right. There's plenty of stuff you can have for dinner: that chicken, most of it's still there and I'm sure one of the avocados must be ripe. And I'll phone Lucy and ask her to keep an eye on you."

"Hah! Lucy! She's not there. And if she was you wouldn't get through. Reporters keep interviewing her."

"Phyl! Why?"

"About her and Malcolm. Tonight she's going to be on the show—introduced."

"What are you talking about?"

"Do you really not know, Mum? He announced their engagement on the mid-morning news."

Despite the fact that the booth was filthy, Rosemary would have sat down on the floor if the telephone cable had been long enough.

"How fantastic! But what . . . ?"

"Don't worry about dinner for Bobby and me: we're going out. Daniel's picking us up in about ten minutes."

"Daniel? How did that happen?"

"Bobby phoned him—about a homework problem, he said. I was studying." Meaning—If I'd known, I might have talked him out of such disloyalty. "So Dad found out you'd gone away for the day. Bobby said to the races in a chauffeured car." Phyl giggled, inviting Rosemary into conspiracy. "Dad was very nice to Bobby. He said he couldn't chat then because he was in a meeting. But he said he'd pick us both up and take us to dinner at the Black Stump. He doesn't know I'm vegetarian now. Mum, I've missed him. I was very mad with him before."

"I know, darling. He'll be pleased that you've decided to talk to him again," Rosemary managed to say, though her voice was out of tune. The warning light began to flash and she couldn't find another twenty-cent coin.

"Mum," said Phyl, "why are you really staying in Lithgow? You can tell me."

But she couldn't—they'd been disconnected.

By the time she'd crossed the road and got some more change from a milk bar and then waited for someone else to finish a call, she could scarcely bear to phone again: Daniel might be there, might answer, might insist on cross-examining her about the day. Might laugh at her for being star-struck and then for being humiliated. Worse than that risk was the risk of Phyl, suffused in the overflow of Lucy's romance, going off with the wrong idea—the right idea—the wrong idea about what Rosemary was doing in Lithgow. It would throw the whole balance of guilt. She dialled, but when she did the phone rang and rang—Daniel had picked them up already.

By the time she gave up trying to reach someone by phone it was nearly eight o'clock. The clamour inside her head was beginning to subside simply as a result of lack of energy; it was time to do something sensible.

The first, so obvious that she was instantly angry with herself for having not thought of it before, was to find out whether there was another train. She soon found there had been one at 7:25 and if she and the XPT ticket collector had not been so angry with each other he might have mentioned it, or she might have stopped and looked at the timetable. By now she would have been safely on her way home. She would have arrived, with the aid of a taxi, not much later than Daniel and the children; perhaps even seen him there and been able to scornfully, casually undo any wrong impressions he might have gleaned about her lapses as a mother or her aspirations as a star.

The only other train would reach Sydney at 12:34. She shivered, chilly in her now totally inappropriate voile dress. It was dark, and the breeze carried an echo of the frosts which had surrounded Lithgow as recently as the previous month, when spring flowers had already bloomed in most other places. The station was deserted apart from a bored-looking ticket seller in a little office.

She had read dreadful reports about gangs of drunk or drugged, seat-slashing youths who terrorised helpless people on late-night trains. If she survived that there was still the prospect of emerging from Central's tiled gloom into the dangerous late night street to compete for a taxi with drunks, muggers, and men with funny eyes.

"You're an absolute idiot," she said aloud.

The next sensible thing to do was find something to eat. This was when she remembered the pub and an immediate picture created itself: smiling film-crew people, standing around a barbecue with glasses of red wine in their hands, eager to welcome her into their group. One of them would certainly drive her at least most of the way home.

But this vision, too, proved disappointing: around the old-fashioned, charmless bar were locals—regulars, obviously—mainly sad-faced middle-aged husbands and wives out for a drink, with little to say to each other or anyone else. Most of them were either trying not to or blatantly staring at a very small group—three men who were so drunk that they had reached the lurching, falling stage and were arguing with the publican, who would not sell them any more. They all swore continuously. As she watched, the one who had fallen over furthest pulled himself up for a few seconds and revealed himself to be Jim Hacket. There would be no lift home either.

Very firmly Rosemary sent herself to the Ladies to fix her make-up and regain control. The corner she'd painted herself into, though uncomfortable, was furnished so simply that the next steps were obvious. All she had to do was stop fighting the inevitable, go and find a meal and a warm bed, and get through the night as quickly and calmly as she could. She had done nothing to deserve this, nothing to be ashamed of. It was good, spine-strengthening advice—had she not been so frivolously dressed, any casual observer watching her walk out of that pub may have mistaken that resolute walk, that firm chin, for those of a Salvation Army worker.

"Australian and Chinese Meals" was the sign outside what looked like the only open place on the main street. Her mother had giggled all the way home once after seeing a similar sign for the first time—inventing combinations like sweet-and-sour witchety grubs, Mongolian goanna, and flied ticks (as opposed to flied lice.) Rosemary, who, even though she now knew that what an Australian and Chinese restaurant really offered was a choice of MSG-flavoured messes made of soft cooked rice and canned button mushrooms, or hamburgers made with possibly old meatballs and definitely canned beetroot, or thin steak sandwiches on white bread, was too hungry to mind. Lacking a jacket, protein and hot coffee were what she needed most urgently to keep her warm. There was little they could do, she told herself, to destroy the protein value of a steak sandwich, no matter what they did to the taste.

It was an obliging establishment. It obviously had an arrangement with the nearby, earlier-closing news agency to take over any unsold papers and try for a few more sales. Rosemary happened to glance at the two almost depleted stacks of Sydney afternoon papers, then gasped and snatched up one of each. They both carried large, fairly similar pictures of Malcolm and Lucy smiling rapturously: she at him and he at the camera. MALCOLM LOVES LUCY proclaimed the banner headline of one, MALCOLM HENRY—ENGAGED said the other. Phyl's news was not only true, it had been true for long enough to have made the afternoon papers.

Thrilled, grinning, wishing she had someone to share this with, she took the papers to a little table and soon, with a cup of coffee at hand and a steak sandwich on the way, began to thaw and really enjoy Lucy's news. I *should* have been there! she thought. I *should* have been there!

The front-page reports were very brief, and both spilled over to a tiny box on page three. Both were obviously very rushed, late-edition stories, but even so the papers must have been aided by the studio in order to get the pictures in time. What a buzz it must have been, with all the radio stations vying to get the news over first!

I could have known before anyone if I'd been there this morning when it happened, she thought. That's why Lucy ran after the car!

Lucy and Malcolm must have been secretly planning this for ages. Months ago—perhaps before the winter—Lucy had come in one night looking as though the world was a delicious snack she'd just eaten.

"We were talking, in his car, still in the parking lot. About Mattie. I was saying she hardly remembers Jack, and he said, 'You should divorce him. It would be very quick and easy.' Just like that! Nothing more, but honestly, it gave me such a thrill."

Then there was the night when, after days of snapping and being mysterious, Malcolm had sworn Lucy to secrecy—as she in turn had sworn Rosemary—and told her that he, too, was still technically married to a woman who had been terribly injured in an accident when he was teaching her to drive. Most of her mind had been erased: she could not talk or move and did not appear to recognise anyone, and for the past eighteen years she had been cared for in a nursing home in North Queensland near where they'd both grown up, where he'd started his career on radio. He paid for her care, through lawyers. That was also the night Lucy realised he was a Catholic. He would not even consider divorce.

"I see it clearly," Lucy said. "There'll always be the three of us: him, his guilt, and me."

These were Lucy's special secrets, the source of pain, speculation, and wild hopes which, in their frequent late-night talks, counterpointed Rosemary's own pain, speculation, and occasional despair. Malcolm must have conquered guilt because of Lucy, Rosemary thought. It's the most romantic thing!

She closed her eyes and let the image of romance run, like a video tape. In the middle of a bright, warm, yet private spotlight she could see the two figures of Lucy and Malcolm twirling and waltzing, as accomplished as Torvil and Dean, making a gift of their enchantment to herself and all the rest of the wallflowers in the audience. Oh, lucky, lucky Lucy.

The day which had started off feeling as though it was going to be one of the most special in Rosemary's life had instead turned into a farce, an embarrassing circumstance that had stranded her in a strange little town miles away from where the most important people in her life were doing really fascinating things. She stared glumly at the steak sandwich which, by now, had arrived. But the steak looked so thin and tough that she doubted if it had any nutritional value at all. Some poor cow had died in vain. The toast had been scorched and then made limp by a large splat of bottled tomato sauce. She pushed the plate away, suddenly preferring the risk of malnutrition. Instead she ordered more coffee to distract herself from cold, hunger, and disappointment in the Chinese-Australian café in Lithgow, where she would never have thought of spending a lonely Friday evening if it had not been for Robert Talbot.

It was time to find a bed. She was beginning to feel angry and disgusted with herself and was seconds away from blaming herself for everything that had gone wrong. Right now she couldn't even get Lucy clearly into focus. Standing at the counter preparing to leave she was too tired to get anything, anyone into focus. She even had a bit of trouble finding her change purse in the recesses of her bag, encumbered, as she was, by the two newspapers.

A man walked in quickly and asked "Have you got today's *Sun* or *Mirror?*"

"No, mate, sorry, sold out," said the Australian and Chinese restauranteur, who was actually Greek.

"I have finished with these—you can have them," said Rosemary, turning towards the man's voice. And then she nearly dropped them because it was Robert Talbot. Behind him, just outside, still throbbing, was the blue Porsche.

"Well! Mrs. Rosemary Quilty!" he said. "What are you doing here? They told me you'd gone back by train."

"I missed it," she said, knowing that she'd lost the struggle to keep relief, delight, and a sudden huge surge of energy from her voice and her face. "I was just about to go and find a motel."

"Wouldn't you prefer a lift home?" he asked. "I was just about to leave, but I wanted to have a look at this first. My local newsagent will have sold out by tomorrow. With any luck."

He took the papers from her hand and grinned proprietorily at the two pictures.

"Well, well. Fast worker, your pretty friend, don't you think? Looks good, hey? Come on, it's late. Have you eaten anything?" The slightly fiddled-with sandwich, still on the table, provided the answer. "Come on," he said, tucking her bare, shivering arm under his warm, dark sleeve. "I'm starving. And it's your fault. If we're lucky we'll get something edible in Blackheath."

"Why is it my fault?"

He didn't answer as he ushered her into the car.

Nine

"Why is it my fault that you are starving?" Rosemary asked again as soon as they had both seat-belted themselves into the Porsche. This time he heard her.

"Because you turned out to be the straw that broke Michael Stoner's back. That's why I had to stay, clear up the mess, go through the rushes. I had to have a beer with the production people and so on. Didn't want a general walk-out!"

"I still don't know what I did." She heard her own voice, smooth and light, as though there was no knotted mass of feelings flipping around and tangling like stockings in a dryer. She had to keep talking, otherwise her limbs would have begun to tremble from emotional overload.

"Well, maybe Stoner was looking for an out. The project had—has some problems. But the screen test—when he heard about that his head fell off and now I'm looking for another director, too." He grinned. "Know anyone? Someone good, brilliant, in line for a first big break?" She couldn't tell if he was being ironic. "Just about everyone is contracted to the thirtieth of June next year. Where were you, by the way?"

"I was there. You walked right past me. I was the sheep in governess's clothing."

"Hah! Must have been a good disguise. Why didn't you say something?"

"It didn't seem like the right moment for a social chat—you'd just told the crew and the actors they were fired."

"Fair enough."

His driving style bothered her; despite the fact that they were going fast up the dark, twisting mountain road he kept glancing at her. There was a hint that he was laughing behind his executive expression. She wondered how he could be so calm, so free of guilt after firing someone who was simply doing what he was contracted to do. Perhaps people like Robert Talbot, who routinely make decisions involving millions of dollars, and hundreds of peoples lives, simply don't allow themselves to feel guilty, she thought. Acknowledging humanity would slow them down.

She envied his calm. Ever since he'd touched her, different kinds of tensions and apprehensions had begun to heave and jostle within, a constant threat to her pretended serenity. What she really wanted to do, what she'd have done if it had been Daniel driving that car, was reach for his strong, black-hair-threaded hand, which would have been more comforting and more direct than the talking they would obviously have to do first. In fact, if it had been Daniel, and if she had been feeling like this, and if they had not separated, she would have got straight to the point by plunging her hand between his thighs. That had always been a good way to drive at night. She had to keep working hard to remind herself that this was a stranger, an eminent person—one whose apparent friendliness was based on a lifetime conviction of superiority.

He broke her tension. "So you didn't do your screen test after all?"

"Probably a good thing," she said. "I only got the script about five minutes before it was supposed to happen."

"Well, at least you got a script! What did you think of it?"

"There wasn't enough of it to judge, really." Your quarrel was much more interesting, she wanted to say. "I heard you lost the script editor."

"Yes, Ed Blackwell, poor fellow. Best in the business. The script-writers he'd got together—some of them have been struggling on, but it's like the Irish Parliament now, with more opinions than direction. That bloody Stoner! He's one of those people who cracks under pressure." Not surprising, Rosemary wanted to say. There's no way of dealing with someone who cancels your contract because he wants his own way and knows he can pay the lawyers! But she continued to listen demurely, and when he spoke again he sounded more puzzled than tyrannical— "I tell you, this project . . ." He shook his head.

"But you're still planning to go ahead with it. Why?"

"Good question, Mrs. Quilty." He made soft whistling noises and other self-involved signs and created a precarious silence. While he'd talked she'd been occupied, delving between his sentences for clues about what he was really like, but now there were no words to prey on the tension inside her. The tension didn't feel like a tangled mass of laundering stockings now, but like hot lava getting close to the boil in a too-long-closed volcano. Any minute it would begin to spill over and flood her mind with the hot lava of sexuality—already it was difficult to take any notice of her mind's prim warning—that few people become terribly rich without being ruthless. To disguise her trembling she stroked her face and her throat, and then realised that was no solution and stopped, and clasped her hands together to keep them out of trouble.

She controlled her breathing and tried to look relaxed. But she knew that if he didn't talk soon she'd reveal the internal struggle. It was too late to speak herself—she didn't trust her voice. Already she felt as though the passion lava was oozing out through her pores, through her eyes, through her hair. Soon he'd see it. He saved her by making a call.

"Excuse me a moment," he said as he reached for the car phone and pressed a few buttons.

"Got stuck in Lithgow," he told the person who answered. There were no preliminaries—it was as though he were paying by the word. "Can't say when I'll be back. Sure. Sure. Righto then." And he rang off.

It was short, but it gave her time to deal with the tension, which she did by acting, a brilliant solution she wished she'd thought of earlier. She simply showed Robert Talbot that she was a relaxed woman with plenty of time. She leaned back in the wonderfully comfortable seat and crossed her hands on her lap, wanting him to know he could trust her. Concentrating on being trustworthy and not terribly interested worked—it distracted Rosemary into calm. Then everything was made easier when he started to tell her about "The Mount Victorians."

At first he talked in the firm, time-means-money voice he undoubtedly used when addressing his senior staff at meetings, but gradually he became involved enough in the story to tell it as though she were someone familiar. And she listened, acting passively at first, as one does when being told information by a teacher. But as his story progressed she became as deeply involved as though it were the early days with Daniel and he was telling her about one of his wonderful schemes.

"The Mount Victorians" started in about 1840. It was set in an inn, a toll-house, and a settlers' cottage made from wattle and daub. Three main families were introduced in the first, movie-length episode which covers about thirty years.

"Children who weren't born at the start are parents by the end," he said. "This covers a lot of development of course: the gold boom, the strife between settlers and squatters for land out west—all that stuff. The pilot ends in 1867 when the railway line was finally connected."

It had taken half a century to solve the railway engineering problems, he told her. She was sure she must have learned this at school: part of a fog of information that had served no greater purpose than to place a dangerous film over the open areas of her mind. But now she was totally receptive to the history lesson—he could have told her anything.

"They had to find a way of getting the train over the Nepean River, around a sharp bend and up to Lapstone, so they built the Knapsack Gully viaduct. It's still there. It was the major engineering feat of the day. In the story, two of the young blokes get work on building the viaduct. Both are in love with the same girl. You've known all three of them, from the time they were born. Then one of the rivals is killed, accidently, though it looks bad for the other fellow—the innkeeper's son. Inquest in the Hartley Valley court-house, all that. Of course, the bloke is cleared but you're still not sure if he'll get the girl.

"Great ending. Oh, great ending: the official opening of the new railway station at Mount Victoria, with the first train slowly steaming in. Hardly had to change a thing at Mount Victoria station—it's still pretty much the way they built it, but dirtier. The pilot runs for two hours. If the viewers like it, it will get them in for years, like M*A*S*H," he said, so eagerly that it confirmed Rosemary's guess that this was his first venture into the telemovie business.

He told her the plot as well as some background history while they were travelling. It took thirty-five years from the first landing at Botany Bay before Wentworth, Lawson, and Blaxland found a route in 1813 from the eastern escarpment through to the western plains on the other side of the Blue Mountains, though people had tried again and again.

One explorer, reporting on the sheer cliffs, ranges, and ridges he'd encountered in an early attempt, had said in a stiffly worded letter that it was like trying to cross London over the roofs of the houses. To him that explanation was obviously sufficiently daunting: he didn't even mention the leeches, the lack of food, the extremes of weather, and how frightened he must sometimes have been by the sounds of large bodies crashing through the bush. Bush-rangers, perhaps, or Aborigines. Or tigers—at that early stage the possibility of carnivorous animals had not been ruled out.

Robert Talbot told Rosemary these things all the way to Blackheath and into a French restaurant where the manager, a skinny, smiling man in black, dashed forward and seized Talbot's biceps as though together they had just scored a goal. Had this been France, he'd have kissed him on both cheeks.

The restaurant was crowded with people who knew who Robert Talbot was —there were nudges, rolled eyes. One man stood up to hang his wife's jacket over her chair back, a gallantry which gave him such a good view that he was able to stare a little at Rosemary, too.

Although every table was full, they were left standing exposed to the

waves of interest for no more than a few seconds. The proprieter arranged for a display of fruit and dessert cakes to be whisked out of an
alcove and for a new little table to be conjured in its place.

"It is small, I know," he murmured, fussing over seating them. "But
soon a transfer, eh? A promotion?" And he glanced significantly at better
tables occupied by less notable eaters.

"No, no, Michel, this is good. Cosy," said Robert Talbot. "Nothing's
going to stay on this table for more than a couple of minutes because
we're both starving. Just bring us a good bottle of wine and tell us what
the best thing is to eat. The best—not what the chef wants to get rid
of!"

Barring the minor interruptions of choosing from the menu, recited
with elaborate emphasis by a tiny, black-skirted person Rosemary would
have called a waiter and Robert Talbot would have called a waitress, he
did not stop talking about "The Mount Victorians."

"The camera work is really great stuff," he said, just as the waiter
brought their entrees. She had also brought a basket of hot rolls. "We
didn't order that," he said, so the waiter apologetically prepared to
remove them, but he stopped her: "On second thoughts . . ."— and
took one and slathered it with butter. "Most of the scenes look like
McCubbin paintings."

His mouth was full of bread but his voice was so full of love that
Rosemary felt she'd been there, part of the story, doing the washing in
half a barrel, making lamb bone soup over the fire and damper in the
ashes.

"In the three commercial TV stations in Sydney, there's really no one
who loves drama. All of us have gone for sport, news, and current affairs
because, let's face it, that's where the ratings usually lie. But some mini-
series are pretty good raters and one or two have even been top raters.
People like them. We try to give people what they want. We claim to
be the best and I want to make sure we damn well are!"

His display of confident energy had the same effect on Rosemary as
a peacock's display of his magnificent, double-layer, multi-eyed tail has
on a peahen. But, like a peahen, she pretended to be unaffected. She
ate tiny mouthfuls while he talked. When her yellow napkin slithered
off her lap he retrieved it, fast as reflex—it may not even have hit the
floor—and put it back on her lap. But she had bent, too, so her lap was
temporarily blocked by her chest, and the back of his hand brushed
across a nipple, sending a thin trickle of nerve electricity through it and
causing a complementary reflex action: her arm jerked up and her nails
lightly scratched the back of his hand.

" 'The Mount Victorians' sounds so lovely," Rosemary said, having delicately cleared her throat.

"That's right, lovely. But the thing is, it's also funny, which is what makes it so different from everything anyone else's ever done."

Rosemary had a quick, shocked vision of the settlers making Alan Alda–like one-liners around the camp-fire or walking into pails of milk or each other's elbows like Keystone Cops in mid-Victorian dress, but he quickly reassured her. "It's funny because of the way the characters handle their situation: although they're tough and life's a hell of a battle for them, most of them have got a good sense of humour. Ed believed that the convicts who made the best of deportation were those who could see the funny side of it and his settlers—their descendants—are like that, too. But it isn't just a laugh a minute—it's got its drama."

The food was delicious; Rosemary, playing the peahen, was able to restrain herself from gobbling, but he was not impeded—very quickly the flounder which had overlapped his plate was reduced to a pile of bones, clean as matchsticks. He also ate all the rolls, each with an air of reproach, yet he still looked so hungry that she was tempted to offer him some of her chicken. She would have if he'd given her a clear signal. Instead, he called the waiter as soon as Rosemary put her fork down and asked for the cake display.

"These cakes are what I come here for," he boomed, impressing everyone in earshot while seriously watching a large slice of pear and almond tart being slid onto his plate. "Try some."

"I'll stick to coffee, thanks," she said, thinking of Auntie Gwen's thighs.

"There's a theory that TV viewers have had enough of bush-rangers, Banjo Patterson—Our Colourful Past. But don't you believe it: people find it much more real than contemporary drama. But it's expensive stuff: some of the sets and effects were way over budget," he added, with the artificial cheerfulness men use to cover things that surprise them. "Can't remember the figures, but just imitating bits of the viaduct cost hundreds of times more than the real thing cost in 1866. Can't just write that off."

"But why would you want to?"

"We don't. No, of course we don't. But the snag is that the telemovie story-line concentrated on the people: babies, weddings, jealousy, how they coped and struggled—domestic politics that had nothing much to do with what was happening in the real world. At that stage we had nothing to do with the production—it was all handled by an independent company. But then"—he interrupted himself with a stern-looking moment of private thought followed by the last mouthful of cake—"we took it over. Bought them out."

I bet you did, she thought. Simply waved a cheque-book like a magic wand and transformed some people's lives.

"I . . . we saw its potential as a mini-series tied in with aspects of history. Mad not to—there are some great stories, specially around the turn of the century. Oh, some great characters: people like James Rutherford, who made a fortune out of Cobb and Co, the stage-coach business. And Henry Parkes, who set up New South Wales economically, but went bankrupt twice himself. Incredible chap, Parkes."

He feels comfortable with me, she realised. This is stuff he wants to say. So she sat there, silent as a flower with petals open, a good listener gladly responding to the buzz.

He's making this mini-series be the thing that interests him, she thought. Like a hobby. I wonder if he's doing it to distract himself from something else? How often does he take a day away from his empire to come to the mountains and get involved? And does he usually have a female passenger? But talking was safer than thinking.

"It must be fascinating. Fascinating, to do research. Like detective work. Like finding treasure."

He stared at her intently—the customs officer look again—then: "I wish some of my staff felt the same way. There's a story that I think would be very good for the next series of 'The Mount Victorians,' about a bloke called William Sandford, who tried to start a steel industry at Lithgow at a time when Australia was bound to import everything from the U.K. He was a partner of Rutherford, I think someone said. But I'm told they can't find out much about him." He looked angry, and Rosemary again got the impression that it would be very dangerous to thwart him, a man so used to the power of his own way. "It's the bloody unions. They killed initiative in this country," he said. "Come on, let's go."

At the very least, Rosemary needed a reassuring look in the mirror. Robert Talbot seemed happy to be left ho-ho-hoing at the front door with Michel. He probably owns this place, too, she thought.

When she'd shaved her legs that morning she had looked critically at the backs of her thighs, which, in the kinder light of her own bathroom, had not seemed as serious as they had three days previously in the boutique. Lucy had explained, in the special voice she got when she was suddenly an expert, that shops have special-effects men to fix the lighting so that clothes at bargain prices look unflattering. This forces people to try on more expensive things to restore their morale, and of course, they then buy them.

The look in the restaurant ladies room mirror was a comfort—no dark circles under her eyes and, as far as she could perceive, no obvious clues about how she felt. The pressure of that bubbling volcano had dispersed enough for comfort. It didn't even feel like a volcano anymore but like a patch of long-dormant seeds shooting up, growing up after a drought.

But be careful, Rosemary warned herself, thinking of the way people had stared in the restaurant. It's always possible to see when people are turned on. They'll read my mind. Sensitive observers will tap into the messages I beam him, like expert CB operators who listen in to police reports and drug deals. Careful.

.   .   .

In the drought of the central Australian desert, all visible life disappears. Only the tribal Aborigines, whose spiritual unity with the environment allows them to perceive no barriers between themselves and nature, are not surprised. They know the secret water-holes. To them the desert is always a garden, sometimes more generous than at others. So, though they are immensely pleased when the rain comes, they are not surprised by what the newer settlers regard as an occasional miracle. It happens perhaps as rarely as twice a century. Not the spattering of light showers which are quickly swallowed by dust as dry as plaster but real rain— enough to clog the earth's pores and stay on top in large, shallow lakes. Then, within days, grass grows, almost quickly enough for you to see the movement. Surprisingly, so do flowers, and within hours, it seems, there are bees and other pollinating insects, all frantically working to a fertility deadline.

More astonishing are the little animals: frogs and strangely shaped fish, which appear and populate the new lake's fringes, feeding on the insects and on a variety of water life whose eggs and seeds have patiently waited deep below the sand's worst heat. News of this spreads: birds arrive, particularly pelicans, by thousands, to feast on water creatures who simply were not there only a few weeks earlier. There is fighting and mating and pollinating and seed setting—all on a speeded up sched- ule. Life is snatched at before the sun boils all the water away again.

It was Rosemary's favourite miracle story, and this night she felt it had happened to her. The rain had fallen. The system had sprung into life. She knew exactly how the night would turn out. From now on her life would be completely different.

Afterwards, she could never even claim that it had begun innocently, though it might have ended that way if she had not been so determined, in the Porsche, to move the conversation away from the safe topic of "The Mount Victorians" and onto more personal things.

Robert Talbot had driven not nearly as fast after dinner, largely because of a series of huge trucks bound for Sydney, full of fruit, sheep, and lumpy bags. Also, she guessed, because he wasn't hungry anymore.

"I'd love to see the feature-length movie," she said.

"Yes, I was thinking of that. You should see that, plus the first few episodes of the series that we've done. We're aiming at having six completed before launching, and so far we've got four, two based around Henry Parkes and two around James Rutherford. The opinion is that it's time we did something with it."

"You mean showing it on TV?"

"No, not yet. Not until the ratings season starts again next year. But it's time to start people talking about it, so we'll fix something up next week, possibly Tuesday or Wednesday, that suit you?—a preview at the channel studio for some of our executives, the advertising people, and a few television journos and so on. I'm pretty sure they'll like it. You'll like it, too." It almost sounded like an order. "Stoner didn't want anyone to see it until the lot was in the can, but he's gone now."

"The ones you've made, are they self-sufficient? I mean, does the last one leave loose ends so you have to have at least one more?"

"No, it's been written in blocks of two episodes each, so if we had to, we could stop at six. We could stop now! But I'd be reluctant to do that. To me the most interesting part comes next, around the turn of the century and up to the First World War."

"Ah yes, the Edwardians," said Rosemary. "I loved that time! Croquet, suffragettes, the first cars and planes. . . ."

"Oh, there was that all right. But there was also the beginning of industrialisation and the establishment of government. Those blokes were so excited about having the power to plan a brand-new country. There were lots of starry-eyed idealists among the hard heads. But their vision was so narrow! And it's left us with a lot of restrictive precedents." He drove gloomily, a man convinced he'd have done a much better job at drafting a constitution.

"Do you usually get so involved in productions—choosing the scripts, choosing the actors? I'd have thought you'd be too busy . . . chairmanning and so on."

"Chairmanning and so on," he mimicked, and laughed. "Have you any idea of what happens in boardrooms?"

But she was used to being patronised. "Well, small boardrooms. Daniel used to get so worked up sometimes that I'd be tempted to feed him raw meat. I suppose it's a matter of degree: in big boardrooms I suppose they get steamed up enough to eat babies."

"Do I look like a baby eater?"

"Sometimes."

"I get involved in lots of things but the closest I've got to raw meat is sashimi. Do you like sushi? "

Rosemary promised to try sushi. She also refused to be side-tracked.

"I really am intrigued. Most of the businessmen I've met run their days to such tight schedules that people have to book them for lunch weeks ahead. But you—and you've got such a huge corporation—you seem to be able to just . . . run away. For the day."

Once more his dark, heavy look threatened the fragile shackles she'd been imposing on her emotions. What's he thinking? What's in his mind?

"I had a meeting at Leura today, looking at some property our people are keen to develop. Lithgow's not much further. Besides, I thought it was a nice day to take you for a ride."

What does that mean? her mind demanded, slightly chilled by the phrase. But her emotions were convinced that it was the first flirtatious remark. He had given her a cue.

Discounting the strictly circumspect dealings she used to have with Daniel's clients, Rosemary's experience with men in prominent positions was limited to articles she had read in magazines. How, for example, would the Duke of Windsor have first made it clear to Wallis Simpson that he wanted to take her to bed? I bet she helped, thought Rosemary. I bet she dropped little lace handkerchiefs and double entendres. And I bet he was grateful, and that his gratitude lasted all his life.

She had been just about to drop the modern equivalent of a lace handkerchief when she reminded herself that he was not royalty. Indeed, not too many generations earlier his ancestors, like hers, had probably been convicts. And besides, it was unlikely that he'd read the same magazines. It isn't easy, nowadays, she told herself. But he obligingly filled the silence.

"And what about you. Did you marry Daniel Quilty straight from school?"

"Almost. He rescued me from college. He was still a journalist at the time and for some reason we thought his salary was enough to go into the baby-making business right away." That, she thought, neatly disposed of the age problem. "And then, five years later, I had Bobby and in between I helped Daniel with his . . . our business."

"Helped doing what?"

"With everything—typing, the books. Banking, making tea, organising promotions and product launches and tours for visiting authors or management gurus, astronauts . . ." she trailed off but he still looked interested. "Administrative stuff, too, of course—seeing printers and bank managers. Phoning people—a lot of phoning. Now Daniel's got quite a lot of staff. He didn't need me as much." That sounds pathetic, she told herself. "So I started doing some of the things I wanted to do: a communications course. And acting again."

"Yes. You told me about the acting." He hiss-whistled bits of a tune. "What about your friend, the delectable Lucy Barlow? Do you think she's a happy girl today?"

"Oh, of course! Though I'm really surprised—she and I don't have secrets from each other, usually. We were all out together for Malcolm's birthday on Wednesday night and they said nothing."

"His birthday, hey? That's a good angle. Hope he mentioned it to the publicity people." Robert Talbot looked very pleased.

It was a simple thing, really. Things that change people's lives so often are.

"Does Quilty get his pound of flesh from all his staff, or did he work you extra hard?" he asked, and she found herself in the awkward position of having to defend Daniel.

"I suppose everyone has to work hard now that jobs are hard to get. But Bobby, my son, says Daniel's doing well. Last time he spent a weekend with him Daniel took him out to sea, just outside the three-mile limit, to a trawler some big group is converting into a casino. It's going to be very big, apparently, and Daniel's got the contract to launch the publicity and handle the promotion. There's a cabinet minister involved and some rich doctors. I was surprised when I heard about that; I thought we—he was going more into direct mail than big promotions."

"In business you grab what you can get," said Robert Talbot like a kindly teacher.

One of the reasons why Daniel had gone off Rosemary was because of her almost total lack of interest in the who's who and the what's what of the Sydney rat race. It had always been her belief that men who became keen on the game of money had merely graduated to an older version of keenness on collecting cereal-packet cards or pictures of naked girls. Having had no father since before she was born and, as a result, no brothers, it had taken her longer than usual to realise that the average male's obsession with competitive acquisition was as normal as the average female's obsession with love. But as a result of her firmly fixed view, Rosemary had believed that once she and Daniel reached the stage of having enough—an enough that suited and would maintain some democratically decided-upon life-style—that he would relax and start having fun with his life. She had sometimes suggested things like flying kites with the kids until Phyl got too old for that. Or going to Fiji during the mango season, or to the races on an occasional Wednesday in spring but there had never been time. She'd even given up trying to have dinner parties because Daniel almost always got involved in a last-minute crisis and left it all to her.

Most of the fights she had had with Daniel had been about the fact that nearly all their energy went into acquiring money and very little into enjoying it. One day the truth had illuminated her confusions. The truth was that, to Daniel, making money was more fun than just about anything, including her. So, in the Porsche, somewhere near the Roseville Bridge, she had felt quite proud of herself for dredging up these details about Daniel's dealings and delivering them to someone who, she trusted, would be at least equally as interested. And that, of course, was the irony.

That was the trap Robert Talbot hadn't even bothered to bait. He'd simply dazzled her bunny eyes and watched her hop through a minefield. Hop from topic to topic (mine to mine)—because the revelation about the casino-trawler was not the only one she made. She was pleased to be entertaining a man whose worth usually made him unavailable to all except a close circle of intimate advisers, pleased to begin to think of herself as one of them. And he talked, too, of course—it seemed like a warm exchange of intimacies. He told her about his fifty-year-old ocean-going yacht made of wood and brass.

"Lovely thing. Sheer luck that I got it—it was for sale in Key West, and a friend of mine happened to see it. Phoned me up and I got him to bid on my behalf, much to the annoyance of some Texan fellow who got there too late. He offered me nearly double the money," he said with grim pleasure. "Of course, it's needed a lot of work—total rebuilding in some parts. But it floats, we got it here, and it will soon be ready to go anywhere. It's like that one in *Some Like It Hot,* where Tony Curtis takes Marilyn Monroe," he said, staring out across the dark road as though he were a be-capped captain and it was a sun-kissed bay.

Rosemary realised all over again that she was not the sort of woman men invited to go around the world in yachts—big, safe yachts too tall for waves to crash over them. The only yachts she'd been on were nervous little racing craft on Sydney Harbour which often threatened to keel over, at which point someone—usually Rosemary—would have to become a human stabiliser, a mere boat-saving object, hanging on straps over the perilous swell while Daniel shouted angry, wind-whipped instructions. She was not the sort of woman invited on large yachts which cruised from places like Rabaul through the D'Entrecasteaux and the Solomons to Cairns; yachts that carried staff to deal with the cooking and the flushing out of the bilge and which had reading rooms with shiny, leather-bound classics and complete sets of *National Geographic*s and visitors' books inscribed with the names and addresses of famous people. The sort of boat Rosemary was invited on usually left her with huge bruises, salt-caked hair and the temper that lies in the ebb of retreating adrenalin. She wished she didn't keep on thinking about Daniel, who, in any case, had sold his boat three weeks before. She remembered how upset they'd all been when they came home to find the garage open and the boat gone—they'd thought it had been stolen until Bobby found Daniel's note in the mail-box.

Rosemary was glad when Robert Talbot got off the subject of his Art Deco–style yacht and his plans to take it around the Solomons when he could get away and onto how restless he sometimes felt in the role his father had created for him. As a result, he said, he had put no pressure on his own son to follow him into tycoondom.

"I sometimes play squash with him, when the time suits us both," he said, and she kindly warned him that for a man of his bulk the occasional, vigorous game of squash could be fatal.

"My doctor tells me much the same. Tells me I've got hypertension. But I indulge in various vigorous body contact sports often enough to keep the heart in trim, I believe." He said this when they'd arrived at Rosemary's house, when his big, heavy fingers were pressing into her arm, when his large, dark face was leaning towards her mouth—her mouth that was as eager and open as a baby bird's. And then, what turned out, after all, to be nothing but a friendly peck on the cheek, had suddenly been bathed in the light of Daniel's car.

.   .   .

Rosemary woke up, startled, to the sound of loud laughter, inharmonious as a metal ratchet grating on a series of cogs.

That first shock turned out to be caused by the kookaburra who normally didn't wake her even when—as she could see in her wardrobe's mirrored door—he was sitting on the balcony railing just outside her window.

She turned to look at the time, and this caused the second shock—

the pain, which wrenched and rippled from her shoulder down her arm and up her neck, leaving her staring, too stunned to move again, at the green digital numerals as they moved from 9:01 to 9:02. Something terrible had happened. It had not been a dream.

She tried to push the images out of her mind: Daniel's wild, triumphant anger. The fall—was it a fall? It had not hurt at all at the time, but now, she felt sure, something was broken. And the shouting. The shouting! Lights had gone on all along the street and the Hermanns from next door had come out to get involved.

Phyl had cried and refused to be touched. Bobby had brushed past her and run into the house, into his room, leaving behind only the impression of huge, reproachful eyes and the sound of a slammed door. And then another slammed door—the Porsche, whose throbbing engine note had receded in direct ratio to the increase in volume of Daniel's voice. Then there were no more images.

I must have fainted! she thought. Someone—Daniel?—must have put me to bed.

Moving very carefully, she lifted the covers and saw that she was still wearing the voile dress. She'd felt so wonderfully sure on the way home in the Porsche. Lying in her bed, Rosemary was engulfed by despair. The tears which trickled into her pillow felt unnaturally hot—perhaps she was ill? Perhaps she had a fever? She wondered if it was possible to die of embarrassment. "You bloody fool," she said. "You bloody idiot!"

"What?" said Phyl, whom Rosemary had not seen coming barefoot over the carpeted floor. "What did you say?"

"I said I'm an idiot. Idiot!"

"You're not, Mum." Phyl stroked her head. "Dad was mean. Do you know what happened? He and Mr. Hermann also had a row and Mr. Hermann threw Dad's keys in the pool!"

"Ouch!" said Rosemary. "I can't move my arm properly . . . there's something wrong . . . my shoulder. No—no don't touch it. Did I faint? I can't remember."

"You did pass out. At first the Hermanns thought you were drunk."

"Oh, why do the Hermanns always get hooked up in my battles with your father? I wasn't drunk, Phyl, I haven't been even slightly drunk for months." Even Rosemary was aware of the regret in her tone.

"Well, you were certainly—what did they do in the fifties movies? Petting? Smooching! Smooching with Mr. Talbot. In the Porsche. We all saw you there—Dad, Bobby, and me—when we came home from the flicks. So Dad just went wild!"

"But I wasn't! I didn't! He just gave me a lift home—otherwise I'd have had to stay in a crummy hotel in Lithgow. And then he gave me a polite little good-night peck on the cheek. Like classy people do. It's just so absurd that you three happened to arrive at that split second—it was nothing!" Which, she told herself, is what was so bloody embarrassing. He must have known how charged up I was, how eager, how easily Daniel could have been right!

Phyl was looking doubtful. "It didn't look like nothing to us."

"But it was nothing! You'd made up your mind that I . . . that he . . . Remember, you said on the phone, 'What's the real reason why you're staying in Lithgow?' And I couldn't tell you, because we'd been cut off. You must have given Daniel the impression . . ."

"Oh, Mum, I didn't! I . . ." But Phyl's easy-to-read face revealed that she was backtracking over her own dinner conversation of the night before. "Oh, how *terrible!* I probably did give him the idea . . . Mum! I didn't mean to. I guess I just wanted him to see that important men still go for you." Phyl's eyes filled with tears. "I'm going to phone him!" she said, and started for the door.

"No, don't. It'll make things worse."

"They couldn't be much worse." Phyl's sturdy, square white hands gripped the door-frame as though discharging their tension into its timber. "I've never seen Dad so furious. He yelled at everybody: Mr. Talbot, us, the Hermanns. He even yelled at Angela, on the phone. He had to take your car—it was too dark to dive for his keys."

Rosemary covered her eyes with the arm that didn't hurt. "Phylly, darling, please will you get me some aspirins. And please, please don't phone Daniel. Don't say *anything* more to him."

"Oh, Mum, I'm so sorry. I'm so sorry. I've really messed it up for you."

No, you haven't. I've done it myself, Rosemary thought but couldn't say. Didn't want to say. Didn't want to think about.

Daniel. Last night he'd turned into Mr. Hyde. She wondered how she'd ever grieved so much for him. Most of all she wondered at the cunning way anger can disguise itself when it needs to escape.

You've really blown it now, she told herself.

.   .   .

Phyl came in with the aspirins and a tray with toast, honey, orange juice, and coffee for a picnic-in-the-bed breakfast, which included Bobby. He followed, still lurching a little from sleep, wearing only underpants since pyjamas are unmanly. His hair was up like Lawrie's shaving brush, his eyes still puffed from sleeping on his face. Without a word he climbed into bed next to Rosemary and snuggled up as though he were still little or as though everything was OK again. She was so pleased, that although he nudged her possibly broken shoulder, she didn't even wince. After nine months of hostility, it looked, at last, as though Bobby had forgiven her. But she felt guilty as she stroked his stiff, wild hair—this was the wrong time for Bobby's forgiveness. She had probably deserved it before but not now.

"Lucy's coming over soon—I saw her in the garden, putting bread on her bird-tray," Phyl said. "Reporters are coming to interview her and Malcolm later. You should see her flowers! Honestly, Mum, her house looks like a posh funeral, and there'll be more today, you bet. We should have sent some, don't you think? And telegrams! There're millions of them. The first interview isn't until just before lunch, so she's got time now. She's having a shower first then she says she's going to take you to Dr. Saxon."

Bobby sat up, startled, which wrenched Rosemary's arm again.

"What's the matter?"

"I hurt my shoulder—my arm last night. I fell."

"Oh, yeah, I saw. It was when Dad and that bloke with the Porsche were yelling." So ugly. A domestic. "But I didn't know you'd hurt yourself. Let's see?"

"I must have tripped," she said blandly, her tone stripped of blame. Carefully she began to peel away the torn dress from her wounded arm and the three of them stared at it in horror. Swelling and dark bruises puffed it up unevenly under skin made unnaturally bright by having had its top layer scratched off. The whole area, from the top of her shoulder to near her elbow, looked as though a piece of some other animal— some exotic reptile—had been grafted onto her. It was almost a surprise to see traces of healthy, dried blood on the maze of scratches. "Oooh, don't touch!" she begged, protectively fluttering her good arm's fingers around the pain. Neither Phyl nor Bobby would have dared.

"Dad was really mad. He swore a whole lot! Mrs. Hermann stayed here with you 'til Dad had gone," Bobby offered.

"Mrs. Hermann was in here? I don't believe any of this!"

"Yes. She wanted to call a doctor last night. But then you woke up, so she decided you'd be okay. She used to be a nurse, you know."

"I didn't wake up."

"Mum! Of course you did. You told us you were fine and that we should go to bed."

I am going crazy, she thought.

"Mrs. Hermann said you were in shock."

"I don't remember anything!" But that's because, she told herself, I don't want to.

"Can you drive with your arm so sore, Mum?" asked Bobby.

"Why? Oh, Bobby! Your dress rehearsal's this afternoon, of course. And tonight's your first night!"

Bobby nodded, warily. "I've ordered the tickets for you and Phyl."

This was a problem. Careful sitting up and careful probing revealed that, despite the aspirins, she could not move the wounded arm without causing sharp flashes of pain. The two children gazed worriedly at Rosemary. This was when Lucy arrived.

"What's the trouble?" she asked, then looked. "Lord, Ro. You should have worn a dress with shoulder pads if you were going to play American football! Oh, shit! It does look awful!"

"Lucy! Lovely Lucy!" Rosemary was eager to get the focus away from her snake-skin wound. "I saw you in the paper! Was it yesterday? Only yesterday? Oh, I'm so thrilled." Rosemary squeezed her hand. "Is Malcolm here?"

"Nope," said Lucy, smiling, smiling. "He's coming later, for interviews in the colour mags and one of the Sundays. It's rough on him: he hates all this."

"And you?"

"I love it! I guess it will pall in due course, when I become an old cynic like him. But now it's such fun—I feel like the princess in the fairy tales. The phone's been driving me mad though; I've left it off the hook."

"How did it happen so quickly?"

"I'll tell you later. Now we've got to get you to the doctor's place before he knocks off. That'll probably need an X-ray."

Phyl helped her mother to the bathroom. The dress was ruined anyway so she cut it off with scissors. Gingerly, she washed the grazes and helped Rosemary most of the way into a white, terry-cloth track suit. Phyl safety-pinned the spare sleeve, and while she was doing it Rosemary noticed her contact lenses were in their little plastic baths in their usual place on the basin shelf. It's true—I must have got up last night! she thought. No one else could have taken them out. How strange that a piece of time can simply be blanked out.

In the bedroom, Lucy was putting down the phone.

"That was Patrick," she said. "He and I have arranged everything."

"Patrick?"

"Yes. He phoned to offer to drive you to Melissa's acting-class party tomorrow. Oh, Rosemary—you've forgotten! You're impossible! Anyway, I told him about your arm so he's coming over. He'll be here when we get back from the doctor."

"Patrick?"

"Rosemary, he's a kind man. He often used to drive you back from the drama class. He likes you! And when he phoned about the party, and I told him about your arm, and that I couldn't help you much today, he immediately offered to drive Bobby to the dress rehearsal this afternoon—and you, too, if the doc says you can go," Lucy added quickly, deliberately avoiding Rosemary's face, since Rosemary's mouth was set in an O of surprise. "I can't take you today, obviously, and Malcolm and I are going to this dinner tonight. Don't look at me like that—it's all right. I didn't ask Patrick—he offered."

"But you hinted!"

"Well, I paved the way. It does seem sensible, doesn't it?"

"Sensible?" Rosemary said in the despairing voice of one who, only yesterday, had felt like a star and then like an orphan lost in the storm and then like a volcano in the blue Porsche. "Sensible?"

. . .

"You've got two choices," Dr. Saxon told her. "You can spend the afternoon in casualty waiting for someone to X-ray this shoulder, after which they'll probably strap you up and send you home. Or you can let me strap you up right now and give you something for the pain. You've got to immobilise it for a while—probably chipped the bone here. It doesn't seem to be fractured." He probed around with strong fingers, making Rosemary gasp and squirm.

"Yes, definitely chipped, I'd say. But the treatment would be similar. If you're still worried about it on Monday, you could have an X-ray then, of course. May be a good idea. I'll give you a note."

"Why should she go to a hospital for the X-ray?" Lucy asked. "I could take her to a private practice. They'd be quicker."

"Those guys don't have to work on Saturdays," he said, trying not to look envious.

Rosemary opted for the strap-now-X-ray-later option and left with her arm in a large, bulky sling which, she felt sure, was going to make her sweat before long. The noonday sun blazed down upon the shopping centre and on the home-going crowd, nearly all of whom appeared to have initiated new, bright sun-dresses, shorts, and strapless tops and T-shirts on this first hot day. She'd have to turn the air-conditioning on for the first time since March if she was going to benefit from the pain-killing, sleep-inducing pills the doctor had given her.

A reporter and a photographer were waiting at the Hermanns' front door for Lucy. Rosemary got a cheery wave from her nurse of the night before.

"You better today, Mrs. Quilty?"

"Yes, yes. Thanks very much for . . ."

"It is perfectly fine. Perfectly. I thought first your husband broke that arm. But it is only sprained, no?"

The reporter—a young woman with frizzy hair, a flowered skirt and lace-up shoes—stared curiously at Rosemary, who was spared further intimate pleasantries by Lucy: "I live around the back," she said firmly. "Please come this way; Malcolm must be there already—that's his car."

From the gate, Rosemary could see that Patrick had arrived already, too, and was walking along the edge of the swimming pool in a pale blue safari suit. From a distance she could see he had his hands behind his back like visiting royalty. Close up she saw smile wrinkles around his eyes.

"Bobby's a good diver," he said. "Could get himself a pearl-fishing job without any trouble. He got Daniel's keys out, one by one—they'd all come off the ring."

Bobby, his hair still wet, his strong body covered in gooseflesh, grinned and towelled himself. "Wow it's cold! We should have a black pool cover, Mum, to solar heat it. It's really icy!" he said. His shivering, Rosemary observed, was at least partly due to nervous tension, so she put her unslung arm around him and kissed his wet ear, though it didn't make him stop towelling.

"You're going to be a great Joseph," she whispered.

"What did the doctor say about you?" asked Patrick. "Can you go?"

This did make Bobby stop towelling, and he waited tensely for the answer, which was the opposite of the one she really wanted to make.

"Yes. Yes, of course. I can't drive, obviously—the BMW's a manual . . . "

"You wouldn't be much good in an automatic either unless you planned to steer with your teeth," said Patrick. "I've got my car here. I'll take you both if you like. But don't you think it would be better if I drop Bobby at the rehearsal and let you get some sleep this afternoon? You don't look much like a theatre groupie at the moment. Is it broken?"

"Is it broken?" Bobby asked, too.

"Chipped, probably. But it hurts like hell!"

"Look, Mum, I don't mind if you're not at the dress rehearsal," Bobby said firmly. "Hardly any mothers will be there, really. They've got teachers and kids from the high school to help with make-up and so on, and you couldn't anyway." She could see he meant it. "You don't even have to come to tonight if you're not feeling . . ." he added more tentatively. This morning's forgiveness had really built a good bridge. But nothing short of hospitalisation for major surgery would justify her non-attendance at the first performance. Besides, she wanted to go.

"I couldn't miss that!" she said. "Not for anything. I'm the star's mother! This is my big opportunity to stand up and yell, 'Look at my boy!' "

"Mum!"

"Truly, I'll be there if they have to take me on a stretcher. Phyl and I. We'll phone a taxi."

"No need—I'll take you," Patrick said. "I'll drop Bobby at the school this afternoon— No, don't argue, please. I've one or two things to do, but I'll be back here before six and then I'll take you and Phyl. Do you think they can find one more single ticket, Bob?"

Rosemary was so amazed, so grateful to this usually self-effacing man, and so laden with guilt and so dazzled by new impressions and by the old ones that had starting spilling out in the last two days from her broken dam of memories, and so tired, that tears filled her eyes. She could feel her nose swelling up, going red and hot. If she'd been wearing her lenses they'd have begun to slide. But Patrick didn't appear to notice, even while she struggled one-handed to extract a tissue from her bag, so that was good.

He strode towards the kitchen with the hearty air of a ranger scout and announced, as though he were a regular at lunch, that he'd heard Phyl say something about sandwiches. And Bobby put his still pool-cold hand in hers and said, "You *really* don't have to come this afternoon. Honest. My costume is fine."

"Dad phoned while you were out." Phyl was finishing off pushing orange halves through the noisy squeezer. She'd made a plate of cheese and tomato sandwiches and decorated them with parsley from the garden and olives from a bottle Rosemary had forgotten at the back of the fridge. "He'll phone again later." Phyl signalled, with her eyes, that he was still upset.

"I suppose it's about the car," Rosemary said graciously, as though the issue was not emotionally laden.

"He didn't mention it. But he did say he can't go to the opening tonight, Bobby. He's sorry. He'll talk to you about going one night next week."

"Yuh?" Bobby bit his disappointment into a sandwich.

.   .   .

Rosemary had taken the first dose of pain-killers while the others were eating, and by the time Patrick and Bobby left she was limp, more than ready to crawl back into her unmade bed. But there, instead of sleep, her new guilt was waiting. Oh, yes, the safety catch of her rage had slipped last night. Her anger at Daniel, so long controlled, was now dangerously ready to wound. Even now, when she was making herself think about it, she wasn't sure of the sequence. Had Daniel started yelling before she got out of the car? Had Robert Talbot waited to hear all the terrible things that Daniel had yelled down the street? Some of them, certainly, because she'd struggled with Daniel, trying to stop him from making dangerous threats:

"There's no one in this town too big to be broken."

"You'd be advised to watch your back."

There were all those other loaded phrases: about casinos and about the politician, and other names she recognised from headlines, and other things that were even less clear but whose significance was revealed in the emphasis and tone of the speakers—or yellers—rather than in her knowledge of where they fitted into the scheme of things. These had all been whizzing around the edges of her memory, confused, since last night's embarrassing melodrama. Clichés. All fights are clichés. It's only the reasons that distinguish them—provided the reasons are understood. Through the noise and her own shock she understood that Daniel believed Robert Talbot's company was trying to take over Patchwork.

She'd grabbed Daniel's arm, pulled him, but his muscles were hard with wrath, his sweat had smelled like metal. When he shrugged her off—brushed her like a blowfly—there'd been enough force to throw her onto the rock garden. Was it then? ("Listen, Quilty, pull your head in. I could break you in so many pieces you wouldn't even be good for fertiliser!") Was this when the Porsche had roared away? And when Daniel had said, louder than all his other shouting, "You already have, you bastard! You think I don't know it! And now you're sniffing around my wife!"

"Stop it, Daddy! Stop it, Daddy!" the children had screamed. But they hadn't been on her side either—not until later, not until Daniel, barred from her bedroom by Mrs. Hermann, had begun transferring his anger into the phone. He'd phoned Angela, Phyl said, and shouted at her. But why? That part was still not clear. Nothing was clear, yet all of it was full of the elements of doom.

For nine months, Rosemary had not only prevented herself from letting out the pure anger, but, with one or two more notable exceptions, she'd even fought against distilling the occasional shot of it and aiming it straight between Daniel's eyes. She'd refused, in fact, to put herself into the sort of clean, open warfare in which all witnesses would have been able to observe that she had given him a chance to duck. When he'd left, he'd taken all the guilt as well, and once she'd understood that, she hadn't wanted any of it back. But she'd got it back now—guilt by the bucketful. More than that—guilt in a tidal wave!

Now that it was over, and enough of the flood of her guilt had ebbed away to reveal the altered landscape, Rosemary could see that the violent shouting had not been about lust at all but about other things that concerned men. She, Rosemary, and that dry little kiss, had actually been incidental. That was so ironic that it left her feeling sick with self-disgust. If that dry little kiss had been followed by a wetter one—one in which she'd participated—there might have been some cause for guilt or blame, though it might be argued that even that would not have represented betrayal. Not betrayal of Daniel anyway—a kiss, however wet, would have been a minor matter in the face of Daniel's adultery, his decampment, his despousement; in the free-thinking, post–sexual liberation 1980s, a kiss that little, though wet, would have been merely a technicality. If the circumstances had been different, she would, by succumbing so eagerly to that kiss, have betrayed no one and nothing except her own determination to stay guilt-free. But in the circumstances she'd betrayed Daniel, and in such an obviously wounded-ex-wifely way that no one would believe her innocent. Certainly not the men. Not either of them.

She had not known Daniel's business was in trouble, though both of them could reasonably believe she had known. She hadn't known, though both of them were undoubtedly sure she did, that her dry-but-maybe-soon-to-be-wet-kissing lover was Daniel's lion. No, that was not a good metaphor—the Biblical Daniel had won. Daniel Quilty looked as though he was about to be—what had his mortal foe said?—smashed into a thousand pieces and used for fertiliser. His mortal enemy, whose power—because of his pull with bank managers, state leaders, judges and federal ministers—was enough to blow a thousand Daniels into pieces without any fear that there would be an inquest into the dust.

As though she'd been plotting revenge or practising spite, she'd given Robert Talbot Daniel's trump card when she told him about the casino and talked about his business plans. To be exact she'd given him Daniel's whole hand—tossed it in, as a small contribution to pass the time between travelling and lust. In nine months, the bottled, fermenting mixture of her rage and hurt had become volatile with its own identity.

And last night, on the journey home, some of it had escaped from her containment, found its own devious way, and homed in on Daniel like one of those heat-sensitive missiles. It had been a possibly fatal blow. The fall-out would be next.

She tossed and ached and fretted and hated herself. There were touches of the fear Pandora must have felt when she opened that box of evils. There was no chance of sleep.

.   .   .

"You haven't slept, Mum, have you? Is your arm very sore?"

"Phyl, where did you come from?" Rosemary asked. "How was I lucky enough to get someone like you for a daughter? I don't deserve it. I seem to spend all my time in tears, or shouting, or being stupid!"

"Shh, shh," said Phyl. "Did you hear the phone? It was Dad. He's crashed your car."

Ten

The green Volvo was smashed. Although she hadn't heard it, Rosemary recognised the sound—it was the rumble of artillery, the first salvo of war.

"Dad is shocked, though, and he's sprained his wrist," said Phyl, and Rosemary had an image of him on a khaki stretcher, a white bandage around his arm and a big red cross.

"One all," she murmured.

"The police drove him home . . . to Angela's place. I told him you were asleep and that you're going to *Joseph* tonight. He says he'll come here tomorrow—he's got something terribly important to talk to you about. Angela will bring him."

"He can't," Rosemary said, slightly panicky, slightly relieved. "I won't be here—I'm going to Melissa's for lunch, with the theatre group."

That was when Phyl burst into tears.

"Darling! Darling! Don't!" Struggling against the bondage of the sling, ignoring the new pain, Rosemary crawled down her bed to where Phyl was sitting, but Phyl shook her head, stood up, and ran out of the room.

"My, God," said Rosemary, fervent as a prayer. "I've failed *her*, too," she said. I can't handle this, it's too much for me, all at once. But she followed Phyl, right up to her slammed door.

"Please go away, Mum. Just leave me. *Please.*"

"I just want to know what's wrong? What's the matter?" But she knew. She had spent the whole day trying to push it out of her mind. Phyl had been a witness, a fellow victim, but one who didn't deserve it. Rosemary tried to brush the wild, vulgar scene out of her mind, believing, as she always had, that problems whose solutions did not immediately present themselves are best left to lie. There was no preventative action possible in a case like this, only distractions.

Rosemary knocked on Phyl's door.

"I don't want a deep and meaningful, Mum."

"What do you want?"

"Nothing."

They both waited.

Rosemary turned the handle and walked in, talking soothingly.

"I've come to tell you about when you were born. I haven't told you that for ages."

Phyl, who had begun to rise indignantly, lay back with a tired sigh and turned to the wall, indicating that this was something she couldn't fight, though when Rosemary took her hand and began to stroke it she stayed stiff, like a museum exhibit.

Phyl's birth had welded Rosemary and Daniel in a unique and terrifying way. They had been married for five months (though even now she edited this out of the story). They were staying at Rosemary's mother's house in Strathfield. Rosemary's mother was away for a fortnight on a cruise-boat holiday that Auntie Gwen and she had planned and saved for. Even now, Rosemary remembered the sense of envy and abandonment she'd felt when they had left on the big, white, streamer-bedecked ship, looking bright-faced with anticipation that had nothing to do with the realities of lumbering pregnancy and a fragile new marriage. But at least Jean had suggested that they stay in her house, which had a TV set and a washing machine and was in every way much nicer than their little unit at Artarmon.

Phyl was not supposed to be born for another month, so that evening, shortly after eating the hamburgers Daniel had brought home, when Rosemary started feeling peculiar, neither she nor Daniel thought of the hospital.

"He was very nice to me—worried, though. Trying to be efficient and then trying not to be cross when things didn't immediately work— you know how he gets. But things didn't get better—I just went on and on squirming around, feeling terrible. Later on, weeks later, I read the book about childbirth your gran had given me, and all the things that were happening to me that night were there, under 'Onset of Labour.' But I'd never read it and never thought of asking questions when Dr. Jensen got me to pee in a bottle every few weeks at the check-up. All that interested me, when he listened to you through my big belly with a thing like an old-fashioned ear-trumpet, was that you were actually in there, with your heart beating. How you were going to get out was something I sort of postponed as a problem for later. Honestly, I must have been mad!"

"I squirmed around on Gran's new couch—she'd just had it re-covered, too, in blue shiny stuff with big pink roses. She and Auntie Gwen adored it. Dad gave me aspirin. Then he gave me hot port-and-brandy which he swore was good for stomach pains. But of course, it got worse. I was so green! I was only two years older than you are now but not as smart—Bobby knows more than I did then. I can't imagine what made you two choose me as a parent!" Phyl, who had gradually lowered the barriers, squeezed Rosemary's hand in response to this commercial.

"Then Dad got that special, serious look, when one eyebrow goes down and his voice gets a speech-making note. You know, when he thinks people might argue. 'I'm going to phone Dr. Jensen and get him to come over,' he said. 'You've got Delhi belly.' I believed him, of course. I believed everything when he talked like that. But while he was dialling, I felt this sort of fast leak—hotter and quicker than pee— run over my legs. I sat up to have a look and it was yellow water. With blood streaks in it, like you sometimes get in soft-boiled eggs. I couldn't stop it—lots of it just poured out, onto Gran's new cover, of course."

"Er yuk. I'm never going to have a baby!"

"I guess that's what I really thought, too, right up to that moment. And what Dad thought, when he saw all that watery stuff, was that I had some strange kind of dysentery and that I was going to die. But at last—and heaven knows, it had taken a while—I'd worked it out and I yelled, 'Daniel, Daniel! It's the baby! For heaven's sake phone him quickly!' I kept thinking 'No, no, not yet. I'm not ready for this. I've got to think about this first. I don't know how to be a mother.'"

"Yes, you do."

"Well, now, maybe. A bit. Sometimes, anyway. You've turned out OK! But eighteen is much too young for motherhood. I didn't even know how to look after myself, let alone someone as little as you. But you, fortunately, were born knowing how to cope."

This had the opposite effect from the one she had intended—Phyl began to cry again, so that what she had to say came out all wet and in bits. It was that she was tired of being seen as efficient and practical and clever and smart—it meant that everyone else around her could go off and be reckless and have fun and leave her to deal with the consequences. "I'll turn out like your Mum," Phyl said. "Working so hard, all dreary. Having no one except—someone like Auntie Gwen. All the others will fall in love with boys, have fun . . ."

Rosemary realised she should not have been surprised that sharp Phyl had defined the relationship between her widowed grandmother and "Auntie Gwen," who, of course, was not an aunt at all. Rosemary herself had been inclined to avoid thinking about it and certainly never talked about it. But that would keep. "You are going to have the most fun, Phylly. It is incredible that you don't know it! You're so beautiful, funny, clever—clever with people as well as things . . ."

"Don't. You don't have to," Phyl sobbed. "No one likes me at school. I'm not part of anything. You know that!"

For a moment Rosemary was shocked, believing Phyl and believing that she herself had been even more blind and self-involved this year than she'd imagined. But the truth bubbled through the doubt. "Phyllis, look at me."

"It's no use! I know what you're going to say and it's all crap!"

"Phyl! Will you just stop? I can tell you right here, right now, exactly what's wrong, because there is not a sensitive person in the world who doesn't go through this at about the same time. You're scared, that's all. Not of not being loved, but of being loved and then being hurt. Scared of the down side. It can't be much fun watching Daniel and me all teeth and claws around you, but it's not always like that, you know that."

"We used to be so happy!" Phyl wailed.

"Well, it's different now. Even though we don't want it to change—didn't want it to change—it has. We can't go on pretending. And we'll be happy again, you'll see." Rosemary was quoting Lucy here rather than speaking with conviction, but saying it surprised her—it felt more true than it had for all the time since the breakup.

"Your gran didn't fall in love again—with a man—because after the war there weren't many around. That's what I think. My father died too young. They hardly had time to learn how to be married. It was terribly tough for her, though of course I really didn't realise that until I was about your age—even then, not really. It's hard to think of a parent as vulnerable." They both had to think about this for a bit.

"I think my mother was shy—scared. Maybe being . . . friends . . . with Auntie Gwen was a compromise. We never talked about it. But *you* won't compromise, darling! You never have about important things."

"I just wish you and Dad would get together again."

"Yes, I know. But we won't. Not anymore—not after last night. Sometimes in all those months when I wasn't talking to him, I felt I'd . . . forgive him eventually. But it really is over. With him and me, not with him and you and Bobby."

"I miss him so much," said Phyl. "I used to think he loved me."

"He still does." This was the hardest part. Her own loss seemed partly deserved: her refusal to become Daniel's fantasy lady, had caused him to go off and seek one somewhere else but the children had been innocent in both behaviour and expectations. "He does really love you, darling. Honestly. He's got a new lover, but no one can replace his kids!"

"Yeah. On alternate Saturdays, going to watch him play golf or freeze and drown in that stupid little boat full of advertising yuppies drinking gin! And that Angela, who wears eyeshadow even when she's bailing out and scraping paint! I don't know how Bobby can stand it!"

But despite this outburst and more of the same, there were signs that Phyl's storm was calming. Any slight new rumbles Rosemary was able to deflect by soothing and reassuring, as though Daniel's defection was as normal and easy to deal with as a failed exam or a lost match. After a bit of this, Phyl looked as though she felt sufficiently cherished so Rosemary decided to be jocular: "And as for you, Miss most-unpopular-girl-in-the-class, it might sometimes be a blessing if you were! The rest of us would be able to sometimes use the phone, or have a bit of the fridge door to stick our invitations on. Certainly we'd see more of you at weekends!"

Phyl smiled feebly. "It's weekend now. And here I am!"

"Only because you turned down two things for your brother's play!" She stroked her daughter's shining hair. I'm not the one to be comforting you about love, she thought. One look at my disasters is enough to put you off men for life.

"I know what you're going to say next," said Phyl. "You get that look. You're going to say, 'Somewhere, darling, there's a boy, just for you.' " Phyl made her voice dramatic in a way Rosemary hoped hers never was. " 'One day soon—sooner than you think, your lives will cross. . . .' "

"I wasn't going to." Rosemary lied.

"Good."

Rosemary looked at her watch: nearly five o'clock. Soon Lucy and Malcolm would arrive. She started to move away but Phyl said, "Aren't you going to finish telling me about . . . I was about half-way born. You can't leave me there!"

"Where? Where were we?"

"Dad was dialling the doctor."

"Ah. Can you imagine him? Not being able to do it right, because of terror? His whole body was shaking as though he were limbo dancing. He got two, three, wrong numbers! Like a nightmare—so slowly, on the one hand, and so fast, for me. I was lying there, getting more and more involved in having you, and Dad was swearing and shouting at the phone. But when he got through, it was a recorded message with an after-hours service number—Dr. Jensen had finished for the day!"

And by the time Daniel had reached the after-hours service and was screaming at the unimpressed woman at the other end, Rosemary was panting, pushing, doing things that suggested themselves to her, much too involved to be very scared anymore.

"All Dad could remember, when we talked about it afterwards, was that he thought that if he didn't do something quickly, I'd die. But I remember that we had a fight about hot water. I couldn't talk much because big, strong hands seemed to be pulling me around inside. It is weird, contractions. You know your muscles are doing it, but you can't stop them or even breathe properly when it happens. So it feels like an invasion. No, not an invasion—an expulsion. Like the opposite of rape."

"Have you been raped?"

"No. No, no. But, you know, how you imagine it: something against your will, pushing in from the outside? In birth, it's something you want, though the process is beyond your will. And pulling from the inside.

"There's a rest between pulls, though not much. But in the rests, Dad and I talked. Or we yelled. He said, 'What should I do?' I still had water leaking out, so I said, 'Get a bucket.' Then I said, 'Get a dish. Get a towel. Phone the police. Hurry. Hurry.' And he did each of those things immediately, as though we were playing Simon Says. But while he was doing them, he kept yelling about boiling water: 'I've got to boil the water. I've got to boil the water.'

"I said I didn't know what to do with boiling water and he said, 'You should know, you're the woman!' Just before the police arrived, you were born. The kettle was screaming! You know those metal ones that sit on gas stoves? We were so amazed by you: you were very small after all that time, that big belly and that struggle. So small, with your face screwed up as though you'd tasted something fairly disgusting—which you probably had, I guess. You looked like a doll someone had dipped in beetroot and sour cream. . . ."

"Oh, Mum!"

"Lying on a wet patch on the couch with the long, slippery cord still joining you to inside me. You didn't look like a real person to us, even though you had all the right things—hair, fingers . . . Then you waved one of your little purple arms and made a sound like a bathroom toy squeezed under water, and we realised that we'd had a baby! And then it was just so incredibly exciting. You can't believe, when it happens, that such a wonderful thing could be. Something that was microscopic—

a speck of jelly a few months before—comes out as a person, looking as though it's entitled to be there and the world should make a space for it.

"There were two policemen, very young. They walked in just when you cried. They looked so shocked, white faces, very serious, though one of them knew a bit about babies. He tied the cord with some of my mother's knitting wool and cut it with a vegetable knife." Politely he had held the bucket and tugged a little at the end, and in a minute, the red, liverish placenta had plopped out. "We didn't think of asking what he did with the afterbirth. But I'll never forget how he stood there, like a butler, at the untidy end of me, holding that slippery rope. He looked so polite!"

His name was Phillip, and the other policeman, the one who'd switched off the kettle and phoned the ambulance, which rapidly arrived in a flourish of bells, was Charlie, so Rosemary and Daniel had named their baby Phyllis Caroline. "Phillipa would have been more exact. But I hate names that are simply female versions of male ones. I used to say, 'Joshuaette. Rogerelle. Craigeen.'"

Later that night, both policemen had gone to the hospital at Daniel's request and the five of them had posed for a picture to accompany the "We did it ourselves" story he wrote for the *Sun Herald*. A yellowed cutting was in Phyl's album, and Rosemary took it down to look at again. Once there had been dozens of copies left over from the stack Daniel had brought home to send to friends and relatives, but this was the last one left.

Daniel looked so fresh-eared, so thin-necked, so vulnerable, and she, despite the sweeping sixties eye make-up, pouting, pearlised lips, and beehived hair, revealed fear and smugness in about equal proportions. Phyl looked surprisingly alert for an hours-old baby, staring with apparent interest at the camera, and Constables Phil and Charlie looked embarrassed.

"Poor Dad. He vowed he'd never do the trendy thing and come into the labour ward. You and I tricked him." It was their little joke, one Phyl had adored when she was five.

"He's so worried, Mum. He said Patchwork is in trouble. It's . . . it's being attacked. Sabotaged, he said. Most of the biggest clients have just . . ."—and Phyl cut her throat with her finger.

"Yes."

"He says he's losing all his clients. He's even lost Glen Rossfield!" (The winery. Their first major account.) "He was trying to be funny about it—you know Dad. He told it to us like 'Ten Green Bottles Hanging on the Wall.' "

And I, thought Rosemary, by blabbing about his secret plans for a casino, cut the string on the last green bottle. She wished everything would stop happening for a while—enough time to let her get her grip and her balance back. Everything now seemed to suggest urgency, but everything was detached from her. She felt the way a mother would feel, looking through glass at her silently screaming baby: she should pick it up and deal with it correctly, but she couldn't even reach it.

She had another look at the rusk-coloured newspaper picture of the thin, confident young man who used to be Daniel and felt the fear, light as a cat lick. Disaster had started, even before Phyl brought the news of the car crash. Something catastrophic was preparing to happen.

.   .   .

Rosemary and Phyl were still holding hands, friends again despite their fear. This time there had been no point in Rosemary's usual promise that everything would be OK because there was no evidence to support it. Things that had seemed temporary, or sure, were different now.

"Hullooo! Anybodyome?" Lucy called, as she always did when there was no one in the kitchen. "We've got rid of the paparazzi and come for a drink with real people! Hullooo!" She found them there, in Phyl's room. "Oops. A heart-to-heart. This is a bad time."

"No, no," they both said, moving quickly to demonstrate energy, pleasure, and the appropriate mood for an engagement celebration.

"Wonder what the loser looked like?" Malcolm said, nodding, smiling at Rosemary's sling.

"Ohh, that particular part of the rock garden will never tangle with me again," said Rosemary, karate chopping the air with her good arm. "Phyl, there's that bottle of champagne in the fridge . . . would you get it, darling?"

"More champagne," growled Lucy, smiling. "I may die from it!"

Mattie had come, too, and had placed herself firmly between Lucy and Malcolm, twisting her mother's new pale, square-stoned ring, wriggling, humming, drumming her heels. Rosemary wished Bobby were there—Mattie was inclined to glue her shadow to his and he minded it less than he pretended. She was pleased to see that Malcolm's hand was resting lightly on Mattie's hair; he had already made some progress along the step-path, though with that difficult, somewhat hyperactive little girl there was sure to be some rough track ahead.

"What I want to know is, how did it happen so quickly? I mean, had you decided when we went out to dinner? When did you get the ring?"

Lucy and Malcolm glanced at each other and smiled, and Lucy extended the aquamarine for Rosemary's inspection. "Malcolm had it: his mother's. We picked it from a little trove she kept in a black enamelled box. Isn't it gorgeous? Set in the thirties, though you'd think it was last week, in Double Bay. That's if, like me, you don't know much about how stones are cut, of course. A modern cutter would have tackled this one very differently, I'm told."

"Mummy was on TV," said Mattie, grabbing the attention like a soccer ball. "Did you see her?"

Rosemary glanced at Lucy, hoping for an I'll-tell-you everything-later look, but she was gazing at Malcolm with an expression as clear, wholesome, and old-fashioned as an advertisement for honey.

"On TV, hey. Did she look nice?"

"Yes," said Mattie, squirming more, thought Rosemary, like a five-year-old than a nine-year-old. Mattie fancied the itsy-bitsy-girlie role, usually lugging dolls around and shoving them in adults' faces in lieu of conversation. Phyl had spent most of that age up a tree, in a go-cart, or reading.

"Lucy's really something on the box," said Malcolm. "I've got the announcement on video—I'll show it to you next time I come. She's got star quality. Someone'll snap her up, you'll see. First the weather, next the late news . . . stay tuned. Next it'll be her own daytime show. . . ."

"Oh, Malcolm, don't talk rubbish," said Lucy, who could not have looked more pleased.

"How's your book going, Lucy?" Phyl asked.

"Book? Oh, about divorce." Lucy giggled. "I've been right out of the mood for anything that serious."

"It wouldn't sell," said Malcolm in his guru voice. "I told her to stop wasting her time."

Lucy shone, like newly sculpted alabaster.

The conversation stayed light. Lucy must have told Malcolm about the day on the film set and the subsequent accident, but he made no reference to it until they were leaving—which coincided with Patrick's arrival and a flurry about lateness.

"Pity you haven't got a Porsche tonight," Malcolm said, grinning at Rosemary. "That'd get you to your son's play in plenty of time for the first act!" Rosemary was embarrassed and she knew it showed, which made her cross, so when Malcolm leaned towards her to kiss her cheek, she shrugged him off a little—just enough not to be sure, afterwards, what he'd murmured. Something like "people mover" she'd heard, but not the rest, though his tone implied a warning.

· · ·

"Please pour yourself a drink," she said to Patrick. "The weekend papers are here—I haven't even unrolled them today! Phyl can help me into something a bit better than this track suit—we won't be long. We've got to be there by seven-thirty, so if I hurry we'll have about half an hour to grab something to eat on the way."

"I've got an excellent digestion," Patrick said. "Years of eating and running from the lab to the university—I'm used to managing hamburgers while I drive. But don't you think it would be nicer to forget about dinner first and have something afterwards? All four of us?"

He was right of course: it would take the pressure off the time. So she didn't even argue, instead she brought him a tomato, a chunk of Havarti cheese, and a packet of sliced black bread. It was only while she was dumping them on the table near him that she realised how unusual it was for her to give a guest things in packets: normally she'd have transferred them onto little plates, added parsely and table-napkins, and sliced the tomato instead of presenting it whole with a sharp knife.

"Would you like some wine?" she asked.

"Only if there is some open." There was. "Don't worry—I'll help myself," he said. He was disconcertingly un-guestlike, relaxed in his blue suit, one leg crossed high over the other knee so that his bright red sock showed beyond its top—a stretch of pale, sinewy calf. He had on black shoes. He must be colour-blind! she thought, and smiled politely at him.

Dressing carefully around the obstacle of the sore shoulder she thought again of the non-conversation with Malcolm and Lucy. She should have told him how pleased Robert Talbot had been by the headline announcements in the *Mirror* and the *Sun,* but she couldn't bear to think of Robert Talbot.

It bothered her that, although they'd seen each other nearly every day in the past week, Lucy had not told her how Malcolm had come to terms with his guilt about his wife. Or when he—and Lucy, for that matter—had started divorce proceedings against their spouses. It was a bit weird. Almost everything that had happened in the past two days was a bit weird.

· · ·

In the car, Phyl and Patrick did most of the talking, mainly about hydrology, which was his subject, and which Phyl knew enough about to keep the talk going. She knew, for instance, that a hundred years ago Sidney Kidman had observed, while droving cattle through the dry emptiness of central Australia, that the periodic flooding of north Queensland's big rivers sent the overflow thousands of miles across the central plains. Then the water would sink and be stored underground— liquid assets, more precious than gold. So Kidman bought properties, one after another, in a chain of potential oases that virtually stretched from the the top to the bottom of the continent and this became the most valuable stock route in Australia, maybe even the world.

Though Rosemary noticed that both Patrick and Phyl shared her fascination with the phenomenon of deserts that can be made to live, she did not get involved—she was preoccupied with dread. Details she could have dealt with. If there had been a program of what was going to happen she might have been able to debate herself into a state of preparedness. She would have begun to cope. But this measureless, directionless terror was exhausting. On the one hand she needed to know what Daniel had to tell her, but on the other hand she didn't ever want to know. By the time they reached the school and had edged into what already looked like the last parking place—despite the fact that the curtain would not go up for another forty minutes—Rosemary's hands and neck were wet with tension sweat.

The noise that emanated from the school hall would have ripped through a state of unconsciousness; certainly it temporarily obliterated her unease. With Phyl and Patrick she picked her way through swirls of excited children, most of whom ran whenever they needed to move. She was very glad to be here, in a nice, safe, recognisable atmosphere of theatrical fantasy.

Other parents had placed bags, programs, and jackets on front seats to reserve them—like most school halls it was not sloped—and had then gone outside to drink sweet, chemical orange squash, urn tea, instant catering pack coffee, or water from the bubbler, which were the choices. Some she recognised but didn't know well enough to care about the curious looks they gave her arm. And the curious looks they gave Patrick, who walked as closely and protectively as though he'd been caring for her for years. It didn't help to create a space between them— he kept closing it.

She was not exposed for long in this embarrassing way. Most of the parents and grandparents looked happily expectant, a little patronising, and a little stunned, but that was not how Rosemary felt—she had a role in this. She left Patrick and Phyl to guard the three chipped blue-enamelled hire chairs which were their seats and fought her way behind

the stage and through the thickest knot of stage-door johnnies and
jennies jostling for a peek at the costuming process. Inside were three
noisy and only partially effective prefects, whose job it was to keep non-
essential people out. They didn't dare quibble with a mother.

Bobby, waiting to be made-up by one of three overworked teachers,
was gleaming with pre-stage energy, and, as usual, its overflow made
him tremble. He barely glanced at Rosemary, since his peers and fans
were around, so she adopted a suitable mode: neutral, verging on humble, and touched him like a professional dressmaker or a valet, not a
mother. "Costume all right, Bob?" she asked.

"Yeah. Spose." They both knew how pleased he'd been with it when
he first tried it on and had stunned himself by his reflection: Joseph, a
youth of stature, swathed in opulence. "Dress rehearsal was up to shit."

She'd given up on his language. "Were you OK?"

"Yeah—no. No one was really OK. The dancing was the worst. Mrs.
McWilliam had a fit all afternoon. Geez, she's a shrew!"

"Familiar. Most directors are torn up at dress rehearsals. And you
haven't forgotten—a lousy dress-rehearsal means a good performance?"
He was not comforted. "Did you eat anything?"

"Nah. Someone nicked my money."

"Good grief! Can we get something here? You'll be famished!"

"Stop fussing, Ma!"

"Milk bar over the street's open, Miz Quilty," said a muscular, be-
spectacled boy who didn't seem to have any real reason for helping to
crowd the dressing room. She decided to give him one.

"You're . . . ?"

"Mike. Mike Aronson."

"Mike! Could you do me a huge favour? If I give you the money,
would you go over and get Bobby—Bob—a hamburger with the lot?
And a strawberry Moove?"

"Sure!" he said, delighted. No prefect could bar him now and as well
he scored a chocolate Moove for himself. Bobby pretended not to hear
all this while dealing with a few more fans and mockers who had slipped
past the prefect barrier, but Rosemary knew he was pleased. She fiddled
one-handed with his make-up, which he endured while screaming the
odd obscenity past her ear at anyone he particularly liked, and without
embarrassing him she managed a sort of semi-hug. "You'll be divine!"
she said. "I'm so proud of you." He'd heard, she knew. She left just as
Mike, the hamburger, and the Mooves came triumphantly in. "Watch
the sauce on that robe!" she called over the tumult. Anyway, it was
predominantly red.

The orchestra was made up of individuals so supercharged with importance that they all looked like soloists. Its conductor, a teacher famous for the brown curls which sprang damply from her unsleeved armpits and for her little squeaky voice, surprised Rosemary by bringing them to order with just a look. And the show began—for Rosemary a golden blur of sound and pride.

Her head and throat felt full of soaking, swelling rice, which is how an excess of mother-love feels in public, and bits of its excess trickled down her cheeks through Bobby's main solo. His clear, high voice and strong gestures made him look like a young priest, or the vision of a saint in an old stained-glass window. He was perfectly in control, a message she received with humble gratitude: from the beginning he'd always seemed to her too vulnerable for real survival.

With him it had been a better class of pregnancy, with expensive maternity dresses, a Macquarie Street obstetrician, and plenty of fuss. But both Daniel and Rosemary had been so afraid of another impromptu home delivery that they were alert to every twinge. From the seventh month they'd arrived at the hospital, suitcase in hand, no less than five times. Eventually the obstetrician had taken pity on them and induced Bobby in his thirty-ninth week, leisurely, in a labour ward. Which was fortunate—he'd had the cord around his neck, and quick and skillful things had had to be done while he was being born. Secretly Rosemary still felt apologetic about having rushed him into the world before he was quite ready. He'd always been so much more volatile, so much less trusting than Phyl.

Rosemary had always ascribed the keys in which both children played their lives to the circumstances of their births, but now it looked as though, in both cases, she had over-simplified: Bobby was tougher and Phyl was frailer than she'd ever allowed herself to believe before this extraordinary day.

The finale filled the stage just as it should, and the violinists, right next to where Rosemary, Phyl, and Patrick were sitting, looked as though they'd saw themselves in half in their efforts to keep up with the volume. Fortunately they couldn't. The singing transcended them, and Rosemary—perhaps only Rosemary—heard Bobby's voice rise clearly through the chorus. A year of effort, much of it intensely emotional, had become a loud and tender triumph.

Neither the cast nor much of the audience wanted them to stop, so they bull-roared the final song as encore number three and would have done it again if Mrs. MacWilliam hadn't stepped on the podium for the rescue. Her cast clearly had enough energy for not just four but forty-four more performances she said, and they agreed at great volume. But it was the teachers and parents she was thinking about. "They're saints, or mad, these teachers who take on so much," Rosemary said to Patrick, and he smiled brightly, having probably not heard over the cheering.

She was so tired that she felt dizzy and as though her joints were filled with dry chemicals. Her arm throbbed and ached—she was sure it must be cracked. The prospect, now, of being cheerful at dinner with Patrick was the worst thing she could think of; had it still been the old time, with Daniel, she'd have begged off and let the three of them go without her. But now there was nothing to compare her life with any-more—everything was out of her control.

"Are you feeling all right?" Patrick asked in the shock of fresh air outside the hall. "Your arm . . . ?"

"No, fine, fine," she lied, the female tiger making sure of her children's nourishment. For them she would endure.

He had booked a table at a Mexican restaurant, a touch of quiet efficiency which Rosemary found impressive. It meant he had discovered the time the play would end and that he knew about children's appetites. He must have made the necessary phone calls while she was dressing. Daniel was efficient, too, but he crowed like a cockerel about his every doing and always invoked the assistance and loyal support of at least one admirer, if not a claque, in every undertaking.

Patrick left her sitting in his car, and he and Phyl went to help peel Bobby away from his cloak and his friends and enemies, and she was left with Daniel, who was still in residence in her head. He had filled it so firmly with memories and fear that everything she experienced was coloured by his presence, totally altering her view as though she were looking at the world through a sheet of Daniel-coloured cellophane.

It was worse than the worst times of marriage, without, any longer, even the faintest hope of kissing and making up afterwards. Perhaps, she thought anxiously, he'll be there forever, a ghost in my head, ready to haunt all comers. It was worse than grief, this sense of unfinished business that could stay there, unfinished, forever, clogging up the paths to progress.

Once she got to the dark, over-warm restaurant full of people enjoying themselves, Rosemary felt better. And then dinner with Patrick turned out to be not just bearable but interesting. Bobby was on a such a high that he had charm to spare, and Phyl had never been short of it, so between them they ran most of the family's contribution to talk and

Rosemary was free to float. She'd known Patrick for over a year, but this was the night she discovered he was a scientist, that he was widowed, and that he had a son.

"Geoffrey. Geoff. He is sixteen now."

"Where does he go to school?" Phyl asked. They were the same age; their paths could have crossed.

"A special school, near where we live, in Lane Cove. He's handicapped." Before the pause could become uncomfortable, Patrick easily continued. "He is very sweet, Geoff. Mad about animals, so I keep quite a menagerie for him—all sorts of things, some of which I'm sure we're not allowed to have, like bandicoots. Couple of little grass snakes, too, who are always scaring the . . . the babysitters." Rosemary noticed that he was shredding the edges of his paper napkin and rolling very thin snakes as he talked. "Even got a duck that thinks Geoff's his mother. Follows him everywhere, and I mean everywhere, so the carpet is full of progress indicators."

Bobby looked puzzled.

"Duck poo," said Rosemary and Phyl in chorus, and the children shrieked with laughter. All tension ceased as though it had been switched off with an ignition key.

"Geoff's good now—easier to be with. He's learned to see to himself —use the toilet and so on. The school has been marvellous for him. He's learned to play some of those games on a computer and spends a lot of time zapping the various chewy monsters."

"That's clever. It's clever to do that," Phyl reassured him, and he nodded politely, one used to being told things he knew.

"Ah, gee, I want one of those," said Bobby, zapping imaginary monsters with his teeth and fingers. "Zuh! Zuh! For Christmas, maybe?" and he wiggled his eyebrows hopefully in Rosemary's direction. She ignored him. They had already discussed the fact that this was to be a budget Christmas. Discussed is too polite a word—they had yelled at each other until Lucy, who was visiting, had said, "Lay off your mother, you little rat!" and then felt ashamed for interfering.

"Geoff comes home at weekends, usually, though sometimes if I've got something else to do he'll stay there on Saturday or Sunday or sometimes both days. Then I'll fetch him for a couple of days during the week instead."

"Like this weekend?" said Rosemary, remembering the 'one or two things to attend to' he'd mentioned at lunch-time. Taking the Quiltys to the play had become important enough for Patrick to change his retarded child's usual program. Patrick looked right at her, seriously, blue-eyed.

"Yes," he said.

No, she thought anxiously. Red socks! Be kind, she thought. Think how proud he'd have been of Bobby.

So she was kind, laughing at his jokes and beaming at her children. Bobby was noisy, verging on rude in his excitement, but she kept smiling at him. What the hell—he needed to feel glorious. So there was a lot of laughing as they worked their way through the crisp, cheesy mounds of enchiladas, tortillas, refried beans, and avocado and crêpes and ice cream: enough food, Rosemary said, to keep them proteinated for three days.

"There's no such thing as proteinated," Phyl said, glancing at Patrick for scientific corroboration.

"There is now," said Rosemary and was fairly pleased to observe that he didn't take sides.

.　　　　.　　　　.

"Bed! Bed! Bed!" she said as they reached her house, just in case Patrick was hoping for coffee. Or just hoping. So he escorted her to the door and said he'd pick her up next day at eleven for Melissa's lunch at Palm Beach. Then he went back to his blue-grey Holden Commodore and didn't see her read the note that Lucy, who had a spare key, had stuck on the hall mirror:

"Daniel says no matter when you come home you must phone. Sounded more than urgent. Don't like his tone, so you won't. I'll be home around midnight if you need a shoulder or, better still, another good hand with a gun."

Anxiously she reached for the phone. Then: But I can't! she thought, almost relieved—I haven't got his number. Then: Stuff him anyway, she thought. What a father, expecting me to be home on Bobby's big night!"

So she went to bed instead. But there she couldn't sleep.

I wish I could have phoned, she debated. Daniel needs me. He wouldn't let Bobby down for nothing. Then: Needs me? Bugger him!

Eleven

"Bloody hell!" Rosemary said aloud. It was two-thirty and she was still tossing. She wished she could phone Daniel. She was glad she could not. She was glad she'd burned the phone number and flushed the ashes.

She got up and went to the kitchen to make some hot milk, and when she switched the light on three medium-sized cockroaches dashed out of the sink and hid under the dishwasher. So much for show-room cleanliness.

"Blast you!" she said, and did, using so much killer from an aerosol can that it made her sneeze. It was trendy, she knew, to pretend to ignore cockroaches or even to welcome them. She'd heard how clean they kept themselves, grooming their little feelers straight after coming out of the garbage. But it was their sneakiness she hated, the role even the little ones played right from hatching: stealing, thieving, leaving their droppings like burnt toast crumbs to show where they'd been. Not even the hospitals were free of them, she'd heard.

She took the milk back to bed when the sneezing stopped, but then she had to deal with streaming eyes and a runny nose for a while and that woke her up even more thoroughly. And her arm ached and ached despite the pain-killers. What did he want? What could possibly have happened to make Daniel so determined to see her? He had been on his way when he crashed the car. She half expected, half wished the phone would ring and that it would be Daniel, to get it over with, however bad it may be. And she wished she could sleep.

It must have been about four o'clock—the sky was lightening already—when Rosemary finally did fall asleep, so heavily that if the kookaburra came she didn't hear him, even in her dreams. Daniel's phone call woke her and Phyl up at ten, and they both answered it on different extensions.

"Rosemary? Where the fuck have you been? Didn't you get my message?"

She heard Phyl put her phone down and didn't blame her: Daniel's voice was heavy with menace. Rosemary quickly put up the defence of mild good manners: "I haven't got your home number, Daniel."

"Have you any idea how serious this is?"

"No. But you sound upset. Is it about the car?"

"The car? Fuck the car! That's nothing! Listen, where the hell were you last night? I tell you, I don't like the company you keep!"

"I was where you should have been—at Bobby's opening night."

He paused, but not for long. "And then?"

"It doesn't matter. The children were with me. What is it that's so urgent? I can't take much more of this yelling and screaming, this mystery, this accusation. . . ." She was doing well, she thought— he could not have heard the effects guilt was having on her heart's pumping.

"I'm coming over right now. There is a lot to talk about and most of it is bad news."

"No, no. You can't—I'm being picked up in less than an hour, and it's too late to cancel now. Tell me on the phone."

"Bugger that! If you go gallivanting off again you'll regret it," said Daniel.

Rosemary put down the phone. "No, I won't," she told the disconnected receiver. "Whatever it is could not be as bad as having to put up with you in that mood." But it was bravado: her heartbeat had become even louder. Feeling slightly dizzy, she leaned back against the headboard and cuddled her sore arm with her good hand. What the hell did I do that for? she asked. I don't even want to go out with Patrick. I could have got out of Melissa's damn party—she'd have understood. I could have known the worst. Got it over with. I'm a bloody ostrich. I'm a bloody coward . . .

"Mum? You OK?" It was Phyl at the door.

"Yes. Oh, yes," she lied. "It wasn't anything much—he's feeling a bit guilty about not being at Bobby's play last night." In fact it sounded convincing enough to be the truth—it was possible, even likely, that Daniel was being melodramatic still, absurdly jealous about Robert Talbot. The worry lines slowly smoothed away from Phyl's face.

"Have you got a lot of homework, darling? I'm going to this end-of-term do at Melissa's. You could come if you like."

"No, no. I'll be fine. I was thinking of going to the Domain this afternoon, anyway—quite a lot of the kids from my class will be there.

We're supposed to go to the Art Gallery—which we'll do quickly and then go for coffee somewhere near the park."

"And Bobby? Will he go with you, my poor unpopular child?"

Phyl grinned but otherwise ignored the jibe. "No. I heard him on the phone yesterday, talking to Jon Rankin. Jon's dad is taking them surfing at Collaroy. We'll be OK. Just leave us some hamburger and bus money. We'll both probably be back on the six o'clock bus."

Phyl helped with the showering and dressing. It worried Rosemary that her arm was still so painful, especially when she had to move it away from her body, even slightly. Phyl had had to thread a soapy face-cloth between Rosemary's arm and her body and pull it back and forth, as though her mother were a gun barrel. It was a painful process that left Rosemary's nerves splayed like unconditioned hair. She was not ready when Patrick arrived: her hair had been a problem Phyl couldn't solve and Rosemary couldn't cope with, and they had started snapping at each other as they both got more and more anxious. Rosemary's eyes were full of tears of pain and irritation because the brush kept on becoming entangled so that every attempt to free it pulled at the fine hairs around the edges.

Phyl's efforts had resulted in an over-teased style Rosemary hated—it was much too high on top, and, she thought, old-fashioned. But, one armed, there was little more she could do to flatten it than bash it with a brush. It was while doing this that she looked out of the bedroom window and saw Patrick. He was dressed in a co-ordinated beige leisure outfit of the sort middle-aged male models display in glossy summer catalogues—or had done, two years before. He was looking pleased with himself—fresh-faced, healthy, and well-rested.

"Oh, Lord!" Rosemary murmured. "Here we go."

"Did you sleep well?" he asked as they drove away.

I must look pretty ghastly, she thought, and said, "No. I tossed for hours, doing something that I've been bothered with for the past three days, which is remembering things. I've been sort of haunted by my own life. You know how they say people's lives flash before their eyes at the instant of dying? I'm having a three-day instant."

"And not dying."

"Not yet. Not physically, anyway. But I have this weird, strong feeling that my life—the way is has been up to now—is dying. That I'll be—have to be—sort of reconstructed."

This is dangerous talk. He'll start seeing a role for himself, she thought. So quickly, before he could respond, she said, "I shouldn't be going to this party. Daniel phoned. In fact, there was a message from him last night when I got back. He wants to see me urgently, but I put him off."

"Are you worried? I mean, would you rather not go to Melissa's?"

"No, no," she said, with argument-proof charm. "Maybe it's not about anything serious. Money, probably, or arrangements about the car. He's very upset because I got a lift back from a job interview on Friday night with someone he doesn't like and he happened to arrive at the same time."

Patrick was amused. "Not Robert Talbot by any chance?"

"How on earth did you know that?"

"Something one of the children said last night—about you in a Porsche, coming back from Lithgow. A young neighbour of mine happens to be one of the sound people on the set, so I know Talbot's making a film there. I put two and two together."

"Well, so did Daniel, but he's come up with five. Or even seven. I get so mad! I mean, he went off with . . . with whatsername. The secretary. But he still feels like a . . . pasha about me. As though he's bought me by paying the children's food and school bills. He's ridiculous!"

He glanced at her, perhaps checking her face for bitterness. She didn't know what he had seen there, but whatever it was she decided to change the subject. "Since this is a reunion party, do you think Melissa has invited Terry the Pregnant Man and Friend?"

"No. Melissa went right off Terry. Right off Australia's Harold Pinter."

"Did she call him that?"

"Yes. In fact, once, when she was really drunk, she compared him with Beckett."

Rosemary laughed but then suddenly felt depressed. Stage-managing *Mother Love* and acting in *Cat on a Hot Tin Roof* had seemed so important at the time. The theatre group and the other things she'd made herself do for all those months had given her a sense of independence. "See," she'd been saying to the world, "I can have an interesting life even without a husband." It had also helped to blot out any deep feelings, since the involvement had occupied every minute, every brain cell, every muscle. But all that time Patchwork PR had been in trouble. What had Daniel called the theatre group? A geriatric play school? He wasn't far wrong. Daniel must have needed her—needed to tell her about what was happening to him and to the company, and she'd been too angry to let him. If it hadn't been for her pride and her hurt and her anger she could have helped him save it. Poor Daniel! But I mustn't be too hard on myself. He did go off with another woman. And he didn't try very hard to contact me. Daniel is never put off if he really wants to talk to someone.

But somehow the case for herself sounded hollow in her own ears.

"Look at that," said Patrick, waving his arm towards the sea. They were going around the bush-banked S-bends near Bilgola, the rough, bright green of the tree-tops forming a dense, bumpy carpet that looked almost safe enough to walk on between the high road and the butter-coloured beach. The blue-green sea ended in a strip of white, frothy as a flower-girl's petticoat, against a curve of headland. There was a scattering of distant people—bright-coloured ants, their beach umbrellas like pretty winged creatures just landed. Sun-feeding creatures, she thought. By dark the world will belong to itself again.

"Palm Beach'll be packed," said Patrick, as though he'd read her mind. It was. From Avalon to Palm Beach the traffic would have looked, to any passing super-hawk, like a lumpy snake or a slow-moving necklace. At least half the cars carried surf-boards or sail boards or trailed boats.

"Could we leave early? Before most of them? We'll be stuck forever in this, otherwise," she said.

Melissa's father's house was in a street near enough to the beach to make parking attractive to some of the hundreds who overflowed the council lots, and her driveway was already full of guests' cars when Patrick arrived at the gate. Melissa, who'd arrived at the door to greet a previous carload, waved her gin at them. "Get in anywhere. Bugger the 'No standing' signs. If the worst comes to the worst, you'll get a parking ticket, but it's better than going home without a drink!"

For as far as they could see, the side of the road was full of vehicles, many of which would have to scratch themselves and each other to get out again. Or wait. Rosemary felt a splash of panic. But Patrick was immensely calming, and, to her amazement, a car moved out of a perfectly legitimate spot hardly any distance from the house, in the shade and out of danger, just as they reached it.

"Positive thinking," he said, laughing at her.

Melissa had vanished from the front door when they got there, but they followed the noise through the vast, cool house out onto a big wooden verandah. This was full of long trestle tables covered with glasses and drinks. Apart from two bowls of peanuts, there was no visible food. The verandah opened onto a cobbled patio enclosed on three sides by the house's wings and over the long view of a majestic, old-fashioned garden was Pittwater and the Pacific Ocean.

Dark headlands and islands curved into it, providing jigsaw shapes as a foil for the hundreds of little white triangles that flitted on it: the sails of a random flotilla of small and large boats with a combined value probably worth more than Australia's national debt. The water was bright as polished sapphire through the clean, semi-tropical air. Although they were only an hour's drive from the heart of Sydney, mangoes and flame-trees flourished, and even in the heat of the day the sound of birds was loud and various. There were frangipanis like explosions of cream stars, their blooms so dense that the ugly, stunted branches were completely hidden. Her mother had chopped down a struggling frangipani from their back garden at Strathfield—it had seldom bloomed and was usually covered in a coating of black dust from the nearby traffic. She'd said the tree looked like old men's dicks, but here, in its right surroundings, the frangipani tree looked like a wedding day. Hibiscus in bridesmaid colours and a few late roses dotted the lawn between the massive trees. Melissa's father must have started the garden in the thirties, Rosemary decided.

Melissa had set small tables and beach umbrellas around the patio between large white pots of brilliant red, blue, and purple petunias. As though posing for a painting or a magazine cover, her friends sat in attractive groups and looked happy. People waved and shouted.

"What a setting this would be for a restaurant!" she said to Patrick.

"Yes. They could do it, too. You should see the kitchen—massive, brilliantly equipped, like a three-star hotel without trying."

"Patrick, you naughty person! What *have* you been doing to Rosemary?" This, with a sweaty hug, was Melissa's welcome, and it had the effect of bringing people around them to exclaim over the sling and, to Rosemary's embarrassment, to give pleased and knowing looks about the fact that she'd arrived with Patrick.

"Sorry about the parking," said Melissa when the sling had lost its novelty value. She was wearing a flowing black cotton robe she claimed a Bedouin had given her in exchange for her rubber thongs on a trip to Morocco, in circumstances which grew more bizarre with each telling. "In theory, we could turn the front garden into a car park. But would you cut down a hundred-year-old angophora to make life easier for your friends? No! You'd make them suffer, like I do. Put them to the test—see if they're prepared to survive the traffic for love."

"Oh, we are," said Rosemary solemnly. "We do." She took a tall glass full of floating fruit and the effluvia of rum which Melissa offered. An apricot-coloured hibiscus flower was attached to the blue plastic drinking straw in hers and after the first sip she noticed that a stream of black ants, like bumper to bumper traffic, was marching out of the heart of the flower. The drink was syrupy and over-strong. She would have preferred mineral water, but there didn't seem to be any.

"There you are, you two! Hello, darlings," Martha called, pink-cheeked

and beaming with pleasure. Rosemary glanced at Patrick for confirmation that Martha had been matchmaking, but he was turned away, smiling
and talking to some of the other people who had been in *Cat on a Hot
Tin Roof.* He seemed hardly to notice his aunt as she hurried towards
them, splashing her gin on the brick paving.

Martha nearly always wore a little hat. Today it was a white beret—
a token to summer perhaps—but usually it was a close-hugging, dark
grey thing that was known, behind her back, as Martha's cat. She never
said and no one mentioned that they knew it was because there was a
wig under it—one whose parting was, perhaps, a give-away. Rosemary
walked towards her, widening the gap between herself and Patrick.

"Traffic bad?" Martha kissed her cheek.

"Yes, fairly. But I probably held Patrick up a bit, having got up late
myself. You look like a teenager in those polka dots!"

"Pretty flashy, huh?" Martha preened. "Strapless. Not bad for sixty-
five, what do you say? I mean, this is all me here—no bones, no falsies."
She pummeled her chest with a wrist ringing with silver, copper, and
turquoise bracelets. "You look good, too, apart from that," she lightly
touched the sling. "Colour co-ordinated to match. I've always liked
broderie anglaise."

"It suits my current virginal state," Rosemary said quickly, hoping
Martha would get—and perhaps even pass on—the message. Then she
realised she could have sounded regretful rather than content so added
primly, "It was so kind of Patrick to give me a lift. My car's out of action
at the moment."

"He's the nicest man I know. Though I shouldn't say that about my
blood relation, should I?"

"Why not? He's very kind—drove me and Phyl to Bobby's opening
last night."

"Ah, his Joseph, of course. And he was a triumph?"

"I shouldn't say that about my blood relation. But yes, he was."

"He's your son, that Bobby. You all over again, with added testos-
terone."

Rosemary was so astonished that she could not speak for a few moments and by the time she could, Melissa had stolen Martha away.

People kept on attracting her attention, and she kissed, smiled, chat-
ted, laughed, finished her drink, and took another, having decided that
the taste was not bad if she didn't breathe while sipping. She waved
hello to Melissa's father, a short, thin old man in white who had the
attention of some of the younger girls.

"I was fifteen, thereabouts, when I first went to sea on a merchant sailing ship," she heard him say. "Had my first mate's ticket by the time the Great War broke out, but I managed to miss that. Never liked the steam." Two of the girls began to wander away, and Rosemary was amused to see him make an effort to win their attention back again, this man in his eighties, peering cunningly at them over wet, pink rims.

"Come and have a look at my non-rent-paying tenants. Messy, beautiful devils they are, the lorikeets—they live in the big lillipili tree around the back." He walked determinedly away from the party and, after glancing at each other, surprised, amused, three young women followed him. Rosemary decided to tag along, too, though she was not near enough to hear any but the loudest of his ornithological gems.

"The fruit's not ripe at the moment, but when it is I think it ferments and goes to their little brains. You should hear them! The currawongs like the fruit, too, but the lorikeets don't like the currawongs, so there's screeching and shrieking—my goodness, they sound like drunken pensioners on a bingo outing! Or full footy fans on The Hill. Motherless they get, hanging upside down swinging by the claws. You'd swear they was bats, what a sight!"

Rosemary hung further back, feeling dizzy from the rum, the heat, the lack of food and sleep. Bright lorikeets and rosellas flashed by overhead and from trees farther away the currawongs engaged in their continual loud, tuneful conversations. Then, just as she became conscious of her aloneness between the party of familiar people and the bird-watching group, a rosella landed less than two arms' lengths from where she stood, vivid and unafraid.

Rosemary stood, entranced, gazing at its story-book prettiness, its clever design in vivid blue, scarlet, orange, green, yellow. Who could rosellas be so designed to please except each other? And how could anything so beautiful seem so unaware of it? Rosellas ate at her house, too, but she'd never looked so closely at one before.

Bobby had often seemed like an alien to her—she'd sometimes even thought of changelings when he was little. And Martha had said, bland as a weather reporter, that he was like her!

There was something in the grass the bird liked. Sunflower seeds, she recognised after peering. One by one, in its thin, dark claw, it lifted them to its beak and then very efficiently removed the husk from the sweet kernel. It was such an exceptionally neat operation with such awkwardly designed equipment that it made her think of sex. Or perhaps it was the rum.

"I've been an actress all my life," she'd said to Robert Talbot, and it was true. She was an actress, playing the ever-changing role of Rosemary

Quilty in a drama being written by strangers. Maybe this was true of
Bobby, too? If so, in his life, perhaps she was one of the strangers.

The rosella gazed indifferently in her direction and continued finding
seeds. Other people think they know me, she told it. Do I?

No more rum, she said.

Why the hell not? she asked.

She sat on the grass, not caring about staining her white skirt, enjoying
being alone on the shaded lawn with the sound of her friends partying
in the background. Her swollen arm had ached steadily in the car despite
a daytime dose of pain-killers, but the strong drink seemed to be blurring
the pain now and she began to relax. At any time she could go back
and belong to that party, but right now she felt closer to the trinket-
coloured bird with the insatiable appetite.

The light breeze carried an embrace of scent from the frangipani tree
and reminded Rosemary again of Jean, her mother, about whom she
felt such a long-established guilt that it had become part of her, like a
mole or even a birthmark.

We were just beginning to be friends, she confided wordlessly to the
bird. How illogical, how wasteful, that she should have died before there
was any reward for her life.

.   .   .

Jean was born in 1918, even before Grandmother knew she'd been
widowed. Grandmother, always good at dressmaking, had made this
their source of income. Rosemary's own dim memories of her were of
a set-faced, grey-haired lady in blue, wearing thick-lensed, wire-framed
spectacles as she bent over an always-going treadle sewing machine.

Grandmother, who had been young at the time of the suffragettes,
had been determined to give her own child a better opportunity. So,
through the Depression years, Grandmother had kept on sewing and
Jean had finished secondary school, matriculating to university. What
Jean really wanted to be was a writer, but her mother thought that was
frivolous if not illogical, since Jean had scored more marks for chemistry
and mathematics than for English. Grandmother had had a lot of faith
in logic.

Because of the continuous struggle for money, and because Jean and
her mother could not agree on the course she should take, she had
decided to find a job instead, work for a few years and save—and secretly
write in the evenings. Though jobs for girls were hard to get, she found
one in a chemist shop and during the night she wrote poems, two of
which were published in the *Women's Weekly*. She also wrote stories,
one about a family of happy, efficient ants who lived in an anthill in a

suburban reserve and one about a little yellow truck that kept going backwards and embarrassing its driver, a red-faced, tight-collared priest. These Rosemary had found many years later and read with a strange mixture of emotions: surprise that her serious-faced, ultra-grown-up mother could have had such delightful fantasies, and something like resentment or even guilt that that part of her mother's nature had been obliterated by the demands of duty.

When Jean was eighteen, she'd met Douglas Cooper, a newly qualified pharmacist who'd been employed by her elderly boss to be trained to take over the chemist shop so that he could retire. Douglas fell in love with Jean and after a while she fell in love with him and they became engaged.

At about that time, her father's brother, an old lawyer who had kept a watchful eye on Grandmother's business, died and left Jean his stamp collection. He'd also left Grandmother enough to buy a little cottage and give up dressmaking except when she felt like it. It was, or would have been, if not for the war, the beginning of good times for the family.

The best of Uncle James' stamp collection was worth enough for a deposit on a house but Douglas had had a better idea: he talked Jean into enrolling in a pharmaceutical course because then, when they were both qualified, they could start the first of a chain of chemist shops and soon be well off. So she enrolled in 1939.

The war whisked Douglas away and kept him for the whole of its duration and nearly killed him: he'd been taken prisoner by the Japanese. There was more than a year between his second-last letter in 1945 and the pale, scrawled note announcing that, though ill, he was soon coming home.

They'd brought him off the troop ship, a rack of thin bones on a stretcher, and rushed him straight to hospital where the medical staff had been sure he would not survive. If it had not been for Jean's constancy, the rationed eggs she brought him and the fresh fruit she traded with Italian growers in the next suburb, he probably would have died. He was in hospital for six months.

Jean, who had qualified as a pharmacist and then started a little shop in rented premises one street away from Douglas's mother's house, had spent all her free time with him. It was the business of making plans for the future that gave him something to cling to through months of therapy for a withered leg—there'd been doubt that it could be saved at all—and treatment for colitis, the legacy of years of dysentery.

It had taken two years before he was prepared to declare himself a man and not a parasite. They had married in October 1948, just as soon, he said in his bridegroom's speech, as he no longer looked like a bloomin' scarecrow in a suit. But in May, when Jean was seven months pregnant, having conceived Rosemary on the wedding night or thereabouts, Douglas died of pneumonia despite antibiotics and all Jean's love.

Grief and shock had started her labour and only control had saved them both: Rosemary's mother would otherwise not have been able to summon up the energy to even care for herself, let alone the scrawny, squeaking, premature baby. It is likely that Rosemary's earliest memories were of her mother weeping in the bed beside her.

Jean had worked hard, saving and controlling every inch of the way, so by the time Rosemary was ready for high school there was enough money to send her to a private one in the eastern suburbs. They had had terrible fights. All Rosemary's friends were going to Strathfield Girls High or, if they were Catholic, to the convent. But her mother had won, sending her reluctant child to a school where, Rosemary believed, every other pupil would be the daughter of a snobby millionaire and hers would be the only parent who needed to exercise daily control over a tight, tight budget to keep her there.

Actually, it was not too bad after the first few tearful months, when she found a little circle of girls as bright as she. Despite herself, Rosemary worked quite hard, and, by the end of the first year, the school offered her a part-scholarship which did much to relieve the fiscal strain and Rosemary's terrible conscience. But when Rosemary was about Phyl's age, she'd diagnosed control as what it was that had imprisoned her mother. Jean's university degree, of which she was so proud, doomed her to work in a chemist shop forever, looking a bit more important than the younger women who were only qualified to sell toothpaste and specials on Nescafé.

At sixteen, Rosemary had been desperate to leave school and start doing all the things she knew the world offered to those out of uniform. She had pined and raged so much and so often and wept about her lost opportunities and complained about her teachers—who had in turn complained about her—that at last her mother had given in and allowed her to leave, after which Rosemary's life began to brighten and Jean's to go into eclipse. But that was an old guilt now.

Rosemary at thirty-four felt exactly the way she had at sixteen and before that, at four—willing to take risks providing that meant she could avoid routines likely to become dull. Now it looked as though the plot of her life had led her into a narrow, optionless corner. Just as her mother had had to do, she'd have to find a job and accept routine and impose control. But, unlike her mother, she wasn't qualified even to sell Nescafé. Her own education had been taken, through babies and hard work in the company, in a series of grabs at courses both formal and informal. As a result it had a good deal of gaps, just as a steady stream of teachers had predicted it would if she didn't knuckle down to something. But apart from marriage and, of course, motherhood, Rosemary had never knuckled down.

So, whatever I do will have to be an adventure, she told the rosella, who had eaten most of the sunflower seeds and was now picking through the spent shells with the concentration of a diamond sorter. But have I got the energy? Have I got the guts? Maybe it's in the genes, she told herself.

She felt content, floating between wakefulness and sleeping, and would have spent the rest of the day in that cool shadow, feasting her eyes on the rosella and the distant sea and drinking the sweet, dangerous juice if Jeremy hadn't come to say hello. That frightened the bird away.

"You OK, my darling?" He took his heavy glasses off and stroked his nose.

"I'm OK, your darling."

"You're lying. I can tell."

"It's the sling, isn't it? A dead give-away. I should have been more subtle—worn an eye patch perhaps. Or a wheelchair."

"You going to say what happened?"

She realised then that Patrick had not told them and was surprised, relieved, and obligated all at once. "No big deal. I came home late Friday night, a bit tired and emotional, and slipped on some of my trendy landscape gardening. It's sore but probably nothing much. Got to have it X-rayed tomorrow, that's all."

He gazed at her as steadily as she'd gazed at the bird but with less satisfaction. "You can't fool me, Sister Woman. Something dark's worrying you."

"Stop being so sweet. I'm OK. Got a bit of the single-parent blues, that's all."

"I'm a really, really good listener."

"I know, darling Jeremy. But I'm not bottled up because of a need to spill, truly—the one thing I'm rich in is good listeners. I've been quietly coming to some conclusions about myself, that's all. About the way I've done things up to now."

Jeremy was chewing the crisp end of a blade of lawn. Graciously he offered her one.

"Trying to give them up," she said.

"Yet another test of strength, huh? And what's been so bad about you, anyway? You always seemed like a real honey-bunch to me."

"Honey-bunch? That's nice. I'd thought I was more like a toaster. Or an iron."

Jeremy laughed, a high, popping sound that made some heads turn at the tables. "A toaster. A toaster?"

"Yes," she said firmly. She had not meant to get into this. "Some sort of potentially useful appliance that is inert until plugged into a current which, in my case, is a man. I worked when I was with Daniel. I've been—idling. Faffing around. Playing, living on dreams since he's gone."

"I beg your pardon, Mrs. Q., if I might be so bold. Those dreams were pretty good examples of a particular kind of reality. By which I mean, if you'd like me to spell it out, that you are a very good actress." Most of Rosemary's confusion was due to the fact that she didn't believe him but knew it would be rude to say so. But he went on, as though she was not blushing and shaking her head. "And as for idle, don't make me laugh—we were all afraid you'd wear your little bones out, carrying the world on your shoulders while running at a steady trot." He laughed again. "Toaster! I love the image! You running around trying to find another man to plug yourself into—what a vulgar expression!—in the absence of the one you're contracted to. It's the best reason I've ever heard for looking for a fuck!"

"Jeremy! That's not what I mean at all!" she said, aware of the fact that her blushing had spread down her throat and along the tops of her arms. "I was talking metaphysically."

"Like hell you were!" he said. "Do you remember James Thurber's aunt in his story? She thought electricity leaked out of empty sockets, so she went around screwing in dead light bulbs to keep it in."

"You're horrible," she said, beginning to laugh herself. "My god, am I so transparent?"

"Of course. Isn't everybody? Haven't you noticed that what is uniquely tragic to you is a cliché everywhere else?"

"Yes."

"Well, don't you find that comforting? I mean, you can laugh at death if it's not your own!"

But it must have been clear to Jeremy that Rosemary had no intention of laughing at death or at much else. He did mention that she had never needed Daniel, or anyone else for that matter, to prove herself efficient and capable—he called her a natural organiser—but she put her head

in his lap and started playing 'This little piggy' with his sandalled toes
so he gave up. And stood up with a wobble.

"What in hell, I wonder, did Melissa put into this punch? Come on.
Let's pretend that I've reformed, and that we're going to be married in
the spring," he said and pulled her up, too. For such a light-boned man
he was surprisingly strong. "Enough of the Deborah Kerr."

"What do you mean Deborah Kerr? She never played melodrama!"

.   .   .

Rosemary needed to be busy before the rum triumphed, and so went
into the kitchen which was almost as big as Patrick had claimed, and
chaotic. Supermarket bags, partially unpacked, stood among their contents. Ashtrays overflowed—there was ash on the butter—and clean
and dirty cups and glasses took up all the space.

"I'll wash the salad things," she announced to no one in particular
and turned her back on the mess. Cleaning lettuce one-handed was
going to be an absorbing challenge.

The house was about fifty years old, built in the low, heavily shaded
style Somerset Maugham would have recognised. The kitchen was kept
cool by a marble-tiled floor, and she took off her shoes to enjoy it. She
wondered how it would feel in winter, though.

All around her the theatre group people gossiped, sounding deeply
knowledgeable about the sex lives and drug habits of everybody out of
earshot. She'd heard it all before, hours and hours of similar conversations during the long waits outside rehearsal rooms or in the costume
sewing bees. She had thought it witty, charming, and insightful at the
beginning, but now it seemed like nothing more than a parade of in-
securities overlaid with spite. As soon as she was out of earshot, she
knew, variations on the theme of her broken arm and her arrival with
Patrick would be fervently discussed by people who believed themselves
to be her intimates but to whom she was really just another walk-on
character in the dramas of their own lives. She knew the game—she'd
played it herself. Now it didn't seem like fun anymore.

Half drunk and one-handed she made a lot of mess with the water.
She giggled, splashed radishes, and tossed washed tomatoes at some of
the others who had volunteered to cut things. She pointedly did not
join the gossip despite numerous overtures. It was a risk, making herself
an outsider—they might make her suffer for it later. But this time she
didn't care, though she didn't know why.

The pig man came in every now and again, fussily looking for things:
a long-handled fork, a knife sharpener, some warmed platters. He was

a professional party caterer who had brought along a portable, gas-fired
rotisserie with a suckling pig to cook on it. He had also brought along
an air of reproach, making it quite clear, with his little sips of tap water,
what he felt about people who drank. He was very slow—lunch was
not ready until almost three.

"Should have been an undertaker, not a party cook," whispered Jeremy, who had come in to help in the hope of speeding things up.

"He is. A porcine undertaker," said Sue, who'd played Maggie the
Cat.

"All very well for you to talk—you're a poncy vegetarian. I've been
looking forward to the deceased."

Patrick, pink-cheeked with pleasure, drink, and sunshine, also appeared in the kitchen, and with an Ah-there-you-are! look, hurried to
help Rosemary. But she'd just finished dressing the two large salads
which had resulted from her labours and was able separate herself from
him by thrusting one into his hands. "It's for the the big table on the
verandah. Unless that's got full of empty bottles again—someone cleared
it earlier." She brushed him off a few more times after that, but he
caught up with her when she'd stopped at Martha's table. He had his
lunch in his hand, and when he noticed she didn't have any he promptly
gave it to her.

"No. No. No. I insist. I'll get more. What about wine? Do you want
red or white? No? Perrier?" He was soon back with another high-piled
plate. "What's the matter?" he murmured when he was settled.

Normally she would have used a barrier of politeness but that would
have required control. "You frighten me," she blurted. Patrick glanced
at her but was silent, picking at his food. "I'm being—ungrateful. I'm
sorry. But I can't help it right now." He gave her a concerned look and
she managed to fight the impulse to say "Why do you always look, as
though you know so much more than you say?"

She felt mean and then guilty. Then angry with herself. Why was it
that any encounter with any man, any closer than shaking hands, inevitably led to this narrow option of mean or guilty? And how could she
tell Patrick that what irritated her most about him was the best thing
about him—his niceness and his simple presumption that she liked him?
Her bandage felt too tight. So did her throat—she could not eat the
limp, fatty pork now cooling in the salad juices on her plate. In fact,
the look of it made her feel ill.

"Take no notice of me," she said as soon as she could. To add emphasis, she touched his arm in what she believed was a friendly, ideal-

ogically sound, non-gender-specific way. "I'm overtired and—I guess—neurotic. Very."

"You two look very lovey-dovey," said Martha. To Rosemary's relief, Patrick jerked away and said firmly, loudly, "Rosemary's arm's giving her some trouble so I'm going to take her home."

"Christ, you're not going yet?" Melissa boomed, so sozzled that she could not get off the garden swing to see them to the door. "Eat-and-run artists, hey? Or have you got an urgent appointment somewhere private!"

"Don't be so old-fashioned," said Patrick, kissing her firmly on the forehead.

.   .   .

"Thank you," Rosemary said, limp, tired, guilty, getting into the car. "I'm sure you'd have preferred to stay. You didn't eat. . . ."

"I ate enough, thanks, and anyway, I want to know why you're frightened of me."

The alternative to suffering deep embarrassment was to simply answer, so she did. "Because you look so sure of yourself and . . . sure of everything."

"Me? Come on! You're talking to the person Jeremy had to trick into an audition!"

"And then you were the best actor in the play."

"I don't know about that."

"Truly you were. Everybody said so. I don't mean the rest of us were lousy, but you sort of lifted the whole thing from amateur to . . . to something pretty much like professional. It was marvellous."

Patrick drove silently, seriously for a while. Rosemary wondered if he'd notice or care if she fell asleep. Then he startled her by saying, "It was one of the hardest things I've ever done, that play. Truly, I'd been a semi-recluse for years. So perhaps I went a bit over the top. Overcompensated."

"Had you never acted before?"

"Only in school plays."

"Well, don't stop, Patrick, because you're good. Really you are."

"Thank you," he said seriously. He said most things seriously, despite an open fan of deep-etched laugh lines around his eyes, which couldn't have got there unprovoked. "It was nice to be able to do it. But I wonder whether you know how much I'd like to be able to behave like you do?"

"Like me?"

"You're so good in groups, laughing, talking—wherever there's an interesting circle you're right in the middle of it."

"Oh, Patrick, how can you say that? I mean, it sounds nice, but look at me today—I slunk off into the garden, into the kitchen. . . ."

"Yes, but you've got something on your mind. I happen to know that because you said so on the way here. But the rest of them probably didn't notice because you kept chatting and joking."

"I really didn't. You see a much nicer me than I am. I kept escaping!"

"Yes. I know you did. What I'm saying is you did it so graciously that no one else noticed. I only did because it's what I usually try to do myself, only I end up feeling awkward and conspicuous."

"How strange. So do I. But to me you look like a most together person, as though you're holding all the strings that make the rest of us puppets work. So it's a bluff for you, too? Isn't that funny—impressing each other with our suave acts while both of us are quaking inside!"

"It's the third thing we have in common," he said, exercising the laugh lines.

"I'm one of the emotional walking wounded right now," she said. "I don't think I have anything in common with anybody normal."

"Normal! What an indictment!"

Rosemary was not tired anymore. She noticed that Patrick tapped his left foot, where the clutch pedal would have been on a manual car, as though keeping the rhythm of a tune in his head, so she fiddled with the radio knobs and found some Stravinsky.

"Tell me it's none of my business if you like, Rosemary, but why are you upset? What really happened?"

Why does everybody want to know? I had to fob Jeremy off, now you, she thought. Then suddenly she didn't want to anymore. "I haven't been speaking to Daniel. Not for months, properly—just money fights on the phone. But he takes Bobby at weekends and tells him things that Bobby then tells me, mainly about Patchwork, the company we used to run together. On the way back from Lithgow—and it's a long way—making conversation with Robert Talbot, I told some of that information to him. It was a stupid thing to do—I just don't know how I could have been so dumb! The thing is, Robert Talbot's tried to buy Patchwork and Daniel wouldn't sell, so he's been white-anting it. Wooing away our—Daniel's—clients."

"Did you know that?"

"Of course not. But the worst part is that Daniel arrived when we did and saw us together and immediately got furious." Patrick glanced at her slung arm. "They yelled and shouted terrible things, especially

Daniel. Robert Talbot talked about the . . . one of the things I'd told him about. So Daniel knew it had come from me. And he blew up."

Even this lust-free version of the event had made Rosemary's temples throb. She grovelled in her handbag for a tissue and then abruptly switched the cheerful music off. "I didn't know he was losing the business. And of course I didn't know Robert Talbot was in opposition to him. But he'll never believe that."

"Why not? You didn't mean to harm him."

"I must have," she said bleakly. "Because I did."

In the silence that followed Rosemary was convinced that Patrick, having recognised the dangerous sneaky streak in her, was resolving not to pay her any more attention. Well, at least I've achieved that, she thought.

.   .   .

"Can I use your phone?" Patrick asked when they reached her house. "I won't stay."

"At least let me give you a cup of coffee," she said. "You've still got a lot of driving to do."

"I've got to pick up Geoff soon—it's after five."

"Well, instant, then," she said, then felt ridiculous. Minutes ago she had congratulated herself on shaking Patrick off, now she was urging him to stay. "I'm going to have some myself, anyway."

She was surprised to find the front door unlocked since Phyl and Bobby were not due back for an hour. But in the yellow living room they were waiting for her, she was shocked to find, huddled together, their faces as grim as refugees on an appeal poster.

"What is it? What is it?" Rosemary asked, frantically trying to embrace them both with one and a half arms.

"Dad came," said Phyl as soon as she was able to free her head from the clinch. "Just after you left. I tried Melissa's number but there was no one there."

"What is it? What's wrong?" She thought of death. Bobby had struggled himself out of the too-tight hug as well and was looking at her with an expression she had not seen on his face since he was tiny: it was fear.

"The company's got no money. Dad said he's been trying to talk to you since yesterday."

"Yes?" She already knew that—or thought she did. "So why . . . ?"

"Oh, Mum," said Phyl, starting to cry—and Rosemary could see then that both of them had been crying quite a bit—"Dad says the company's gone bankrupt and we're probably going to lose the house."

"Lose the house? That's ridiculous. Impossible!"

"It's true, Mum. That's what he wanted to tell you. He found out for sure yesterday that there's no way of saving Patchwork PR. He was so upset! If Angela hadn't been here he'd have cried, I think." She glanced at Patrick, still standing near the door. "She was even worse. She looked . . . she looked . . . like a dead person, almost, so white! We had to give her strong tea with lots of sugar."

"Why didn't you put rat poison in it?" Rosemary demanded and the children glanced apologetically at Patrick.

"He took his car. That's why they came," Bobby said, answering a question she hadn't asked yet.

"How? I've got his keys, remember. Bobby rescued them from the pool." Rosemary opened her handbag and revealed a bunch of six or seven on an American Express card look-alike key holder.

"Angela had a spare."

"We were at Melissa's father's house at Palm Beach. Her flat's too small for a party. I should have told you. Have you two been here all this time, alone, waiting for me?" They didn't have to reply. "Oh, my poor darlings!" Suddenly Rosemary needed to sit, or lean on something, and Patrick appeared at her side and grabbed her, but she shook him off as though he'd been a wave or a dog and backed to the wall from where she could properly survey her frightened children.

"That's the most ridiculous thing I've ever heard," she said. "Lose the house? How could we? It belongs to me. . . ." Doubt confused her. The forms she'd signed at the notary's office—guarantees for the new computer printing equipment from America, Daniel's little yellow stick-on note had said. Surely not . . . ?

In May or June a courier had brought a bigger-than-usual batch of company documents for her to sign. She'd been surprised, annoyed to find that four of them needed to be signed in the presence of a notary, a pedantic and irritating delay in an already too-tight schedule.

"You have read these documents, Mrs. er . . . Quilty?" the dry little man had asked, peering greyly at her over his half-moon spectacles.

"Yes, yes," she'd lied, reaching for his black pen.

"I have to be assured that you understand the nature and the contents of the documents you are about to sign," he'd said, holding them just out of her reach. She'd seen, then, that impatience was not the answer.

"I went through them for hours, last night, Mr. Bean. My eyes are red from that fine print. It's really perfectly OK. I have signed things like this often."

His expression had not changed as he pushed them over to her— "Sign here, here, initial that correction . . ." —at his own imperturbable speed. Half an hour later she had burst out of his office like a horse through a racing barrier. Later, on that same busy day, she'd posted the big envelope full of forms to Daniel's office and then forgotten about them. Now, as though Mr. half-moon-spectacled Bean were holding them under her nose, she remembered them again: personal guarantees. Another betrayal.

"Rosemary, why don't you phone your lawyer? He's a friend, isn't he? He won't mind a Sunday call." Patrick was still there.

"Yes. But I must think first—about what to say, what he'll need to know. I was such an idiot to go to Palm Beach! I knew I shouldn't have!"

"Oh, Mum! What are we going to do?"

"Do? Fight like hell!" said Rosemary, aware of the pose she was striking with her back to the wall. "We can't lose our house!"

Even Phyl was cheered.

Twelve

It had felt good, standing with her back to the wall and proclaiming that she wasn't going to lose the house, but the feeling was rapidly eroded by circumstance. Patrick tried again to persuade Rosemary to phone Jim Begg, but she was much more concerned about feelings than practicalities at that moment—Phyl and Bobby needed as much comfort as she could offer.

"I'm so sorry. You were going out so it never occurred to me to give you the Palm Beach phone number."

"Dad came five minutes after you left," Phyl said. The late afternoon light highlighted her pale skin and gave the illusion that her cheekbones were stripped bare. It was hard, hugging two children with one arm.

"But he told me he wasn't coming. On the phone."

"He wanted his car. And he was mad—mainly at you."

I can just imagine, Rosemary thought bitterly. He poured it out on you two, then left you here to stew half the day. The bastard!

"What else did he say?"

"It's hard to remember, Mum. We were so . . . About a—a legal document was one thing. I don't know whether this is right: a big company that Patchwork owes money to sent him something . . ."

"A demand," said Bobby.

"Yes. A demand. Three weeks ago. That's why Dad sold the boat. But the boat money wasn't enough, or they wouldn't take it or something. And now the three weeks is up."

"What has three weeks got to do with anything?"

"I don't know. I don't know," Phyl said, sobbing. "It all sounded just terrible.

"But surely they can be stopped? I mean, this is ridiculous!"

"Dad says he's tried just about everything. There's only one thing left and that's something he's going to try next week."

"What?"

"He didn't say."

"He said he'd keep us informed," said Bobby.

It was hard for Rosemary to remember that only a few hours ago at the party she'd been sorry for Daniel. How dare he come and frighten the children like this—use them as weapons to reach her and wound her.

"What's his number?" she demanded, reaching for the phone. Fearfully, the children observed her as though they believed she was capable, in her present mood, of telephonic homicide.

"Bobby's the only one with Dad's home number," said Phyl.

"No, I lost it," said Bobby.

"Blast!" said Rosemary, slamming down the phone. She had a vivid memory of herself burning Daniel's number on the scrap of paper she'd found in Bobby's pocket. When she'd done it, to prevent herself from making any more embarrassing three A.M. calls, she hadn't given emergencies a thought.

.   .   .

"Will they really take our house?" Bobby asked with his mouth full. Not even tragedy affected his appetite which had had to be appeased as soon as Patrick left. They had baked beans and eggs on toast for dinner—what Rosemary called "poverty food." It reminded her of her childhood. Usually it irritated her that the children, especially Bobby, were so keen on the things she felt she'd graduated from, like crumpets, doughnuts, highly coloured, gelatine-based desserts, canned spaghetti, french fries and tomato sauce. But tonight, she knew, it was a comfort, and besides, it was easy for a one-armed woman to prepare.

Phyl had a headache which a hot bath and a neck massage did not fix, so she succumbed to a Disprin, pulling fierce faces about polluting her body with drugs. In Rosemary's opinion, bottled tomato sauce was a much worse pollutant, but Phyl never liked to hear that.

All three of them were in their beds and both children were asleep by eight. Rosemary was certainly tired enough to sleep; instead, like an ostrich on a dry clay bed, she was forced to keep her head up and face things she'd rather have avoided.

"No one can ever get us out of here," she'd said boldly on the day they moved into the house. Fate, tempted, seemed to have a long memory.

She informed herself, as though delivering a fatal diagnosis, that if she really did lose the house it would be her own fault since she'd signed the forms in blind, self-destructive trust. In her eagerness to avoid punishing Daniel for leaving her, she'd punished herself instead. Why do I do that? she asked, tossing uncomfortably, What's to stop me doing it again and again if I can never see or smell the danger? Am I deliberately blind? If so, I must be mad!

She thought about herself as a mad woman. There were lots of symptoms. She cried a lot and lost her temper easily. She argued with herself. These things had bothered her, but she had not before recognised them as ominous indicators of mental collapse. Worse was the fear that there might be other things she was secretly doing to undermine herself.

She suddenly thought of an example—the conversation with Robert Talbot. Why had there been no warning bells in her head when she started revealing things which had a direct bearing on her own and her children's security? Nobody was that naive! If she had observed some other woman blather away her husband's business secrets—a woman in a play, perhaps—Rosemary's stomach would have constricted in recognition of the danger and she'd have wanted to warn her. Why didn't it work for me? Why am I so blind? she asked herself. It can't simply be trust. Did I want to damage myself?

This was a terrible thought—her arm throbbed to underline it—but she didn't duck away from it. She turned it over and over, examining all the evidence it contained until at last she realised that it was a weak idea with holes in it.

I am blind, she told herself, because there has never been any real reason not to be. I've been protected, like a budgie in a cage. Budgies don't even know what butcher birds are—how could they possibly avoid being gobbled up?

Then why, she asked, did Daniel stop protecting me—us?

Because, she told herself, I moved away from his umbrella. It does not extend beyond where he happens to be. He'd never have risked the house if he were still living in it.

And so, gradually, through her second sleep-diminished night in a row, Rosemary transferred the focus of her anger and blame from herself to Daniel. And then, as dispassionately as she could, she faced the future.

It's true, she thought, that I have been marking time. Part of me has been waiting for him to come back, even though, logically, I knew it would never work again. Logically, what is the worst thing that can happen? she asked herself. But logic was a thin shield against the charge of fear which, like unearthed electricity, flowed unchecked through all the most vulnerable places in her nature. But she refused to flinch and continued toying carefully with reality—the source of the charge.

We can lose the house and have to rent one. Is that so terrible?

No, was the brave and logical answer. But it did not help for long— it was drowned by a lifetime's memory of the effort and the love and sense of strength that had gone into having a house of her own.

She had a vision of herself and the children as refugees in some orange-vinyl-walled place where social workers were in charge—the sort of place Malcolm Henry's cameras might probe for a story about domestic suffering. There was a different vision of herself, as a tree about to be unearthed, as though a force as impartial and ruthless as a bulldozer were about to descend and rip her out of her place, leaving her collapsed with little to show except torn and broken roots.

"I won't be able to bear it," she said aloud, and believed it. She kept running through imaginary phone conversations with Daniel. Sometimes she wished she had never burnt that number. Anyway, talking to him would have been futile, like dropping conventional bombs on Hiroshima after the A-bomb.

Eventually, the pain-killers helped and the debate was resolved in her troubled sleep. When she awoke on Monday morning she realised that if she lost the house she would be able to bear it, the way two generations of women before her had borne the unexpected bleakness of their lives.

Perhaps it will end with me, she thought, struggling unaided with the soapy wash-cloth. Perhaps it will be OK for Phyl.

.   .   .

By eight o'clock when it was too late for politeness, she phoned Jim Begg to tell him what had happened.

"Oh, my God, Rosie, you sure? Has he had a three six four?"

"What's that?"

"A demand from the creditor that gives you twenty-one days to pay up, or else."

"That sounds like what Phyl was trying to tell me."

"Phyl? Your daughter?"

"Yes. I was out."

His pause was long enough to reveal what he thought of people who left their children to deal with such vital matters. "When can you come and see me?" he asked. She could hear the clink of a spoon. She had to have her arm X-rayed; she'd ask Eve Everingham to drive her to North Sydney; then she'd take the plates to Dr. Saxon's office, which was quite near Jim's. "About eleven, do you think? Anyway, I'll be in all morning. I'll have some light on all this by then," he said, munching what sounded like muesli. But when she got to his office, the light Jim had promised turned out to be only a dim glow.

"Haven't been able to talk to Dan's side yet, though a friend of mine who does business with some of the people involved says it looks pretty grim. Patchwork PR's got itself into a hell of a mess fairly quickly—just about overnight, God knows how. You spoken to him yet?"

"No. I'd rather not. I'd rather you did."

"Don't be silly, Rosie—it's the shortest cut to knowing where you stand. He's not dangerous, is he? Not likely to, er, lose his cool? You and the kids?"

It was a hard question to answer, sitting there in the bright new sling the X-ray nurse had put on for her, so she ignored it. "What happens about the twenty-one days being over?"

"Well, if it was a three six four—which is a petition to the Supreme Court to have the company wound up—they can probably go ahead now and liquidate."

"Probably?"

"Yes, unless Dan's come up with the money in the meantime."

"He tried—he sold the boat. But it wasn't enough."

"And they didn't accept what he offered as part payment?" Jim whistled through his curled tongue and stared unhappily at a framed print of a Tiger Moth on the wall behind Rosemary's shoulder. "Well, either he owes one hell of a lot more than the boat's worth, or they're gunning for him. Or the kid got it wrong," he added optimistically. "Get onto Daniel right away, Rose-girl, and find out what's what."

"I really don't think it would help. How could it help?"

"Ro, face it. You gotta do what you can to stop them grabbing the house. Those forms you signed—sure you didn't get a copy? It's usual for guarantors to have a copy."

"No. I told you—I just put everything in an envelope and posted it to the office. I never gave it another thought." Rosemary was ashamed all over again, and frightened of the consequences of her own laxness. "It's—it's habit to trust him."

"Yeah," he drawled. "Trustworthy bugger, old Daniel." He paused and stared at her, and she wondered if she looked different now, having lost a husband and a house within the same year. "No worries," he said with a sigh. "We'll get copies from them."

"If it comes to the worst, how long have we got?"

"Well, all they need to do now is get judgement against you both, then along comes the liquidator. That's the legal process. But usually the situation is that you've got forever—that's unless they really are gunning for him, or unless there's something big that we don't know about. Does he gamble, Daniel?"

She shook her head, then remembered the casino, but if her expression changed Jim did not appear to notice.

"It would be a very callous creditor who'd push so hard for his dough that he pushes a woman and kids out of the family home," said Jim, his hands in the prayer position, his tone like a law-course lecturer's.

"So how do they get their money?" asked Rosemary, docile as a first-year student.

"You concerned about them? Don't be so silly. Probably some big public company loaded with dough who'll be suing as part of the routine. Half a million bucks—that about what Dan's down for, you think? Could be fixed in a journal entry if someone wanted to. Chicken-feed. Probably realise most or all of that just from the company's assets, no need to touch the directors' personal stuff. Though how you could put the house up . . ."

"Patchwork hasn't got many assets—most things are leased."

"Yeah. Would be. Still, probably no need to worry. Meanwhile, how are you off for cash?"

"Up to now Daniel's paid all the bills," she tried not to sound like a helpless dependant. Jim stared again for a second or two—enough to reveal that he was concerned, perhaps even shocked.

"So you've got no money?"

"No. Well, yes, about two thousand dollars in a savings account."

"Hang on to that, baby. You'll need it."

"And I'll get a job as soon as possible, of course," she said quickly, to blot out the quick vision of the red dress. It had cost almost a third of her money!

"Yeah. A car? Is that in your name? Hardly likely."

"Hardly likely, as you say. Daniel said it was mine, of course. In fact he gave it me as a fifteenth wedding anniversary present. It makes no difference, anyway—he borrowed it and crashed it."

"Wrote it off?"

"I suppose so. It wasn't a priority when we last talked." Her memory flickered back to that nasty scene, but she slapped a "censored" sign over it.

"Where is the car now?" Jim persisted. "It's worth checking. If it is yours, your own, you'll get what it's worth from insurance. Volvo was it? Fairly new? Worth enough."

Enough to cover his fees among other things, which, she realised, were bothering him on a level she had not yet considered. So even his alliance was under threat.

"I'll find out," she said, trying to sound firm. "There is one thing. The trouble Daniel's in is because Robert Talbot's been taking away his clients."

"What do you mean 'taking away'? Competition is healthy, normal . . ."

"Not this. Daniel says he's deliberately been trying to break Patchwork." Jim frowned. "Daniel told you this? Can't you see he's grasping at straws . . . making excuses?"

"No, I think it's true, Jim. I overheard—I was part of an argument between Daniel and Robert Talbot. They said—yelled—a lot of things to do with business. Daniel was accusing him."

"But how? When . . . ?"

"At my house on Friday night."

"Talbot came to see you at your house?" For the first time Jim looked at Rosemary's wounded arm, about which he had not even commented. "What in hell is going on, Rosemary? How come you're mixed up with Robert Talbot?"

"I'm not really mixed up with him, I . . ."

"Bloody hell!" said Jim angrily. He crashed things on his desk as though his large, red hands were tennis racquets. "Can't you see this is just not good enough? You've got to tell me the full story! I've got to know exactly what's going on!" Judy, Jim's tiny secretary, rushed in looking worried. "It's okay Jude," he said, calming down abruptly. "Cup of coffee's what I need."

"Or camomile tea?" She suggested it tentatively, but there was an underlying note of conviction it would be hard to argue with. Jim nodded as though she'd won at arm wrestling.

"I'm sorry," said Jim. He shook his head hard several times as though to free it from something soft stuck on the outside. Rosemary felt it was important to show him, by means of careful tone and body language, how well balanced and normal she was.

"Robert Talbot offered me a lift back from Lithgow where I went for a . . . job interview. At the time—it was Friday night—Patchwork was still a struggling company. It wasn't, as far as I knew, in liquidation. In any case, we didn't talk much about business. That only happened when we got to my house and Daniel was there. He'd taken the children out. He was furious to see me with Robert Talbot." Her arm was hurting badly and her face felt flushed and feverish. She wished she hadn't come and had to face this absurd interrogation. Even if she had been able to remember every word Robert Talbot had said, it would not have been any more enlightening.

"Whatever happens, it's essential that you and Daniel work together as allies in this, even if only as directors of a failed company," Jim said, regaining his lawyerly calm after a long, earnest look at her face.

"I doubt if we can," she said bleakly.

"Well, try. And it can't do you any harm that you've been able to talk to the man who's liquidating you—it's a contact you should develop."

"But Robert Talbot isn't liquidating Patchwork. A computer company is."

"Sure, sure. But you can be certain that he owns the computer company."

"I don't think so." She breathed deeply to counter a wave of dizziness. "Jim, I don't feel well. I really must go. But I'll find out more about all this . . . liquidation and . . . do what I can."

He nodded briskly—he'd been thinking and not listening. "You see," he said, "you're probably in a good position to plead innocence. You could convince the creditors that you signed under duress. Of course, it would make it easier if Daniel backs you—if he says, 'Yes, I made her sign the forms. No, she didn't read them properly.' It's worth it, to both of you. Otherwise, he'd be cutting off his nose."

.   .   .

Phyl had been too upset and nervous to go to school and so had pleaded pre-menstrual tension. Bobby, in a terrible temper and without a comparable excuse, had gone, because, as Rosemary's explained, he could hardly justify going on stage in the evening if he was too sick for school in the day. Which is why his daughter and not his son witnessed Daniel cutting off his nose. Metaphorically, of course, no blood was spilled on that violent day.

He arrived at noon, looking rumpled and fragile, his normally pale skin like wax with tension. Watching him slowly walk towards the house, his reddish hair glowing like soft flame in the sunlight, Phyl and Rosemary grasped each other's hands in pity.

"So you came home at last," was his greeting. It confused Rosemary for a moment since it had looked to her as though he, tired and beaten, was the one returning to base.

"Do you want tea or coffee?" she asked.

"Whichever's paid for, in cash."

"How bad is it, really, Daniel?"

"As bad as it can get. We've lost the lot by the look of it."

"I don't understand . . ." she began, but he interrupted with a bang of rage: "*You* don't understand? That's fantastic! 'I don't understand. I don't understand.' " he mimicked. " 'Yes, I'm playing around with Robert Talbot. Yes, I know Robert Talbot's out to get Daniel Quilty. No, I don't understand' . . . Shit, Rosemary, how can you be such a hypocrite?" Anger had called on reserves of energy they would both have doubted he had a few minutes earlier, and for the first time she wondered, fearfully, whether he was safe. Sane.

"Just a minute," said Rosemary. "All this has got nothing to do with Phyl. . . ."

"No, no," Phyl interrupted, signalling with quick little frowns that she was as concerned for Rosemary as Rosemary was for her. At least we're two against one, she seemed to say. And we need to be!

Daniel was too preoccupied with what he had to say to notice his wife and daughter wriggling their eyebrows, tipping their heads, and rolling their eyes at each other. Anger kept altering the course of his speech so that it emerged in bits that Rosemary had to try to separate. Clearer than his words was the message of his helpless pain—it emanated from him like the signs of a chronic disease. Daniel had no experience of failure. Somewhere between the lines of his gaunt face she read messages of self-doubt, confusion, and fear that had never been there before, and it occurred to her that for him it might have been as bad or even worse than it had been for her during the past three-quarters of a year.

She gained the impression, a few times, that he felt everything that had happened was her fault—as though it was the household budget that had overloaded his fiscal row-boat. She noticed how carefully his eyes avoided looking at her sling.

Other major themes were Talbot and the computer printer he'd had so much trouble landing from America when the dollar was devalued. "If I'd got it up and running in time I'd have been able to sign up two contracts that would have made Patchwork untouchable. But they messed me around, the bastards—I missed out. Then, when I tried to cancel, they started getting nasty. Now they're putting me under! That fucking Talbot!"

Rosemary knew the best thing was not to argue or question Daniel when he was in spate. She was reluctantly connected to him by an invisible band of tension, as though they were circling boxers. The fact that Phyl was there, listening again, taking the burden of all this, seemed like fate to Rosemary—a theme that kept replaying itself. Again she tried to signal Phyl, but she was gazing intently at her father with an expression that linked fear with pity.

"Daniel," Rosemary said artificially calmly, as soon as she could, "I can't work out what Robert Talbot has got to do with the computer printer company, but whatever it is I want you to know that I am not 'playing around' with him. You simply must believe me. He gave me a lift home on Friday. I had never met him before, and I'm sure I'll never see him again."

"Don't make me laugh!" Daniel said, far too grimly to be in any danger of it. "I'm not blind. Or deaf."

"It's true, though, Dad," Phyl said, and by so doing cut through the tension. "Mr. Talbot just brought Mum home. Malcolm Henry had organised a job interview for her at Lithgow, and she missed the train back."

He hesitated for a moment, then was angry again. "Listen, Phylly, you and Bob and I sat in my car and saw the two of them carrying on like . . . like . . ."

"Mr. Talbot pecked my cheek. The way Jim Begg does. Malcolm does. The way I've seen you do lots of times at parties to women you hardly know. I never thought anything of it."

Daniel and Rosemary stared levelly at each other, then, more calmly, he said, "That man is poison. Worse than poison. He set about deliberately to kill Patchwork PR, and he's done it. He's influenced everyone in Sydney to turn against me."

The word paranoia flashed into Rosemary's head. "But why? And when? It must have taken months. I mean, I only met him on Wednesday." She was so genuinely puzzled that she could see, then, that he was convinced. But although her words were glib and confident enough, they did not erase her own private guilt. She escaped to the kitchen. Making tea, she could hear Phyl's bright, light voice saying and asking all the comforting things she would have said herself in a different time.

"Poor Dad!" Phyl said as Rosemary brought the tray in. "It must feel as though Patchwork PR has died!" And to everyone's amazement, Daniel's eyes filled with tears. He brushed them away and brushed Phyl away, too, as she dashed over to hug him. "I put absolutely everything into that company," he said and then, with his estranged wife and his only daughter, bleakly considered the full significance of what he'd said.

"Well," said Rosemary when she couldn't stand it anymore. "What's to be done? Jim Begg says that even though the computer people are suing, we probably won't lose the house. Not if we play our cards right."

"What would he know? Bloody little suburban lawyer?" Daniel asked, but without real malice.

She explained as well as she could.

"So you tell them you're just a dumb housewife? Signed those forms I sent you, not knowing what they meant, and they dry your tears and let you keep the house? Neat. You know who you'd be sucking up to, of course?"

She pretended not to understand, though it was hard not to be irritated by his new obsession.

A black limousine pulled up outside. Daniel had his back to the window, but Phyl and Rosemary saw it, and Rosemary's innards wrenched in anxiety. Oh, my God, what do I do now? she thought, but Phyl, with no change of expression, picked up the milk jug, headed calmly for the hallway, and managed to pull the door behind her so that it all but closed.

" 'Oh, please, Robert dear, don't let those nasty computer people take the house away from me and my poor little kiddies,' " Daniel said, mimicking a female voice again.

"Daniel, why did you come here this morning? Just to fight with me? We're all in trouble, you know, not just you. The company was what fed all of us. Now, if we're sensible, there's a chance of saving the house. That would be something."

Daniel's shoulders slumped, and the true state of his misery was revealed for Rosemary to see. She realised that much of his roaring had been to impress Phyl with power he did not feel. He said that saving the house was the least of his worries, but, yes, if it were possible to do so, that would be something.

This is a person I used to know, she thought. Lovable, funny, and exciting. It was hard to believe. Presumably that Daniel now existed for Angela, but for Rosemary he wore a mask of enmity, close-fitting as a stocking, and, apart from a few familiar signs of him that she could glimpse through the mesh, he was a stranger. And by the way he was looking at her—a close, frank stare—it occurred to her that he had lost sight of whatever it was about her that he had once loved.

Rosemary had the feeling of being on a railway station platform, watching him about to leave on a journey in a direction she could not and no longer had any desire to follow. It was a relief, an oddly peaceful moment.

Later she wished she'd said something, anything, to detain him— another fifteen seconds would have been enough. But he turned towards

the door and hurried out with Rosemary close behind, and reached the
hallway just as Phyl was stuffing a bouquet of red roses and Rosemary's
large, lacy straw hat behind the telephone chair.

If Phyl had not looked so guilty there is a chance that Daniel may
not have noticed, but she was white and literally panting with anxiety—
obviously she'd been heading for the stairs when Daniel walked out of
the living room.

He moved like a panther and wrenched the flowers out, bending their
stalks in his speed. The hat fluttered to the floor, and Rosemary's heart
seemed to stop beating and to leap under her throat, cutting off her
breath. Daniel ripped open the envelope that was stuck to the cellophane, read it, and went blotchy red with rage.

"A perfectly innocent lift home, hey? Listen to this, you bitches. Yes,
I mean you, too—lying to protect this fucking mother of yours."

The next few seconds were impossible to reconstruct: to Rosemary,
Phyl had seemed to crumple like tissue paper, and she'd moved—perhaps leapt—towards her, but her progress was deflected by a sharp
thump which spun her around so quickly that she slipped on the slate
floor, onto her slinged arm, and heard the bone crack. Through the roar
of shock—there was no pain at that stage—and the shrill of Phyl's
screams, came Daniel's contemptuous voice as he read the note aloud.
It sounded terrible: incriminatingly intimate, a knell to any hope of a
house-saving alliance.

And then Rosemary heard nothing.

.   .   .

She was in an ambulance. Phyl was there, and Mrs. Hermann, so that
it felt like a continuation of Friday night—the same, long nightmare.
There had been a vision of Daniel's face, the feeling that he'd touched
her, but that could have been part of the dream.

"Lie still. Soon you will be fine," said Mrs. Hermann.

At the hospital, through the swirls of reality and strangeness, she saw
Phyl and Mrs. Hermann talking earnestly to a young black-bearded
doctor. He walked towards her and said, "This won't hurt, Mrs. Quilty."
But it did.

Then she was at home again, in her own bed, her arm encased in
plaster, heavy and alien—a parcel she was forced to carry. Bobby had
come into the room.

"Mum?"

"Hello." Her tongue was drug heavy.

"Dad broke your arm! Dad?"

She shook her head. "Slipped. I slipped. Clumsy."

"Phyl said . . ."

"We were just—shouting. Nothing unusual. Just noise. But I slipped on the slate."

He was not convinced. His freckles were bright on his tense face. He ground and grated his teeth—an early habit he had long ago given up. He would not meet her eyes. This is terrible for him, she thought. He must be protected—Phyl, too. But by me? What good am I?

"What's the time, Bobby darling?" She made an effort to sound normal, dull even.

"Five. Is your heart OK?"

"My heart?"

"They thought you had a heart attack."

"Who thought?"

"Mrs. Hermann. Dad, Phyl."

I could have died! she thought. How strange! A few hot tears trickled into the ear she was lying on, but her hands were too numb and far away to do anything about them. Then Auntie Gwen walked in, and Rosemary realised she was dreaming.

"Robert! I told you not to upset your mother!" she said, dabbing a tissue on Rosemary's face. "Get yourself ready, boy. There's some scrambled eggs in the fry-pan—I couldn't do better in the time. Make yourself some toast. Ben's mother will drive you to your play, she kindly offered. At six. And I'll fetch you. What time does it finish?" And Rosemary realised she wasn't dreaming.

"Come here, Bobby. Give me a kiss," she said. "Listen, I'm absolutely fine. Fine, fine, fine. Just dopey. I wish I could watch you tonight—it's the most marvellous show. But I'll be there tomorrow, OK? For the finale. My heart, and all the rest of me, is strong—nearly as good as your voice-box. Truly." Bobby looked less doubtful as he left the room. "Did I have a heart attack, Auntie Gwen?"

"Do you think you'd be here, in your own bed, my girl? Use your sense. You'd be lying in intensive care, bristling with tubes. No. You broke your arm, good and proper. Passed out. That's all." There was concern under her grumbling tone; Rosemary, grown up, could hear that now—but as a little girl she'd been convinced that Auntie Gwen was always angry with her.

"Phyl? Is she all right?"

"Yes, poor scrap. Had a bad fright, but she coped very well. Phoned the ambulance, phoned me . . . She's out for the count now. Your Dr. Saxon gave her a tranquilliser. She'll probably sleep 'til noon tomorrow." She grinned. "I had such a silly conversation with that nice man. He phoned, you see, to say your X-rays showed a hair-line crack and that you'd better have a light plaster support. Well! I didn't know you'd been pushed around earlier by that bloody hysterical man. So he's lost his company, so he comes and shoves his wife around! And whose fault is that, anyway? So Dr. Saxon and I, we had a real mix-up. I thought he was from the hospital—kept telling him to stop being so stupid and look at the records—your arm had already been plastered and it was no hair-line crack at all but a major fracture. . . ."

.   .   .

That first night had been dreadful. Rosemary couldn't lie on her back without the feeling that the broken ends of her bones were grating together. The pain-killers had sent her into bouts of heavy, sweaty sleep until they wore off. Once she must have groaned aloud because Auntie Gwen had appeared like a large pink cloud, her eyes lost in the folds of sleep, and wordlessly built up a horseshoe of pillows behind Rosemary's back so she could sleep sitting up instead. After that she had trouble staying awake.

The next few days were made up of unrelated things, all of which were underlined by pain that ranged from tolerable to terrible and back again and which were swept together by the vigorous strokes of Auntie Gwen's voice. Neighbours visited, bringing cakes, casseroles, and curiosity. Mrs. Hermann, whose name was Hilda and who was, in fact, shy, not snobbish at all, popped in at least once a day with delicious, unpronounceable little snacks wrapped in white linen napkins, most of which Bobby ate. In the background the radio's news babbled at her about violence in the suburbs and hunger in Ethiopia and police corruption everywhere. It all seemed to go on forever.

During that time the first of a long series of grim legal demands arrived. Even if Auntie Gwen had let her try, Rosemary would not have been able to focus on the large print, let alone the fine.

Patrick, Malcolm, and Jim Begg phoned, but Auntie Gwen fielded their calls. Dr. Saxon came twice on Tuesday and insisted that both she and Phyl stay in their beds despite Rosemary's avowal that nothing, apart from her now-secure arm, was wrong and that there were things she needed to do. It irritated her that her eyes kept filling with tears she could not control.

Dr. Saxon sat on the edge of her bed, a man with a young face and old hair, looking authoritative.

"You listen to him," Auntie Gwen growled.

Rosemary told him she was worried about Phyl. She was limp and withdrawn and would not talk about what had happened. He prescribed rest and sleep and a tonic which she knew Phyl would resent taking, certain it was made of chemicals. Rosemary could not tell him how haunted she was by the memory of Daniel's voice reading Robert Talbot's note. She wished she could remember what the note said, but presumably he'd taken it with him.

"How long will this take?" she asked, tenderly tapping the bulky plaster as though it, too, had wounded nerve ends.

"About six weeks. We'll do another X-ray in three, and then we'll see about some physiotherapy. You don't want to stiffen up."

Stiffening seemed an unlikely fate to Rosemary, who felt almost as limp and lack-lustre as Phyl did, but Bobby's needs and the desire to escape Auntie Gwen's vigilant devotion kept her from sinking into the comfort of apathy.

Despite Dr. Saxon's orders, because she'd promised, she went to the finale of *Joseph and His Amazing Technicolour Dreamcoat* and sat groggily, dizzily through the performance, which, this time, sounded far too loud. Auntie Gwen went, too, and held her up, firm as a puppet master.

"Bloody stupid, going out in this state," she said again and again, but Rosemary was too groggy from pain-killers and day-old shock, as well as too determined, to answer.

When they came home from the last performance Bobby went straight to bed, having fallen asleep in the car and Rosemary would have, too, but Lucy was there, visiting Phyl. Rosemary was greatly relieved; she hadn't wanted to leave her, but Phyl had refused to see the show again and had pointed out, reasonably, that she'd often been left alone before.

It was like the evenings they had shared in the winter. Mattie was curled up on cushions, asleep in front of the TV under the faded crochet blanket, and Lucy was knitting a complex landscape sweater in glowing silk, in shades of russet, tan, and ivory. Lucy, who used to wear jeans, sweat-shirts, and running shoes almost all the time, now looked like a lady in a Revlon advertisement. She was wearing an amethyst silk dress with pleated sleeves and black sandals that looked as though they cost four hundred dollars. Her Gypsy look had been brought under glossy control: her satin-black hair had been blow-dried by someone with at least two spare hands and architectural flair. It was a new uniform for a new life-style.

Phyl looked, if not happy, then certainly alert.

A crystal rose-bowl was full of the red roses Robert Talbot had sent, their stalks cut short to even up the damage Daniel had done. Auntie Gwen could not abide waste. The roses were half open and perfectly lovely, and Rosemary was aware of Phyl watching her as she leaned over to sniff them.

"You know what I found in the hall when Lucy came? The note. Dad must have dropped it when you fell, and it got kicked into the corner by the door," Phyl said.

Rosemary snatched it from her and then became aware that they were all watching her, so she tried to look impassive as she read it. But her pulse beat was harsh with anxiety. Then her face must have registered surprise. "Is this it? This all?"

Phyl nodded.

"It sounded so . . . Daniel made it sound, well . . . actionable! Listen—do you think this is a note to break an arm for? Hey?" And in the voice of a secretary reading back her shorthand Rosemary read the note.

" 'Returned herewith: one garment, shed on a very pleasant journey. Will ring you soon about the film. I hope I caused no trouble you couldn't handle. Robert.' "

They were all silent for a moment as Rosemary rephrased it in her mind in the scornful, hate-loaded, innuendo-ridden voice Daniel had used. It certainly made a difference.

"Garment?" said Auntie Gwen, grim as an interrogator.

"My sun-hat. It was in the back seat of his car. Robert Talbot gave me a lift home at night."

"What film? He's taking you to a film?"

"No," Rosemary said patiently, but damning Auntie Gwen, whose relationship to the obvious was like a magnet's to a steel pin. "There may be a job for me on a film his company is associated with. If there's a preview, his secretary will let me know so I can see it. Business, Auntie Gwen. Business." Then her patience finished. "BUSINESS, Daniel!" she shouted. Lucy stopped knitting and Mattie sat up, looking glazed. "How *can* Daniel have the cheek to be . . . to be jealous of me? Suspicious? What a bloody nerve!"

"Shush!" said Auntie Gwen. "You'll upset yourself. You'll upset Phyl again." But she already had—Phyl had darted off to her room.

"It's been like this around here. Like, terrible," Rosemary said limply as Auntie Gwen marched off after Phyl.

"All the things that have happened to you in a week!" Lucy shuddered in sympathy. "How do you know where to start?"

"I don't," she said. There was no comfortable position for her arm except to place her other hand under the cast-covered elbow and help fight gravity. "I've worked out a heading for my condition: I'm a forcibly liberated female. I'm the reluctant liberee."

"Yes, that's good. How does it feel?"

"Weird. Most of the time I think I'm hallucinating. Then Auntie Gwen jerks me back to reality with all the finesse and delicacy of a cheese grater. No, I mustn't say that—she's kept everything going since"—she tapped the plaster. "I haven't been much good. I think I've gone a bit mad, actually."

"That's good," said Lucy smoothly. "If you're a little bit mad you'll find it easier to cope in this insane world. It's like knowing a smattering of the language in a foreign country. Have you heard from Daniel since . . ."

"No. I can't reach him. But anyway I'm too disgusted to think about him—he's carried on like a brat. I felt so sorry for him; just days ago I actually felt guilty, having left him to run the company on his own and having to suffer all its problems. But the bastard brought them all on himself! So now I feel"—and Rosemary cut her throat with her finger. "Stuff him. I've had him. I want to know about *you*. Tell me—everything. The engagement—did Malcolm go on one knee?"

Mattie stirred again, obviously not asleep anymore, and Lucy glanced at her. "I'm dying to talk. But not now. There's school tomorrow, and its been a bit rich for her, too—late nights, a new father-figure. I'm dying to know all about you and Robert Talbot. Talk about dark horses!"

But Rosemary shuddered at the thought of turning her foolishness into an anecdote so she, too, glanced at the wakeful child as an excuse to postpone intimacy.

"One thing, though," Lucy said, and smiled, thrilled and glossy, more beautiful than Rosemary had ever seen her. "They're making a pilot tomorrow of a new mid-morning talk show. And I'm being tried out as a co-host. I actually did some tests today."

"Lucy! That's wonderful!"

Nodding, her eyes shining, Lucy packed her knitting into its grey suede bag. "Just pinch me—or, better still, wish me luck."

"Of course. Of course. When will you know?"

"Maybe immediately, maybe never. You know how they work."

Rosemary tried to look like one who knew.

"Come on, lump. Ooh, too much McDonalds in here, by the feel of you—you get heavier every time we visit." Mattie giggled in her half-sleep, a dead weight in Lucy's thin arms.

·   ·   ·

More demands, petitions, and notices arrived, and these Auntie Gwen whisked away from Rosemary's shocked and tearful gaze and delivered to Jim Begg's office as quickly as though they were bingo numbers and he was the caller.

Auntie Gwen behaved as though there had been a place and a role for her all along in Rosemary's house. The guest-room, with its celadon wallpaper and white cane furniture, had become simultaneously swamped and homey under the drapings of Auntie Gwen's large mauve floral continental quilt, her pink dressing-gown, and a collection of her more precious begonias and African violets which, she said, were happier on the window-sill here where she could test the soil every day, than at home where the neighbour might drown them. "Don't like wet feet, do you, my darlings?" she murmured to them.

She had taken over the grocery shopping—that memory game that is never won because even on the rare occasion when absolutely everything is listed, obtained, and then crossed out, by the next day a new list will have started.

Rosemary had often looked at the other women on escalators down to the parking spaces under the shopping centres, like herself, burdened with white plastic shopping bags full of things that had had to be bought to keep the feeding process going without a hitch. Like ants carrying crumbs twice their own size, women scurried home with toilet rolls and instant coffee and eggs and oranges to fill up the spaces husbands and children so rapidly cleared. It was a job only noticed in default. "Why's there no milk?" someone would ask, bewildered, as though a tap had been cut off by Council. Or, "Do you realise that there isn't a single tomato in the fridge?" someone would say, as though a government had fallen.

Shopping hardly rates a mention on those lists of things wives and mothers are supposed to be—lists starting with nurse, psychologist, gourmet cook, mistress . . . Yet, apart from surface-wiping, shopping is the great, constant inroad on every woman's day, to be fitted in between trips to dentists and schools and jobs, or on the way home from hospital or from rendezvous with lovers. Bad enough when there was time and money to do it, but lately there had been less of both. Shirley Coote, Daniel's secretary, had said Rosemary couldn't have blood out of a stone.

Now Auntie Gwen was doing it. Buying livid green toilet rolls and tinned fruit with added sugar and thin, white, factory-packed spaghetti instead of curls of green or yellow fettucine—but buying it and paying for it. So far, Rosemary's feeble attempts to reach for her purse had elicited such a bounce of refusal that she'd retreated, tired and embarrassed. The problem of reimbursing Auntie Gwen would have to wait until her head worked.

Auntie Gwen's way of being kind—and of course she was being kind—bore an air of judgement. It was hard to be grateful to someone who took over your house like an officer relieving the rookies in a besieged fort.

Flowers—pink carnations—arrived from Shirley Coote. When Rosemary phoned to thank her, she asked, without any hope, about the ownership of the crashed Volvo, and it turned out that it was hers.

"We had to get rid of some money because things were different then—we were looking at paying a hefty lot of company tax at that time," Shirley Coote explained, perhaps to remind herself of better times. As soon as she'd rung off, Rosemary wept with relief from fiscal tension she hadn't even properly acknowledged yet. And also because, no matter what Shirley said, the Volvo had been a loving, personal gesture from Daniel, a gesture which, now that his love was destroyed, seemed as poignant and pathetic as a glow-worm's light in a well.

"Insurance money, hey?" said Auntie Gwen. "They take months, and for once that's a good thing. By the time that comes through all this other business should be settled and the liquidators won't be able to touch it."

"But . . ."

"No buts. They need never know it's yours. Tell the girl to send the papers here and I'll look after them, and if anyone asks you can say with perfect truthfulness that your husband took the car. But they won't ask if they don't fall over it, I shouldn't think. Now listen, I was going to give you some money. Had prepared meself for a fight. But now it can be a loan, OK? I've got some stashed away. Just stop bloody well grizzling all the time. I've never seen so much crying in my life, and I used to be a nurse!"

Rosemary's attempt at a grateful hug was an awkward flop—for someone as fat as Auntie Gwen, she moved very fast.

·   ·   ·

By Thursday Phyl felt well enough for school again and though Dr. Saxon had said she should stay home all week, Rosemary did not stop her; her friends might do a better job of cheering her up than the household could. On Friday morning Robert Talbot's secretary phoned. Auntie Gwen answered. "It's him. For you," she said, her huge hand over the mouthpiece.

"Daniel?"

"Talbot."

"No, I can't talk to him!"

"You certainly can. That's where the strength lies, my girl," she said,

and thrust the phone towards Rosemary so that any further argument
would have been heard.

"Mrs. Quilty? Ah, there you are. Hello. Mr. Talbot asked me to tell
you there's a preview of the first part of 'The Mount Victorians' on
Tuesday at five at the studio."

"Oh, yes?" said Rosemary, feeling trapped.

"Would you like to be picked up, Mrs. Quilty? I can arrange for a
car to be at your house at four-thirty." As she agreed to this convenient
arrangement, Rosemary pondered the significance. Would the other
guests be picked up, too? Was she special? The mood of the red dress
was so remote from her now that it seemed to belong to another person's
life. Yet it had been only a week since her trip to Lithgow.

But he sent red roses. He likes me, she thought. There's no argument
about that. It was knowledge that felt like secret treasure hidden in the
pain and confusion-filled time between the phone call and Tuesday. She
kept thinking of what it would be like to meet Robert Talbot again—
what she could do to save her house. Perhaps her future security, perhaps even her whole life, would change. Red roses! They must mean
something!

.   .   .

On Saturday, Auntie Gwen went home, the neighbour who'd been
entrusted with the feeding of the cats having displayed human frailty
by going to visit her daughter in Nowra.

"I'll be back, never fear. I know all about liquidators, believe me.
Sam was a real bad lot."

"Sam?"

She looked at Rosemary, astonished.

"Sam. My husband. You never knew about Sam? Went off in—must
have been—fifty-two. You were little then, of course. We lived next
door to your Mum's chemist shop and I think she saved my sanity."

Rosemary guessed that her mother's help in fifty-two had not been
nearly as forceful as Auntie Gwen's was now. She stood with the children
and watched the beige Datsun round the corner and felt as though an
invading army had shipped out.

"Come on," she said, taking Bobby's hand and bumping Phyl with
her plaster. "Let's get out of here. Let's go for a walk. Roseville Bridge?
French's Forest?"

"Oxford Falls. We may be able to ride horses if they're not too
booked," Bobby said, but Phyl hung back.

"I don't feel like it. It's too far and I've got lots to do."

"Homework?"

"Sort of."

"Come on. The fresh air will do you good."

Phyl pulled a face but went inside with Rosemary to change shoes and fetch keys.

The phone rang. "Rosemary?" said Patrick. "Are you well? Or better?"

"Yes, thanks. Better enough to be going for a walk with Phyl and Bobby. We've been rather house-bound this week."

"How's your arm? Was it broken?"

"Oh, yes. Yes. It's in plaster now." So Auntie Gwen had not told him the details of Daniel's second violence. "Hurts like hell every now and then, but I'm surviving. Thanks." I'm so rude, she thought. "What about you? And Geoffrey? Geoff, is it? You OK?"

"Fine. Fine thanks. You haven't got a car yet, have you?"

"No. But even if I did, I couldn't drive."

"No. Well, I'm baby-sitting a rather odd vehicle this weekend—a sort of mini-bus. Rather nice, very roomy. I wondered if you, Phyl, and Bobby would like to come out with us tomorrow if the weather's nice. A picnic somewhere."

"Can I call you back? Within ten minutes?"

"Sure." He sounded serene. He always sounded serene.

"Who was that?" Phyl asked.

"Patrick."

"I like him. He's straight."

"I think that's the trouble."

"What?"

"That he's nice. Patrick. So I can't get him into focus. He makes me feel—aware of the bad bits of myself."

"What bad bits?"

"He makes me feel mean."

"You? Mean? Oh, Mum, that's ridiculous. You're such a softy. Such a sweety!"

"Yeah," said Rosemary, simpering like a singer in a Sondheim show. "That's me—sickly icky sweet."

Phyl breathed out decisively and turned away.

"Oh, darling, don't look like that. I'm sorry. The thing is, I don't like that either—being thought of as sweet. I don't want to be sweet, or bitter or sour. Just a nice gourmet mixture that I can't seem to get right."

"You, too? I thought people grew out of being mixed up."

"Maybe some do, but I've never met one. Even Patrick says he's mixed up, but you'd never know it, would you? He wants to take us out in some bus he's borrowed. Yes. Bus. With his retarded son on a picnic. I said I'd call him back."

"When?"

"In ten minutes. Five now."

"When does he want to take us?"

"Tomorrow."

"Well, that's OK. We're not planning anything else?"

"You're the sweetie, really. Untroubled by doubt! I said I'd ring back because I'm having a moral dilemma. This is it: If I go out with Patrick, is it because I'm being sweet to him or because I'm selfish?"

Phyl gazed at her, fascinated.

"Are you two going to stand there gassing all afternoon?" asked Bobby, dressed for adventure. "The sun'll go down!"

"I'd better phone him back. Do you want to go on a picnic tomorrow, Bob? With Patrick? And his son?"

"Sure. Patrick's OK."

So, still uneasy, Rosemary phoned and accepted. Patrick said they'd be around at about ten and that she was not to worry about lunch—his housekeeper was good at picnic hampers. Patrick made her feel the way Auntie Gwen did, as though everything was already worked out and all she had to do was play a bit part in her own life. And she was supposed to be grateful.

.   .   .

On the way to Oxford Falls—a much farther walk than she'd realised, along roads zipping with weekend traffic on its way to the beaches at Dee Why, Collaroy, and Palm Beach—Rosemary tried to talk to Phyl about Daniel, but she simply shrugged. They were silent for a while. Then Rosemary took Phyl's hand and said, "Seeing we're both going through adolescence, let's make a vow to help each other."

"Actually," Phyl said so quickly that it was obvious that she had been waiting for the right opportunity, "I've decided to leave school."

Oh my God. It's me, all over again, thought Rosemary. But now I'm Jean. On the outside she made sure her consternation didn't show. "Tell me why? And what you've planned?"

Phyl, who had been expecting a battle, visibly relaxed. Her plans were vague—she'd get a job, any job. Share a house with people—nice people. She just wanted to get out of being a schoolgirl, of feeling trapped.

"You know, of course, that there's the danger of simply swapping one trap for another?"

"I *knew* you'd say that!"

"Then you know that I'd suggest you find the job first, before you leave, since jobs are hard to find—rather than join the thousands on the dole."

"And you don't mind if I leave school?"

"No," she lied. "Not if you've made a real plan for your next step. Worked it all out and got yourself established."

"I want to be a writer," Phyl said shyly. "You don't need school for that."

"So did your gran. Did you know that? But then she got too busy, looking after me. I've still got some of the things she wrote when she was young—your age. Lovely things, I'll show you. She'd have been great, your gran. You'll be great."

By now they had turned into the Wakehurst Parkway where, even so near the expressway, it looked as though the bushy forest might reclaim the suburbs. Not much further down the road Rosemary knew, from having often zipped along it in a car, that the bush on either side was dense enough to get lost in. Tall pines and other introduced species lived luxuriantly among the gums and banksia and both indigenous and exotic creepers trailed between them. It was thick and lush for much farther than they could see. Presumably, among the possums, flying foxes, and other small mammals whose corpses so often lay along the side of the road, there were nests of feral cats. And she'd heard that people had introduced bird species, too—nest-attacking blackbirds, brought in cages from Europe during the early time of settlement, and maybe others, too.

"What a meddling species we humans are!" she said to Phyl, who agreed, surprised, even gratified, since it sounded to her like a confession.

At the riding stables, Rosemary sat on bench in the shade, watching the children lining up on docile ponies for a controlled stroll through the nearby clear stretches, regularly bulldozed to keep fires contained and controllable. It had been a hot day, and the radio had warned that there was a high fire danger. This whole forest had been an inferno only a few years before—some of the trees still showed black scars under the light green lace of leaves which would soon extend to branches and replace those that had crashed to the ground. Some trees had been too badly burnt and stood limbless—charcoal monuments to the two-day holocaust. But today there was no whiff of smoke, and anyway, they were near enough to the road to escape if it happened again.

Rosemary thought about the cycle of their lives. In turn Jean and then she had felt as Phyl did now—that she could do anything she chose providing that no one held her back. Neither of them could have guessed that such strong belief was so vulnerable to bombardment by circumstance. Jean had lost her belief that she could do anything and instead had begun to believe in control, until it took over her life.

In Rosemary's case, her belief in herself, her judgement, and her lovability had been so minced and battered that she was not sure she'd ever get the pieces together again. She'd said she was an actor and had been all her life. It was true. But now, despite Jeremy's encouraging words, it was almost certainly too late for a career in such an overcrowded profession for which she had no formal qualifications. There was not a chance, unless she continued to believe in miracles, or magic, the way Phyl now did—the way, she suddenly remembered, she had felt in the fitting room when she bought the red dress—as though all that was required was a long but relatively simple acrobatic leap from ladder to ladder.

I leapt, she thought. And I crashed. Now I've got to get up again—I can't afford to crack up.

For Phyl, Rosemary vowed, there'd have to be a better solution: neither Jean's terrible control nor her own blind trust in love. For Phyl it would have to be something that combined the two in a way which would offer options forever.

They took a taxi home from Oxford Falls, having decided that another eight-kilometre walk was more than Rosemary's now-throbbing arm could take. The western sky was washed in glorious bands of apricot, orange, purple, and grey. In the middle the sun was translucent red, like a small child's hand illuminated by a camping torch.

"Must be a real bad bushfire out there somewhere. Blue Mountains it looks like. Or Richmond," said the taxi driver.

Thirteen

Cooking with one hand was a new challenge. It had been difficult enough when her arm was impeded only by the sling, though Rosemary had managed to do all sorts of things with care, angles, and leverage, but with the plaster cast it was much more difficult. For a while, she struggled to peel and then slice an onion, then contributed some wry laughter to the tears its fumes produced. The third time it slipped out of the grip she'd managed with the cast against the sink corner, she threw the knife across the kitchen. The novelty of her new dependency had worn off.

"Help!" she yelled. "Help! I'm starving!"

Phyl and Bobby both ran anxiously into the kitchen and then stood and laughed as, wordlessly, she showed them how she'd been trying to cope.

She set the table and did other one-handed things while the kids cooked under instruction.

"Did you see what Auntie Gwen bought? This fridge is stashed to the eyeballs with stuff I've never seen before. Look." Phyl held up a pale, oval, plastic-wrapped object. "Spiced meat loaf. What do you do with that?"

"You slice it onto white bread sandwiches and eat it with bottled tomato sauce."

"It's luncheon meat," said Bobby firmly. "You've had it lots of times before you became a food snob. I like it. I like all the things Auntie Gwen bought. A bloke gets sick of brown rice and yoghurt sometimes, and salad. And even you still like sausage rolls."

"Home-made, yes. Bought ones are full of cereal and entrails," said Phyl.

"Yah!" Bobby looked confident and amused and not at all outnumbered. "Auntie Gwen bought stuff that's easy to cook—all you've got to do is heat it up in the microwave. It's mad to keep making things you need to chop and stir and mix and wash up when you can't."

Rosemary had a comforting vision of the sort of man he was going to be.

The meal was a compromise between Auntie Gwen's and Rosemary's choices of food, and the three of them felt good together for the first time in weeks.

"I'll get it," said Bobby when the phone rang, then maddeningly ignored her signals to say a name, simply supplying polite monosyllables until the end.

"Patrick," he told them. "The guy lending him the bus has changed his mind because some pensioners need to be taken to Canberra. So the picnic's next weekend instead." He hadn't asked to talk to her. Rosemary felt equally divided between mild relief and mild disappointment.

.   .   .

More ominous-looking legal documents came on Monday and Tuesday and Jim Begg spent more and more time talking to her on the phone. Nothing that she read or that he said reinforced the bit of hope he'd offered her the previous week.

Rosemary started hardening herself against the house. She tested herself in every room, feeling the sunlight through the windows, checking the views, and in all of them there were faults that made it possible for her to love it less. The kitchen, for instance, was on the south-west side, so it was dark in the mornings and hot in summer—often too hot for the air-conditioning to cope with. And it was narrow, and the choice of moulded wooden cupboard doors had never been wise—bits of fallen food crisped into the decorations and had to be scratched out with a knife or scrubbed out with a toothbrush.

She managed to find something unlovely in every room except the yellow lounge and her light, bright bedroom with its long view over soft green bush and its precious glimpses of Middle Harbour. If she could just remove these two rooms and let the liquidator take the rest, that would be bearable.

The only good news was Lucy's, which she told Rosemary on the phone. Lucy was so busy nowadays that they scarcely saw her. The executive producer had told her that they were going to try her out on the weather a few times in December, and if people liked her she'd be given the co-host news job in January. "I feel guilty, telling you all this," Lucy said.

"No, no, you must tell me. Everything. Don't you see," Rosemary said, "you are living proof that a terrible string of disasters could equally well become a flood of delights."

"Oh, it will! It must!" Lucy said.

Rosemary had a vision of Lucy having delicate little lunches with equally prettily dressed new friends, her peers in the industry, with whom she'd find it easy to gossip and swap tips.

.   .   .

There was still the secret treasure of Robert Talbot's invitation to see "The Mount Victorians." It had been the subject of inner debate on at least two levels. Rosemary's prim, reproving side had stated that she could not possibly go, since Robert Talbot was her husband's enemy and, by default and circumstance, hers.

But, she answered herself, surely this gives me the advantage a diplomatic spy has? I can see into the enemy camp?

On a deeper level, there was no debate at all. It wasn't anything that could be put into words without sounding banal and even pornographic. This wordless voice was full of confidence that Robert Talbot signified a way out of all her traps and full of reassurance that Daniel was no longer anyone who deserved her loyalty. So it was the voice that prevailed.

Auntie Gwen came back on Monday, her Datsun's boot full of replacements for the food she presumed they had eaten in her absence.

"I thought I already had the biggest fridge in Australia," Rosemary said, having found that jocularity was more acceptable than gratitude. "But I'll have to get an annex to it!"

"Growing kids. And you're convalescent—need building up if you're going to start job hunting after Christmas."

In a flash of grateful brilliance, Rosemary responded on automatic to this handy cue—she had been worrying about Auntie Gwen's reaction since the Friday afternoon phone call from Robert Talbot's office.

"I just may get one sooner," she said. "I'm going for an interview tomorrow afternoon," she said. "At the TV studio."

"They've got a part for a wounded governess in your soapie then?" Auntie Gwen asked not trying at all to control the ironic flickering of her thinly plucked eyebrows.

"Why not?" said Rosemary firmly. "The script is still being written." Auntie Gwen was silent, but her eyebrows continued their comment.

.   .   .

When the now-familiar black limousine arrived late on Tuesday afternoon, Rosemary was ready. She'd covered the sling with a large, beau-

tifully patterned silk scarf in shades of red, purple, brown, and silver—
it made a striking accessory to her pale grey suit.

"Giving ya tennis arm a holiday, huh, Mrs. Quilty?" It was Olly, who
had driven her to Lithgow.

"Tripped over the cat," she said.

"Nasty that. Me brother-in-law had no end of trouble with his arm.
Just a simple break, they told him. Nothing much. Well! Bone didn't
knit. Months of physio, X-rays and that. He was lucky, but—he did it
at work, see. Barrel rolled on him. So in the end he got a lot of compo—
enough for him and me sister to get themselves a waterside holiday
home at Umina."

A few "Uh huhs" kept the flow of his conversation going and freed
her to think. She presented herself with a questionnaire, a neat trick to
aid confronting things that were trying to slip away, out of focus. It was
more than a week since she'd broken her arm and been warned of
bankruptcy—she could not go on reacting as though the shock was new.
She had to look ahead.

All day her body had been preparing itself. She was conscious of her
nipples against the black lace of the absurdly skimpy bra she'd chosen
to wear. She'd told herself, at the time, that it was because its straps
were detachable so she could put it on easily around the cast. Its lack
of contribution to her body's profile was not important—her right-
angled arm disguised that, anyway. She was perfumed, damp, and gleaming. Through all of the horrible week she'd been sustained by her secret
memory of the way Robert Talbot's hand had felt on her cheek and her
neck—she could almost taste him.

The grey stone building which housed Robert Talbot's TV studios
and offices was built on a hill which should have given it wonderful
views over the parklands that almost surrounded it on three sides. But
the view was blocked by numerous equally large buildings and oldish
houses; this was the heart of a busy, light industrial area. She was half
expecting to bump into Lucy, if not Malcolm, among the groups of busy,
interrelating people. But there was an air of sombre calm about the part
of the building she was ushered into: a reception room crisply managed
by two elderly women. Rows of black leather chairs were full, mainly
of grey-suited men who looked as though waiting was not something
they were good at. Advertising men, she thought, or lawyers, maybe.

A private bus full of happy-looking middle-aged women pulled slowly
past the double glass doors and many of them waved, still under the
cheerful spell of whatever show it was they'd earlier been brought to
watch.

A thin young man in black clothes very much too big for him came quickly down a curved staircase. He moved as gracefully as a ballet dancer, and all but the most world-weary of the waiting people looked at him, expecting that he was a TV star they should know. He had five small, sparkling earrings up the side of one lobe and a white clipboard in his hand.

"OK," he said, like a prefect. "Will the following people please come with me." Rosemary's name was one on a list of about twenty.

On the way up the stairs, one of the group touched her shoulder. "Rosemary? Rosemary Quilty?"

She stared hard at the man's lined face.

"Trev! How nice!" She hoped she'd hidden her surprise at the way this former youthful colleague of Daniel's had aged. It was not just the fact that the front part of his long, dark hair had vanished, leaving the rest like a skirt around his blotchily tanned dome. Years of cigarettes and long lunches had sagged and crumpled his skin, which looked as though it had emptied itself of some bulky softness which had since slipped to his belly where it was divided up and down by a thin belt.

"What are you doing here?" they both asked at once, then both laughed. "I'm an adman now—sort of. The public relations company I started when I left Daniel—it grew like Topsy." See what you lost? his expression said. "Merged with the ad company last year. You knew that?"

"Of course! Terrific!" she lied. "And I'm here because Malcolm Henry wangled me an invitation. Lucy, of course, is my neighbour."

They were led into an ante-room of the preview theatre where pretty girls with trays of drinks circulated. The volume of sound began to rise.

"Things going well with you? I heard Daniel and you aren't together anymore?" Trevor asked. Having taken two whiskies off a passing tray, he poured one into the other and returned the empty glass. Rosemary chose mineral water.

"No. What about you? Still living happily ever after with . . ." What was the name of the bride at that long-ago wedding?

"Oh, no. Janine and I split while Dan was still dabbling in video seminars, Ro. Or shortly after, anyway. I've lived happily ever after with three nice ladies since then. Not all at the same time, mind you. Though maybe that's an arrangement that would have solved some problems; they could have scrapped with each other instead of me. No, I've given away the husband game for the time being. What about you? You fancy-free?"

The appalling thought occurred to her that he was planning to ask her out. "Not really, no," she said firmly.

"Old Daniel, hey. You never can tell, can you? Those quiet ones. I'd have been prepared to put a bet on him being the 'til-death-us-do-part type." Rosemary was surprised to hear Daniel described as a quiet one— the echoes of his voice had only just begun to die down in her head. "Mad to give up a bird like you," Trevor continued. "Kids of course, too. How're the kids?" He wasn't even trying to sound sincere. "So he ran off with the delectable Angela McLennan, hey? And what's she doing now—I mean apart from . . . ?" He pumped his hand up and down and she politely pretended to be amused. "I once predicted she had a real future in soapies. Did you see that ABC series called—some god-awful name—'Teen-Times' or something? Couple of years ago?"

Fortunately she did not have to answer because two other people she assumed were admen pounced on Trev and loudly claimed his attention. She moved quickly away. Angela in a soapie? He must be mistaken.

She had glanced around a few times, hoping to see Robert Talbot, and finally did, deep in the heart of a knot of men who, by their confident stance and dark suits, proclaimed themselves to be among the bosses. He did not look her way.

He invited me, she reminded herself.

His secretary did. He was keeping a promise, that's all.

.   .   .

They were ushered in to the theatrette and the man in black, who turned out to be Mervyn Thomas of publicity, stood up to welcome them. He said the pilot had taken a long time to get off the ground for lots of boring reasons not worth going into. They might be interested to know, though, that some of the early scenes were shot as long ago as three years. "It's been a difficult birth," he said. "But worth it, as you'll see. Anyhow, we're pleased with it."

Murmurs and giggles from the advertising people around her made Rosemary think of the bad fairies in bedtime story christenings. Smart people in a group always manage to sound as if they already know things.

"Everyone got a full glass? Everyone OK? Right, Dave, we can start."

"The Mount Victorians" had all the ingredients and qualities Rosemary had expected from Robert Talbot's telling: superb scenery, close-ups of cute wombats, startled baby possums, lovable wallabies, the odd wildflower. Tall, light-freckling trees were full of the sounds of whip-birds, bell-birds, cicadas, and other creatures who obligingly filled the soundtrack between lines of dialogue.

The people, especially the settlers' family, were terrific, instantly endearing in the humour-filled and purposeful way they tackled the ardours of living in a wattle-and-daub hut in the middle of nowhere. Some of the lines were very funny, and there was gratifying laughter around her which made her feel relieved on Robert Talbot's behalf. Daniel had told her that the first trick was to get the press to laugh out loud, then they were with you all the way.

During a scene that looked as though it were painted in oils, in which the mother and her daughters were all dressed in the muted tones of faded cotton, their long skirts brushing the twigs and leaves, their white caps and aprons flashing contrast against the dark wood structure of their lean-to kitchen, Trevor nudged Rosemary from behind and whispered, "There she is. Angela. In the blue."

And there she was. The oldest daughter, the one who had been spurning the advances of the nice boy from the inn. Of course the face had been familiar. Faces on TV always are. Trevor must have thought that she knew Angela was in the mini-series. Or perhaps he wasn't sure she knew, and couldn't resist making a little contribution to her pain.

Most of the rest of the two-hour movie was lost for Rosemary. She was fascinated by Angela, who seemed so fragile in her porcelain beauty when there were snakes and strong young men about. Yet when a horse and its rider fell down a gully, killing the horse and breaking the young prospector's back, she was the one who pulled him out, her sweat mingling with his blood, her hair pulled, whisped and dusty, over her urgent face.

Then she'd been steadfast as a nun, nursing him through the worst, gritting her teeth through his pain, and weeping privately. She'd even bullied him a little, so humorously, so gently that her words could have been the beating of the wings of a butterfly. And in the scene where the innkeeper's wife stuck her hat-pin into the injured young man's foot and he didn't feel it—which made him turn his face to the wall, determined to die—it was she who wheedled him into eating and who massaged the limb and urged and encouraged, until the wonderful day when she tickled his foot with a feather and it made him laugh. Then she'd been like a Madonna—or perhaps a virgin princess.

He'd fallen in love with her. No man could have resisted her. She'd turned him down, of course, but so kindly that his ego, far from being bruised, was probably enhanced.

Angela McLennan. She knew how to be irresistible.

Rosemary felt like a voyeur, gazing at her husband's lover as she revealed her full emotional range on the blown-up TV screen. If she was so good at acting, why the hell was she working at Patchwork, handing out name-tags at book launchings? How much did Trevor know? And all the other people here—the ones who sold the soap that made soapies possible?

Maybe it was no more than a bizarre coincidence that Daniel's new woman was in the old part of "The Mount Victorians" and his old—or rather his former—woman was hoping to be in the new part. Rosemary felt like a bee trying to fly through glass: frustrated, vulnerable, doubting her instincts, and drowning her reason in buzz.

. . .

At the end, when all the others clapped, Rosemary noted how cleverly the script left the plot's ends just touching rather than tied. Most of the other guests left fairly quickly, avoiding Mervyn and his obvious appetite for feedback. Others murmured enthusiastically in groups for a while, though from what she heard in passing, they were discussing interest rates and offshore investments more than "The Mount Victorians." But those who spoke to Robert Talbot must have said the right things because he looked pleased. I can't hang around here waiting to be the last, she thought. What now?

"Rosemary Quilty?" She hadn't noticed Mervyn glide towards her. "I've got a message for you. There's been a hold-up about your transport—it might be half an hour. Sorry about that. Look, let me find you somewhere comfortable to wait and have some coffee." So that was it. Robert Talbot was not even going to acknowledge her presence. This man had probably lost her her house by sending her a bunch of red roses—the costliest flowers in the world—and she was being left to pay the price. But she let nothing of this show.

"Maybe Lucy Barlow is still here? I could get a lift with her—she lives next door to me."

Mervyn delegated one of the girls who had earlier served the drinks to try to find Lucy in the huge place. But it was well past eight: Malcolm's program had finished for the night, and they had both left. To Rosemary, who had been led into a little reception room which offered a pile of old *Time, Bulletin,* and *B&T* magazines, a coffee machine with an "Out of order" sign on it, and a phone that the switchboard didn't notice, it was *déjà vu*—a repeat of the night she was abandoned in Lithgow. But, just as he had there, Robert Talbot walked in, so she should not have been surprised.

"Mrs. Quilty," he said.

"But not for long," she answered, quicker than thinking, and then blushed as her brain struggled, like an off-guard policeman, to catch up with her tongue.

"No, I suppose not. Pretty rough time you've been having with Daniel Quilty," he said, and lightly touched the silk around her plaster cast. She watched his strong hand, willing it to stroke the skin of her other hand which had got into the habit of lying protectively on the hard cast forearm, but he delved into his pocket. "Broken? I was worried about that. How bad is it?"

"I'll be trussed 'til Christmas. Like all the other turkeys," she began jokingly. Then she outstripped her control again and blurted, "Actually, it's bloody awful. Sore—which is bad enough—but it gets in the way. It's the worst time for it to have happened: I can't cook—I'm forced into helplessness. I can't even drive." She bit her lip. Whatever she said sounded accusing or whining but she could not stop. "Unless your new script-writer gives her a broken arm, I couldn't even be the damn governess!"

"I was going to offer you a drink. . . ."

"I'd accept. Thank you," she said, mastering her manners. "And I'm not drunk, unless Mervyn spiked the mineral water."

"What's so bad about being drunk?" he said and ushered her into a much more luxurious room—obviously the one he used on studio business visits. Pale carpet, neither grey nor lilac, softened a floor that seemed half the size of a tennis court. At one end were cream-coloured chairs and a business-like, low table and at the other was a cluster of deeply comfortable black leather armchairs around a giant TV screen.

"What will it be?" he asked from the bar which had been hidden behind prim padding on a wall unit. "I'd recommend a shot of medicinal brandy."

"Will it cure madness? With dry ginger and ice, please."

"Madness?"

He gave her the drink and sat with his own on a nearby chair looking polite, puzzled, businesslike. Bugger you! she thought.

"Madness, or dreaming. It's been the worst couple of weeks in my life. You know that I'm probably going to lose my house?"

"What? Because of Quilty's company?"

"Yes."

"Jesus!" he said, and stood up. "You're sure? You got someone working on it? A good solicitor?"

"Jim Begg. He's been a family friend, a neighbour, for years."

"Never heard of him," he said, as finally as an executioner. He walked around the room and his restlessness and energy seemed too much for it—he could have been a hawk in a tiny cage. "Look, I don't know what Quilty has been saying to you but . . ."

"That you did it," she said flatly. "Took all his clients away."

He rubbed a hand across his face as though removing a layer of tight skin. "Well, he's partly right. The reasons don't concern you. But I do want you to know that the point it's reached—of liquidation proceedings and of threatening your personal property—that's not my doing."

"Maybe not directly, no. But aren't you connected with the computer company that's going for the house?"

"No, no. Not at all," he said. But she was sure someone as rich and powerful as he lied easily. She told him the computer company's name and watched him for signs, but he shook his head once, quickly, as though he'd soon be bored, if not irritated.

"They supplied the huge computer that Daniel needed for printing and direct mailing. It's got lasers," she said. "He would have been able to pay for it if it weren't for . . ."

"And he put the house, the family home, against a company debt? Was it that Jim Begg who advised him to that?"

"No. Jim's my solicitor. Daniel makes—made—his own decisions."

"Let me get the picture. You're a director, too, right? You sign the forms, you don't question much . . ."

"I'm an idiot, is what you're saying." She put her glass down and lowered her head. "I can't blame Daniel. Can't blame you."

Quickly, silently for someone so big, he crossed the room to her and lifted her chin. The feeling of his hand obliterated all other sensations—she couldn't hear him or think, so gently she took his wrist and moved his hand away.

"Being a loyal wife is not generally regarded as idiotic," he said.

"Unless the loyal wife's disloyal husband has left her and gone off with a pretty girl half his age. Then she's an idiot not to read the forms she signs. That's what Jim Begg says, and he's right," she said, flushed.

Robert Talbot had walked away again. She finished her drink fairly quickly, nervously, and went on talking.

"Anyway, it turns out that I'm not such a loyal wife. I told you things I shouldn't have, wouldn't have, if I'd known you were trying to take over Daniel's business."

"And you didn't know?"

"Of course not!" she said crossly, aware that she was still blushing. "I know it probably looked like that—like petty vindictiveness. But I'm not like that. If I had wanted to wound Daniel, I'm sure I could have thought up something with less-damaging consequences. Less damaging to myself and my children, is what I mean. I would never have put the house at risk."

"The house was at risk from the time you guaranteed it."

"But Patchwork was so strong."

"When did you sign the guarantees?"

"I'm not quite sure—sometime in the winter. July, perhaps."

They looked at each other.

Of course, she thought. You'd been thoroughly undermining Patchwork by then—it wasn't strong at all. Daniel was desperate, and he let me take the risk.

She felt anger mix in with the other emotions Robert Talbot was stirring. Most of the anger was for Daniel but some was for him, too, and she didn't care if it showed in her face. There was a rush of words she didn't even try to edit before they reached her lips.

"Daniel came to see me three days after you . . . were there." She stroked the silk of her sling, aware that his eyes were on it. "It was stormy, of course. But then we'd sort of agreed to do what we could to save the house. He would have gone to the liquidators. No, that's not true." She made sure his eyes were on her face. "He'd have gone to you. But then your flowers arrived." He stared at her intently, then finished his drink at a gulp. "Red roses," she said. "He thought . . ." She wished she had another drink to fiddle with, to drown her words, since his complete lack of expression did not help at all.

"He thought?"

"That you . . . and I . . . "

She could not look at him but waited for him to say, "He's right, of course," which would make everything right in its wrongness. Instead he was silent for more strain-filled time. Then he said, "Those 'business secrets' you told me—the casino plan, which, by the way, was absurd and unworkable—they were nothing I didn't know already. You could call them the actions of a desperate man." He said it kindly, as though offering absolution and as though the desperate man was someone neither of them knew. He offered her another drink.

"No brandy this time, thanks," she said, feeling light-headed enough already. "Just dry ginger and lots of ice."

"Don't be hard on yourself," he said, handing her the icy glass. "Quilty hasn't actually treated you like rare silver, has he? He's lucky you didn't scratch his bloody eyes out!"

"What? And have a blind as well as bankrupt ex-husband?" She felt rewarded by his smile.

"Give me Begg's number," he said. "I don't guarantee I can help, but . . ."

"If you can't, no one can," she said, and her intense sincerity complicated her one-handed struggle with the clasp of her handbag. He rescued her with a pen and another of his cards, printed side up this time, and she smiled at him.

"There may be little, even nothing, I can do at this stage without being too conspicuous. My company is among the creditors, even though it's not the major one. Damn! You should have phoned me!"

"To say what? 'Why are you attacking Patchwork?' "

"Just a friendly call. You got your hat back?"

"Yes, of course. I should have thanked you, but I couldn't because . . ." And then she could not go on; a sense of pride made her not want to damn Daniel even more in his eyes. He didn't seem to notice—he was pacing again.

"Why I've been doing what you call attacking Quilty's company is purely business, and business, as you've probably learned, is a form of war. You've been an innocent victim." He came and sat on the arm of the chair closest to her so that his knee almost touched her. "Usually I wouldn't know and wouldn't care about what happens to someone in your position. Wives, kids—I never know the personal repercussions. I happened to meet you, though, and it makes a difference. You're . . . an extraordinary woman."

A tendril of sexual tension stretched across the silence between them, but he snapped it with a cough.

"Come on," he said, looking at his watch. "I'll drive you home."

.   .   .

"I loved it," said Rosemary. "And so will everyone. Honestly, I haven't seen anything that—involving—since *Seven Little Australians.* But this is better, somehow."

"It's in colour." Was he teasing her? Or perhaps he thought she was being sarcastic, since *Seven Little Australians* was more than ten years old. She tried harder to demonstrate her sincerity—"Lovely colour. And it's got something for people of all ages. Whole families will watch it together." I'm gushing, she told herself. But he didn't seem to mind. She opened her mouth to mention that she knew—that she'd met— Angela, the star of the show, but then closed it again, since she would then have to explain that Angela played a role in her life, too. Now was not the moment to discuss the morals of his leading lady.

"What about the end?" Robert Talbot asked. "Don't you think that's pretty final? For something that's supposed to continue?"

"No. Not at all. Why must it be a cliff-hanger? By the time people have seen the first part they'll know the characters. They'll be clamouring to see more. Look at 'Hill Street Blues.' That's not a continuing drama; it's just the characters—what they do, where they are—that brings people back again and again."

"It's interesting that you should mention 'Hill Street Blues'—it's one of the examples I used, arguing with that stubborn Stoner. M*A*S*H, too—now there's a commercial success. Man like Stoner, locked into one small world, tends to lose his vision."

So he thinks I'm smart. That's something, she thought. By breathing consciously, carefully, she distracted herself from the desire to stroke the hairs on the back of his hand. I've got to stop this. It's adolescent.

"There's not a chance in hell, by the way, that there'll be any more filming this side of Christmas. So—er—don't get your hopes too high about the Governess role." He smiled. "With or without a plaster cast. The new script-writers are beavering away, but I don't expect to see anything worthwhile until January, February." He paused and left her to register this new disappointment, then suddenly added: "But if you're interested, I'm told they could do with a researcher."

Thank God, thought Rosemary, I thought you'd never ask.

"I know it's not the same as acting," he said, "but it's work you could do fairly easily, isn't it? With one hand?" He grinned at her, and serene, comforted, feeling absurdly secure and strong, she grinned back. From now on they were allies, and from allies it was only one step into bed.

"I'm sure I'd enjoy it. Thank you," she said, smiling, and touched his hand.

He didn't respond. Momentarily she had forgotten about his war with Daniel. So after a few seconds, feeling foolish, she clasped her hands in her lap, cleared her throat and said, "Where will I work? At the studio?"

"Yes, I suppose so. They've got an office there. There're three of them—two women and a man." He told her their names, and she convinced herself that they were familiar. "You'll probably spend a lot of time in libraries and so on."

She had not been watching the route which he took with the speed of habit. Now, glancing around her, she was surprised to realise that there was dense bushland on either side of the car. Then he turned sharply right along a short branch road, travelled to where a dark void indicated the end of the bush, the edge of the world with sea beyond, and stopped the car abruptly.

"Want to look? Have some air? This is my favourite place."

"Where are we?"

"Near West Head."

He took her hand and walked confidently over the dark rocks and rubble, giving her no option but to do the same and to hope that she didn't twist an ankle or fall at his feet—not any more than she had already done, anyway.

He led her to a flat rock overlooking the sea, which, now that her eyes had adjusted to the lack of headlights, showed its white edge far below.

"Glorious, don't you think?" he asked, and the strong breeze carried his words along in short chunks like items on a factory production line. She folded herself around her arms to ward off the chill.

"Bit nippy up here," he said and, kind as a boy scout, enveloped her in his arms. She felt exultant—safe, secure, vindicated—it had been a mutual attraction after all.

When he kissed her, she felt herself melting, like strawberry gelato too near a strong lamp. "Mmm," he said, and firmly stroked her hair away from her face. She could not talk. She put her head on his chest and fought back the flood of relieved tears. Glorious. Absolutely glorious. She didn't care that he'd offered her a job for charity. She wanted the kissing to go on and on, here, by the edge of darkness, on the rock, and for the lamp heat to continue until they had both melted onto the rock. Then there would be the next step and the next and the next . . . It took a moment in the turmoil of her responses to realise that what had just begun for her had just ended for him.

He was calm, with the air of a man whose mission is accomplished. He held her, but lightly, and so, gradually, the whirling in her head and the thumping of her pulse settled to something approximating decorum. She shivered in the cool wind, reclaimed by separateness. She wasn't going to show him that she was mystified and hurt, because she suddenly realised why he had chosen this exposed and uncomfortable spot—there had never been anything more on his mind than a comforting kiss for his victim.

As they drove back along the narrow track, a car with four people in it passed them. If Robert Talbot had melted, too, on the rocky ledge, that carload would have arrived just in time to illuminate a scene that would have featured his distinctive, initialled Porsche in the foreground and his eminent white bum jerking up and down in the background. It was such a deliciously shocking thought that she had to cough to disguise what would otherwise have been hysterical laughter.

Fourteen

A taxi ambled ahead of them along the Monavale Road and suddenly Robert Talbot accelerated the Porsche, overtook it, and signalled for it to stop.

"You don't mind, do you?" he asked Rosemary. "It's getting late. Besides, there seems to be a distinct danger of flying fists at your house!" He patted her nose with a finger, as though she were a good Labrador. "I'll be in touch," he said, and gave the driver a twenty-dollar bill, which did much for his indignation at having been hijacked. There was no salve for Rosemary's indignation, which, in seconds, turned to self-disgust. All the way home she told herself that she was an idiot. But her self was too numbed to be affected any longer by either reproach or shock. Or so she believed.

"Well?" said Auntie Gwen. "Did you get the job?"

"Job? Oh, yes. I did."

"You look surprised. Didn't you expect to?"

"Jobs are hard to get nowadays, Auntie Gwen,"

"Specially one-armed governesses." Rosemary pretended not to hear. She didn't feel like the heap of sliced ham, mayonnaise, and tomato salad that awaited her under a sheet of plastic film.

"Ah ha! Been living it up, hey? Caviar at Talbot's table!"

"More like crumbs," Rosemary murmured to herself, heading for bed.

I've gone mad, she told her reflection. That's what's happened. So now, nothing can really affect me.

It was a useful attitude for ensuring a good night's sleep, but by the next day it was obvious that she could not escape the responsibilities of her tottering world nor the self-doubt bordering on self-loathing which was what Robert Talbot had left her with on that unlovely rock.

I turned thirty-four in May, she told herself grimly. That's half a lifetime. Yet I still only know how to behave like someone of eighteen. I stopped developing when I got married! She was so ashamed of having tried to seduce Robert Talbot that she slammed her mind's door on the thought of it every time it tried to present itself. This was difficult, since his job offer was the one nice thing that had happened to her in weeks, and she wanted to think about that a whole lot.

Jim Begg phoned, insisting that she come and see him as soon as she could. She told Jim the good news that she had a job, though she couldn't answer his questions about the salary and the starting date since she didn't know these things herself.

"Robert Talbot offered it to me. I'll be working on the mini-series his company is producing."

"Robert Talbot, hey? You really do have smart friends."

She had half expected another sarcastic outburst and was surprised that Jim sounded quite respectful. She said she'd be at his office as soon as she could get there, which might be a while since she had no car.

"Take a cab. I'll pay for it from petty cash," he offered.

"No thanks," she said piously. "I don't want to be indebted to you more than necessary."

"Well, my morning's pretty free, so I'll see you when you get here."

This was useful flexibility. It gave her time to take Robert Talbot's advice and phone the major creditor—the Sydney office of the computer printing supply company that had liquidated Patchwork.

It took half an hour and a series of calm, persistent arguments with increasingly senior and confidently obdurate secretaries before she was permitted to speak to the chief accountant. He coldly told her that it was irregular, that he would not, could not, see her without impropriety.

"I'll take the risk," she said. "You don't know what this means—my children and I are likely to lose our house. We have no money and, literally, nowhere to go. . . ." Her transmission was interrupted by the static of impending tears and his anxiety increased exponentially.

"Surely Mr. Quilty should be dealing with this matter? Surely there are remedies he can take? All we want is our money, Mrs. Quilty; we're not in the business of taking the roofs off people's heads. But we have a duty to our shareholders. . . ." He said this in a speechifying tone, then crumpled with a sigh. "Mrs. Quilty, the real problem is, as you possibly know since it's been in the financial papers this week, that our company is fighting a take-over."

"I didn't know, I've been too busy—upset—to read the papers. But why should that make a difference?"

"It does, believe me. With respect, Mrs. Quilty, your problem is comparatively in a minor league. I don't mean we are without compassion . . . but . . ."

Before the call, she wasn't sure what she'd hoped to achieve. Now she knew there was no hope.

.   .   .

She walked the five kilometres to Jim Begg's office, observing that the bright side of her recent disaster was that she was getting fit. This body Robert Talbot had spurned was now one with good firm thighs and clear skin. Her broken arm and the new worry lines that had started around her mouth were marks against her, of course, but before the non-episode on the rock, she had believed he'd gone beyond the packaging, so to speak, and actually liked her. Now, of course, the truth was obvious—he had gone beyond the packaging and didn't like her. Her self-esteem, especially sparked up for him, had turned out to be fragile, transparent—and readily crushed. The job offer to which she now clung as though it were the last canteen of water in a long desert walk—it could be just as casually denied. But she refused to linger on that new fear. She had to have the job. He owed it to her!

"What I don't understand," Jim said, "is why Daniel is just letting things slide about the house. I mean, *no one* loses a house in a thing like this. I've found out for sure now that he's down for less than half a million."

"I can't talk to him. He wouldn't do anything. He's got the idea that I'm to blame—partly, at least."

"That's ridiculous, surely?"

"Yes. But there's some circumstantial evidence that makes it impossible to convince him." She sighed. She wished she didn't have to tell the shabby little story again, especially now that she could see how little she'd ever meant to Robert Talbot. But she told Jim as much as she'd told Patrick, and he listened as though in pain.

"Hmmm," said Jim. "Looks like Daniel has a point."

"But I didn't mean to harm him!"

"Hmmm," he said again, looking at her the way the other disciples must have looked at Judas after the event. "You usually go around telling Daniel's business plans to people you've just met?"

"Now look here," she said, suddenly angry. "Are you on my side or not? I mean, Daniel himself told all this stuff to Bobby, for heaven's sake. Aged ten. Bobby wasn't sworn to secrecy—for all I know, he's told every kid at his school about the casino." Her face felt hot. "We've—we never used to have secrets unless something wasn't finalised. In fact, talking about the things the company was doing or planning was good for business! If anything, I suppose I thought I was being helpful!" Her eyes glittered with hurt, angry tears.

She convinced herself so entirely of her innocence that she left Jim with his hands over his head saying, "OK, OK, OK. Just being devil's advocate." He made it sound like an apology, which he followed with a thoughtful pause. "I'm still puzzled, though," he said. "OK, so I accept that you didn't deliberately sell out Daniel to Robert Talbot. But you say Talbot offered you a job?"

"That has nothing to do with Daniel or the business. It was a pure coincidence—I met him through Malcolm Henry and Lucy."

Jim stared at her as though her face were a finely drawn map with no cross-references, and he was trying to find a very small town. Finally he sat back in his chair and sighed like one who hadn't found it.

"What I want to know," he said slowly, "is where you stand now in this. How you feel about it all. Jesus, Rosemary, I don't mind telling you, I'm out of my depth a bit here."

"Don't you be out of your depth, too, Jim, or we'll both drown!"

She was considering asking him if he'd prefer to hand the whole messy problem to someone more experienced, but there was no way she could think of suggesting it. He'd have to offer and then help her find someone who'd accept her in her current indigent state, and both of these events seemed highly unlikely.

"How do you see your future, Rosemary?"

It was the question she'd spent most of the last year avoiding, so the words were hard to round up. "I love my house"—she began, then had to fight to keep talking and not become a mess of tears again—"more than I can tell you. We built it up together, Daniel and I. It's all Bobby's ever known. Phyl, too—she was so small when we bought it. I live here. I belong in the community—my friends . . ." She blew her nose. "But I'll lose it. I've known since . . ." she rubbed her plastered arm. "Daniel can't be reasoned with now, and by the time we're talking again it'll be too late. So. We—the kids and I—we'll do what other people do: get by. My mother was a single parent and so was my gran, so struggling and supporting kids is in my heritage." She sighed. "I thought I'd broken the mould. I thought I'd found security."

"Security doesn't exist."

"I never knew what that meant before," she said, though he probably didn't hear, as his phone was ringing.

"I said no calls, Jude," he said firmly into it, then his expression changed and he glanced at Rosemary. "Oh, really? Yeah, yeah. Put him on." He covered the receiver with his hand and murmured, "Talbot's solicitor." Then, "G'day. Yes, yes. She's here, matter of fact, right with me."

This was followed by a string of "Uh huh's" and "Right's". Once he said, "But they'll attack that, surely? It was a prior . . . Oh, yes. Yes, I see."

Rosemary waited, resigned to being handed very small pieces of a puzzle and no picture. "Well, thanks for that," he said. "I'll get back to you." He steepled his hands and gave her another searching look.

"So Talbot is making an attempt to protect you. Pretty low-key, but an attempt, certainly. Why would he do that? Be honest, Rosemary?"

How you'd love me to say "It's because I'm his girl-friend and that's why Daniel left me and that's why Patchwork is being liquidated," she thought. "I wish I knew," she said, sure that he could not doubt her honesty.

"They think that between Daniel's solicitors and us, if everybody moves quickly, we could draw up a divorce settlement that puts the house in your children's names. Pre-date it to before the liquidation process started. Irregular, of course." He looked guilty. His large, red fingers played a bar or two on the edge of his desk, as though it were a piano. "If we get away with it, it will change the game. At least it will stall things, maybe long enough for Dan to get out of trouble. It's the spirit of the law," he added belligerently, as though she'd argued.

"Well, most of the settlement details were drafted long ago," she offered humbly. "You did that, in January? February? It's not as if Daniel's solicitor doesn't already know what we were discussing. The house, the children's support, access . . ."

"Quite so," he said, and played a final chord. "Judy!" he yelled. "Bring me the Quilty vs. Quilty file, will you, there's a darl. And coffee. Milk, no sugar for Mrs. Q."

"But would it work? Surely the liquidators would argue . . ."

"Yes, yes," he said, waving his hands as though he'd been promoted to conductor. "Of course. They'll kick up a bit since they've already established that you and Dan jointly own the house. But the Family Law Court is a separate entity, much more concerned with the protection of the innocent." His eyes gleamed. She'd never seen Jim so interested. "The ideal scenario would be to pre-date the documents and hope Family Law will accept them, because if they do, you end up with the house, no worries, and the liquidators go whistling for their money."

A rush of feelings made Rosemary's throat tighten. In the midst of joy and relief was acknowledgement that this was how corruption worked.

She'd have to be a saint to pass up a chance like this. But if she gained her house by lying to the Family Law Court, she would have to abandon the image of herself as a good person. I'd be doing it for the children, she told herself.

Oh, yeah? replied some sceptic voice from deep inside. It would not be silenced by quick sips of coffee.

Jim was still talking. "Anyway, even if the Family Law people don't accept old documents, we could still bombard the liquidating company about the divorce settlement and we might still succeed in muddying the water a bit. It would gain us time if they have to start all over again."

Rosemary swallowed again and put her destiny in his big, fidgety hands.

"We'll have to be quick, though. If the liquidators decide to apply for summary judgement they'll almost certainly get it, and then there's nothing we can do. And Daniel would have to co-operate, of course."

"You'd have to ask Daniel—I can't," she said, and knew that he'd recognised an unarguable note in her words.

"I'm sure Dan'll be reasonable," Jim reassured himself. "After all, no matter how upset he is, no one wants to lose valuable property. What's his number?"

She told him.

"Is that home or office?"

"Office. I don't have his home number. It's probably best to phone him at lunch-time or just after five because he has a very tough secretary who might take it upon herself to protect him from you, since you're my solicitor."

"Righto," he said. "What's this dragon's name?"

"Shirley Coote."

"I'll try now," he said bravely. "It's near enough to lunch-time. Judy!"

Judy, fine-boned as a quail, sped in on adrenalin, took the number and instructions, nodded as though her little, black-curled head was battery operated, and rushed into her adjoining office without a smile. Soon she was back, worried, as though everything was her fault.

"Mr. Quilty's not in Sydney," she said. "He left last week. Mrs. Coote couldn't tell me when he'd be back. I tried to leave a message but . . ."

"That's all right. Thank you, Judy," Rosemary said as kindly as she could, hoping to erase some of that dangerous anxiety. But it didn't help—Judy went off to lunch like one destined for indigestion.

"Bloody Shirley Coote!" Rosemary said as soon as Judy couldn't hear. "She's been using that not-in-Sydney line for years. What do you bet she's got a crush on Daniel!"

"Then she'd be eager to see him divorced, surely," said Jim dryly.

"Why?" Rosemary snapped. "She's married. And he's got Angela. It would make no difference to bloody Shirley!"

Since Rosemary did not know Angela's address or phone number, they decided to send Daniel a telegram to his office.

" 'Please Phone Urgently About Arrangements For Children' might help," said Rosemary.

"It would pack more punch if it came from you."

"Yes. But then he probably wouldn't phone, or if he did, he'd be nasty."

So they sent it without much hope, with Jim's name and telephone number on it. Then, because they couldn't think of any more stones to turn, Rosemary accepted his offer of a taxi ride from petty cash. After all, she'd already compromised herself.

She got home ten minutes before Jim's sad-voiced phone call: the liquidators had got judgement against her, Daniel, and Patchwork PR that morning.

This time even Auntie Gwen cried.

.   .   .

"Thought I'd just warn you," said Jim when he phoned again a little later. "The Department of Corporate Affairs doesn't look kindly on directors who flit off without warning when they're going bust. Stands to reason. So don't you be tempted to do any vanishing acts. Oh, and by the way, you'll probably get a call from the liquidators."

She did, and was relieved that Bobby's school sports day was on the only morning the man could come.

"Never you mind," Auntie Gwen said. "I'll deal with the bugger. You take the Datsun—you can surely manage an automatic now?" She could, barely, by steadying the wheel with her cast-arm while putting the gear into drive. She hoped there would be an easy, nose-in, nose-out spot at the school so she wouldn't have to reverse park, but there wasn't. The tension of an unfamiliar, rather quirky car gave her a headache and Bobby, who came in third in three events, hardly seemed to notice she'd come. Then, when she was tensely, slowly, pulling out from the parking spot, an old man with thick glasses and a new, light blue Honda bumped heavily into her door.

"Stupid woman driver!" he yelled. "Where'd you learn t'drive?" The bump did no damage to either car, but it jerked her arm which, having recently settled into a dull ache, was shocked into harsh pain again. This pain made her tension headache worse and by the time she got home she was white-faced and nauseous.

But the liquidator was still there. In fact, he'd arrived late, having been delayed at the office, so he'd only been there long enough for a "very pleasant" cup of coffee and a scone with Auntie Gwen.

"Just a formality," he said to Rosemary and, simultaneously detached and intimate as a gynaecologist, he began slowly doing what he called "Crystallising the company situation."

He was a short man with strong, white teeth, a small black moustache, and one built-up shoe which did not quite compensate for a limp. His skin was almost transparent, white and shiny as though it had been bleached with strong chemicals and then stretched thinly to dry. His breath smelled of spearmint and his smile was a matter for his lips alone. Most of his crystallising took the form of a cross-examination with questions Rosemary felt ranged from banal to impertinent.

Policemen who interrogate spies probably use this approach, she thought. He believes I'm holding back some information that could be useful to him. He can't believe someone intelligent and fairly classy like me could really be a victim.

This theory of Rosemary's was given weight by Auntie Gwen's fussing over her with aspirins and the quick, protective way she gave comic-opera grimaces and other elaborate signals Rosemary could not comprehend but which the liquidator seemed to understand perfectly: they always made him redouble his probing efforts.

Auntie Gwen was often first with the answers to the liquidator's questions—the wrong answers. Then she and Rosemary would have a debate:

"Of course Daniel has an office here, Rosemary—what about the little room with his desk? And all those files?"

"Auntie Gwen, that's the study. He used to use it, right in the beginning. But those are old files from the seventies, or Phyl's and Bobby's old school projects." What the hell are you trying to do to me? Rosemary hoped her tone implied.

Auntie Gwen looked at her as though she were stupid and the liquidator insisted on going through the study, where he spent an hour carefully thumbing through their earliest records and correspondence, making notes about such things as banking accounts that no longer existed. He admired Phyl's vivid drawings that filled her eleven- and twelve-year-old school-books.

"Quite an artistic family," he said, and Auntie Gwen glared.

He limped back to the yellow living room.

"Just want another look at your fine pictures," he said. "That a genuine Nolan?"

"No," said Auntie Gwen; "Dobell," said Rosemary. They spoke at the same time, so it was hard to know which answer he heard.

He made Rosemary a speech that could have come from a religious tract about how there was no malice intended, that liquidation was not enmity but a fact of business life, and that he hoped they could be friends despite the painful circumstances. He handed her a document on which the word "demand" was one of those in large type.

"A report for you to complete. No hurry. Post it to me within the week, that will do, in this stamped envelope. About the company affairs."

"But there's nothing more I can say on this than I've said already." Rosemary found it hard to conceal her irritation. "I stopped working for Patchwork over a year ago."

"Actively."

"Yes, actively."

"But you're still a director. Your signature is on documents dated as recently as August."

She closed her eyes and wished he'd go away.

"It's a very nice house," he said when he finally did. She thought his attempt at a sympathetic tone very feeble.

Auntie Gwen and Rosemary turned on each other as soon as he'd gone. Most of what they said was lost in the overlap, but Rosemary gathered, in stray phrases, that the liquidator had said on arrival that he could only stay for two hours because he had an appointment elsewhere, so Auntie Gwen had found ways of wasting his time to keep the focus off Rosemary.

"You made him think I'm a crook!"

"No. Just a fool. Don't you see, you're safe if he thinks you're a fool? You won't bother him. He'll reveal his hand and go straight for what he wants."

"You live in fantasyland!" said Rosemary.

Just before she slammed her bedroom door she heard Auntie Gwen yell: "You're the one to talk!"

Rosemary had never witnessed a nervous breakdown and so was not sure of the symptoms. She felt dizzy and almost uncaring. The woman who stared at her from the mirror had parchment skin, like the liquidator. Nothing was bright about her except her eyes, which gleamed like a night animal's and frightened her.

I can't cope, Rosemary told herself. This is it. I can't take any more.

It sounded true. There was every reason for it to be true. She lay down and wondered, without much interest, whether the children would miss her while she was away in the mental hospital.

She fell asleep and woke to find herself covered by a light cotton blanket. There were sounds of a meal in progress. Dinner! she thought. I've slept all afternoon!

She was even more surprised to find that it was breakfast, that Auntie Gwen was just leaving with the kids for school and that she could cope with the next bit of bad news which Jim Begg pointed out on the phone. It was a small piece in the business part of the *Herald* about the fact that Patchwork PR was in liquidation and that no one knew where Daniel Quilty was. Though blandly written, it seemed to Rosemary that it rang with innuendo.

Lucy saw it, too. She came over, white-faced, and hugged Rosemary without a word.

"Don't," she said. "You'll start me off again. My eyes have only recently stopped looking like tomato salad."

"I just don't believe all this is happening to you," said Lucy. "I wish there was someone I could kill!"

"You'd ruin your gorgeous shoes. Blood looks horrible on peacock blue."

For a change Lucy was in no hurry. She sipped black coffee and kindly did not smoke while Rosemary ate two bowls of muesli and yoghurt, a scrambled egg with bacon on toast, two halves of a muffin with butter and honey, and three cups of milky tea, with absolutely no thought about her thighs.

"What the hell will you do now, Ro?" Lucy asked.

"What I've been doing all year, I suppose—lurch from day to day and try to duck. At least I've got a job, or I think I have—I'm waiting to be told when to start and so on. As a researcher on 'The Mount Victorians.' Robert Talbot offered it to me the night I went to the film preview. You'll have to tell me how to be a researcher."

"Great! Terrific! Clever you! Sure, I'll give you some tips, but it's dead easy—you'll do it with one hand tied . . ." Lucy began, then looked at the plaster-cast and laughed. "Like you do everything. What I want to know is what's going on with you and Robert Talbot."

"Nothing," Rosemary said firmly, and hoped her tone did not convey regret.

"Hey, I'm Lucy! You can't bullshit me."

"Truly nothing, though I would have been willing for it to have been . . . something." Willing seemed like a neutral kind of word. To put Lucy even further off the track that ran beside her bruised feelings, Rosemary said, "He thinks he can buy and sell people."

Lucy's small black eyes squinted at her through the post-breakfast cigarette smoke. She shouldn't do that, Rosemary thought. She'll get horrible lines.

"Of course he can buy and sell people, Ro. It's always been like that for the rich. It's because people are willing to be bought, in the hope that it will make them rich, too."

"Or else they refuse to be bought."

Lucy gazed at her as though trying to see which category Rosemary belonged in. Rosemary, who was even more confused, gave her no clue.

"I've just thought of a good definition of democracy," said Lucy. "Hot off the press. Democracy is when people have the right to refuse to be bought or sold. That's all. That's the only difference between us and Russia or China." She tilted her chin and stroked her throat, delighted by her idea. "Democracy is more complicated than communism because those who refuse to be bought often wonder if they'd have been better off if they'd accepted."

"Well, I wasn't bought," said Rosemary, relieved to be sure. "He has a guilty conscience about Daniel. That's all."

"Well, you know the gossip, don't you?"

"Gossip?"

"What the journalists are saying in the pubs. They really do think you're on with Talbot."

"Oh, Lucy!"

"Don't be surprised if you get a few calls from old mates in the media. I'm sorry," Lucy added in reaction to Rosemary's expression. "But I thought I'd better warn you."

"Oh, God, I wish I could just go away!"

"Like Daniel? No, that's not the answer." She lighted another cigarette. "Actually, I was rather pleased when I heard about you and Talbot—it would certainly have solved your problems if it had been true." She misunderstood Rosemary's expression, which was not surprising since it was created by numerous conflicting emotions. She put her hand up like an official. "I know what you're going to say—that you'd never have an affair with a married man and so forth."

"But . . ." said Rosemary. Lucy could not have heard. "I'm a feminist," she said. "We both are," she added generously. "Not by choice. What did you once say?—we were forcibly liberated. But do you know what that freedom really means? It means we're free to tag onto the turn-ups of society because men are still in charge. The libbers haven't changed that."

"Turnips?"

"Turn-ups. Of men's suit pants. A really dumb woman, married to a company lawyer, has access to his friends, and they could be politicians and chairmen of boards or interesting arts administrators. Anything. And wasted on her! But the wittiest, most brilliant woman married to a dull man is stuck with his friends, who probably won't even try to talk to her. And it's even worse if she's not married at all—she never gets to meet anyone except widows and aged spinsters."

"That's cynical. And how can you be sure it's true?"

"Of course it is. Look at you—how many top people have you met since Daniel left? One. And that was through Malcolm. Truly, Ro, the important thing is to realise that strong men want certain things from women, and the women who give them what they want then have a toe-hold on power."

"But," said Rosemary. Then suddenly she was suffused with her old certainty, her old truth which, like a chronic illness, appeared to go away from time to time but which was, in fact, incurable. It was the truth that she was not beautiful. Lucy had what it took to attach herself to the turn-ups of the powerful and even be elevated into their arms. Being unbeautiful, Rosemary would forever be in the way of their pointy-toed boots—unless she was smart.

"But what about women who become powerful in their own right?" she asked, smartly.

"Name one."

"Jane Fonda. Germaine Greer. Doris Lessing."

"Yes," said Lucy politely. "But they started younger. Besides, men probably helped all of them at various times."

"Well, why not?" Arguing felt good. Rosemary began to feel better about her lack of turn-up attachability. "OK, so men shape our lives. But we shape theirs, too—or try to. When relationships work well, surely it's because each takes from the other what they want?"

"Yes. But most men just want one thing."

Rosemary rolled her eyes.

"No, no," Lucy went on. "Not sex. That's easy. I mean admiration!"

"Sure," said Rosemary. "But then, so do women."

Lucy had to admit she hadn't thought of that, and when she left, Rosemary, though plain and unsophisticated, acknowledged to herself that sometimes she was pretty smart.

· · ·

The vehicle Patrick was baby-sitting for was a shiny, light-tan-and-gold eight-seater bus which he drove so close to the edge of Rosemary's garden that a wheel mounted the curb. Rosemary, Phyl, and Bobby, equipped with a cooler full of drinks and fruit and a batch of folded directors' chairs were waiting on the front path, as was Auntie Gwen, who stood at the door and boomed greetings.

"Don't think I'll come," she said as though she'd been invited. "Thought I'd stay and polish the silver. See my new car?" she pointed to a used-looking blue station-wagon half-way up the drive. "Traded the Datsun for it yesterday. Real bargain and nearly as roomy as yours!"

Geoff—it must have been Geoff, though there were two large teenage males in the bus—was sitting next to Patrick, bouncing like a four-year-old, grinning and clapping his hands. His chin was wet. His face had an oddly squashed look as though it had been made of skin-coloured plasticine and then dropped. He made sounds like speech played at sixteen r.p.m. and moved with no plan, lunging into other people's space without warning. His body was bulky and rather shapeless, and the look of him made Rosemary feel acutely uncomfortable, but, she was pleased to see, neither of her children looked as though they shared her feeling.

"G'day, Geoff," Bobby said, and shook his hand.

"And this is Andrew O'Reilly. Andy. He's coming, too."

"G'day Andy," Bobby said. Andy, a bright-faced boy of about seventeen, was in a seat in the next row, leaning forward confidently on his elbows, obviously at ease in Patrick and Geoff's company and perhaps everywhere else as well. He wore glasses that slipped to one side and his thick brown hair flopped over his slightly spotty forehead. When he moved to take the drink cooler and help Rosemary into the back door, she observed that there was a lot of power in his frame and muscles. Phyl had glanced at him and then looked away but seemed content to end up in the seat beside him.

Rosemary and Bobby took the next two seats. The sun-roof was open and so were the large windows that slid along both sides, so unless Patrick turned to face her when the red lights stopped the bus, and then boomed like a tour guide, she could not have a conversation with anyone but Bobby. And Bobby was more interested in what Andy had to say about computers, rowing, karate, and school. Andy had two more papers due the following week and then his Higher School Certificate would be over and he'd go to university the next year and do computer science. Or vet science, though he doubted if he'd get the mark for that even though Patrick had been helping like mad, coaching him in maths and science. . . .

"We usually go to Lane Cove Park, but I thought we'd cross the bridge for a change and go to Nielsen Park," Patrick yelled. "It's such a nice day—hot enough for a swim. Did you bring your swimming togs?"

The children had. Rosemary would not have dreamed of exposing her blue-white flesh to public gaze and the risk of cancer.

Geoff made strange, raucous singing noises as they drove and banged his hand rhythmically to the non-tune. It was a not-unpleasant background sound to the murmur of more intelligible voices.

They had passed through William Street, where oldish buildings were being given the cosmetic surgery of dark-glass fronts and showing up the wizened, faded, tan brick shops-with-flats-on-top of Darlinghurst and Woolloomooloo. Then, past the quick glitter of King's Cross's neon signs on the left and after a dive through the underpass to Rushcutter's Bay, Rosemary began to enjoy the scenery. The masts of hundreds of moored yachts looked like a bunch of pick-up sticks stuck in the silver blue bay. Tiny glimpses of the bright blue harbour were revealed down some side-streets between a succession of commercial buildings that ran most of the way to Double Bay, but after that the road climbed in large curves and the view was almost unobstructed. Each turn revealed a different arrangement of the grey-toned city skyscrapers and the bow of the bridge. In the foreground was the harbour, busier than the road itself, its traffic mainly comprised of white-sailed racing yachts following the water's invisible road signs as they carefully negotiated buoys and small, tree-covered islands. From where Rosemary sat, the white-sailed or brilliant-spinnakered boats looked as random and purposeless as butterflies. In between the boats and the islands, ferries ploughed their way, and once, across the middle of the vast water-scape, a hydrofoil sped, its passengers visible as bright dots of colour against the white deck. If I could live near here, Rosemary thought, I'd look at this all day long and get nothing done.

It took a while to find a parking spot big enough for the bus and near enough for Geoff not to have too long a walk. Patrick's patience astonished Rosemary—she'd have started getting cross at the delay. She was loudly outraged by the rudeness of a mother in a small car who ducked quickly, nose first, into a spot Patrick was lining up to reverse the big vehicle into.

"Never mind," he said, as Rosemary maintained a reproving glare at the woman who refused to look at them. "It was a bit of tight squeeze, that one. We'll find a better one." Which they did. Throughout, Geoff sang and thumped, undistracted by anything.

Rosemary began to see, when their group had straggled through the trees to the edge of the shark-proofed swimming enclosure, that Geoff's pleasure was genuine, without guile, as though he really were a small child. And, listening carefully, she began to understand some of his speech: "Simmy poo'. Simmy poo,' " he said when he saw the water and immediately started struggling with his T-shirt.

"Ocean, Geoff, not swimming pool," said Andy, helping him out of his clothes. Geoff's pants were closed with velcro strips, so they were easy to remove.

"Osha! Osha!" said Geoff.

"Why don't you all go and swim, and Rosemary and I will put the lunch out," said Patrick, and they all obeyed without a word, even Phyl, who'd been ambivalent about swimming in the shallow and fairly crowded sea pool—a pool created among the rocks by a row of shark nets that made swimming safe in this part of the harbour.

"Is Geoff OK in the water?" Rosemary asked, watching her slender daughter walk self-consciously away in her pale skin and blue bikini.

"Yes. He loves it—dog-paddles, splashes around. The trick is to get him out; I usually end up using bribery," Patrick said and held up half a watermelon.

"Andy is very good with him."

"Yes. Marvellous kid. Lives nearby. He's known us for years—as you can see, he's sort of Geoff's self-appointed minder. His parents are rather dull and ancient." He was unpacking the hamper: home-made pies, sliced carrots, cherry tomatoes, chicken legs, thickly filled sandwiches. No plates would be needed.

"What happened about your house?" he asked.

"I've lost it."

"Just like that?"

"It does seem ridiculous, doesn't it?" She sighed. "If someone arrived with the right-sized sum of money and paid off the company's debt, we'd be OK. But we don't know anyone rich." Well, actually I do, she thought. I know someone very rich, who won't allow himself to help, even though he caused the loss.

Suddenly she remembered how pious she'd been when Lucy started falling in love with Malcolm—she'd warned against the dangers of getting involved with the boss. What a hypocrite I am, she thought. Then she became aware that Patrick was watching her, leaning over slightly, one hand on a hip.

"How much do you need?" he asked with the air of a man with resources. She knew he would be shocked even before she told him the amount.

"I'll buy a lottery ticket," she said to comfort them both. "Maybe that's the answer."

"It really is a lot of money," Patrick said. "For someone on a salary it sounds—unbelievable."

"Yes. It is rather. And ten years ago we were scratching to find enough to live on."

Suddenly she felt like weeping again and turned away. Patrick calmly busied himself with plates and knives and mayonnaise. "It's been hell for you," he said quietly.

"Yes. But its my own fault. I tried to shove it all aside, you see. When Daniel left I was too angry to deal with the truth, so I didn't. I've spent the past year doing everything except actually face the fact that my marriage was over and that I was in charge of my own life. You saw me—losing myself in the plays. Rushing around doing, doing, doing, and not thinking. So I've got into a terrible mess, and not just financially, either."

Patrick squatted next to her like a tribal Aboriginal, his hands loosely between his knees, and looked interested. She wished he did not look interested.

"Now I think I've . . ." She stopped. She'd wanted to say "paralysed my emotions," but that sounded frightening. "I cry at the slightest thing," she said. "It's like a dam break that I can't mend, and more and more keeps filling the dam and I feel as though I'm drowning, in a way. I can't trust myself to be right about things. Everyone else seems so sophisticated! Everyone else seems to know who's wearing the black hats and who's wearing the white, but to me they all look grey."

For some reason this made Patrick laugh, which was disconcerting because she'd hoped he would realise how dangerous she was and then keep at a safe distance. She noticed he was opening a bottle of champagne. That would make it easier.

"Daniel's probably going to be investigated. God knows what he's done, if anything. But Jim, my lawyer, says there're usually some technical irregularities in busy companies which they'll find if they're gunning for him. I want to warn him, help him—but I can't. Apart from anything else, no one knows where he is. Besides, I'm still so disgusted with him for shoving me around. He was never like that."

Patrick's tendons were obviously tireless. He squatted with the champagne bottle in one hand and his coloured-plastic stemmed flute in the other, nodding, raising an eyebrow, or shaking his head in slow sympathy. There was no sign that he was bored or impatient.

"I told the kids—told myself—I'd fight like hell for the house. But I'm helpless. Numb, almost. God, I'm boring," she said, and quickly drank half her champagne. "Great talk for a picnic."

"Go on," he said calmly. "You don't have to do a song and dance routine for me."

"I'm sorry," said Rosemary. "My life is as topsy-turvy as Alice's was when she went down the rabbit hole. Everything's changed. It's all zipped around so quickly that I can't keep up with how I feel, and that's the truth." She wanted to get away from talking about her disaster. She picked at the threads of grubby gauze which protruded from the plaster cast.

"You'll get through it, you know. You're a survivor," he said.

"How can you say that? You hardly know me."

"I've made a study of you, Rosemary Quilty."

She looked away from his grin, feeling even more uncomfortable now that she'd told him so much.

"You're obviously a survivor, too," she said. "Tell me about Geoff?"

He turned to look at the shining bow of sea water which had edged its way, in time, into a generous gap between the craggy grey rocks of the headland park to form the small, neat beach. The water was shallow and safe in its belt of black shark nets, and Patrick looked relaxed as he watched his child splashing, jumping, and having a good time.

"It was what you said—topsy-turvy, Alice in Wonderland. My whole life got twisted into a new direction and it took—oh months—maybe years, to catch up with myself. I don't think I'm as adaptable as you are."

"Will you tell me? I mean, do you talk about it?"

"Sure. It's long ago now—more than sixteen years. Everything seemed fine in my life—career—I was twenty-six, had my doctorate. Christine and I had been married about two years, and we wanted a baby. We moved in with her widowed mum—into the house where Geoff and I live now—and that was fine. But then Geoff was born and the birth went wrong and Chris was the one who died."

"Was it the birth that made Geoff . . . ?"

"Partly at least, though who knows for sure? He certainly was without oxygen for too long, but he was probably physically handicapped in the first place."

"How did you bear it?"

"Well, I didn't, of course. I lived in a daze. It was self-pity—I kept asking, Why me? I hated Geoff—or feared him is closer to the truth. If it were not for his grandmother, he'd probably never have made it through infancy. He had sucking problems, a milk allergy, and hardly any resistance to disease." He looked again fondly towards the sea where

Rosemary's two children and Andy had joined Geoff's splashing, shouting game as though they were all three- or four-year-olds.

"But you got over it."

"No, I don't think so. You live around it, you assimilate it. But it changes your life's direction."

"Like a knot in a tree?"

"Yes, I guess." He liked that. "Knots in trees. Makes the foresters avoid them like plague."

"Yes. They'd only want the ordinary ones—straight up and down, for making packing cases and kitchen shelves!"

"Yup. The ones like me get chopped up for firewood."

"No, no. They get left growing! Looking interestingly eccentric."

He was silent. Perhaps he didn't like being called eccentric. Well, she told herself bravely, that's tough. I'm tired of pussyfooting around men's feelings. She couldn't stop herself from blurting out: "You've come too soon into my life. It's too cluttered—there's no space for you."

He was startled, then he quickly smiled and said, "Can I book? Be next on the list for a space?"

It was an extraordinarily romantic thing, said in his precise and gentle voice. Then he laughed, which was fortunate because she didn't have to answer.

I really am frightened of you, she thought, as he poured more champagne for her. She looked at his kind, square-chinned, blue-eyed face, his light, thinning hair, his emerald green T-shirt, his reddish-tan pants, made of some material that shone in the sunlight—and which, she noticed, had no turn-ups—and his black, round-toed, lace-up shoes.

"You seem needy," she said. "And too real. I can't explain. Oh, I'm being horrible." She drank the whole glass. "I mess up people's lives."

"Whose?"

"Daniel's. My kids. My mother's—all the people I love—loved—most." She saw him look at her hands, still twisting in her lap, and understood that he wanted to touch her but had decided not to.

"I can't speak for your mother. But what I've heard about Daniel, he appears to be doing a fairly good job of messing up lives. And as for your kids, they're marvellous. You know that, surely? One of the nicest things about you is the way you are with Phyl and Bobby."

Embarrassed, she glanced towards her children then—"Look!" she said, urgently, pointing at the sea pool. Something had happened, because Phyl was standing with her arms protectively around Geoff and Andy was furiously running through the water after two large, black-haired youths, with Bobby splashing along in his wake.

Patrick moved with the speed of a snake, grabbing a towel in one hand and a bar of chocolate in the other, and Rosemary ran, too. By the time they reached the beach it was all over: one boy was lying grunting, holding his leg, and the other had got safely away though Bobby had not yet stopped chasing him. Phyl had brought Geoff gasping, coughing, bellowing, to the water's edge.

"They ducked him," she said, out of breath with indignation. "He'd been splashing. The hoons!"

"He's a fuckin' monkey," said the black-haired boy, struggling to his feet. "Shouldn't be at a decent beach. Should be locked in a fuckin' zoo wiv the other animals." But he made sure to keep out of Andy's way.

When Bobby came back from his hopeless chase he was trembling so violently that his teeth chattered and his breath came in gasps. Rosemary had not brought his towel, but, very conscious of what Patrick had said about her qualities of motherhood, she tried to warm him by rubbing her hands vigorously up and down his arms, and she murmured about his courage.

The black-haired boy slunk off limping, making increasingly bold threats as he got farther away. Geoff ate the chocolate, refusing to share despite Patrick's gentle suggestions and touches, and soon his wet chin and bare chest were brown with slick dribbles.

"Thanks, mate," she heard Patrick say to Andy as they walked towards the spread-out lunch. "And you two as well. You're a game bloke," he said to Bobby and ruffled his wet hair. Phyl was rewarded with a smile.

Nobody felt like going back into the water after lunch. Patrick produced a blow-up ball, obviously a favourite toy of Geoff's, but he only joined for a little while and then settled down with his back to a rock and, like Linus, rubbed his face with a corner of his towel while sucking the back of his other hand. Rosemary wondered if he was having a delayed reaction or whether he could even remember what had happened.

"This is a tired boy, aren't you, Geoff?" Patrick said. "He'll sleep in the bus," he announced. He tapped his lips with an index finger, a habit Rosemary had noticed during rehearsals, usually when things were going badly.

"Look, what I'd like to do is take him home. He might just nap for a while and be fine when we get there, but he could sleep for hours. So, why don't we have afternoon tea there? You could show Phyl and Bob the animals," he said to Andy.

"Yeah. And the computer games."

Rosemary could hardly refuse.

The house was in Hunter's Hill, with a large, bushy garden that needed pruning and a low-roofed, colonial-style verandah which overlooked the Parramatta River. Rosemary suspected that if it had a second storey, like others in the street, the views would include the bridge and the city skyline. Geoff, who had slept open-mouthed on a foam mattress at the back of the bus, woke up bright-eyed when they reached his home.

"There's my house," said Andy, pointing to a neat, primly maintained white, red-tiled double-storey across the street and two doors along. Rosemary was struck by the contrast. Patrick's house looked as though it were trying to disintegrate back into the earth from which it had sprung. Timbers were bleached and splintery, tiles cracked, steps worn, and the inside was dark and smelled of the dogs, which, after exploding out of the door barking and wagging menace, curiosity, and welcome, clicked back in over the uncarpeted, parquet floor to occupy every chair, mat, and sunny spot. A fat white duck greeted Geoff with flapped wings and a scolding squawk, then set itself behind him, its beak never more than six inches from his ankle. It followed him. Everywhere. Phyl and Bobby thought it was hilarious.

The small front windows took very little advantage of the view. The house was a renovator's dream. She became aware of Patrick's amused expression—what she thought about his house was probably written all over her.

"Come and meet the menagerie," he said.

A long, sunny back verandah enclosed in louvered glass showed the only obvious signs of a builder's touch within the last twenty years. A rubber-tiled floor sloped gently towards a central drainage hole. Sun and fresh air filled the room, as did the smell of animal urine, despite a busily functioning extractor fan at one end. Along two walls were large cages full of a variety of small, bright eyed, healthy-looking animals.

Geoff headed for a cage, awkwardly opened it and then, with the utmost delicacy, lifted out a little white rabbit and stroked it on his cheek.

"Mum! I don't believe this! There's even a wombat!" Phyl's face was alive with pleasure, her words almost gabbled. "It's fantastic! What do they eat? Who feeds them? Where do you get them? Oh, look, look how cleverly the cages are designed—the droppings just get washed out into that back part, do they? And then out?"

"Great for compost," Patrick said solemnly. "Neighbours have to be put on a roster system—all clamouring for bags of wombat poo for their native shrubs. There's also pig, gerbil, grass snake, rabbit . . . old Clarrie, next door, swears there's nothing to beat it for his grevillea."

Andy was eager to answer Phyl's questions—he often did the cleaning when Patrick was busy. Bobby and Phyl would be able to help that day with chopping carrots, measuring wheat and sunflower seeds, picking herbs and leaves from the tangled garden, gathering slugs and snails— hosing, too, if they felt like it; he usually hosed on Sundays.

At one end was an array of fish tanks in which rainbow-coloured, fan-shaped fish, gasped meaningfully in their green stage lighting. Rosemary was not very interested in the fish, though Andy insisted that she look at the axolotl that stuck, like a little rubber monster, on the side of one tank and glowered coldly at the world.

At the other end were doves, rosellas, cockatoos, galahs, bantams, and little spotted quail in a long cage that continued beyond the wall into an external aviary. They all went outside to look.

Higher than the house, the aviary encompassed two fairly large trees and numerous dropping-splashed shrubs.

"See," Parick said, pointing, "Plenty of room to move around in there. Nice food, nice company. Look at all those magpies up there on the roof, and the pigeon. They'd love to get in!"

"But do all these pretty ones live normally in the cage? Breed and all that? Don't they want to migrate when the time comes?"

"When does the time come?" he asked, and looked at her seriously, as though there was some deeper meaning to the question.

If there was, she tried to ignore it: "Isn't it instinctive?" she asked.

"Probably. But perhaps it's just a reaction to environment. These seem quite happy here, don't you think? They use the house to build nests, shelter from bad storms, or repair themselves if they're sick, and they fly around out here as though it's the whole world. They've got it good here—regular meals, the illusion of freedom, no predators." Once again his eyes smiled at her.

"Talking about predators," said Rosemary, in the tone of one asking polite questions at a formal garden party, "surely a burglar could stroll through here, then through the doorway into the house? He'd only have to cut the mesh there."

"He'd be dealing with quite a welcome committee," said Patrick. Two of the younger dogs were frolicking around, and as he spoke a black Labrador jumped up to try for a face lick. "Apart from this nong there's a sharp-toothed red setter, the two boxers, the kelpie, and Mick, the German shepherd. And don't think the birds would keep quiet about it! No, we're safe here." He smiled. "I haven't got too much of value anyway. Why would they bother with this house when most of my neighbours advertise by leaving Mercedes and BMWs in the drive?"

"Oh! What's that one? That little green one?" Rosemary pointed to a bird on a low branch in the cage.

"Which one? The one with the . . . with the . . . ? Very carefully positioning himself behind her, Patrick crouched a little so his sight-line could exactly follow her finger. It seemed an odd thing to do so she stepped aside.

"There. It's just fluttered up to the higher branch. Oh, gorgeous! Green on top, yellow underneath, blue *and* red on its wing. There— you can't miss it!"

But he wasn't even trying to look anymore; his face, even his array of laugh lines, was crunched in concentration. He tapped his lips.

"Could be a turquoise parrot. Is its face turquoise?"

"Yes, look," As though displaying itself for examination the little bird swooped to the side of the cage near them and paused for a few seconds, holding the wire mesh in its claws.

"Oh, him!" Patrick sounded relieved. "Yes, he's a turquoise parrot all right. Greedy thing—he knows I mean food. A pretty rare bird— not a threatened species but close . . ." He was looking distinctly more comfortable, but Rosemary continued to be curious.

"How did you recognise it?" she asked.

"That patch along the wing. Yes. Very distinctive."

"It's red, the patch. Bright red."

"So I believe," he said wryly. "I'm colour-blind. I thought you might have worked that out—you always look at me as though you'd like to rip my clothes off. For all the wrong reasons!"

"Bobby?" Rosemary called, aware that her voice was a little strangled. "Where are you, darling? Gosh," she added, not daring to look at Patrick, "those computer games . . . they take over children's minds!"

.   .   .

Geoff did get tired and flopped as totally as a bean-bag with no beans. Patrick carried the man-sized child to bed in a room also fitted with rubber tiles and also smelling of urine, though more faintly. Bright alphabet posters, pictures of trains, cars, and aeroplanes, and pages torn from magazines and coloured comics were roughly glued and overlaid upon each other on all the walls—a casual, visual scrapbook that served as wallpaper.

"You can see Geoff isn't colour-blind," he said, watching her look around. "To me all this appears as various shades of grey, apart from the blue tones. I think I've learned which grey is red and which is green."

"No you haven't," she said, grinning at his clashing clothes.

Geoff's bed was very low, and a large rug made of sheepskins lay beside it—he'd land softly if he fell out of bed. A small bathroom, also a fairly recent conversion, adjoined the room.

Patrick stroked the sweating, snoring child. In sleep he looked less ugly to Rosemary. Or perhaps, she thought, he's growing on me.

"You really love him, don't you," she said, lightly touching Geoff's wild, curly hair.

"Yes. I do now. For years it was just guilt."

.   .   .

Bobby was the only one who didn't help feed the animals and clean the cages, though he was obviously torn. But the computer and its games had won, for him. He didn't even feel like stopping for a drink under the trees in the back garden.

"Give him the word and he'd move in tomorrow," said Rosemary, amused and exasperated, having struggled to lure him into the bus. He knew she wouldn't yell in front of Patrick and Andy.

"Yeah! Yeah!" said Bobby.

"Any time!" said Patrick.

Andy stayed to study and keep an eye on Geoff, and Patrick drove them home.

Fifteen

It was past seven when they reached the house. Bobby ran in first carrying the chairs, having yelled, "Thanks for a great day, Patrick! See ya later!" He gave the air of one intent on homework, but Rosemary knew he wanted to watch "World of Sport" on TV.

Rosemary wanted to tell Patrick something but couldn't put it into words. It was to do with the fact that she felt more at ease with him, after the day together. But she feared he might misunderstand—that he might be too encouraged. She didn't want to encourage him. But she didn't want to discourage him either. It was all too complicated for a street-side speech, and besides, Phyl was there. All the way home Phyl had eagerly talked about the animals, about the picnic, about Geoff—everything and everyone, in fact, except Andy.

Then Bobby ran, yelling, out of the house:

"Jesus, Ma! We've been burgled! Shit! They've taken everything!" and Patrick's hand closed on Rosemary's good arm as though he was arresting her.

.   .   .

"Where the hell is Auntie Gwen?" Rosemary demanded while dialling ooo. No one knew. "How'd you get in?" she demanded, while hugging Bobby with the phone crooked into her neck on the plastered side.

"I—just opened it. I didn't have a key."

"Blast her! She just went out and left it unlocked! Hello? Hello? Police please."

Patrick could not stay—he had to wake Geoff and feed and bathe him, then get him back to the school before nine. So he left, looking more shocked and upset than Rosemary yet felt.

Two polite, bored young policemen were there when Auntie Gwen came home. She had locked, she said. She always did. She'd popped out just for an hour, to see a friend at Mona Vale Hospital and then had car trouble and the friend's son had had to fix it. She'd tried to phone—there'd been no reply. One of the policemen found that the window to the laundry had had its catch smashed.

"Cool cheek!" said Auntie Gwen, who had just discovered that her new portable AM/FM stereo bedside radio, her Canon camera and both its lenses, and a purse containing a hundred and twenty dollars had gone. "Must have carried it all out of the front door!"

"Ask the neighbours if they saw anything," said the senior policeman. "Give us a call. No point trying to get prints from this—he's wiped them. You insured?"

Rosemary nodded, too upset to speak. After they had gone, Auntie Gwen insisted that Rosemary take one of the tranquillisers Dr. Saxon had prescribed when she broke her arm.

"What's the use ferreting around tonight? What's missing will still be missing in the morning, and you'll have a clearer head."

"The paintings!" Rosemary grieved. "The Dobell! The Fred Williams! I was depending on them—they've been the aces up my sleeve! Oh, and even my sad-eyed lady—why would he take that? My darling picture!" But it wasn't until Phyl discovered that her gold locket was gone that Rosemary broke down. It had been Jean's, and it had a picture of Rosemary's father in it.

"I can't stand it anymore. I can't!" she sobbed, hugging Phyl, who felt the same way. "I hate this house now."

"But you've been burgled before," said Auntie Gwen with an I-can-do-nothing-with-them expression.

"This is much worse. It's like rape."

"What difference, though, does it make, really? It was either some wretch of a burglar that got your stuff or the liquidators. It's just things. Things! Not health, or life!"

Rosemary and Phyl removed themselves from Auntie Gwen's insensitive gaze and Bobby went out to quiz the neighbours.

.   .   .

The insurance assessor was a brown-eyed, wavy-haired young man who looked as nice as an ABC newsman. He made notes on a form while Rosemary talked about what had happened. He asked mild questions— "Which items belonged to Mrs. er . . . ?" He got Rosemary to sign the form.

Then he said, "Now, I must explain to you that under this policy only the insured's possessions or those belonging to a spouse or children living in same house, are covered. . . ."

"You mean my aunt's things . . . ?"

"No. You see, the company assumes that people insure their own possessions." So, if they're stupid enough not to . . . his look added.

Rage rippled through her like a current. Why didn't I lie? Why was I so moral? So gullible? Why did I sign first, without asking? Again? she demanded of herself, feeling vulnerable as a country mouse fleeced by clever city slickers. She had not sensed the danger behind his innocent-sounding questions—she'd trusted his handsome face. How would she ever win in a world that played by these twisted rules?

What she actually said, coldly, was, "I think it's disgusting. You can't rely on anyone!"

The handsome insurance man chose to believe she was talking about the burglar. "We are supporting a drug-based alternative economy," he said. "It's probably bigger than this whole, huge insurance organisation and all its property, business, and investment assets. Do you know that last year we paid out in claims more than we got in premiums? My opinion is that money this big can't possibly be in the hands of amateurs—some very smart people are playing behind the scenes."

"What do you mean?"

"Politicians, judges, bank managers. Point the finger where you like." He shrugged. "It's people like you—and I, Mrs. Quilty—who are manipulated. And there doesn't seem to be any solution."

He left his card. He said the claim would take a while to process.

"How long?"

"Weeks. Couple of months, perhaps. We have people in touch with the big art dealers, and they'll be looking out for the paintings. It's fortunate that you've got these photos—many people can't even describe, never mind identify, their own property."

So the cheque would come after the company was wound up and the house was gone. Rosemary wondered if the liquidators would fight her for it then. It would be all she had left from half a lifetime's effort.

. . .

Officially, Auntie Gwen had moved back home again three weeks after Rosemary broke her arm. Her left hand was fairly useful again—she could hold things to slice, open doors if the handles were not stiff, and manage the little containers for her lenses without spilling fluid all down her front. It was partly because of the increasingly less-gentle exercises the physiotherapist had led her through and mainly because of impatience. She would have got over the stress and driven regularly if she'd had a car.

Auntie Gwen's visits usually lasted two nights at a time and resulted in a fridge full of casseroles. Her style of cooking had begun to include more of the things Rosemary said were good for people, though she'd grumbled more than Bobby did about brown rice and salads. "Like that time I gave Weight-Watchers a go. Proper disappointment I was to them," she said, licking red jam off a large spoon.

But the wordless nutritional compromise they'd struck meant that for every salad, there was a compensatory dessert—what Auntie Gwen called a sweet—thick with cream, rich in short-crust pastry, chocolate, custard, and syrupy canned fruit. Auntie Gwen's cheesecakes were three inches high and scarcely quivered when sliced. Her pavlovas were strawberry-and-passion-fruit-encrusted clouds. Bobby adored Auntie Gwen's sweets, despite Rosemary's and Phyl's prognostications about acne, and neither Auntie Gwen nor Bobby appreciated the moral conflicts Phyl and Rosemary endured, resisting slices.

When Auntie Gwen was away, neighbours with school-age children solved most of Phyl and Bobby's transport problems, though the price the children had to pay was to be delicately, horrifiedly quizzed about the fact that their Dad's business had gone under.

"I feel like a leper," said Phyl. "As though what we've got is catching."

"Tell them to mind their own business!" said Auntie Gwen.

"What? And catch a bus? No, I just look sad until they stop."

.   .   .

Robert Talbot's secretary solved Rosemary's transport problems when she phoned to arrange for her to meet the producer and the scriptwriters prior to starting her new job. The call came on the very morning Rosemary had decided she must have dreamt Robert Talbot's job offer.

"I'm sending you a Cab-Charge card," the secretary said. "No need to keep records—they bill us. Just use it for everything."

The producer, whose name was Kim Haymes, hardly remembered Rosemary from the day at Lithgow. He was thin. Even his head was thin, and this was accentuated by over-large tortoise-shell glasses and a pointed adam's apple that leapt up and down like an express elevator. He'd been a production assistant then, and this job was obviously his first big break. He seemed confident enough, though it occurred to Rosemary that Robert Talbot might have been having trouble finding experienced people to finish the mini-series.

In Lithgow, Kim had come into the make-up caravan at one stage and teased, tickled, or cuddled just about everyone and then gone off with half of Carol's fruit-and-nut chocolate bar. Rosemary liked him. He made her think of Woody Allen, twice the height.

"I'm used to hiring my own people," he said. Rosemary looked demure. She knew he had to say it. "I plan to build a team. Know what I mean? I don't know anything about you, Rosemary Quilty." She looked sympathetic.

When he said it must be nice to have friends in high places, she looked wistful. When he said there was a lot of hard work to be done, and in very little time, she looked efficient. When he said the project had been a bloody disaster and it was up to them to pull something good out of the rubble she looked like a good soldier, and when he finally offered her a cup of coffee, she looked thirsty. Then he looked friendly. She'd passed, and he hadn't even asked her about her qualifications for the job. She supposed he realised it made no difference—no doubt he'd heard the gossip.

Rosemary started work on the last Monday in November, one of five researchers helping three writers, one of whom was acting as script editor. Debby was the editor and Barb and Peter the writers. They had been there for three days thrashing out the story-line.

Debby was a large, dark-haired girl who made Rosemary think of Jo in *Little Women*. Her olive-skinned face was long and plain, her teeth were crooked, and her eyes were almost lost in deeply recessed sockets. But her dark, glossy hair hung in bouncy, uneven curls around her shoulders—curls that could only have been natural. It was hair that shone and gleamed as though it were the repository of all good vibrations. Rosemary, trying to visualise Debby without it, thought of Marmee, the hard-working, moralistic mother of the four little women, who, when her daughter cut her own hair off to sell as an act of charity, had made what Rosemary thought was the most insensitive remark in literature: "Oh, Jo!" Marmee had said. "Your only beauty!"

Peter was a big man whose body was relaxed, but whose head was not. He said very little but glanced around in quick jerks in reponse to other people's talking, as though following a ball in a soccer match.

Barb looked like a young boy, though Rosemary guessed she was about thirty. Her mousy hair was roughly cut short as though by someone drunk and in the dark. Her faded red T-shirt protruded under a chopped-off, once-white sweat-shirt whose ribbing had been ripped off, leaving an edge of loose threads and little holes like bites. Her sandalled feet were dirty. Her single earring, which swung from a well-used hole in her left lobe, was a silver question mark. Barb chain-smoked, and the others flapped their notepads and coughed without expecting to be taken seriously.

If Rosemary had had to guess their professions before talking to them, she'd have put Debby down as a missionary, Peter as a tennis umpire, and Barb as a political radical living on unemployment benefits. None of them fitted her image of what script-writers look like. This she put down to the fact that she was really a lousy judge of character.

A large electric coffee-pot stood keeping its contents warm on a small table which was strewn with styrene cups and the paper plates and other remains of the last two meals. She wondered where—or if—they'd slept.

A researcher called Simon arrived to give Barb some urgent information and stayed for Rosemary's first script conference. Simon was a pink-faced Englishman who would have looked more comfortable in a suit than in huge jeans and an uncrushable linen shirt. He had a very classy accent and an assured air, which, Rosemary soon noticed, was applied, like make-up. His style was not to ask questions but to make bold-sounding statements that began with "Of course . . ." and then to nod impatiently as he was corrected. He made long notes on a lined pad like the one she'd been given. He mentioned that he had a degree.

Rosemary gathered that the researchers spent most of their time working from home or in libraries, once they knew what was needed—bringing, phoning, or sending information in as soon as they could. So she probably would not meet the other researchers except by coincidence or unless a major conference was called.

Everything about the script conference was strange and fascinating and not much like the slow, polite one at Film Australia her communications class had once been allowed to observe. This crowded, smoky room full of people who never sat still reminded Rosemary of her children's games when they were little. Being used to working with business executives who claimed that time was money and who therefore expected a high degree of application and speed, at least until lunchtime, she was enchanted to be in a group who paid due regard to imagination. They teased, gossiped, repeated things, lost notes, and said "Bullshit" or "No, no, no. This is better, listen . . ." Yet ideas suggested and then criss-crossed with counter-suggestions quickly developed into recognisable bits of the lives of the people they were inventing. Scenes of the story took shape.

Eileen, a middle-aged secretary who smiled a lot and said little, patiently typed and re-typed and re-typed and re-typed, because at the end of day each writer would have to take home a scene break-down to work on.

Everyone, even Simon, made comments and offered new angles about everyone else's scenes. At first no one seemed to be in charge, but then Rosemary realised that Debby really was aware of everything that was going on despite looking relaxed to the point of detachment. And Kim observed constructively, as though he were the leader of a small orchestra left to get on with practising harmonies until he was ready to tap the baton.

This second part of "The Mount Victorians" picked up in 1897, thirty years after the movie-length part had ended with the opening of the railway station at Mount Victoria.

Sybil, the character Angela had played, and Frank, the boy from the inn, had married and were now an agreeable middle-aged couple who lived in Lithgow, where he worked as the manager in James Rutherford's office. Angela in a grey wig, soft padding, and etched-on lines—the vision pleased Rosemary.

They had a son, Charles, now twenty-five, who was a member of the New South Wales Citizens' Bushmen Corps. The writers had argued about that: Debby had wanted him to be a horseman, but then Simon had produced a book which quoted a letter written in 1900 from a lance-corporal who was waiting in a camp at Randwick, hoping to be enlisted in this very popular corps. The letter said they slept in sand and ate stew for dinner and that it was usually covered in flies.

"Yeah," she'd agreed. "We can make something of that. Randwick's not too far from Lithgow for furloughs and weekends. And he'd have worn a slouch hat?"

"Yes, indeed, slouch hat. And, of course, he was married, too, don't forget. And twenty-five, which would have made him older than most candidates. His chances would not have been very good unless he impressed a superior officer." Simon said 'superior' as though it had only two vowels.

"Yeah, that's right," said Peter, writing and talking at the same time. He seemed to be in charge of the war scenes. "Good with the pistol. Tell you what, why don't we just have him tame a runaway horse, win a race on it, and then say 'with acknowledgements to *Gallipoli*' in the credits?" Debby threw a pencil at him, and then needed one and stole Rosemary's.

Sybil and Frank had two daughters, too: Catherine, twenty-eight, with young children of her own, married to manager—er—Bert, they decided. Albert was a very fashionable choice for the time. He worked at the colliery. Susannah, the youngest, was seventeen and very beautiful.

"Clarice would have been what? Fifteen, sixteen then? If we make Susannah her friend, schoolmate, or whatever, we can get rid of that ridiculous governess idea," said Kim, and for a moment Rosemary was back in Lithgow, in the dark green dress, preparing to be a TV actress. A lovely dream, she thought. But—easy come, easy go.

"Sybil and Frank's family will pull together a lot of loose ends," Barb explained to Rosemary.

"Especially the title," drawled Peter, reminding them of an old battle. "Mount Victoria is simply a way station from now on—most of the action is in Lithgow," he explained for Simon and Rosemary. "We've left the married sister up there, to keep the link."

Barb went on as though Peter had not interrupted.

"About twenty thousand Australian soldiers went and fought in the Boer War in 1900. Can you imagine that? I mean they didn't even have to—they damn well wanted to. And that was out of a population of what? Four million in the whole of Australia? Not even that many, unless you counted the Abos, who were not likely to volunteer.

"But Charles will go, of course—a good dock-side weeping scene, love letters from the veldt, and so on. Probably he'll get killed if we need a death later on, in 1902 or 1903. But first there's federation coming up in 1901, so there's a lot of political activity—very interesting stuff, Kim keeps telling me, since I'm the one picked to do that! Debby's doing the Lithgow characters: Rutherford and the Sandfords."

At the end of the day, all three of the writers looked pleased though exhausted, and Rosemary had her assignment, which was to delve into the life of William Sandford—the man Robert Talbot had so enthusiastically talked about in the Porsche, while she'd sat, supercharged with sexual expectation. I don't give up easily, do I? she asked herself. Still, this job will be a pretty good consolation prize—if I can do it.

Debby caught up with her as she waited for her cab. "Quite a first day, huh? Look, don't take much notice of all that in there—a lot of it was just, you know . . ." She stirred the air with her palm. "For writers the real work's done at home, each of them glued to their little word processors, night and day."

"I loved it!"

Debby regarded her seriously, and Rosemary had the feeling she was being perceived as a character. What was Debby seeing? A gushy mum playing at work? An attractive, graceful woman who revealed little and who was going to age well? Robert Talbot's lover? At one stage, referring to the budget—which was much tighter than it had been under Stoner's direction—someone had said, "The trouble is, there's always someone in power with a big name and no talent," and in the short silence that followed Rosemary realised they were talking about him and thought she might be offended. Or a corporate spy. But she had pretended not to hear and the moment had passed.

It was obvious that, in the industry, talk of the high cost of making the first episodes was already a legend and she would have loved to have had some allusions more fully explained. There had, for instance, been a staggering percentage of OB.

"I've got your number, you've got mine. Phone me if you have any problems," Debby said, turning towards the car-park.

"Wait!" said Rosemary. "What's OB?" She had blurted out her ignorance. She was aware that she was blushing. But Debby did not look particularly shocked; on the contrary, her large, heavy face suddenly looked almost gentle.

"Jargon," she said. "Shorthand for location filming. It comes from 'outside broadcasting,' from the days of radio—it's another way of saying 'costs a bloody fortune.' "

"Thanks," said Rosemary.

"No worries," said Debby, and with a cheery wave, left Rosemary, with a stack of notes and scribbled-on draft scripts and eye-strain to start her new career. Which was another thing: so far no one had told her how much she would be earning, who would pay her, and when. Kim had just said, waving a hand, "That's all fixed by head office. Let me know if you don't hear anything in a week." And, instead of getting worried about this vagueness and feeling the urge to work out budgets on scraps of paper, she had just accepted that in due course there would be a salary and that that would be a huge improvement in her life.

Rosemary had never thought of God as some sort of super-father she could chat to, so, unlike her mother, she could not and did not pray. But on the way home her gratitude for this absorbing, distracting, and economically essential job overflowed her own containment. She had been in greater danger of losing the duel with stress than she'd acknowledged, but now, having been given a weapon, she could directly fight the things that threatened her. And those she could not fight— like Daniel—would be obscured or even obliterated by the demands of healthy, creative time-filling work.

She felt exultant. She wanted to thank the whole world—yes, even Robert Talbot, in whose arms she had so humiliated herself. After all, a bit of humiliation was nothing after the things Daniel had caused her to endure all year, and the reward was magnificent.

· · ·

There was no listing for William Sandford in the state library. She tried 'Iron' and 'Steel' and 'Lithgow.' A few titles looked promising and most, fortunately, were on the shelves—ordering titles from the stacks looked too daunting for a beginner.

By noon she had found out more than anyone writing a popular script would need to know about metallurgy. But then things picked up: Sandford was mentioned in a commemorative publication paid for by the people who'd bought him out in 1908. She also found the photocopier and the Ladies. And she decided to ask a busy-looking librarian for help.

"You'd be better off in the Mitchell," he said. "Know where it is? Down the passage. They've got most of the historic stuff."

Gold fever probably feels like this, she thought, running through the filed cards in the Mitchell's thick wooden trays. There, clear and uncomplicated, was "Sandford, William. Two boxes, papers, cuttings, etc." She was almost too excited to fill in the requisition slip.

"You haven't put your reader's ticket number here," said the young woman at the desk. Original documents such as these were only shown to people with reader's tickets, she explained. No, not hard to get—just a matter of filling out a form and getting two referees to sign it. It would take a day at the most.

Rosemary tried to phone Debby but got an answering machine in reply. She'd have to take the form home and do it all later.

Disappointed, frustrated, she went and had a sandwich in a crowded little coffee shop and then got thoroughly wet on her way back to the library. An accumulation of dark clouds that had hovered around most of the week had suddenly decided to pour semi-solid sheets of rain through the crowd of lunch-time people, who quickly vanished as though they'd been swept into the rapidly overflowing storm drains. In minutes the street edges were ankle-deep with water and there was nothing to suggest the rain might stop.

Rosemary bought a *Daily Telegraph*—a handy size for an impromptu umbrella since her own was still in the check-in cubicle at the library—but it was reduced to papier mâché by the time she got across the street and into the main foyer.

She decided to spend the afternoon going through copies of the newspapers of William Sandford's time—perhaps there'd be something about him there? And next time she came, she decided, she'd bring her own lunch and, if it wasn't raining, eat it in the Botanical Gardens opposite the library's main doors.

She spent the afternoon drying slowly while poring through the tiny print and unfamiliar layouts of the microfilmed papers. There seemed no logic to the presentation of news at the turn of the century—official Treasury notices, announcements of warehouse sales, births and deaths, and the embarkation dates of ships interspersed what she would have regarded as important: reports of the war with the tsar, for example. It looked as though the printers had just put things in as they arrived.

She loved the microfiche. There was an odd sense of power in being able to make a whole week pass with a flick of the wrist. But by the end of the day her eyes were strained and her back was sore from leaning over the reading machines. And though she felt steeped in the right atmosphere, she also felt she hadn't earned her as-yet-unspecified salary.

The Cab-Charge idea was fine when there was no competition but, she'd stood on a corner for thirty minutes under an inadequate umbrella—it kept rain off her front or her back but not both. In the end she'd caught a train to Lindfield and taken a cab outside the station.

"How was it?" Phyl asked when Rosemary arrived wearily home.

"Both hard and easy. I don't think I'm much good at it though."

Auntie Gwen had left a pile of messages to phone people. The liquidator's office—about the burglary, no doubt. The insurance company—about the liquidation, no doubt. Jim Begg, about both, either, or something worse, no doubt. She wished they'd just all talk to each other and leave her alone.

She scurried past the white patches in the hall where pictures had been and would not even look into the sacked living room. It did not feel like her house anymore but like some roadside stall where strangers felt free to finger possessions that had once been private property.

When Patrick phoned, she was in the bath, and though he asked for her to call back, she decided not to. Apart from anything else, Phyl was murmuring into the phone to Andy and Rosemary didn't want to interrupt.

Next morning Rosemary dealt with things much better. She sent her reader's ticket application form to Kim by taxi, telling the driver to wait and bring it back again and then take her to the city. She phoned the liquidator and the insurance man and both of them surprised her by being almost ingratiatingly nice. The things they wanted to know were minor details—things they'd been told already and forgotten in the mass of paperwork their jobs entailed. The insurance man laughed self-consciously and apologised twice for wasting her time, and the liquidator talked to her as though she were his Sunday school teacher and he hadn't learned his verse. In both cases it was a total reversal of their previous behaviour. Why were they both being so nice? It was as though a message made up of jigsaw puzzle pieces was trying to assemble itself for her to understand.

The Spanish-sounding woman who answered Patrick's phone said, "Dr. Price was a' work and she didda no' know number."

Dr. Price? Rosemary thought. Is it usual for hydrologists with Ph.D.s to call themselves doctor? Then she remembered he'd said something about commuting to the university. Obviously he had some academic post, too.

How annoying nature's trick is, she thought. I was attracted to Robert Talbot, but he didn't fancy me. Patrick is attracted to me, but . . .

Actually, she thought, if there was some guarantee that he would never make a pass at me, it would be lovely to spend more time with Patrick. He is interesting and kind and surprising and fun. What a pity there just isn't that Wham! Shazam!

.   .   .

Rosemary was eager to get away from her doomed house and its troublesome telephone, as though the plague were there. By contrast, the library offered peace and mental health. There, at least, in that darkwood furnished room full of information, was something at which she might succeed.

She'd been in the Mitchell Library only once—the previous day—but already it felt like a possible haven. Obviously it already was to some people, who had set themselves up at the smaller tables and created demarcation lines around themselves with piles of folders, books, microfilm boxes, and sweaters. Already Rosemary knew better than to wear steel-tipped high heels as she'd done the previous day—she had clicked conspicuously over the marble-tiled floor.

The weather had looked promising so she'd brought cheese and salad sandwiches and some fruit as well as her umbrella. And, after requisitioning the Sandford boxes, she had lunch in the park where a blowfly, three or four sea-gulls, and a long-legged, sharp-beaked, dark-feathered bird tried to share it. An ibis? she wondered. She'd check in the library's wonderful brain.

Despite its better manners and its bony, back-to-front knees, the possible ibis managed to do quite well in competition with the squawking, hissing gulls. They allowed themselves to be side-tracked from the occasional crust Rosemary chose to toss by being more concerned with politics. Matters of territory and pecking order were obviously more exciting to them than the food, which was just an excuse to set them shrieking anxiously over each flying bit and then scolding whichever bird caught it. The odd thing was that the more tense they appeared to be, the more relaxed Rosemary became. They looked so silly, caring so much about who won, while the backward-kneed dark bird simply concentrated on getting as much whole wheat bread and butter into its system as it possibly could.

The park was beautiful. Full beds of calendulas and other bright early

summer flowers made focal points of the vast, curving lawns over which
a high sprinkler arced, rhythmically creating a rainbow at the same spot
on each backward and forward journey. The water wasn't really necessary in Rosemary's opinion, since it had rained so heavily the day
before, but it was a welcome addition to her almost private enjoyment.

In the vast, smooth, brilliant lawns there were clumps of roses here
and there, pearlised and pastel-coloured in the clear air which was filled
with the scent of herbs and small-flowered climbing things. No more
than four blocks from anywhere important, the gardens were surprisingly empty. Apart from a man in a once well-cut suit who was curled
up on a nearby bench, sleeping off the effects of a bottle of something
which lay empty in its brown bag, and apart from three old ladies in
pink, green, and blue with delicately matching hair, frailly helping each
other on a little walk, Rosemary, the birds, and the blowfly virtually had
that part of the gardens to themselves.

To reward the gulls for consuming her tension, Rosemary threw them
the last of the scraps in a sweeping arc of distribution that left them
wide-beaked and shrieking like evil spirits. Then, calm, feeling nourished, and sun-kissed, she went back to the library and was given the
Sandford papers.

.   .   .

They were in two sturdy, dark grey cardboard boxes reinforced with
cloth, probably made by hand by a man with bookbinding skill. A handwritten note on one of them said they had been presented to the library
by Clarice Sandford, William's daughter.

Most of the papers were glued into large, bound journals of the sort
bookkeepers used before computers. The pages were hand numbered.
There were smaller items, too: an old-fashioned birthday book, nearly
empty, and some tiny pocket books, absolutely full of closely written
pencil notes. Commemorative programs and promotional leaflets, printed
in the curly, open-faced type the early Edwardians obviously thought
very tasteful, had been preserved along with various letters, many of
which had federal or state government crests and addresses.

The large notebooks contained hundreds of pages of closely typed
documents. It could take the best part of forever to get through them,
Rosemary realised. How much time could she spare for this first part
of her job? There was no deadline apart from "as soon as you can."
There was no yardstick about the quantity of information she'd need.

Gently fingering the pages which, perhaps, had not been touched
since Clarice Sandford pasted them down, she experienced a flickering

thrill, the way a hunting dog must when it first catches the scent of the fox. Or like the way Daniel had sometimes made her feel by running his tongue around her earlobe.

Clarice's careful choosing and pasting had been done at least fifty years before—fifteen years before Rosemary herself was conceived. Someone whose life had never touched on hers was communicating to her through these papers which, odd phrases revealed, were full of protest and justification. The angry urgency that must have prompted Clarice to put the evidence of her father's story on record lingered like old perfume in the boxes. Rosemary sensed it would be fascinating. Even if Robert Talbot hadn't told her about William Sandford, Clarice was doing so now.

Rosemary tried to picture Clarice sitting somewhere, alone, in a quiet room, perhaps late at night, carefully reading and choosing the bits of her father's life. Perhaps it was winter and a fire flickered in the nearby grate and perhaps Clarice crumpled up and threw in there all the letters and photographs and documents that were irrelevent or too intimate for this story intended for a wider public. And as she sat there, her head bowed in concentration, Clarice probably tried to imagine people in a future time looking carefully through the boxes and sharing her indignation. Or perhaps it was no longer indignation by the time Clarice did the pasting, since most of the events described in the documents had happened thirty years earlier, in the first seven years of the century. By that time her indignation had probably settled into a chronic desire to put the record straight. She might have thought in terms of an official biography—she'd probably died before television.

In a state of quiet excitement, Rosemary read until her eyes were so strained that she had to swap her lenses for her glasses. There had certainly been a good reason for Clarice to keep the papers.

Rosemary had been told she could not photocopy anything from the boxes because the process was cumulatively bad for the pages. They could be photographed but that would take weeks because there was a small staff and a big backlog. It was the first time in her life that she regretted not having concentrated more in the secretarial course her mother had sent her to after she'd left school—shorthand would have been a blessing now.

Writing as small and as closely as possible, Rosemary filled both sides of every page of the notebook she'd brought and could have done with another one. Her right hand began to suffer from writer's cramp and ached much more than the healing left arm.

Quite late in the afternoon, Rosemary stopped to phone the children to tell them not to wait for her—they were latchkey kids today. They were to heat up the chicken casserole and cook some beans and rice and leave her some to microwave when she got home.

"When'll that be?" Bobby asked.

"I don't know yet. I may stay until the library closes if I don't get too tired. Why? Do you need something? Help with homework?"

"We don't have homework anymore now that the exams are over," he said in a tone that suggested she should have known that.

"Well. Will you be all right, you two?"

"Yeah. Spose," he said.

"Love you," Rosemary offered brightly.

"Yeah," he said.

Phyl sounded less glum. In fact she sounded over-bright; Rosemary correctly detected an asking note in her voice.

"If I pass my learner's test and get L-plates, Andy will teach me to to drive," she said. "Isn't that great?"

"You're not old enough to drive, darling!"

"I will be on the thirtieth of March—three months before my seventeenth. He's already showed me how the gears and things work. It's easy."

"Well, don't you dare start driving around until you have got L's! Apart from anything else, that car of Andy's doesn't look road-worthy and it's just the sort of thing the police will pounce on, to check the brakes or something. And drag you both off in chains!"

"Oh, Mum!" Phyl said. It could have meant anything. "I'm going to feed the animals on Sunday," she added before Rosemary's uneasiness about the car could focus itself in words. "Andy arranged it with Patrick. Andy's got his last paper on Monday and he needs to study. Bobby's been invited, too. Is that all right?"

"Of course. Yes. Lovely," Rosemary said, though it felt more odd than lovely that they should be making independent plans to visit Patrick's house. "Don't forget it's Bobby's birthday on Monday. I think we can scrape up enough for a restaurant unless he picks French."

Rosemary left the library when they switched the lights off. She was tired, but it was good, creative tiredness, not the crushing, ageing tiredness of grief. She planned to be back as soon as they opened in the morning, to make sure she had the complete story for the Friday script conference.

"I've discovered the joy of workaholism," she told Lucy, who'd found her already in bed when she visited on Thursday night, though it was still light enough outside to read by.

"You've been practising for years."

"This is different. This isn't work, it's fun. This man I'm finding out about also lost everything—much more than I am losing, because he was rich and powerful in the first place. And his poor daughter! It makes what's happening to me seem manageable."

"I still don't know how you're coping," said Lucy, whose personal problems seemed more and more to revolve around finding the right dress designer and propitiating Mattie for seeing so little of her. Lucy's social calendar could no longer be contained in a hand-bag diary: she carried a quarto-sized, leather-bound executive planner full of closely written notes and assignations. For instance, she was going to have her tarot cards done that very evening by a wonderful woman in Willoughby who had squeezed her in at nine.

"Bobby's not mad about this latchkey business either. But, for us, it's that or starving," Rosemary said, aware too late that in guiltily justifying her own position she was being tactless.

"At least he's got Phyl."

"Yes. And Auntie Gwen's here a lot of the time. And Mattie can come here as much as she likes if Eve has no objection."

"Yes, thanks, I know. But Eve feels a bit put out if Mattie comes over and leaves Ben there, and she won't let him come because she's nervous about your pool. I mustn't be late, Ro; don't let me miss the time." They switched the radio on, too quietly for its well-pronounced disasters to interrupt, but loudly enough for the time signals.

"I've just got to have my cards read to see whether Malcolm's right. He says I've got a real future in the industry. He's helped me so much!" Lucy said this while putting dark red lipstick on, using a little gold compact mirror into which she satisfiedly smacked her lips before snapping things back into her bag. "I've been meaning to tell you, in case you wondered, that I haven't had time to finish your jumper."

"That's OK, Luce, we're getting into heat-wave weather. It will be wonderful for the autumn."

"Yes." Lucy sounded dubious. "I could be too tied up then, too, if what Malcolm's talking about happens."

"What?"

"Me being a co-presenter on his show," she said, her gleaming eyes completely destroying her attempt at casualness.

"How fantastic! How . . . perfect!"

"Yup. What a year. This has been the—oh—greatest, sublimest year of my life. Just incredible. And it's all Malcolm's doing." Lucy lighted a cigarette.

"No, Lucy!" Anger and urgency suddenly combined in Rosemary's tone, startling them both. "It's you! It's your talent!"

"Yes, of course," said Lucy, hiding her surprise under a deep inhalation and a reasonable manner. "But he's the one who . . ."

"*No!*" Rosemary interrupted. "Don't you see what you're saying? You're saying that Malcolm's your . . . sculptor, like I used to think Daniel was mine. Lucy, you're the star. On your own you're the star, believe me. If Malcolm walked out tomorrow you'd still . . ."

"How can you say that?" Lucy was suddenly angry. "How can you ill-wish us like that?"

"Ill-wish? Luce, Malcolm's not going to leave you. I only meant . . ."

But the radio signalled, and Lucy was in too much of a hurry to know what Rosemary meant. "If you like," she said at the door, "I'll give you the jumper to finish—the back and front are done, it's just the sleeves and the neckband now and it's really easy."

"You used to knit because it stopped you smoking." Rosemary said.

"Yes," Lucy smiled politely. "I did, didn't I?"

You're my best friend, Rosemary tried to say with her eyes. Please don't let's lose that.

.   .   .

With her full, fat notebooks plus copies of a few things the Mitchell librarians had deemed invulnerable to the light of the photocopier, plus a head so full of information about the Sandfords that no chink of her own anxiety had space to reveal itself, Rosemary went to the script conference on Friday and found Debby had virtually decided to scrap the Sandfords.

"Oh no, no, you mustn't," Rosemary said, standing up, leaning forward, gesticulating. All of them looked at her as though she were stripping or singing, but she didn't care. "It's wonderful stuff. So interesting . . . Sandford was the first man in Australia to smelt steel. He had this vision of making Australia a great new manufacturing centre in the world—another Pittsburgh—instead of just exporting raw materials to make other countries rich. But it caused tragedy for him . . ." Then, suddenly seeing what they were all looking at, she trailed off.

Kim, Debby, Peter, and Barb—Simon was not there that day—were all looking at the appointee of somebody in power with a big name and no talent. Somebody who had made a special point of having the Sandford story mentioned. Somebody upon whom their jobs depended. Rosemary felt a gap begin to form between them and herself, as though she was drifting off in a small boat and they, her new friends, were safe on an island. And then there was no choice, no question about where she wanted to be—Clarice would have to wait.

With a metaphysical "wait for me!" Rosemary leapt back on land again—"Take no notice of me," she said, laughing shyly. "The story is probably not all that wonderful. Just over-enthusiasm, I guess. It's the first time I've done this sort of investigative research." Then she bit her lip. Had the others, apart from Kim, known she was a novice? Their expressions didn't help. Peter, particularly, looked at her as though through a microscope. "I've just got carried away," she said to bridge the dangerous gap. "I think I fell in love with William Sandford at that dark table in the Mitchell!" She tried to reassure everyone with brilliant smiles that she was part of the team and would do as she was told. Then:

"Well, hell! Love!" Kim said. "We can't do better than love! I'd thought Sandford was just some dreary old fart of an industrialist— someone to give employment to our characters and a daughter the right age for romance. But if you think . . ."

Rosemary wasn't entirely sure if he was being sarcastic.

"Go on," Debby said kindly. "Give us the high concept."

There was so much. Rosemary thought quickly, sorting through what she'd just learned. "Well, apart from Clarice, William Sandford had had a son, too—Roy—who was killed in the war." No one said anything though Barb raised her eyebrows. What would sell them on the idea? Quick! Quick!

"William was a very private man, but one thing I found that . . . well, it could be something. A birthday book with his children's and his wife Caroline's birthdays in it. And there is only one other one—just initials: A. I. M."

Kim and Debby looked at each other as though their brains were linked telex machines. "There's your secret romance," he said. "A mistress in Sydney, a . . . a singer. Popular entertainer, big bosom, ostrich feathers. What you wanted. He could visit her and secretly take her to all the places you wanted to do—the Tivoli or whatever it was."

"Yes," said Debby. "The brass band in Hyde Park. And it could get him into trouble at home with the wife."

"A. I. M.," said Barb. "Amy. Better still, Aimee. Aimee Iris Morton."

"We're talking about a real character here. We can't just invent people's lives," said Peter so seriously that the other writers laughed.

"Get off the bus, Pete. The day you stop inventing people's lives is the day you open a sandwich bar at Dulwich Hill station."

"You know where Talbot got this Sandford bug, don't you?" Kim asked Debby. "In Lithgow. There's a bust of the old bugger at Eskbank House. They say his daughter did it," Kim said.

"A sculptor? Clarice? That's perfect!" said Rosemary, feeling the excitement rise again. "One thing I'm sure of—there are no direct descendants in Australia because Clarice never married and Roy was killed. William did have a son called John who lived in Devon, in England, but I'm sure he must have been from a former marriage." Then she shut up abruptly. For someone who'd hardly opened her mouth on Monday she was fairly dominating the scene.

Barb scratched her boy-short hair noisily with all ten nails at once. "Well, I don't know," she said. "I still can't see what it is that grabbed you about it. Can you, Kim? Deb?" Seconds ago both of them had been Rosemary's allies, now they looked neutral.

"Convince us," Debby said kindly. "Wait! First some coffee. Anyone else? Then we'll make ourselves comfortable and be a viewing audience of two thousand million people—that's the U.S. market and Japan," she added like a teacher. "And you can dazzle us. OK?"

Rosemary had some coffee, too. She felt quite calm, fatalistic in fact, as though this was the moment when her future would be decided. It would be a performance, unrehearsed, off the cuff. There was a thoughtful silence, but Rosemary plunged right into it, not caring whether they did think she was Robert Talbot's bed-mate.

I've been an actor all my life, she reminded herself.

She told them about William Sandford, the English steel worker who had arrived on a contract to make fencing for a big New South Wales company and had recognised the opportunity to manufacture steel in the little town of Lithgow. It would be the first such industry in Australia. She told about his struggles to make the business viable, about the impressive, flashy banquets he staged in order to impress politicians and financiers, and about his vision for Australia as a great manufacturing centre—a southern-hemisphere Pittsburgh. She told them about his years of struggling and about his kindness to his employees, who were given the opportunity of buying their little mine houses on easy terms. And she told them about the night the first steel was poured, at a great banquet where every lady had been presented with a cast-iron rose. She must have done it right.

"I've seen one," said Peter enthusiastically. "Perfect kitsch—a shiny black rose at Eskbank House. You should go and see it, Rosemary!"

"What do you think about Sandford now, Debby?" Simon asked.

"Well, I think we'll have to keep him," she said. "Bits of him, anyway.

But don't get too carried away about the declining business and so on—it did decline didn't it?" Rosemary nodded. "We don't want any too many downers in this episode. And see if you can find something for us to pin on to Clarice to bring her into the story, too. We need some love interest around 1900. She'd have been eighteen at that banquet, wouldn't she?"

I'm in! thought Rosemary. I've passed!

Sixteen

Auntie Gwen was there when she got home. What Rosemary wanted
was a hot bath and bed.

"Nice, riding around in taxis," Auntie Gwen said. "How much longer
does that plaster have to be on?"

"Two weeks, maybe three. I've got to have another X-ray on Tuesday
to see how its getting on, but I'm sick of it—it itches in there and I'm
sure it stinks. And the exercises still hurt like hell!"

"What side of bed did you get out of today?"

"Me? Do I sound ratty? Actually I'm in a wonderful mood. Where
are the kids?"

"In the rumpus room," Auntie Gwen said after a thoughtful look.
"Phyl is, anyway. That young Andy is here. Didn't you see the funny
car outside? It's a German DKW, thirty years old, probably the only
one in Sydney! He's done it up, he says, with a bit of help."

"Yes I know. I don't like the look of it one bit; it's the one he's said
he's going to teach her to drive in."

Auntie Gwen raised one eyebrow. Rosemary was not sure what it
meant, but in case it was a hint of criticism she said, "I'm so glad about
Andy—he's just what Phyl needs right now."

"She'll need to go on the Pill, I reckon."

Anger, bright and sharp as a camera flash, exploded in Rosemary and
turned everything black and white.

"Auntie Gwen! Why do you have to be so . . . so gratingly unroman-
tic?"

Auntie Gwen, who had been sitting in an armchair, heaved herself
into a good levering position and then got up. If she'd been a turkey,
her feathers would have stood out.

"Listen, Rosemary Quilty, although you're so good at being deliberately blind, even you can't seriously pretend that teenagers don't go straight from 'go' to 'whoa' nowadays. The papers are full of it. Hell, they even teach contraception in schools. Phyl's a healthy girl without too many hang-ups, as far as I can see, and if she takes after either of her randy parents, she's heading for trouble just by being alive!" Rosemary was too furious to speak, even if she'd been given the opportunity. "What I want to know is," Gwen continued, her angry voice seeming, to Rosemary, to bounce around the room like large balls, "why do you, an apparently grown-up woman, persist in calling me Auntie? When we're not even related?"

It was the fight that had been waiting for years to happen. They glared at each other through an almost visibly charged field, red-faced, breathing hard, joined as though by an invisible lasso.

"For someone who's not even related, you do an awful lot of bossing around."

"Well, someone's damn well got to. I've never seen such a lot of fools as you and Daniel, running around like headless chickens, destroying everything you've built up. Sometimes I think you forget you've got kids to bring up!"

"How dare you! How dare you!" Tears of anger squirted from Rosemary's eyes, as though little water pistols had been squeezed in there. She was half blinded. "That's so unfair!"

"Unfair? You even talk like a bloomin' child! Whatever's fair?"

They yelled at each other for fully five minutes about domestic things, minor things, attitudinal things. Gwen—she was now Gwen—resented the way Rosemary left instructions on notes. "You've got a tongue in your head. What's wrong with asking?"

"Nothing. But, unlike you, I don't go barging into people's bedrooms when they're asleep and start talking to them about toilet cleanser and onions and and light bulbs. What's wrong with a polite note, anyway?"

"Nothing. But yours aren't polite—there's never a please or thank you!"

But even in anger Rosemary could not say "I hate you because you're fat. I hate you because I had you instead of a father. I hate you because I thought that I might turn out to be a . . . that I might also become a . . ." Because . . . And the realisation made her crumple into softness and freed her from the hold of anger—all that was nonsense now.

"I'm sorry," she said shyly. "You're the last person I should snap at. You've been so bloody nice to us . . . and . . ." And she burst into tears.

"Now, now enough of that," said Gwen, who disposed of her own anger by immediately enveloping Rosemary in her huge, soft arms. Rosemary felt in no danger.

"Come on. Dry up," Gwen said. "You've done a very good job of hanging on to your marbles through all this nonsense—don't let go of 'em now." But Rosemary sobbed some more, luxuriating in the relief.

Gwen poured them each a drink—a large whisky for Rosemary, a few teaspoonsful for herself since she didn't like the taste of any liquor except red wine and she didn't think half a glass justified opening a whole bottle.

"Want some cottage pie? A sandwich?" Gwen offered.

Rosemary shook her head. "What about you?"

"No, ta, the kids and I had something earlier."

"A cheese biscuit, then?"

"No. Haven't you noticed I'm cutting down on between-meals?"

"I hadn't, no. I'm sorry. You're right—I am very self-absorbed."

"Hardly surprising," Gwen said magnanimously. "Fighting World War Three single-handed."

"Yes." Rosemary laughed. "I suppose I am, aren't I?" The quarrel had left an oddly comfortable feeling. They both kept glancing, with little smiles, at each other.

"Where did you say Bobby is?"

"Oh, around. He's eleven on Monday. Don't fuss so!"

"Do I fuss? I often feel I neglect them both."

"Time will tell." Gwen sighed. "I've watched a lot of parents and all I can say is I'm glad I wasn't one. Too many people in the world already, I reckon, and all blaming each other for the way their lives turned out. What one kid thinks is fuss another will think is neglect. You, for instance. You broke Jean's heart, getting pregnant at seventeen. Nobody could have been a better parent."

"Oh, Gwen, I wish she was here now. I miss her so much."

"Don't you start blubbing again!"

"No. No, I won't. It's just that earlier, when I was angry with you, I realised *why* I went off with Daniel. I was looking for . . . for a different pattern. I suppose I was saying to my mother that I didn't want to be like her. Like you and her," she added, in case the woman she was now going to have to call Gwen missed the point.

"You are a very coy woman, Rosemary, do you know that? Very coy. This is supposed to be the permissive eighties. Tell me," Gwen said, wheezing and coughing into an incongruously small handkerchief. "Now that we're having this heart-to-heart—this first-ever heart-to-heart. Did you make it into the cot with Robert Talbot?"

"Oh, hell, you're the end!" said Rosemary, standing up again, full of indignation. But once up she couldn't think of anything else to say and despite herself began to giggle. She sat down again. "No. But if I had, it would have been on a rock, not in a cot."

"The night you went to the film preview? I thought you looked churned up. But you came home in a taxi."

"He put me in one."

"Where?"

"Where? Why?"

"Where were you? Where was this rock?"

"Somewhere near West Head. Past Bobbin Head. I don't know. Does it matter? The taxi was in the Mona Vale Road."

"Ah ha! You were the curtain raiser. The so-to-speak curtain."

"Talk about coy! And arch! What is all this?"

"My friend Doris—who is in the Mona Vale Hospital, and who I did not, of course, visit on the day of the burglary—her daughter is a manicurist and she does the nails of a certain very fine-looking woman who used to be married to a certain State opposition leader. Talbot's been visiting there for months—pulls straight into the garage which closes behind him and makes him think the neighbours haven't noticed. Lovely place, she says. St. Ives, overlooking the Davidson Park. Hop and a skip from the Mona Vale Road."

So Lucy's media friends were right—right gossip, wrong lady.

Rosemary gazed at Gwen, this remarkable new old friend. The news about Talbot simply speeded up the process that had begun when she'd visualised the headlights illuminating their coupling on a rock—it put a shape to him. No longer was he a vast, random, all-powerful force but a bumbling, vulnerable romantic. Like anybody. He had come within an ace of cheating, with Rosemary's co-operation, on his mistress. Which would probably have made him feel as bad, or worse, than cheating, with his mistress's co-operation, on his wife.

I really could have been his mistress, if the position had not been taken! she thought and, quick as a special effect, an image of protected indolence formed itself in her vision. She glimpsed herself chatting to friends on the phone, closely guarding her confidences but letting delicious hints drop anyway. There'd be money for beautiful clothes and presents. She would sit, during the days, in a sunny room with white cane furniture, with David Hockney prints and Ken Done paintings on the walls and massed azaleas flowering outside the window. A woman would come to sculpture her nails while she read novels. She'd have facials. She'd do yoga in private, under the benign eye of an utterly sexless, elderly male instructor. If she got depressed, she'd have hypnotherapy. Some nights Robert would come and they'd eat smoked salmon and drink champange and then go to bed.

Then the image was forced out by one she could not prevent: the long, empty hours, the lies she'd have to tell. There would be the loneliness of being forever available for someone who may not turn up for weeks. What if, on the night he'd put Rosemary in a taxi, he had arrived at his lover's house to find her waxing her legs, or out? If he got jealous or bored or angry, her life-style would be at risk.

All other friendships would have to be placed on hold or kept at arms' length, and how would the children fit in? Dinner parties would require her to be matched with someone safe—someone's eighty-year-old father or a gay corporate boss or judge. She'd have to stick to a set of rules which Robert, paying all the bills, would make. No. It would be a very small cage. It would not suit at all. In fact, she felt she'd had a lucky escape, and took a deep, healthy breath.

Much more intriguing was the hint Gwen had so clearly dropped.

"Where did you go, then, if not to the hospital?"

That was when Bobby walked in, sweaty, dusty, and rumpled, munching a stick of celery, and took over the conversation.

"You gonna tell her, Auntie Gwen? You said you weren't going to tell her."

"I changed my mind."

"Tell me what? What does Bobby know that I don't?"

Shining-eyed, chewing with his mouth open, Bobby was obviously enjoying himself.

"About the stuff," he said. "The pictures, the silver. The burglary. There was no burglary. She took it."

Gwen sat looking solemn, like someone with a good defence lawyer and a hopeless case.

Rosemary could not believe what she'd heard.

"Truly she did. Nicked the lot," Bobby said.

"What the hell did you do that for?" Rosemary yelled, angry all over again. "What an idiotic . . . !" Gwen looked determinedly innocent. "Christ! I could be charged for fraud! What if the insurance company finds out?"

"They will. They will. In good time. I'll confess everything when the liquidator and the auctioneer have done their dirty work. I'll be your dotty old senile relative who's had this kleptomania for years, or whatever you think. They won't mind. The police won't mind. But I summed up that little rat of a liquidator—didn't like the way he was looking at your stuff. He'd have sold it for threepence ha'penny—to himself, under the names of Tom Smith and John Jones, if you ask me."

"She's hidden it," Bobby offered. "Won't tell anyone where. Not even me."

"But they're not going for anything except the house," Rosemary said confidently, then trailed off—"I think . . ."

"You never know," Gwen said, like one who was sure she did. "Anyway, I wasn't taking any chances since that little lizard said he's sending the auctioneer fellow here next week to have a scout around. I heard him talking on the phone to him when he thought I wasn't listening. Much too friendly, I thought."

"But Jim said nothing like that would happen. Auctioneers coming and so on. Not for . . . oh, months."

"Jim Begg! What'd he know? He's only used to parking fines and conveyances. You can't leave important things to other people."

"But the liquidator knows now—he's seen my things. He'll go for the insurance money, surely? I mean, if the house money is not enough. Or if he legally can—Jim says . . ."

"Jim says, Jim says," Gwen interrupted. "I could see that liquidator's eye—he was too keen on your pictures for my liking and people like that have ways around the law. People like him take first and ask after if it's easy enough to do, no questions asked. I made it hard for him, that's all. He'll back right off now is my bet. It's amazing what you can learn about a bloke by watching him eat a couple of cream scones!"

"You are incredible! Just incredible!" said Rosemary, and she began to laugh. And she laughed and laughed until she had to press the plaster cast hard against herself to stop her belly aching. Bobby laughed, too, spraying celery pulp, and Gwen started muttering about hysterics.

"So Bobby knew," Rosemary said, when she could speak again. "This is my third box of Kleenex this month! Bobby, but not me." Bobby looked delighted. "And Phyl? Does she know?"

"No, not Phyl. Bobby found out. One of the neighbours saw me ferrying some stuff, so it's good the policemen didn't do their own asking around. Why d'ya think I bought the station-wagon?"

"I didn't think anything."

"Well, I knew you could be bluffed. But sharp ears here couldn't."

"I still don't know why you didn't tell me."

"Because you're the lousiest liar I've ever met. Everything you think is written on your face in block capitals. You wouldn't have fooled the police or the insurance company for seven seconds."

Rosemary was stung by this. Shaken, in fact. How could she be an actress if she couldn't control her expression?

Bobby came and sat beside her and patted her plaster cast with his dirty hand. The cast had almost become part of her, she realised. It was hardly an impediment anymore. In fact, it was going to feel strange without it. "Auntie Gwen means you're too honest," Bobby said, snuggling up to her.

Rosemary put her hand over his and smiled her thanks for his reassurance. "A real twit, you mean. Got to be looked after," she said.

"No, Ma. You're real tough. Honest."

"You'd better get ready for bed now. What were you playing, cricket?"

"Soccer. Some of the guys from the high school, just kicking around on the field. It's only just got too dark."

This pleased Rosemary greatly and she hugged Bobby, who had been skulking around alone indoors too much in the past year. But her next question wiped the look of amused contentment off his face.

"Did Phyl ask you what kind of restaurant you'd like to be taken to on Monday night?"

"Yeah," he said and walked away.

"Bobby?"

"Listen," he said, and whirled around crossly. "I don't need a birthday treat, Ma. OK? I'm not seven." He mockingly blew out some invisible candles, clapped his hands and grinned like a clown. "Just let's cool it. OK?"

Rosemary glanced at Gwen, who narrowed her eyes at her. Leave him, her face said.

"It's Daniel, of course," Rosemary said when Bobby had gone. "He always made such a special thing of Bobby's birthday because it's so near Christmas. I wish I knew where he's gone. You don't suppose something's . . . happened to him?"

"Nothing's happened to him. Don't be silly. He's just got out of the way of the flack, that's all."

"But it's not like Daniel to run away."

"Oh, so now you're an authority on Daniel, are you? A year ago you'd have said, 'It's not like Daniel to go off with another woman.' I'm telling you, he's buggered off somewhere out of range, that's all. He's never been out of his depth before—it's a new experience for the cocky bugger and he doesn't like it."

Rosemary could not argue. "All the same," she said, "I *must* get hold of the bastard! We can't go on in this ridiculous way!"

"You and I have been talking for long enough for all kinds of things to have brewed in that rumpus room," said Gwen. "I'll make the coffee and sandwiches, and you go and make a noise at the door."

Andy, his face shining with enthusiasm, his large, knuckly, boyish hands making patterns in the air, was talking about star nebulae. Phyl, curled up like a kitten and almost close enough to be touched, was rapt.

"We're going to the observatory at the weekend, Mum," said Phyl. "I've never been there before," she said in the voice of one on the brink of great adventure.

"It's not bad," said Andy, as though he owned the observatory. "But, really, Sydney needs a planetarium."

What a super kid, Rosemary thought, watching the pair of them scamper, chattering, up the stairs to the kitchen. But Gwen's probably right about the Pill.

.   .   .

Rosemary went to Lithgow on Sunday morning, came back on Monday morning, and didn't miss any trains. Instead she made some wonderful discoveries, which had been the best of luck, as she and Gertruida agreed at length over Viennese cakes in Gertruida's pretty cottage in Roy Street.

"I never go to Eskbank House anymore. Seldom. Seldom. But I wanted to have another look at that remarkable music machine. Nothing like that have I seen before coming here in Lithgow!" Gertruida said.

Rosemary had gone to Eskbank House, which was peacefully a museum again now that the film crew had gone. She wanted to examine the black iron rose and see if there was anything about Clarice in the collection. The rose was a long stemmed, thin-petalled creation of deathly exactness. It's craftsman must have been very proud of it, she'd thought, twirling it under the eye of the attendant, who, she could see, would have preferred her not to touch but didn't say so.

Rosemary imagined the ladies at the banquet for the first steel tapping, splendid in their bustled and trained, gem-coloured gowns of brocade or satin, trimmed with lace or feathers, cut low to reveal their soft white necks and shoulders and their husband's diamonds. They would have tripped along through the cooled slag in buttoned boots, their way lighted by lanterns held on long poles by grinning, dark-clothed mill workers especially assigned to the job.

The women, dutifully following their men to observe the history-making moment, would have covered themselves against the chill evening air with silk-fringed shawls. Some of them would have brought their cast-iron roses from the table—conversation pieces to be admired during the wait—and then perhaps regretted not leaving them beside their printed souvenir menu cards when their artificial but nevertheless sharp thorns entangled themselves in fringing or curls.

Was this Clarice's rose? Rosemary wondered. She half shut her eyes, hoping to conjure the image of the eighteen-year-old girl she was searching the past for, but the attendant's face, both concerned and bored, blotted out the possibility.

And Rosemary had seen a white plaster bust of William Sandford: a large-headed man whose nose was long and wide with an abrupt ending that hinted at a snout. He had a short neck and massive shoulders, which contributed to her impression of him as a powerful domestic animal. Did Clarice make this? she wondered, reaching out to check the bust for a signature. But the attendant found his voice and importantly told her not to touch.

Rosemary and Gertruida had been the only visitors at Eskbank House. Gertruida was a tiny lady with a pronouncedly bent back and high-heeled shoes which still placed her at not much more than the five-foot level. She looked as though her fragile bones had been pushed down steadily from above by a large, heavy hand. Her face was finely wrinkled, yet a pink-and-cream European complexion was still apparent even though she was probably in her sixties. Her fine beige-coloured hair was carefully set and sprayed in place and she wore lipstick, a mauve lace blouse, pearls, and a good suit. She could have been a wedding guest.

Gertruida was looking at a long, highly polished wooden music box with a multiplicity of carefully placed pins and hammers, decorative and mysterious as the insides of a clock, when Rosemary asked about Clarice Sandford. The attendant knew nothing about Clarice Sandford, he said proudly, though he was happy to run the music box through all eight of its delicately harmonised, harplike tunes. And after that, Gertruida invited Rosemary home.

"I have some of Clarice Sandford's paintings, yuh? Maybe these you would like to see?"

"Paintings? She was an artist? I thought she was a sculptor."

"Both. Both. I have some small cakes. We will have coffee, huh? I show you."

.   .   .

Three walls of Gertruida's house were full from floor to ceiling of solemn-looking academic books in dark bindings, many in French or German. There was a librarian's ladder nearby, covered in an Arabian saddlebag to make it look less utilitarian when not in use. Gertruida's husband had been a professor of philosophy and she, when she was much younger, had been a tutor.

"Here we came when my father-in-law was old, to look after him. Ten years he lived, and after—well, why should we move? For me Sydney was always too hot and here I have my books and some good friends."

During William Sandford's time, when Gertruida's father-in-law was very young, he had been a clerk at the Eskbank works. He was slightly older than Clarice, the boss's daughter, and like some of his more senior colleagues, he had bought a few of her paintings when she came home on visits from Julian Ashton's art school in Sydney. They bought them because they liked her and because it was probably good for staff politics.

Gertruida had three of Clarice's paintings: a portrait and two landscapes. They looked competent, Rosemary thought without much confidence. None were pictures she'd have chosen. But it was marvellous to have this new dimension on Clarice, the independent young lady with a developing career of her own, living in respectable digs in the Big Smoke all week.

"I had another picture," Gertruida said, as Rosemary helped her hang the three back on their hooks. "My husband bought it before the war— we were newly married then—at a small exhibition Clarice had somewhere . . . Mosman, I think. Very different from these—these are the work of a young student, of course. That other, I am told, is a better painting. "Well, my husband has died now and is not here to tell me what to do, and so I sold it. Many years ago. I sold quite a lot of things at the time and went overseas with the money and I do not regret it!"

While she talked, Gertruida rummaged through two shoe boxes and pulled out some photographs which Rosemary believed were of that distant trip and which she would endure as a small fee for enlightenment.

"Here are some of the things I sold. I thought perhaps the photo is here, too, of that picture . . . This desk. Nice, hey? Georgian. But for me, too light. It does not suit." All the small room's furniture was of the tall, dark, frowning variety with lots of scrollwork and multiple drawers from which Rosemary suspected some of the house's musty smell emanated. The old books were responsible, too.

"Beads, amber beads. Very fine, but I am too short for such things. And this samovar, but what do I want with a thing from Russia? Ah, here her portrait is."

Rosemary took it as casually as she'd accepted the others. And then she screamed, as one touched by the finger of fate.

Gertruida, white-faced, clutched her chest and sat on the edge of a table. "You give me such a fright!"

"I'm sorry. I'm sorry." Rosemary had stood up. "I'm sorry. But—I *own* this painting. It's mine! My sad-eyed lady! I just can't believe it's Clarice." She paused anxiously, testing herself for wakefulness. For madness. Hallucination? But it all seemed real—this tiny woman, fanning herself back to normal in a house that hadn't heard screaming for years, if ever. She felt chilled. She felt awed. Most of all, she felt excited in an extraordinary way, as though she'd witnessed an act of magic. She kept glancing at the photograph to see if it was true. It took a while before either of them was able to speak properly.

"Nobody would believe this!" Rosemary said.

"The *Reader's Digest*. Send it to them—they like that sort of story about coincidence." Gertruida's colour was normal again.

"I've never been able to read the signature. It looked like Lawford or Sawland. Sandford! How incredible!" Rosemary hestitated to use the word omen. Some people were funny about acknowledging the patterns of good and bad that form to make coincidence. "I'm actually quite dizzy," she said.

"Me, too. Shock," said Gertruida. "I get some water. You want, too? Or coffee? Or maybe some sherry?"

"Water will do fine, thank you."

"And you bought the picture?" Gertruida asked from the adjoining kitchen.

"Yes, at an antique shop at Lawson."

"Lawson, yes, that's right. The man did not want to take the painting, he preferred the furniture and bric-a-brac. But then he said why not. I forget what he gave me for it—maybe much less than it is worth."

"Clarice is not famous," Rosemary reassured. "She's not even known anymore."

Gertruida came back with two little cut-glass tumblers of cold water, each on a saucer with a paper lace doily. Rosemary took a glass and quickly drank the lot.

"You have shock because you have experienced synchronicity," Gertruida said, sipping hers more decorously. "And I," she added, "was shocked by your experience. You know about synchronicity? No? Read what Jung says. Very interesting. There are patterns like the sea tide in what happens in the world: the same, the same again—but always also a little different."

"Synchronicity? That's nice. I'd thought of it as magic!" said Rosemary. "If I'd spent a year hunting through books and old places I would never have met anyone who actually owned something of Clarice's!"

"I have also met her, when already she was old. Very elegant woman."

There was so much to tell that, of course, Rosemary stayed for dinner.

While she talked, Gertruida cooked chops, eggs, and cabbage. Although Rosemary did not want to miss a word, she also wanted to be a good guest, so she went out and bought the best bottle of red wine the town had to offer, plus some fist-sized white mushrooms which she sliced into a salad and dressed with yoghurt.

Clarice had been a confident girl, Gertruida told her, brought up in the exciting environment of her father's passion for his steel-making venture. She was talented at drawing and painting, which she did at home while helping to run the house and be her father's hostess. But her school education had been at an exclusive girls' school in Sydney, and eventually she must have persuaded him to let her go back to the city to live so that she could go to art school.

"I don't think it would have been usual for young women to leave home in those days, do you?" Rosemary asked. Gertruida didn't think so either.

"Mr. Sandford was having a lot of business worries at the time. I remember my father-in-law used to say always there was trouble with the steelworks: one day it was transport, one day it was raw materials or equipment. Only the workers gave no trouble."

There had been hope for William Sandford late in 1906, when he'd got a big contract from the New South Wales government. On the strength of that, he'd built a huge, modern blast-furnace. But then the contract was cancelled. "Terrible for everybody," Gertruida said. "Many men lost their jobs that day."

"If that was about the time when Clarice left home, it would have made it much worse for him," said Rosemary, whose dinner was getting cold while she wrote.

Gertruida hunched her thin shoulders and drank the second half of a glass of the wine she'd said she would only have a small taste of, and didn't protest as Rosemary topped it up again. Clearly this was fun for her, too. "You know Clarice won a scholarship to a very good art school in St. John's Wood, in London?" she asked. "This, I think, will have made her father worry even more. But she went—he let her go—and what an experience for a young Australian girl!" Gertruida waved her glass in ladylike bonhomie. "What I know was from letters and postcards Clarice wrote to the wife of the senior clerk who was her close friend here in Lithgow, and this news would go to all in the office. This is how my husband's father came to know. I remember he said that on the ship to London, at the captain's table, Clarice met Dame Nellie Melba who was of course not a Dame at that early time. And Melba took her under the wing and introduced her, in London, to the full society."

"Wonderful! They'll love a London scene!" said Rosemary.

"Then there was a scandal!" Gertruida said. "Ah, yes. Clarice fell in love. And with whom? A European count—a man in exile from his own country!"

Rosemary closed her eyes and breathed deeply.

"Perfect. Perfect!" she murmured, then tried to write as fast as Gertruida talked.

"I do not know the country of this count, or his name. Maybe Clarice did not say in her letter or maybe the senior clerk's wife was a little bit discreet. But not discreet enough! Soon Mr. Sandford has heard also this news and then he was very angry. Of course, it may be that Clarice herself told her father in a letter—I do not know. But Mr. Sandford was very angry. Very, very angry. He had a terrible bad temper! He went straight to England on the first ship and brought her back here."

"Oh, I can just see it, can't you? Sandford's company is in crisis, he doesn't know which way to turn. Then he hears about this love affair— his only daughter—so he rushes off to the salons of London. It is the centre, the peak of the Edwardian social scene. He finds her and brings her back to Lithgow. She'd have been—what? About twenty five then, not pretty, her father on the verge of bankruptcy. The Count would have been her last chance at love. Maybe her only chance. I wonder why she came back? What power he must have had!"

"It was different then—a man was the head of the house. Even now, in most families."

Rosemary hardly heard that. "Poor Clarice—to be brought back from that wonderful life—back from love, from elegance to a small, cold town. William Sandford had been a king here, and he lost his throne. The year 1907 would have been the very worst time for him to go away because it would give his enemies a chance. It was horrible of William to break up Clarice's love affair!"

"Horrible? Ah, it was tragic. Most tragic. When they arrived back here, father and daughter, there was a telegram to say the count had died in a shooting accident."

Rosemary was jerked into that long-ago grief. "Oh, poor Clarice. Oh, poor, poor Clarice!" she said, awed and moved. "Poor William! Both father and daughter utterly lost what they most loved. It must have maimed their lives!"

She was a little drunk with alcohol as well as with shock and sentiment, and it expanded her capacity for happiness so that she felt vast and light as a balloon.

This is what I want to do for the rest of my life, she vowed to her glass through the first really happy tears in a year. This kind of work, for this kind of thrill.

"Yes, poor Clarice," said Gertruida, who had caught some of Rosemary's excitement. "They say that the Sandfords had to leave their house after the bankruptcy. They say her paintings were all on the walls, big frames, you know? Heavy. She and Mr. Sandford left in such a hurry, so much with a broken heart and such shock, and she took a sharp knife and cut all her pictures out of their frames. She rolled them up and took them."

They were both silent, imagining the cool, proud-looking woman full of determined viciousness, slashing out the symbols of her early contentment to take them into a life that offered nothing.

"She looked after her father until he died," Gertruida said. "He got a lot of money from those who took over his business—enough to be quite comfortable, a little bit wealthy even. But nothing, no business for him, no marriage for her."

"They bought him."

Gertruida was puzzled by the expression but kept talking. "Clarice went on painting, of course—the portrait was done when she was already a mature woman. He had enough money, Mr. Sandford, so she did not have to earn her own living. But I think for the pleasure of her talent she went to people's houses and painted their portraits."

"Apart from that, nothing else except looking after her father," said Rosemary in mournful pity. "William Sandford died in 1932, aged ninety."

"Yes, and later she went blind. She died less than ten years ago, you know, in a nursing home in Sydney."

Rosemary tried to visualise the sad-eyed girl grown old and blind, sitting in a dressing-gown and slippers in a little sunny room. Where were the paintings now? There'd been no relatives as far as she knew.

"I still wonder why she didn't fight her father when he went to London to fetch her. She was of age, an educated, modern woman. There was a liberationist movement throughout the world—lots of women were explorers, artists, doctors, scientists, and politicians. Even here in Australia there were women in politics. . . ."

"So? There is women's lib here, too, now. But how liberated are most women? We women, when we are liberated, we are liberated from protection only."

It was not an argument Rosemary was prepared to enter into with this tiny, bright widow, who, after all, was foreign. So Gertruida had the last word: "Do you think Clarice did not know her father's business was in bad trouble? He was how old? Sixty? A weak heart maybe? And this count—who knows? Catholic perhaps? Maybe married? If he was a man of good reputation, would William Sandford risk his business and go all the way to Europe after his daughter?"

.   .   .

In the morning before leaving her motel room for the station, Rosemary phoned Bobby to sing "Happy Birthday." He didn't sound happy at all, and she wished she knew what to do about it. Daniel had done enough wrecking—he wasn't going to hurt his son any more if she could help it.

She spent most of the train journey thinking about William and Clarice, planning what she would say at the script conference to which she'd have to go, straight from the station.

What a relief to have discovered the joy of work, she thought; it is the only really socially acceptable drug. I'll just have to be careful not to get hooked, like William Sandford did. He suffered all the side-effects: emotional blindness, stress, and dangerous bad temper. What terrible withdrawal pains he must have endured when he was forced to go cold turkey!

Suddenly she had a brilliant idea for a development. Caroline, Sandford's wife, could have run the office. She could have done the accounting, balanced the books with care, stuck to budgets, and left William free to develop his sales network and his technical expertise and deal with premiers and prime ministers and state officials and his affair with Aimee in Sydney. This would have been during the time of prosperity. Then Caroline would die, in childbirth, and it would be after that that William Sandford would begin to depend on Clarice to run the house and be the hostess. And that would be when the company would start its decline into eventual liquidation.

Rosemary began to write it down, scribbling with eagerness, proud of her inventiveness, then suddenly she put the pencil down and chuckled wryly. It wasn't inventiveness at all.

.   .   .

When she told the writers at the script conference about the portrait—Gertruida had given her the photograph to produce in lieu of the real thing—they were not as bowled over as she'd expected. They liked the Clarice story but they accepted it simply as another ingredient for the magic they performed routinely every day. Right now, everyone's attention was focused on plans to celebrate the proclamation of Federation in 1901.

Rosemary felt justified in leaving early, having worked most of the weekend—certainly they would have called it work.

"Great stuff, by the way, Ro," Debby said, glancing up. "Keep it up! You can get into Edmund Barton, the first federal PM, next."

For a moment it felt like betrayal—the Sandfords belonged to her now. Then, of course, she realised, I'll go on from here. There'll be plenty more treasure in the library. But she wondered if she'd ever feel quite the same about any other people whose lives she researched.

Seventeen

Shirley Coote was still determinedly chilly on the phone. She acknowledged that Daniel was back in Sydney indignant—an indignation Shirley shared, by the way—that people would have thought he'd run out when all he was doing was trying to raise capital in Melbourne and Adelaide in order to save the company. Rosemary did not resist the impulse to suggest that it would have been sensible to let his lawyers and his creditors know his whereabouts; it would have saved a lot of unnecessarily destructive speculation. To this Shirley replied that most people were small-minded and some were bitches.

It was obvious that Daniel had not raised the money to save Patchwork—he or Jim Begg would have told her news like that.

"If you can get hold of him, please give him a message, Shirley. It's Bobby's birthday. He may have forgotten. Bobby has done nothing to hurt him—he's been fantastic. In fact, both kids have been! And it's really important that Daniel should see him—or at least phone him. Please. OK?"

Shirley said she would see what she could do.

In the late afternoon a courier arrived with a birthday card enclosing a twenty-dollar note.

> Eleven, hey! Chin up, boy-o. And good luck, love Dad.
> **XXX.** Buy yourself a treat

the card said in someone's spiky, slanty writing. Bobby held it in his hand for a long time, then put it on the coffee table and went and had a twenty-minute shower.

Despite Gwen's luscious chocolate cake adorned with eleven candles in the shape of naked ladies—she'd bought them in Kings Cross—and Phyl's gift of her Walkman that Bobby had coveted all year, and Rosemary's gift of an Italian racing saddle for his bike, bought with a Bankcard she'd fervently hoped had not yet been cancelled, he was not cheered.

One of Patrick's setters was pregnant and Bobby had been told he could have a puppy if Rosemary agreed. She'd agreed. "But it'll have to be on condition Patrick will let it go back to its mother if we have to move into a flat," she said. Then she wished she'd simply agreed.

Rosemary had been going to tell them all the Clarice story, but it would have got lost in the mood so she saved it for later. After the dismal birthday dinner, she sat beside Bobby's bed and murmured to him about the wonderful things that had happened in his life before and the wonderful things that would happen again and about how Daniel was fighting for survival at the moment and could not manage to do that and show love at the same time but that the love was always there, and that he'd taken Bobby and Phyl to dinner only a few weeks ago and would surely do so again soon. Bobby's long, pale eyelashes had fluttered and then succumbed, just as they used to when he was a baby fighting sleep.

.   .   .

A week and a half before Christmas Lucy came over for a celebratory and goodbye tête-à-tête drink. Rosemary was delighted—she hoped the visit would bridge the gap that had been developing between their over-full lives. It was public knowledge now that she would be the co-host of the new mid-morning program during the second half of January—there had been a flattering interview under a large, glamorous picture in the *Sun Herald* and an even bigger one, in colour, in *TV Week*. The other papers' TV pages had also already mentioned it or planned to do so soon. Lucy was becoming a celebrity.

"You're amazing! It's like watching a comet!" Rosemary said. "Next you'll be on the best-dressed list. You've no idea what a thrill it is to be a friend of the famous!"

"It's not such a big deal." Lucy laughed, and lighted a cigarette. "January's the silly season, when people switch on a canister of reruns in the morning and go out for the rest of the day. Nobody watches. Nothing to watch."

"All the more reason why everyone in Sydney—and quite a lot *don't* go away, you know—will flock to your bit. I certainly will!"

"Oh, please, yes. If more than three people watch me I might have a chance for something permanent—or as permanent as TV gets!"

She and Malcolm were leaving next day on a slow cruise down the coast which would culminate in Tasmania a few days before the Sydney-Hobart yacht race ended there in the first week of the new year.

"You're the one who really needs a holiday, Ro, not me, but I can't wait!" said Lucy, who, despite the evidence of many weekends spent preparing Malcolm's boat—a glorious tan and thighs like a Barbie doll—and despite her delight about her own career, had strain lines around her eyes. "Being happy ever after is pretty full-on. Though not, of course, in the same league as . . . as . . ." She waved her hand to encompass Rosemary, the oddly barren living-room and drama in general.

"Oh, me. I feel as though I've been put into a blender with a wide range of ingredients and turned on high," Rosemary said. "Your news is the one sane thing I can hang on to."

She topped up their glasses from the bottle of Chardonnay Lucy had brought over in an ice bucket. Such delicate burdens were possible now that Lucy was using the gates to visit and not the squashed fence near the black bean tree. Apart from the fact that she was usually dressed in non-athletic silk and expensive stockings, both she and Rosemary were on good terms with the Hermanns now, who no longer peeped through the curtains but waved and said, "And how are you this day?"

"A blender," said Lucy. "That's good, a good image. You can't undo what a blender has done. I've been thinking about you such a lot. I know you didn't consciously plan all this, but if, deep down inside, you'd wanted some change in your life, couldn't you have done it without sacrificing your security?"

"You think I did this deliberately?" Rosemary asked, yet she was less surprised by the idea than she might have been a few months earlier. Lucy watched her steadily as Rosemary sat, her chin up, her eyes half closed in thought, her free fingers patting the now-limp, grey-edged plaster cast on her other arm. "I suppose there's some truth there," Rosemary said quietly. "I'd got hooked into the habit of my marriage and I guess I'd never have had the strength—the courage—to break away without some outside influence. In a state of what I thought was security I was becoming too—what did I say before?—house-dumb. Too house-dumb for this complex world. But Angela supplied the opportunity, I suppose." She laughed. "She chucked me into the street."

"Well, not really . . ."

"No, I'm exaggerating. But it was what started everything. I guess that if I'd really wanted Daniel, I'd have fought for him instead of freezing him out."

"But Ro, you 'froze out' everything! Your husband, your house, your life-style . . ."

"Ah, but you see, of the three, only the house had any value," Rosemary said in a joking tone, trying to lighten the mood.

But Lucy was still intent. "It's hell about the house," she said. "I still don't believe there's nothing you can do."

"Nothing. If those bloody red roses hadn't arrived when they did, Daniel and I probably would have come to some sort of civilised arrangement like other people do when they get divorced. I'd probably have got the house, he'd have got the business. But he was—is—so mad at me. He's so sure that I was involved with Robert Talbot—that I caused Patchwork's liquidation—that he'd do nothing now to help."

"What about Robert Talbot? Didn't he say he'd do something?"

"That's the impression I got, but perhaps there isn't anything he can do. In fact, the less I have to do with him, the better. Are the media people still gossiping about me?"

"Oh, no. I mean, they probably still believe you and he are on, but you know what gossip's like—there've been two, three good stories since then."

"Good! I had had two phone calls—from people who were copy girls when Daniel was on the *Herald*. One's a features editor on a glossy now, and one's on the *Telegraph*. I literally haven't seen or spoken to either of them for years, but suddenly . . ."

They sipped in silent sympathy. "What did you say to them?"

"Nothing. I never spoke to either of them. Gwen kept answering and making excuses, and I think they've given up."

"God, you've had a time! Was it only three weeks ago that she was in here, nicking all the pictures? She's so wonderful!"

"Wonderful!" said Rosemary, rolling her eyes. "Yes, well, we're good friends now. Phyl's got her locket back. My paintings are safe, or so I believe—she's not saying where they're stashed, though I've asked her to bring Clarice back so I can show Gertruida next month when she comes to visit."

Rosemary had phoned Lucy at the TV station to tell her the story about Gertruida and the painting that had reached out from the past and Lucy had loved it. Lucy found it easier than Rosemary did to believe in magic, mystery, and coincidence. "Do you know what Malcolm said when he thought all your stuff was going to be auctioned?" she said. "That he'd bid for the sad-eyed lady and give it to you for your next birthday. Can you see why I feel the way I do about him?"

"Oh, Lucy, how lovely you are! Both of you!" Rosemary's eyes filled with sudden tears. "I'm so lucky to have you!"

"It works both ways. You're a good mate, Mrs. Q." Then, in case the mood became sentimental, Lucy added, "At least you can't say all your dramas haven't had their funny moments, Ro."

"Maybe they'll be funny to me later, when retrospect has had a chance, but I still expect one of those oily young men in a three-piece suit to arrive, smiling like a butler, with a warrant for my arrest! Gwen took the silver, the Royal Copenhagen china, all my Waterford, most of the linen . . . three station-wagon-loads of stuff, unaided, while the kids and I were out."

"Out with Patrick."

"With Patrick. Yes." Rosemary avoided Lucy's inquiring eye but volunteered that Phyl and Bobby adored going to his strange house.

"You're not sure about him, are you?"

"What's there to be sure about?" Rosemary demanded. "He's just a nice man who happened to be in the same theatre course and who's been kind to me because I broke my arm. Honestly, the way you all carry on—you, Gwen, the kids, Martha—you'd think . . . you'd think . . . "

"I'd think he was one of the ingredients in the blender," said Lucy.

To Rosemary it seemed like a good time to change the subject.

"What you've never told me—we've seen so little of each other in the past few weeks—is about you and Malcolm. The engagement. Your plans. I'm dying to know."

Lucy gazed steadily at her. "What don't you know?"

"Anything. Where you'll live. Whether I'll be bridesmaid . . . That's a joke, by the way."

"It's all a joke. I thought you knew. How long were you in PR?" Lucy lighted another cigarette and blew smoke to blur the image of Rosemary's shocked face. "You know he can't marry me—he's got a wife."

"Yes, but I thought . . ."

"He's Catholic. I mean, very Catholic. He wouldn't. He couldn't. I thought you knew that."

Rosemary's stare made Lucy uncomfortable enough for her to turn away, serious and defiant. I can't believe she'd do this, Rosemary thought. But she remembered Robert Talbot's pleased face when he took the newspapers from her at Lithgow and saw Lucy and Malcolm on the front pages.

"Talbot . . . ?" she started.

Lucy nodded quickly. "It was his idea. Phoned in the middle of the night! It was a boost for Malcolm's program in the pre-Christmas ratings time. And it worked, it really worked! Did you see the ratings? We were right up!"

"So it's all just a publicity stunt?"

"No, of course not." Lucy's seldom-used frown lines were brought to play. "It was just—fun. Mal and I were planning to live together, anyway. I mean, what's marriage anyway? We've both had that, you and I—the white dress and the contract."

"Mine wasn't white."

"Mine either, but you know what I mean."

"What will happen about you and Malcolm?" Rosemary asked after a pause.

"We'll just have the world's longest engagement. And I'll get auditioned for daytime shows. If I play my cards right, and if my luck holds, I'll be right up there . . . late-night news . . . current affairs . . . maybe, eventually, my own show!" Lucy's whole person had changed in the past year—there seemed to be more of her. Not in weight—her slight, elegant, dancerly body was slimmer now if anything—but in self-possession and glow.

"It's all been good for Malcolm, too. You can see it in the fan mail—gorgeous young things are writing again, making offers while there's still time! He'd begun to get only the mums. I mean, the mums still love him—we've had over two hundred offers to make the wedding cake. But there's a balance now, and he can see the value in that. Poor Mal, he loathes Talbot! He calls him 'the tinpot people-mover.' " She puffed smoke again. "I'm just surprised that you didn't work it all out."

"Don't be surprised. I've been too self-absorbed to notice anything outside my immediate orbit."

"You don't approve, do you?" Lucy didn't want the answer. "It's worth it to me. I love him, and it's the way to get where I want to be."

Who am I to judge? Rosemary thought. I'd never have got my job if it weren't for the fact that I had the hots for Robert Talbot!

"Look," said Lucy, "You're the only one who knows, apart from me—and the lawyer who sees to the money, of course. It is the most deathly, deathly secret. Don't ever forget!"

"Luce, you know you don't have to say that."

They looked at each other, and Rosemary wondered if Lucy was also thinking that it was only a year ago that theirs had been a shared orbit—the closeness of lonely women.

"Must go," said Lucy. "I've left my house key with Eve in case of *real* burglars, but get it any time if you want a retreat or a cup of sugar or anything. I would have lent you my car, but it's become part of a highly complex deal which will result in my Christmas present from Malcolm. Did I tell you? He's paying the difference between what it's worth as a trade-in, and a new car."

"How lovely! What?"

"I don't know. He says there has to be *some* surprise. All I've speci-
fied—well, suggested—is that I like bright red. And a sun-roof. And
ivory leather seats. In something that will go like a rocket!" Lucy looked
very happy. The price is right, Rosemary thought, amused but a little
detached.

"Bye, Ro. Have a wonderful Christmas. And I hardly need to say I
hope next year is happier than this one! I must go—I've promised Mattie
I'd be with just her, for the whole night. A quantity- and quality-time
mother for a change. Usually it's only quality time," she added, as though
Rosemary had asked. "Mattie is actually looking forward to Christmas
now, thanks to you. I just wish she could have come, too, but nearly
two weeks on a small yacht. . . ."

Rosemary didn't answer. Her friendship with Lucy was based on lots
of shared things but not on their attitudes to their children. To Rosemary
it still felt as though an invisible umbilical cord attached her to Phyl and
Bobby: she would be unable to run unless they ran, too, at the same
speed and in the same direction. What she believed was that as they
grew older the cord would stretch to give everyone enough freedom
for different directions while still maintaining connection. But, though
it was obvious that Lucy loved Mattie, it was a detachable love in Rosemary's opinion.

Two days before, Lucy had made an Early Christmas for Mattie,
complete with a stocking full of pretty things which included a real pearl
necklace—something Rosemary thought rather too old for a nine-year-
old. As well as Rosemary, Gwen, Phyl, and Bobby, Eve, Tom, and Ben
had been invited. It had not started off as a good night for Rosemary.
She and Phyl were speaking only as much as necessary, to not draw
attention to the fact that they were furious with each other.

On the previous Thursday, the second last day of school for the year,
Phyl had told the headmistress that she would not be coming back. She
had mentioned Daniel's bankruptcy and said her mother approved of
the decision. Then she'd gone out with Andy without warning Rosemary,
who was unprepared for the phone call she'd got that night from the
headmistress. Though sympathetically wrapped, there was accusation in
the content of what she said, and whichever way she handled it, Rosemary felt sure she'd sounded like an uncaring parent.

She and Phyl had had a terrible fight in which "But you said . . ."
"Yes, but you knew I meant . . ." figured a whole lot. Both were still
hurt and aggrieved.

Everyone got a present at Lucy's early Christmas and Rosemary was
bedazzled by her generosity; after years on a researcher's fairly modest

salary, she now felt rich. She gave Phyl a wafer-thin portable typewriter and Bobby a little computer complete with a set of games. *Just what I would have given them if I had been able to afford to,* Rosemary thought, swallowing with difficulty.

Lucy gave Rosemary a beautifully cut, sexy night-gown and negligee set, in cream with pale-peach-coloured silk lace straight, as the accompanying note explained, from a daytime movie. "This removable prop is guaranteed to supply at least a year of blissful romance," it added.

Mattie was showered with goods, present after present, which she lined up around herself and tried to enjoy all at once. But all of them were discarded in a brush of joy when Malcolm arrived late and presented her with a large, framed, coloured photograph of a pale young horse, galloping with flying mane across a pretty field.

"Strawberry?" she asked, clutching the picture.

"Yes. And she's yours."

"You mean I get the horse as well as the picture?" Mattie asked, virtually swooning with surprise. Her pleasure was perfectly real—she went into a dancing frenzy, yelping, "Oh, oh, oh, Strawberry," while everyone watched and laughed. But while Rosemary joined in enjoying Mattie's pleasure, she felt some pity, too. *She's been bought,* she told herself. *You're jealous,* she told herself.

Rosemary's children were not expecting anymore surprises this Christmas. In fact the prospect made her think of *Little Women* again, when the odious Marmee gave each of her four daughters a copy of *The Pilgrim's Progress*—with different coloured binding. For someone on a budget, that had always seemed so silly to Rosemary—at least Marmee could have got them each a different book so they could share them.

One nice thing was planned for Christmas. Lawrie had amazed Rosemary by inviting the three of them to spend a few days over Christmas with him at the house at MacMasters Beach. It was where they'd sometimes gone before as a family. But Lawrie was, after all, Daniel's relative, not hers.

"When do you bring Strawberry?" Mattie asked Malcolm as soon as she'd calmed down enough to talk.

"We can't have her here, darling," said Lucy. "She'd hate it—all the cars and nowhere to run! She'll stay on the farm, of course." Mattie's face fell.

"But she'll be yours," said Malcolm. "In your name. Every time we go there you can ride her until you're both exhausted. Meantime, Ted will look after her, with the other horses."

"Can we go tomorrow?"

"No, dear. Not tomorrow. But in January, soon after we get back. We'll go there for a whole week."

"But that's such a long time. Long after Christmas!"

Rosemary was surprised to hear her own voice, which seemed to start speaking without reference to her mind. "I've got a good idea. Why don't you come and have Christmas with us at MacMasters, Mattie? It's probably less than an hour to the farm from there and we could all go and see Strawberry. You could show Phyl and Bobby and me around the farm. . . ."

There was a stunned silence which Eve broke first, rather huffily. "We've already made plans for the days before Christmas, Rosemary. Ben and Mattie are going to . . ."

But Malcolm interrupted. "It's a great idea! Great! Why didn't I think of it? You all go there and spend a day or two. Or stay as long as you like! When's Christmas? A Sunday? Perfect! Ted and his wife will look after you . . . No, go on, I insist!" And in the midst of a babble of voices—Rosemary's, trying to retreat from rashness; Eve's, politely demurring in case what she'd said could possibly have been construed as a hint; Tom's, being "really pleased, old chap, always wanted to have a look at your famed country seat, old chap, make a nice outing"—Malcolm got up and phoned his farm manager.

There would be some surprises after all.

.   .   .

"What I thought was that you and Bobby and Phyl might like to spend Boxing Day with us." Patrick said. "Let me rephrase that. I already know they would like to. What about you?"

Rosemary rested her chin on her hand and looked at him sitting crossed-kneed and steeple-fingered in one of the armchairs opposite and a few feet away.

"Tell me the truth. Why do you like me?"

It was his turn to stare. Then he stood up from where he was and sat down where she was in one smooth, arched movement that could not have been interrupted. "You can't expect me to answer a question like that from the other side of the room," he said and took her hand, freed only that day from the plaster.

She tried to pull it away. "It's ugly!" she said. "Ugh!"

"Ugly? It's healed beautifully." He stroked her forearm between his thumb and fingers with the sort of professional air that made her stop struggling.

"It's so thin, my poor arm, and grey—the skin looks filthy, though I scrubbed with a loofah. And my hand—hanging like a big brown crab at the end of a stick!"

"Why do I like you, huh? Sometimes I wonder why you *don't* like yourself."

"Don't I?" Rosemary withdrew her hand in shock, but he quickly reclaimed it. "I think I do." Is that it? she thought. Is that why I make such a mess of my life? I don't like myself?

"Don't look so worried!" Patrick said. "Hey!" But she'd got up, too disturbed, for lots of reasons, to stay sitting in such warm proximity to him.

"I'm going to make a cup of tea. Want some?"

"No, thanks. But, to answer your question, one of the reasons I like you is that you're surprising. I'm never sure where you'll jump next."

"Neither am I," she said, and laughed. "Usually flat on my face. Do you want some toast? I'm starved! I keep missing meals in this job."

"No toast, thanks. Phyl and Bob cooked dinner for Geoff and me. Great cooks, your kids! We had an excellent mushroom omelette and Bobby's avocado salad. Even Geoff liked it, and he's never touched avocado before." He'd followed her into the kitchen and now leaned against the door, his arms folded.

"I haven't even thanked you for having them," said Rosemary. It was the Wednesday before Christmas, a week into the school holidays, and she'd been at work for most of it.

"You don't have to thank me. It's good for Geoff. Good for Andy, too—I think being the local saint was beginning to pall and that he regards meeting your lovely daughter as his just reward!"

"He's nice."

"The best," he said, proud as a coach. "He and I gave Phyl rather a hard time today. She hasn't had a chance to tell you yet." Rosemary whipped around to watch him talk, which he continued to do serenely. "About leaving school. She said you didn't mind if she dropped out." She opened her mouth to explain about her policy of non-confrontation, then closed it again as he kept on talking. "She said she wanted to be a nurse-aide. Andy was pretty scathing—he said it was 'a callous waste of intellectual resources.' I was expecting him to add, 'And a crime against society!' " Patrick's smile mostly involved the muscles around his eyes. "Andy and I did the tough cop, nice cop routine. I was the bad cop. Half the hospitals would go on strike if they'd heard me. I said, among other things, that as a nursing assistant she would simply be a uniformed slave. You know—no future, awful pay."

Inside, Rosemary was a cocktail of feelings, shaken and stirred. She walked towards him, aware that her face was hot, and the cocktail fizzed over in what looked and sounded like anger: "Now can you see why I'm scared of you? Now can you see?" she demanded.

But it was obvious that he could not. If anything, at that moment the fear was mutual. But then, very casually, as though this was something they did often, he gathered her into his arms. "Don't be so silly!" he said. But his voice was far from parental. She felt his body tremble. He wanted to kiss her but she pulled away, working hard at cooling down. Let's be friends, she hoped her body was saying as she poured the tea, buttered the toast, sliced the cheese. Friends. Friends.

Patrick cleared his throat. "Shall I take that?" He reached for the plate and the cup.

"No. You switch off the light, thanks."

Very polite. Like friends. And this time she sat on an armchair, not the inviting sofa, and felt safe, eating her toast and cheese and sipping her hot, milky tea until the feelings stopped stirring and she could think again. She just made sure not to look at his probing, clever face.

"I'd felt really helpless about Phyl. I dealt with it the way my mother should have dealt with me—which was to call my bluff—but it didn't work with her. Phyl left school, on the last day."

"Yes, that was pretty smart; she did the exams first, so she's made it easy enough to re-enlist or whatever it's called. Plenty of kids do it."

"So you think she might decide to go back?"

"Yup," he said. "Pretty sure. Give her time to get a bit bored and doubtful. It'll help that it's a new school—she won't have to make an apologetic comeback."

"Yes, I think you're right. But, oh, God, all that business lies ahead—where to live, new schools. At least I've got a job."

"Did Phyl tell you she's teaching Geoff rhythm? To drum with his hands on bongos? He's getting a real kick out of that."

"That's lovely!"

"Yep. Your kids are a lot of fun."

That's it! she thought. The kids. An extended family. That's what he likes me for! Probably, if his wife hadn't died, they'd have had five by now. But this was not the sort of topic she felt safe discussing with Patrick, whose physical presence continued to disturb her. Primly, her ankles crossed, she told him about Clarice and the picture and Gertruida and the music box at Eskbank House, and it was obvious that he enjoyed that.

"I think you'd actually like to write the script yourself—you're so keen on the story," he said.

"Me? Oh, I can't write! But you're partly right—I'd love to produce it! I have such clear ideas about what the scenes should look like, where the people should stand, the colours, the shapes, the sounds . . ."

"Is that why you joined Melissa's drama class? To produce?"

"No, no, I thought I'd like acting. And I do, of course, on an amateur level. But then Melissa got me into stage-managing, which I knew nothing about before, and I loved it! I loved being on the film set, and I love the planning—the whole business—at the script conferences. I'd love to . . . to work in the industry, and learn more and more about it. . . ." She trailed off, embarrassed by her own enthusiasm. She was much more accustomed, in conversations with men, to listen rather than talk, so, even though he didn't look in the least bored, she changed the subject. "Why did you join Melissa's school? I know you said once that Martha pushed you into it, but . . ."

"That really was the reason, the one and only reason—good old Auntie Martha's patent remedy for curing unsociability. It's working, I think," he said seriously enough to be teasing, so she talked quickly, in case he was.

"But you're so good at acting, you really are. You should do more,"

"Well, thanks, you're very kind, but I don't know about doing any more. I mean, after I had been psyched out of my terror, that Big Daddy role was fairly easy, in that it felt fairly close to my own experience of thundering away at engineering undergraduates. I really don't know how well I'd do at anything more subtle—or with longer lines!

"You lecture?"

"Yes," he said, looking so surprised that it was clear he must have talked about this before in her presence. I'm so bloody rude! she thought. I've spent the whole of this last year inside my own head!

"I'm a visiting lecturer in the water engineering department, seconded by my own department. Actually, I don't do very much anymore— they've changed the curriculum—but there are still odd days when I have to front up and pretend to be a wise man."

"You do that as well as your full-time job?"

He told her about his main work, which involved Sydney's water supply, and Rosemary was surprised to find that it was interesting— previously her total knowledge about water was that it came out of taps.

He said he'd like to take them all to the Warragamba Dam catchment area one day and show them what he believed were the most wonderful views in New South Wales, areas not open to the general public. He liked his work, but, he said, he'd have preferred to work in places where water was scarce, like Central Australia or Fiji. Geoff had kept him confined to Sydney.

"But things are easier for us now—not only is Geoff coping better, but my work is less demanding. I'm in a good position to delegate somewhat, though this is a pretty recent development; there never used to be any spare time. So now I'm starting to branch out a bit in a few directions."

"Which directions?"

"I want to start travelling a lot, short trips at first and then more adventurous ones, round the coast, into the centre. . . . I've tried Geoff in the mini-bus and he really likes it. So I've decided to buy it, and get some camping equipment. And I've been trying my hand at writing a play."

"A play? You write?" How could I ever have thought you were dull? Rosemary wondered.

"I'm trying to, though it's not easy. You keep coming across little obstacles in the story that wouldn't exist if it was real life."

"What do you mean?"

"Well, for instance, there is the business of coincidence. It happens often in life, but in fiction it seems unrealistic."

"Yes, I wonder why? What's the play about?" Rosemary was intrigued.

"A group of city kids who set out to live in the bush and a group of tribal Aboriginal kids who set out to live in the city. They all get caught in a bushfire half-way and end up in a cave together. It's partly about survival and misunderstanding, and there's a lot about how one culture can erase or dilute another, but it's also about how people can learn things in unexpected ways. It's pretty rugged, some of it. I need to lighten it a bit."

"You mean make it funny?" Rosemary asked, thinking of Robert Talbot's desire to have elements of "M*A*S*H" in "The Mount Victorians."

"Not funny. Just lighter. More colourful." He grinned. "Colour is my problem, as you know."

"That comes from writing a black-and-white play," she said promptly. "Can I read it?"

"If you like. It needs some more work first, but I'd like your opinion."

They smiled at each other. Rosemary was surprised to find she was enjoying this. How lonely he must have been, she thought, watching his graceful movements as he lifted his tea mug, found it empty, and put it down again.

"More tea?" she asked. He nodded and smiled, and she rose to take his mug. "How did you manage all alone with Geoff when he was little?"

"Ah, Geoff. He used to be very sickly—lots of chest infections. There was one terrible year . . ." He shuddered. "But since puberty he's been much better. He doesn't have tantrums so much anymore. And being able to use the toilet—you can't imagine what that means. To be able to take him out in public . . . but it's still not easy. I've never tried a restaurant, for instance."

She told him about the dream she and the children had had, soon after Daniel left, of travelling around Australia in a caravan and of the terrible fight she'd had with Bobby. This whole conversation happened from opposite sides of the coffee table, and they both laughed quite a lot. We're friends, she thought. Isn't that nice? Isn't that a relief?

"You haven't answered about Boxing Day," he said as he was leaving.

"We'll be catching a train back from Gosford. I don't know the times yet."

"We can fetch you in Gosford and picnic on the way back if you like, somewhere on the Hawkesbury River."

It seemed silly to argue.

.   .   .

The next day, the Thursday before Christmas, had been her last at work until the third of January. It had been busy, rushed, and interesting, and Rosemary had reluctantly pulled herself away from the impromptu party Kim had started at about four—by sending out for champagne—because the Mitchell Library had phoned to say the photographs she'd ordered of original letters and documents from the Sandford boxes were ready.

"That can wait!" Kim said. "Champagne's much more important."

"No, no, I'd rather get them. We're going away and I'll read them on holiday. Besides, the kids are expecting me." She was surprised and pleased by the fact that the others also urged her to stay—despite Robert Talbot they obviously liked her.

The holiday traffic had involved a slow detour through the city, which had sent the cab-charge bill into double figures. But she'd asked the driver to keep his meter ticking as she dashed into the Mitchell Library; there would be little chance of another cab in a city full of hurrying shoppers aware that, after tonight, there was only one and a half days to go. Rosemary had not even done her little bit of Christmas shopping yet—the hurly-burly would have to be faced tomorrow.

To her the carbon monoxide fumes and the bumper-to-bumper grind were worth it for the crisp, white photographs which half filled a shoe box. There'd be plenty to read when conversation palled over the Christmas weekend.

At the house that no longer felt like home, Rosemary lay in a hot bath trying to relax enough to sleep because the next day would be terrible: shopping with a mean, tight budget through the panicky crowd. It would probably be a steaming day. There would probably be long queues for taxis. Then there was the wrapping and packing because they'd leave early on Saturday for Malcolm's farm. She wished she'd kept her mouth shut—she'd been wishing it heartily ever since. A day and a half of Tom and Eve, unrelieved, and in a strange place—she must have been mad!

She'd been paid that day for the first time, there having indeed been some hold-up at head office, and then she'd had to query the amount on the cheque because it was nearly three times what she'd been expecting.

"No, that's right," the wage clerk had said on the phone after going away and murmuring to someone else. "That's right, according to the memo we received." There was a note of astonishment in the clerk's voice—she'd obviously never had a query like that before.

"Made out to you, is it?" Gwen had said when Rosemary phoned to tell her of this bonanza. "I'd have thought the least you could have done was give yourself a different name. Oh, well, endorse it over and I'll cash it. No need to get your bank manager any more excited than he is already."

"It's a hell of a lot of pay for three weeks!"

"Least he could do," she said. "Bastard!"

.   .   .

Gwen had made her own plans for Christmas. Her friend Nola was out of hospital now and they'd drive together to Mollymook to Gwen's little shack for a week of fishing, scrabble, and detective stories. Lawrie had said 'Bring her along!' when Rosemary told him Gwen was staying.

"No *thank* you!" Gwen had said. "That imitation Aussie! Ruined at a young age by over-exposure to Errol Flynn movies. Randy old coot— he nearly had me once, in the little laundry off your mother's kitchen."

Not having Gwen along meant they could all go in Tom's car. Eve had lost weight, but there was still plenty of her, and Tom, who drove, was a hefty man, so there was only enough room for three on the front seat if one of them was Phyl or Rosemary and the other Ben or Mattie.

Eve denied resenting the fact that she had to sit in the back, in the middle of the ongoing fight between Bobby, Ben, and Mattie. Any two of them usually got on well together, but they were like Iraq, Iran, and Syria for the trip.

Phyl sat in the front enduring Ben in the middle, who kept swivelling onto his knees to lean over the back of his seat to keep up his end of the fight, in the process knocking Phyl and endangering the pavlova she'd made—"high-class poison" she called this first-ever effort, which she was carefully nursing in a plastic cage arrangement on her lap. She had justified the life-endangering white sugar and cream on the basis that if one became too much a slave to the stomach, one was submitting to tyranny. Andy had told her that.

"Please sit still, Benny," she pleaded. He ignored her, but Eve said "Phyl, if you don't like it in the front, why did you insist on sitting there?"

"Bobby, if you say one more word to Mattie, I'll clip you, so help me!" said Rosemary.

"You mean it's OK for her to kick me? I've just got to sit here and take it? She's a bitch!"

"Bobby!"

"I won't let you ride Strawberry for being horrible to me," Mattie wailed.

"Erh, big deal. You already said that before. You can't take something away twice. Anyway, who wants to ride your stupid horse?"

"He's not stupid! I'll tell my mummy!" Mattie yelled, then wailed again at the yawning emptiness of this threat. "I want my mummy!"

Rosemary, as her de facto mother for the duration, felt obliged to try and cheer her up. A story didn't work because Bobby didn't want to hear *Snow White and the Seven Dwarfs,* but he had to. And Ben did want to hear but couldn't without turning around and crushing Phyl.

A song didn't help much either because they'd only got through Old MacDonald's seventh animal when Eve announced she had a migraine. So the fighting resumed until, on the Gosford turnoff, Tom suddenly yelled "Jesus Christ!" and slammed on the brakes, at which the pavlova sailed off Phyl's lap and smashed into the dashboard. White snowflake meringue, passion-fruit, strawberries, and whipped cream erupted onto the grey carpet. Tom had veered off the road into a rest area in order to lay down the law to the children, but instead demanded of Phyl, "What the hell did you bring that stupid thing for?" Rosemary bristled, prepared for defence, for which there was no need.

Phyl turned around to her usual baby-sitting charges and said in a voice they obviously knew well,

"See what you've done? And I'm not going to make another one unless the three of you clean this all up perfectly!" Then she stepped out of the car and walked briskly away into the bushes. Rosemary followed, and so did Eve's voice, saying, "Cheek! What a cheek!"

Phyl was leaning against the other side of a tall tree, her shoulders shaking, when Rosemary reached her. But it was laughter, not tears, and the two of them stood there giggling soundlessly until tears actually did begin to run. Every time they set off back to the car it would start up again and they'd have to clap their hands over their mouths and duck out of sight. Bobby found them there, his eyes sparkling, too.

"I knew Phyl would break up!" he said. "I nearly did, too!"

There was a new order for the rest of the journey: Eve in the driving seat, Mattie beside her, and then Rosemary. Tom was delegated to control the boys, which he did by playing cards with them while Phyl pretended to doze, though she couldn't stop the smile from twitching at her lips.

"There you are," Tom said in his capacity as navigator. "Strickland State Forest. Should be the next turn-off to the right, then we reach the village. Do you think we might buy some more egg white and stuff, girlie?" he asked, tickling Phyl's chin. He hadn't been fooled by her sleep act. She nodded without opening her eyes, accepting his apology.

The farm was much lovelier than Rosemary had imagined, and her dread and tension melted in the welcome from Ted McLeod, the manager, and Meg, his wife. In seconds the younger children, accompanied by the McLeod's son, Mark, had charged off to the stables. Ted followed, yelling a series of comments, each of which started with "Don't." Phyl watched them go.

"I've brought the stuff to make a pavlova. Can I use the kitchen please?" she asked Meg, a woman whose large, pink face was wreathed by wild, oiled grey curls. From a distance her greyness and a certain care in her rolling walk made her look like a grandmother, but close up it was obvious that she was not yet forty.

"Sure you can, love, if you feel you need another one—I made one, but. As well, as a sherry trifle and a coupla cakes."

"In that case . . ." Phyl said gladly, handed over the groceries, and headed quickly to where the riding was.

"A cup of tea? Coffee? What about a drink?" said Meg.

"I'd rather explore. It's such a lovely day," said Rosemary. "Is that a river over there?"

"Creek. They said rain but it cleared up nicely, didn't it? Prob'ly rain for Christmas, but. There's a nice little rocky climb other side of the creek if you've brought old shoes."

Tom elected to explore, too, and Eve to have a cup of tea and a rest in the huge, zebra-skin-covered bed which was obviously Malcolm's when he was at home. Eve did not look well.

The long, low bungalow was smaller, inside, than it looked, with only two real bedrooms. But there were seven divans along a wide back porch open to the stars except for floor-to-ceiling fly-screen netting. Rosemary supposed there were clip-on windows and shutters for winter or heavy rain.

"Plenty of hammocks, too," Meg said. "Hang them from side to side on these hooks. Low for kids, high for show-offs."

Rosemary would have preferred to walk on her own, but Tom seemed determined to come, too, despite her suggestion that Eve might need company. "Like a hole in the head," he said cheerfully. "Peace and quiet, that's what she craves. Peace and quiet."

Light green grass dotted with yellow daisies extended in every direction, interrupted here and there by single trees and, on the creek side, by a thick cluster of lush shrubs from which huge willows bowed.

A similar thick cluster in the opposite direction partly concealed a red-brick cottage—clearly Ted and Meg's—and to the right were the stables and a barn, and stalls for other animals. The horizon was defined by soft purple hills in one direction and by the black-green line of a pine forest in another.

What was best about the place was the smell—fresh, cool, and with a hint of peaches—and the quiet. Rosemary relished it, standing on the rocky heap, her feet still wet from the clear, shallow creek. Tom had not climbed, using his city shoes as the excuse, but he'd started panting as soon as the ground began to slope. Now he was sitting on a rock near the bottom, talking to her. She couldn't hear—the fruit-flavoured breeze blew his words away.

She visualised Malcolm and Lucy standing here watching the sun go down, then wading back—perhaps in winter he carried her—to a log fire and a tête-à-tête dinner they hadn't had to cook. How romance could flourish here!

". . . admired the way you cope . . . absolutely terrific . . ." she thought she heard Tom say.

"Pardon?" Rosemary had climbed down to within earshot and Tom gave her a bewildered look. "You didn't hear what I said?"

"It's windy up there."

He looked tired and crumpled, a determinedly city man on an uncomfortable perch, but when she was near enough he shocked her by firmly grasping her hand. "What I said was, you've got very nice legs."

"Oh, Tom," she said, jerking her hand away. She knew she sounded like a school teacher. She had to stop herself from saying "Not you, too!" Why was it that men she'd hardly even noticed except, perhaps, to sneer at, were the only ones who found her attractive? Exasperated, verging on anger—after all, what did he think could be achieved by making a pass at her here, minutes away from where both their families waited, even supposing she had ever given him any indication that she was interested—she started stomping off towards the house.

"No, wait, Rosie. I didn't mean to . . . to . . ." he said and hurried, panting, after her, but she ignored him and hurried on. She fervently wished she had never agreed to this ridiculous excursion. It's a pain being broke, she thought, her eyes stinging with tears. Other people go away on yachts, or to nice resorts, and we have to accept charity, in the company of dull and foolish people!

When she got to the house the kids had taken over the living room, turned the TV on full blast, and were consuming a pre-dinner warm-up of pizzas, chocolates, chips, and Coke. There was no sanctuary.

Rosemary would have loved an early night in the fresh, airy room, alone with her Sandford papers, but it would have been obviously rude. Instead she joined in and played cards until Ben grizzled and was put to bed in a hammock. Mattie looked tireder and tireder but would not go to bed until Rosemary insisted.

"I want to sleep in the small bedroom where I always sleep," she said. "Not outside, where the monsters are."

Bobby was insulted until reassured that she meant real monsters—leopards, Dracula, coral snakes, and so forth—who could have easy access to the porch. Not him.

"What about a blow-up bed in the same room as me?" said Rosemary.

"You have the blow-up bed. I'll have the real one."

The tyranny of the abandoned child, she thought. Ho hum! And was about to settle for the blow-up bed when Bobby said, "Tell you what. You sleep in a low hammock and I'll sleep in one just above you, with one eye open and this lethal weapon"—he took a butter knife off the tea trolley—"and if you hear anything or see anything you think I might not have noticed, just stick your finger straight up in the air and it will poke me in the back."

Mattie thought she'd try out this back-poking first, which she did with enough giggles to wake Ben, and it sooned turned into a romp. But ultimately all of them, even Phyl, settled down to sleep. At last Rosemary was able to lie in bed, enjoying the sensation of having her arm free. One more day and I'll be free, she told herself, and fell asleep with her hands clasped behind her head.

Eighteen

Spilt sugar and crumpled cornflake packets were evidence that the children had already had breakfast, though it was only seven-thirty. Strawberry was clearly having a good work-out. Rosemary, buttering a slice of whole grain toast, was just wondering where Tom and Eve were when Tom came in.

"Listen, Rosemary, I . . ." he whispered, but she cut him off loudly, cheerfully—"Hello, Tom. Sleep well? Want some of this? It's a lovely day, isn't it?"

"I . . ." he said, then noticed Phyl at the table in the next room, seriously typing something on her new machine.

"Here, it's still hot," Rosemary said, handing him one of her toast slices with what she sincerely hoped was a no-nonsense smile. So he gave up trying to say whatever it was and went off, toast in hand, murmuring about sunburn and saddle sores, in search of the younger children.

"What's that you're writing?" Rosemary asked Phyl, who was gazing at her in an embarrassingly enquiring way.

"Just . . . notes. Sort of a journal. Are you cross with Tom about something?"

"Keep your voice down, honey! Of course I'm not!" Rosemary said, hurrying to Phyl's side as an aid to privacy.

"Because if it's about him shouting at me yesterday, I don't mind."

"You're a good kid," Rosemary said, relieved.

"But on the other hand," Phyl said very solemnly, "if it's for any other reason . . ." and Rosemary realised she was teasing her. I'm not at all subtle, Rosemary thought. I overdid that cheerful early morning toast business. And I do take myself awfully seriously!

"Phyl, just you wash your mouth out," she said, and laughed and kissed her daughter on the top of her reddish curls. Phyl had put Tom's silly behaviour into a simple, ordinary perspective, and Rosemary felt greatly comforted.

Tom had found the children, who didn't have sunburn or saddle sores but a new enthusiasm: Mark had taught them to play poker for real money and so far Mattie had won four dollars.

"You know what?" Mattie said at lunch, "Something's just occurred to me. We haven't got a Christmas tree!"

"You're absolutely right!" boomed Tom in his holiday voice. So he took her and Ben out on a hunt for the perfect tree, which, Mattie said, she was going to pay for with her winnings.

"I'm doing turkey, baked potatoes, chrissy pudding, all that," said Meg. "And I'm sure we've got some spare tinsel. Mark, be a gem and get into that old hat box of Gran's; it's in there, I think, if the moths haven't been at it, behind the hot water."

Her thirteen-year-old son, who, like his father, looked more like the wire frame for a clay model than a gem, catapulted his sinuous self into the gap behind the water heater.

"You shouldn't be waiting on us like that at Christmas! I feel very bad. . . ." Rosemary said to Meg.

"Nonsense! Living here is like being on holiday all year round. It's a treat to have people!" Meg said. She'd already persuaded Tom and Eve to stay for Christmas day as well—"I'll leave something cold," she said.

Rosemary phoned Lawrie to tell him not to expect them until late on Christmas morning and not to cook much.

"Standing me up, huh? Well, I hadn't beaten up the breakfast omelette yet so I guess there's nothing lost. But drive carefully now—there're lots of idiots on the road."

Rosemary wrapped her presents, not one of which had cost more than twenty dollars, and most of which had cost much less. The small children's things came from a trick and magic shop—it would be a Christmas eve of rude noises under cushions, rubber spiders on necks, and reappearing ink-blots. She'd bought Tom and Eve a bottle of wine and for Lawrie there was a Mozart tape—a ten-dollar bargain with the clarinet concerto in A on one side and the flute and harp on the other.

For Phyl there was a crisp new ream of typing paper, a ring binder, and a paper punch and for Bobby a treasure he'd yearned for and was now old enough for—her father's Military Medal: "Lieut. Douglas Cooper" it said. "For Bravery in the Field." Plus a little bag of gold coins made of chocolate.

Tom, Ben, and Mattie came back with a very nice tree plus a selection of plastic Santas, glitter-covered pine-cones, and glass balls—all the newsagent had left. There was also a set of gnome, elf, and reindeer lights that didn't work.

"Let me try," Bobby said after Tom had sworn a few times, and in a quiet corner, with pliers and tape, he cut and rejoined and tested and tested until all the duds were gone and the rest worked.

"Flashing or plain?" he asked casually.

"Flashing! said the Tom, Ben, and Mattie.

"Plain!" said Rosemary, Phyl, and Eve.

"It's got to be one or the other."

"You have to decide then. You've got the casting vote," said Eve. And Bobby gallantly settled for plain—a constant, colourful glow instead of the on-again-off-again, headache-triggering flashing.

They all had a surprisingly nice time.

. . .

"Ben's mum says if it's all right with you I can stay here with them and Strawberry and go back in their car tomorrow," Mattie said on Christmas morning, giving Rosemary a lift to the spirits that might just as well have been gift-wrapped.

"Sure you want to? Rather than the beach?"

Mattie nodded.

Whew! thought Rosemary.

"Come along for the drive, anyway, and see where you'd have stayed." This time there was no fighting in the car.

Mattie didn't think much of Lawrie's house. After sticking her nose into the room full of knives and stuffed swordfish and some immensely detailed blow-ups of photographs he'd taken under water, Mattie went and sat in Tom's car and refused to get out. One picture, she told Phyl and Lawrie, who'd gone to comfort her, was really scary: a thick-lipped, prickle-faced, small-eyed monster who had stared dangerously from its full-colour blow-up.

"It's just a little bitty thing, really. Only so big," Lawrie said. "It kissed the lens." But Mattie clenched her eyes and shuddered.

Eve had brought their cold Christmas lunch and would have needed little urging to combine hampers for a picnic on the beach, but on the way through Terrigal, Mattie and Ben had seen a line-up of brightly painted pedal boats on the lagoon and really wanted to go there.

"It's Christmas Day—feller might not be operating,"

"Yes! Yes! I saw one going," Ben said.

"Anyway, there's always row-boats," said Mattie, whose territory this was.

So they left, and within minutes Phyl and Bobby had dragged Lawrie's battered Windsurfer out of the garage and headed for the beach.

"Daniel phoned me about that," Lawrie said, pointing to the wrecked E-type Jag that still occupied most of the garage space. "Said he might come up today or tomorrow and have a look at it, to see if it's worth anything. I told him you and the kids would be here."

"Oh, Lawrie! Is he coming? I couldn't bear that."

He shrugged, leaving her uneasy. They followed the children to the beach.

"Right," Lawrie said, settling himself in the sand beside her. Rosemary began the slow, meticulous business of covering every exposed scrap of herself with total sun-screen. "Tell me what's happening with you?" He didn't stop for the answer. "I know Dan's gone bust. I knew about that. Tried to get me to bail him out, but it was too late by then—it would have wiped me out, too. Better, I told him, for me to hang on to what I've got 'til the dust settles."

Rosemary could just imagine the anguished visit—Daniel snatching at such straws as the house he'd given Lawrie, and Lawrie obdurate, boiling up to anger.

"What's the point, I told him, chucking everything down the hole? I thought he'd throw a punch at me."

"He's done a bit of that lately." Rosemary rubbed her arm.

"Yeah? Roughed you up?"

"Accident, partly. It wouldn't have been so bad if I hadn't slipped." She glanced thoughtfully at his turned-away face. "You don't really have any idea about what's been happening with us, do you? I never contacted you. I thought—I suppose I thought Daniel was confiding in you."

"Nope. Not until the silly bugger got desperate." He drew a daisy in the sand. "I'm at fault, I must say. I've been preoccupied up here—fishing, writing, mainly doing a lot of reading. About religion." He glanced at her quickly and then added a stalk and leaves to his sand daisy. "You been into that? No? Well, seems I've been so busy with the theory of Christianity that I haven't paid much attention to the practise. Been a bit neglectful of my relatives, haven't I?"

"What a surprising man you are!" said Rosemary. "I always thought you were some sort of crook. Or a wicked CIA man."

Lawrie's laugh was a brief, small explosion like the popping of a champagne cork. "I should watch my mouth," he said. "I told Dan a lot of Walter Mitty stories. Seems he couldn't tell the difference between fact and fiction." He lay back, smiling, on the sand, yielding to it as though it were a comfortable bed. His crumpled, greyish eyelids half covered his ale-coloured eyes, making him look like a wise ape. From a distance Rosemary had always assumed that the pinprick-sized black spots that lined his deep mouth-bracketing creases were blackheads, but now, closer to him than she'd ever been, she could see they were tough bits of beard stubble which a razor had blurred rather than sliced. He had always looked dirty to her, but the greyish tinge to his skin was its natural colour, not dirt at all. She could see that now. For a moment he reminded her of someone, but the impression vanished when he spoke again.

"I should have guessed there was something bad going on. You two have always had your differences, of course—you're both pretty tough nuts. But I didn't know for a long time that he'd left you and the kids and gone off with a bloody secretary."

"She's an actress, actually." It's odd that I didn't think of telling him, Rosemary thought. Perhaps if he'd really been Daniel's father—or behaved more like his stepfather than a big brother or a best friend—I'd have phoned him right away. That would have been a way of communicating with Daniel when I was so mad at him. So, despite all those months of doubt, I really, really didn't want to! The realisation was comforting. Rosemary relaxed in the fine, warm breeze and turned her now totally protected face to the sun.

But Lawrie still had a burdened conscience. "There's nothing worse than that state a feller gets into," Lawrie said. "I remember it meself. Daniel was a natural candidate, of course—pushing forty . . . "

"He's only just turned thirty-seven!"

". . . Yeah, well, I was precocious, too—just about thirty. And it was different with me, 'cause I guess Geraldine had sort of replaced my . . . well she provided some family life I'd had to do without." He was silent, remembering old pain. "Guess I was about ready to grow up—to find someone of my own generation; anyway, that was what impelled me. With Dan it was the good old mid-life crisis, a copy-book example, can't you see that? He'd worked hard. Successful business, nice house. People started treating him in a particular way; he started to think, Is this all there is?"

"Isn't it enough? What he had?"

"That's not the point. The first thing that goes is perspective. He starts to remember that he never sowed more'n a trickle of wild oats before taking up the ploughshare of marriage. Married, when his friends were still sowing plenty in Spain, California, Bali, or Khatmandu. 'I missed out on that,' he says. 'Hey! I better hurry up!' But how's he going to justify it? Well, he takes a look at the nice lady he married.

He's used to the way she looks by now—what used to be an addiction is now a habit. 'Hey!' he says. 'If it weren't for her, I'd be having fun!' "

"You talking from experience?"

"Yup. Geraldine got a little sensitive about her looks, and she had a few women's problems. I guess I took advantage of that. Hey! This is real Christmas talk, real Merry Christmas talk!" Rosemary did not respond. Lawrie trickled sand through his fingers, unconsciously destroying the daisy he'd drawn. "She got sick. She died."

"She had a stroke, I always thought."

"Yup. Dan was twenty-one. It was like she'd said 'Daniel doesn't need me anymore. And Lawrie surely doesn't need me anymore.'"

"Lawrie, it wasn't your fault!"

"No? Tell it to the judge," he said, and tipped his chin to the sky. "Time I made another visit to the house of the Lord. You wanna come, you and the kids tonight? Christmas service?"

"Why not?" she said, still surprised by this new angle on Lawrie. His lips, she noticed, were very red, as though he'd been sucking mulberries. She'd always thought him ugly before.

Lunch was a fruit binge. Lawrie fetched a striped umbrella to keep off the sun, which, despite Meg's prophecy, was hot and strong. He also fetched a card table, folding chairs and a plastic icebucket for the French champagne which was his present to Rosemary, and the four of them sat on the wheat-coloured beach, watching children and puppies playing in the sun-glinting waves.

They ate black cherries, so perfect that they looked like the artificial ones on old-fashioned hats, and golden mangoes whose juices leaked down their wrists and whose scent was like love-making and like ozone from the open sea. There were slices of crisp-soft watermelon and white-fleshed early peaches and even lychees, which Rosemary had not tasted before and which she claimed were the eggs of *brontosaurus australianus,* a believed-to-be-extinct mini-species lurking in the nearby trees, nearly wiped out by the magpies, who sought them out because they believed them to be good for their vocal range. "It's the fertilised lychee that gives them that wolf-whistle call," said Rosemary, trying to imitate the notes which resounded from the nearby trees.

"You're as bad as Lawrie!" said Phyl.

The pyramid of fruit on the table was like a display at a harvest festival, and it hardly seemed to get any smaller. There was cheese too: a ripe, flowing Camembert and a pale slab of Jarlsberg, with Lawrie's dark bread, unsalted butter, and a choice of crackers. He'd brought his brilliant yellow, plastic-coated AM/FM cassette deck and played the tape Rosemary had given him—haunting, pure music that made their group private and complete to itself. And he told them wonderful new lies about his adventures underwater. One was about the giant marlin that had strayed from North Queensland waters and got itself trapped in a cave only he knew about. He'd signalled peace to the giant fish by doing exactly the opposite of what it was doing.

"Stands to reason—he was panicking, see, and that made him lash his tail. So what's the opposite of panic to a fish? Smooth gliding. So I kept my legs still and swam, arms only, like a turtle. Very hard to do with scuba gear on, I tell ya. Then he was dashing left to right, left to right, twisting around, like a fat man in a barrel. Well, I swam kinda serene, you know—long strokes—to the way I knew he could get out, and I whistled . . ."

"Whistled?" Phyl and Bobby glanced, solemn mouthed, at each other.

"Yes. Haven't you whistled under water? Nothing to beat it!"

"Through your mouthpiece?"

"Oh, you do it like this." Lawrie clapped his hand over his mouth and nose and hummed, a high, fluting note and then ignored further giggling interjections as he told them the happy ending: how the marlin had grown to trust him and had followed him through the tortuous, narrow caverns to the path back home.

"I could have killed that mighty creature with my bare hands, I was that close. I'd have had my name in every record book in the world. But how could a man do such a thing?"

"No," said Bobby. "You sent it back to the Great Barrier Reef so millionaires in speedboats could do it for you." Then he ducked and giggled as Lawrie hit at him with a strip of watermelon rind.

"Where's ya soul, boy? Where's ya soul?"

"This is bliss," said Rosemary, reaching for a slice of pineapple.

"I've worked it out—Adam and Eve took bits of Eden with them when they left," said Phyl.

Rosemary agreed, though she kept glancing towards the street that led to Lawrie's house. The serpent Daniel could slither along at any minute.

"How'd ya go with the Windsurfer, boy?"

"Good. Fell off thirty-eight times, then stayed on."

"Phyl?"

"Fell off thirty-eight times, then stayed off."

"We'll soon fix that. You want to try, woman?"

"No, thanks," said Rosemary. "I'll read—I've brought work that keeps on being interrupted by having a good time."

She lugged home as much as she could of the lunch remnants, made herself some coffee, closed the bedroom door against serpents, and fell into a deep sleep.

Some tiny sound, or that bit of sixth sense we have which, like wisdom teeth and the coccyx, has not quite disappeared from the animal evolution made her open her eyes. A man was standing at the open door. A thrill of horror coursed through her body, but she managed not to cry out.

It wasn't Daniel, it wasn't a burglar, it wasn't even Robert Talbot, though in the half-light and in her half-sleep there had been a second when she'd believed it was. It was Lawrie, looking at her oddly.

"I didn't mean to give you a fright. Sorry, Ro."

"How long have you been there? Watching me sleep?"

"Just came in," he said. There was a pause—a long enough pause for Rosemary, who was waking up now, to become aware that it was a pause with intent. Lawrie seemed to fill the room with the power of his plan.

It was such a simple plan. Such an obvious solution—or resolution—to what had started on the night when, splendid in her new red dress, she'd met Robert Talbot and made a secret assignation of the senses. She could think of no argument but merely lifted the sheet when he felt sure enough to cross the floor to her. She hardly felt surprised—in her dreams this had happened before.

He kissed her, and she felt deliciously, warmly drowned in the sensation. He began to tug at his clothes, and she had a clear visualisation of the next step—when she would submit her smooth, white self to his strong, thin, dark body.

Then, "No! No, Lawrie!" she cried urgently, and suited the words to action, struggling violently to evade his seeking fingers. "We can't! I can't. We mustn't!"

"Don't be silly," he soothed, entrapping her with the angle of his body. "The kids aren't anywhere near. We're"— he was panting—"healthy, consenting adults . . ."

"No!" she shouted, slightly fearfully now. He was very strong. Desperately she played what she hoped was a winning card: "This is adultery!" He did not falter. "It's . . . oh, Lawrie, we can't! It's incest!"

It worked, but not for the reason she thought it would. It was his sense of humour more than his Christian conscience that caused the almost instant collapse of his aspirations.

"Heavens!" he said, still laughing at her as he pulled his shorts on. "It would be hard to know which of us is the greater hypocrite!"

When he'd gone, she burst into tears. What's the matter with me?

she wondered. It takes just about nothing—and just about anybody—to get me so aroused. It must show, in some way. I must look available.

There was an element of regret, too, in her shocked tears. Why does everything have to be complicated? she thought. It would have been so nice. Wrong, but so nice. It took quite a while before she was sufficiently unshaken and unstirred to go back to sleep again.

.   .   .

Her coffee was cold, a drowned fly stuck in the cream, when the sound of the returning family woke her up.

"This train terminates here," Lawrie yelled, banging at her door. "Everybody off!"

I dreamed all that! she thought and was relieved. Then Lawrie looked into the room and winked lewdly and she knew it had not been a dream. Oh, hell, how embarrassing! she thought. But Lawrie didn't look embarrassed.

"Evensong starts in about half an hour. I'll delay those scruffy kids and you can get the top of the hot water. 'Cause if they get in first, you'll be left with cold." From his voice, no one would guess anything had changed, and to Rosemary's great relief, that's how he continued to talk.

.   .   .

The little stone church was lit with candles and decorated with dozens of old-fashioned bunches of flowers. Most of the small congregation was made up of elderly women—widows probably, living in retirement. Families would have come in the morning.

It was obvious that Lawrie was known there, but there were curious glances at her and the children—as well there might be, she thought guiltily. Both children had cherry-coloured sunburn all over their faces and shoulders—Phyl's nose looked blistery already and she'd had to have an aspirin before they left. Bobby was squirming and his eyes were half shut from swollen lids. What an irresponsible mother I am! Hats and sun cream, the drill from baby-hood—since Phyl and Bobby were both such fair-skinned people—had been forgotten in the new pleasure of sailboarding. I should have reminded them, she thought, and sighed. When do you stop having to look after them? she wondered anxiously. Ever?

There was a choir of solemn men who, despite their black robes and white lace surplices were more striking for their individuality than their uniform. Two little boys who looked like cricketers were the sopranos. Though supermarkets had been Muzak-ing carols since early October, so that Rosemary was heartily sick of the whole range, the boys' clear, innocent sound gave new beauty to "O Come All Ye Faithful" and especially to the descant in "The First Noel." It made her feel serene and mundane at the same time—an oddly peaceful combination.

"If it was always like this, I suppose I wouldn't be a—what could you call me?—off-hand agnostic," she said on the way home.

"If it's just entertainment value you're after, you wouldn't get much out of it, true. I guess I'm luckier than you in that regard," Lawrie said.

"It's the preaching I don't like. They're always going on about the seven deadly sins and how you should avoid them. But to me that's nonsense —normally they're what makes the world go round. They're the motivators of the human race!"

In a school-teacherly voice he said, "Can you list them?"

Rosemary came up with eight, after some thought.

"That's not right—you've got two of them twice," Lawrie said, having scribbled them in his writing man's notebook as they walked. "Gluttony is greed. And lechery is lust."

"No, it's not. Avarice is greed," Phyl said.

"Covetousness then?" Rosemary offered.

"That's the same as envy. So that's four. I'll give you that—lust, gluttony, avarice, envy, they're pretty good motivators. The other two as well—anger and pride."

"All that sermoning stuff was political—designed to keep the serfs down in feudal times. It's totally inappropriate in a material world," said Rosemary.

"Two points you miss, woman. One is that what the church gives can be appreciated for itself, never mind the message. It offers fellowship— what shy and lonely people need in the world of fractured villages. It spans history and it links generations. Have you no love for tradition and history?"

"Oh, yes. Oh, yes! Haven't I told you? I've gone mad about Australian history. Not dates, treaties, all that. But people!"

"Don't start her off," Bobby said. "She'll spend the next hour raving about William Sandford."

"Well, I'd certainly like to hear all about the feller. But back to what I was saying—my other point. Which is that the seven deadly sins come from Chaucer. Bet you thought it was the Bible, huh?"

Phyl had been lagging for the past few yards. Being careful not to touch her painful skin, Lawrie hooked her arm in his. "I've just thought of the last sin," she said. "Sloth. And boy, is it a motivator—all I can think is bed!"

Rosemary gave Phyl and Bobby each a salt tablet, then thought that that was probably the wrong thing to do and so urged them each to drink two large glasses of lime cordial, which made Phyl gag. Then Rosemary gently patted camomile lotion on their shoulders while they gasped, squirmed, and even screamed a little from the shock of the cold. She fanned Phyl's face until she fell asleep. She pulled Bobby's sheet off when he sweated and put it back on again when he shivered, and all the time Lawrie watched, hiding his guilt under mutters about over-protected city young.

At last they slept peacefully and Rosemary wished she could, too, without having to talk to Lawrie alone. What an extraordinary weekend, she thought. First Tom, now Lawrie. But Lawrie behaved as though nothing was different. Good, she thought. Neither of us will ever mention it again, and soon it will be covered by time and forgotten.

"OK," he said over a glass of sherry and the Christmas cake Meg had packed for them. "You still haven't told me what you're going to do."

She checked his face. Nothing in it looked like the man with sweat-damp curls on his forehead, who'd kissed her and touched her and panted for her in her little, narrow, guest bed. He looked like safe Lawrie, who was just as likely to talk sense as to tell a wonderfully adventurous lie. Would she, Rosemary, become the subject of one of Lawrie's stories? Probably not, she decided. He preferred to cast himself as a serious, winning hero and certainly not as a man spurned for making foolish assumptions.

"I don't know for sure what I'm going to do," she said. "I've got a job. If I get a cheap house—a flat if we absolutely have to—I could manage. I'm sure I could. Of course, Phyl has to change schools, but she left that one, anyway, in a big flurry of independence—she was going to give up being educated."

He grimaced. "Another female with a head full of Swiss cheese holes!"

"But she's been talked into finishing. She's got one more year."

"Then it's best she does it at the same school, isn't it? Same teachers. Knows where the ladies room is."

"Lawrie, I couldn't manage the fees. She can go to a state school or the tech . . ."

"Hear me out," he interrupted. "I still own the house in Darlinghurst. Remember? I bought it after Geraldine died. No, don't interrupt. What if we clean it up? You could have that—you and the kids."

"Darlinghurst?"

"My first idea was that you three come and live here—this is the kids' house after all—and I go there. That was my agenda for tonight's li'l meeting. But if you've got a job and Phyl's got her school, you should go there. Get Bob into Fort Street High when he's ready—he's bright enough."

"Darlinghurst? I thought you sold it."

"Nope. Couldn't. Or, rather, didn't think it was worth it; Department of Main Roads earmarked it for some expressway that may never happen, but you know what it's like—you can't get a price on a place that's DMR-affected."

"So who lives in it?"

"No one. I had an old Dutch lady who paid me enough to cover the council rates, then she died. Meals on Wheels found her, stiff as a brick. Then, squatters. I got them out. I put bars up. Yes, you can look like that. It's lousy. A lousy house in a pretty lousy area. But free, to you."

"But . . . ?"

"Tell you the truth, I haven't looked at it for a while. I guess it might need some fixin' but there's a sock full of money under my bed for just such an eventuality. Why don't I give you the key? You go and have a look—feasibility study, huh? Tell me what ya think."

"Lawrie, you're very kind," she said "But . . ."

"No, no. I've lived in paradise here. Phyl said it herself, today. And I've had this pleasure because of you and Dan. What you expect me to do? See you sleeping in the park?" He stood up, looking, suddenly, quite angry. "Hell, I just can't understand Daniel. Help me fill the gaps. Because really, I can't make out what's gone wrong with that boy."

"That's not what you said earlier."

"Ah! The testicular imperative. But that's just part of it. Marriages survive these excursions—they're just oat-sowing flurries. Why hasn't yours survived? Or will it? Are you two just playing a wilder game than most?"

"I never . . . I haven't," Rosemary began, aware that it was a certain hypocrisy which was causing her to blush and stammer. But Lawrie, who did not, could not, know about Robert Talbot, absolved her with a wave.

"That's only part of what I'm talking about," he said. "I mean the game of jealousy and hate and destruction that married people dabble in when they get bored. Oh, sure, sex plays a part in that nasty game. It's a weapon, or a gambling stake, but it's seldom the reason. In fact," he added delicately, deliberately, "it seldom matters at all. People put too much on it." This left them both silent for a while. "Well, Daniel's a fool to lose you, I don't mind telling you," Lawrie said, crumpling suddenly with fatigue. "We'll check the train times in the morning."

"No need—I forgot to tell you. A friend is picking us up at about eleven," Rosemary said, and with one raised eyebrow, Lawrie gave Rosemary the impression that he understood something perfectly.

. . .

In the morning the children both felt even sorer, and all they could wear were the previous day's swim-suits, which didn't touch the burnt parts. They sat glumly eating cornflakes while Lawrie surreptitiously checked his watch. He'd be out in the surf or somewhere along the coast, into the rocks by now if it weren't for them.

"None of us will be able to go out today, Lawrie. You go—why not? We'll be fine. Patrick and Geoff will be here at about eleven and I'll just hang the key on the nail."

Lawrie did not protest and Rosemary was glad to see him go, relieved that he would not meet Patrick and fill the air with a jabber of communication, both verbal and non-verbal.

Now, if Patrick would hurry and take us away quickly before Daniel arrives, this can be as happy a Boxing Day as yesterday was a Merry Christmas, she thought.

. . .

"Peaceful!" Patrick said, stepping down from the golden bus into the the quiet, bushy street.

"Most of it's not very grand," Rosemary said. "The finger of gentrification has only recently started tickling this street. But look, if you stand on your toes, you can see the sea."

"You forget I don't have to stand on my toes," he said, very close, as he gazed over her head at the view. Then, "Ha! Roast adolescent!" he said, catching sight of Phyl and Bobby. "Had a typical Aussie Christmas, did you?"

Geoff had clambered out and he began shouting joyfully in his odd, crackly voice. He hurled himself at Phyl.

"Careful! Careful! Oooh!" she gasped, then closed her eyes in pain as he hugged her. She kissed his cheek and said apologetically, with a little grin, "Well, it's a friendship worth suffering for!"

"I'm glad we're still only on handshaking terms!" said Bobby, standing well away from the risk of hugs.

"No Andy?" Rosemary asked.

"He's at the Gold Coast, Mum, with his aunt and cousins," Phyl said before Patrick could reply.

"Is this all you've got?" Patrick picked up two pieces of their little pile of luggage. Then suddenly, to Rosemary's great discomfort, Lawrie was there with a bucket full of cleaned fish—he hadn't been able to resist his curiosity. But she need not have worried—the man who shook Patrick's hand was an ideal stepfather-in-law.

On the pretext of packing the fish in ice, Lawrie took everyone into the house. And once Patrick and Geoff saw the weapons display they looked as though they'd stay forever. Patrick seemed to know almost as much as Lawrie did about the origin and functions of the artifacts, especially those from New Guinea and Indonesia, and the two men asked eager questions and exchanged anecdotes and information as though they'd been working together for years on a project. And Geoff was so fascinated by the swordfish that Lawrie eventually took the huge thing off the wall for him to cuddle, mounting board and all. Rosemary had no way of hurrying them up.

At noon, complete with fresh fish on ice and, in Patrick's case, a pile of books and pamphlets he promised to return soon, they said goodbye again to Lawrie. When it was his turn to kiss Rosemary, he looked at her seriously from under his wrinkled lids.

"Daniel's missed you. He's too late," he murmured.

. . .

Patrick had brought a guitar and some hand drums so the children could provide music for the journey home, which they did in the back of the bus. Though uniformly loud, Geoff's rhythm was indeed terrific, and, apart from the occasional 'ouch!' or 'ooh!' as Phyl or Bobby bumped a burnt limb or back, peace reigned.

"Comfortable?" Patrick smiled at Rosemary.

"Bliss," she said. "How was Christmas for you?"

"Oh, nice. Martha cooked the whole, traditional thing, and Melissa came and got very sloshed. She was pretty funny for a while, fooling around with the animals. Geoff thought she was marvellous. But then— you know how she can get."

"Big sobs, followed by big rages."

"Yup. Martha dealt with that. But Geoff tried to put party hats on the dogs, and Sultan snapped at him, which gave him a fright, so he took a bit of settling down."

It seemed unfair to tell him about the much more lovely time she, Phyl, and Bobby had had, so she edited it substantially. However, she did tell Patrick about the Darlinghurst house.

"You said you were going to have a peaceful two days, be a vegetable—wasn't that the expression? If that's your idea of a peaceful time. . . ."

"Oh, I tried. I tried, believe me. This morning I got stuck into my Sandford box at last—don't you think that's peaceful? Sitting at a knife-scarred table reading old letters? Well, it wasn't."

"The roof fell in? The garden hose turned out to be a viper? You found a will amongst the Sandford papers, and you're the sole heir? No? I give up."

"It's the letters themselves. I got so excited by them—it seems a pity to just sort of pop William and Clarice into a mini-series. It should be something more—a documentary maybe. No, no one would watch that. A feature film, that's what it should be. There's enough there: human drama, human interest. William Sandford believed he was conned, you see. Late in 1907, when he'd built the huge, modern blast-furnace that could really start efficient production, the state government agreed to guarantee him a loan of seventy thousand pounds. He had no more money and he'd mortgaged his house to guarantee bank loans for wages and materials."

Patrick glanced at her but said nothing.

"The money was to be a sort of advance against orders, since the government had signed a contract with him for all sorts of iron and steel things for public works. But the bank the government nominated fiddled around and fiddled around about finalising the loan while poor William had wages to pay, and he kept getting more and more desperate and he kept getting messages from the government and from the Ministry of Works saying not to worry. To hang in there."

She paused, thinking of the aching, stretching slowness of legal matters. Jim Begg often said he was fighting for her, but it had not seemed like a fight—more like a dream-dance through some thick substance like molasses. William Sandford would have had the same feeling, waiting for the bank, for the government, for the contract, for the hope.

"Then suddenly he heard that a rival iron-making company—a firm called G & C Hoskins—had made an offer to take over his works and the government had secretly agreed. All these arrangements were made behind William Sandford's back—he was presented with a *fait accompli*."

"And what happened to William?"

"Nothing. Angry, hurt retirement. Twenty-five years of life with his unmarried daughter. The Hoskins got their come-uppance eventually, in about 1934: they were swallowed up in a merger. But that was too late for William—he was dead."

" 'Swallowed up in a merger,' huh? I suppose you know you're talking about BHP?"

It was her turn to frown. "Well . . ."

"Well, what your story says is that Australia's biggest company started with a shady deal!"

"Does it? I didn't think of that. But how could BHP be blamed for something that happened thirty years before?"

He smiled at her seriousness. "OK. I'll resign from being a script consultant."

She smiled, too. "You're right—I am taking it all rather personally, aren't I?"

They travelled in silence for a while, then she said, "You know what William Sandford wanted most, when he was very old? To fly over Lithgow in an aeroplane and look down at the ironworks. But Clarice wouldn't let him."

"You're really enjoying this job. You had the same look when you were stage-managing."

"Oh, yes. It's great. I feel so lucky! Just a couple of months ago I was thinking of myself as someone half-way up a ladder to nowhere, with the choice of starting right from the bottom at something new or making a wild leap to the middle of something else. And here I am, safely in the middle of the nicest ladder I could have imagined!"

They were crossing Broken Bay, and the water gleamed dull and smooth as aluminium under the warm, cloudy sky. A myriad of slender sticks protruded from the calm surface; oyster farms, whose shadows, earlier in the day, would have made patterns like Japanese script on the water. Now, shortly after noon, there were no shadows—there would not have been even if the day had been bright. A train made tiny by perspective eased smoothly over the distant railway bridge, too far away for the sound to reach them. It looked delicate in the silver air—a vehicle of elf-land.

Geoff's enjoyment of anything usually lasted longer than anyone else's, but even he had got tired of drumming. Phyl and Bobby had long before lapsed into a more-or-less comfortable silence. Then Geoff began to wail.

"Oh, no! Not on the expressway! I can't stop now!" Patrick said anxiously, trying to see what was going on by re-angling the rear-view mirror. Phyl scrabbled in the remains of yesterday's picnic and produced an apple for him, but Geoff snatched it and threw it out of the window. Juice? Lollies? They went the same way.

His croaking wails grew louder. He began to kick the side panels, his wild arms striking at his flinching companions. Phyl tried the guitar again, but he wrestled with her for that, clearly wanting to throw it after the apple.

Patrick, looking more worried than Rosemary had ever seen him,

moved into the left-hand lane and then the safety strip and slowed down.
Then he speeded up again.

"No, that's crazy! He wants to get out and there'd be nowhere to run
except into the traffic. We'll just have to go on to the Brooklyn turn-
off." He chewed at his lips. He kept glancing in the mirror, and Rosemary turned back, too, to see Bobby looking frightened, fending Geoff
off. Phyl had backed away, too.

Rosemary unbuckled her seat-belt and worked her way down the
mini-bus, talking soothingly: "OK, that's OK. That's enough now, Geoffy,"
she repeated in what she hoped was a firm, cheerful voice. She signalled
with her eyes for Phyl and Bobby to move forward, which they quickly
did. He is big. And strong, she thought. I couldn't cope with anything
physical. But she didn't stop the soothing, cheerful litany. He's only a
four-year-old in that big ugly body. And it's nothing but a tantrum. And
it was true that Geoff's flailing arms and legs were not directed at anyone—
she just had to be careful to keep out of the way.

"OK, Geoffy," she said, though she doubted whether he could hear
through his clackering cries. "OK, baby." Very lightly, quickly, she ran
her fingertips down his cheek and tickled his neck. He stopped bellowing
for a second and his faced registered the moment of surprise, but then
he bellowed again. So she did it again and he paused again, and again,
until gradually the tickling became a gentle massage and the yells became
intermittent sobs.

She stroked and soothed his face and shoulders, sometimes letting
her hands brush over his eyes so that he had to close them. Poor thing.
Poor thing, she thought. How Patrick must have loathed you for taking
his wife away.

In a few more minutes Geoff would probably have fallen asleep, but
they reached the turn-off and, thereafter, a wide grassy strip beside the
railway embankment and soon he was charging around being an aeroplane, a tractor, and just a noisy boy. But he didn't look like a noisy
boy having fun—he looked and sounded like an alien creature intent
on menace. Rosemary became aware of something Patrick had lived
with for years—the hostile stares of other people.

"Why's that man making that noise, Gran?" a small child asked.

"It's because he's mad in the head. You keep right away, Carreen."

Patrick did not appear to have heard. He was leaning, arms folded,
one knee bent up, against the vehicle. It was past lunch-time, Rosemary
realised. And she and the kids had had nothing but cornflakes for breakfast. So, with food negotiations in mind, she walked back to him and
saw that he was watching her and that his look was of intense pain and

needing. Her instinct was to walk into his arms, murmuring 'It's OK! It's OK!' and to take away his stress, just as she had with Geoff. But— What am I? The whole world's mother? she asked herself. Instead, from a safe distance, she said, "What's for lunch, boss?"

He strolled towards her and was his usual smiling-eyed self by the time he reached her side.

"Thanks for that, with Geoffy," he said lightly.

"Don't be silly. It was nothing. There's a shop open that we passed. Maybe they do hamburgers?"

Patrick gave Bobby some money and sent him off to find whatever he could.

"This is not what I had in mind for a fun-filled Boxing Day," Patrick said.

"It's fine, lovely," Phyl said, smiling politely and trying not to shiver. Rosemary persuaded her to pull a soft cotton sweat-shirt carefully over her burns.

Bobby brought back a cooked chicken, some crisps, and an assortment of fruit drinks, all of which they consumed fairly quickly and, in a subdued mood, drove the rest of the way home. All three children slept until they reached Rosemary's house.

"I won't bring Geoff in," Patrick said. "So I won't stay. But I'll phone you later. You can keep my piece of Lawrie's fish in the freezer for some other time."

There was a burden between them of unsaid things.

.   .   .

Bobby checked the post-box. "Just some Christmas cards. Nothing from Dad," he said, and went straight to his room. Soon afterwards, when she had helped put things away, so did Phyl.

Well, Single Parent, you survived Christmas, Rosemary said to her reflection in the hall mirror.

.   .   .

Patrick did not phone that night. In fact, it was not until she got a telegram from Jim Begg next day that she realised her phone was cut off.

He told her, when she phoned him from Eve's house, that having it put back on again would not be a simple matter of paying the bill and a re-connection fee, since the bill was now part of the winding up of the company. Of course, he'd do what he could, but probably the quickest way would be to re-apply in her own name and pay a new connection fee.

"But we'll be leaving."

"Well, even if you do—and that's still not a hundred per cent—it will be some months and you can't manage in the meantime without a phone."

.   .   .

During the next few days, Rosemary went through every room of the house again, to see if she really could separate herself from it. It was easier this time. She thought about the time she'd spent drawing decorating plans on sheets of squared paper after spending hours sifting through magazines and brochures for better and better ideas and for the perfect combination of colour, layout, materials, and serviceability. I did it before, I can do it again, she said to the rumpus room, and turned her back on it. Lawrie had given her a trump card—she must go soon and look at the house in Darlinghurst.

But the living room, Mr. Menotti's cedar-finished living room—that would always be hard to leave. That she would never forget because it had been the scene of the best of her times here. And of some of the worst—it was the room in which Angela had appeared.

"Bobby?" Rosemary called. His sunburn was starting to peel, making him look as though he'd been dipped in sawdust. "You're good with the camera. Won't you please take pictures of the house? All the rooms, from different angles and the garden and the pool . . . we'll make an album for later."

"Yes, OK. Sure. Should we get Auntie Gwen to bring back the paintings? It would look better without those white patches."

"No! Shhhh! Never mention the word paintings, darling; there're meanies waiting around every corner, ready to snatch them and anything else not nailed down." This was not true, of course, but it was easier to joke than to say that the missing pictures made the house definitely transitory and therefore easier to shrug off. But Bobby did not find it funny. In fact, he had not found anything funny or even particularly interesting since sailboarding at Lawrie's at Christmas, and Rosemary was glad she'd thought of the photographs.

.   .   .

Lawrie's house was on a fairly busy street at the East Sydney end of Darlinghurst. It was narrow, a terrace in a mismatched row like teeth in need of orthodontic attention. The gate was missing—a cast-iron one which had matched the railings on the upstairs balcony and which now, no doubt, had found a more appreciative home in a better-renovated suburb.

The short concrete path, which hadn't been new since the 1920s, was criss-crossed with cracks so long established that moss had almost beautified them. Rosemary didn't happen to like that particular shade of green. Neither did she like the snails, arrogant clusters of both the big, brownish-grey ones and the little, harder-shelled, harder-to-kill pearly ones, which had glued themselves companionably to every level of the front steps and around the necks of the two chipped terracotta urns which flanked the little front verandah.

What she liked least of all was the smell which burst out like bad breath from the house once she'd won the battle with the two sets of deadlocks. Mould, dust, urine, drains, humidity, and other, less-recognisable scents had fermented together in the closed house, so thoroughly permeating the structure that it bordered on visibility, like phosphorescence. She wished she'd brought someone with her. There was a sense there, strong as the smells they'd made, of transitory, dissatisfied people.

The front, small room faced the street and Rosemary looked out of the grimy window to find herself eye to eye with a heavily whiskered, very dirty, vagrant old man who had obviously been attracted by the possibilities suggested by the open front door. When he saw her there he cursed, spat, and lumbered on.

Rosemary exorcised him and all the other malign influences by jumping efficiently on the floorboards. They surged but did not splinter. Neither did the ones in the passage, where swathes of faded wallpaper arched away from the high walls, creating curved shelves for dust which lay thickly enough to obscure the patterns.

The living room was sound, too, though darker than the inside of a car in an underground parking station and not much bigger. The stairs, which rose steeply across its back wall, felt promising—no child would crash twelve feet through rotting timber on the way up to bed.

There was no doubt that, despite its tininess, the house had possibilities. In fact, she was amused to find herself placing furniture and visualising Phyl and Bobby at a table in the cleaned-up version.

But the visions were shattered in the kitchen, or the cooking alcove—*kitchen* was too grand a word. Two grey terrazzo laundry tubs stood on bricks against a mould-stained wall and underneath them both a permanent puddle stagnated in a deep dent worn through the linoleum and into the cement. A small and lumpy table, once painted light green, now chipped and streaked with dirt, provided the only working surface. A gas stove with a leak, which in this part of the house dominated the cocktail of bad smells, stood caked in grease black as tar in which cockroaches had died face down.

The water supply was from an incongruously shiny chrome-plated tap and from a green hose which snaked in from where, she guessed, a wood-burning stove must stand in the adjoining alcove. And that adjoining alcove turned out to be the shower: a mould and soap-grimed stall from which nearly all the tiles had fallen off the wet wall. The toilet had no seat and smelled so bad that she jerked her head away. Then she sat on the little kitchen table and tried to be strong.

To put in a kitchen and bathroom that were clean and worked, to have the wiring checked and, no doubt, fixed, and to have a proper water supply installed would be, what? About ten thousand dollars? Add another two, three thousand for painting. Then she'd need carpets, cupboards. Would Lawrie have seventeen thousand dollars or more and if so would he spend it on a house that was likely to be demolished or, worse, lost in the shadow of an express flyover? He may never recoup.

And a car—she'd need a car for the job; it would have to stay in the street, where vandalised hulks proclaimed how unreliable some of her neighbours were likely to be. Would it all be worth it?

No, never, she said. It's haunted. It'll always be. There's evil in these walls. Rubbish, she said. They're just walls and, furthermore, my own. Once fixed, it'll be quite cute. Small, and tight—we'll struggle to fit in—but we'll be safe. Relatively safe.

See! See! said her negative voice as Rosemary inspected the three little rooms upstairs and found the signs of some bad trips in one of them; slavering faces, quite well drawn but luridly coloured, leered from all the walls of the room she had in mind for Bobby. A broken guitar case in the corner was full of rubbish—a sand-shoe streaked with dry blood lay among small, tightly wrapped parcels that could have been bandages. She was sure there'd be syringes in there among the crumpled bits of newspaper and the McDonalds wrappings if she looked.

But she didn't look. A contract cleaning company would have to deal with that and with the marked and stinking mattress in the room next door—and with all the old carpeting and linoleum, and everything, but everything, in the kitchen area. That would help for a start.

She phoned Lawrie, reverse charge, from the only unvandalised call-box, and told him.

He hesitated. Then, "Well, the money sock's fairly big. But get some quotations. And cut some corners—it doesn't have to be another show-place."

"Lawrie, it couldn't be, not if you spend three times that. I'm not thinking of making a silk purse out of a sow's ear—just a sow's ear we won't catch AIDS in. Maybe you'd better come and have a look."

"No, no, no. Too busy. Got a deadline to meet by the end of this month," he said, as though rushing to oblige editors was a normal priority. Rosemary guessed he just didn't like the city.

"I'll get Bobby to take some pictures and we'll send you copies."

"You do that, woman."

She also left a message with Patrick's Spanish cleaning lady but doubted if she'd understood the word "disconnected."

"It was cut off. My phone."

"Butter?"

"Cut off. Cut off. Listen, please just say Rosemary says hello. OK?

"Rosamara. OK."

Nineteen

Rosemary felt pleased to be going back to work, even though for the first time in ages she'd experienced the working mother/holidaying schoolchild nightmare. Phyl had not let the lack of a telephone at home interfere with her wonderful friendship with Andy—she'd taken a twenty-cent piece, borrowed Bobby's old bike, and ridden to the shopping centre to a public phone that worked. And as a result, Andy had picked up her and her guitar for the day.

Bobby had not wanted to go along, even though he was invited. He'd squirmed and scowled when Rosemary urged him. Then, "Shit, Ma!" he'd roared. "Gimme a break! It's great there, I tell ya! In one room, Phyl and Andy looking googy-eyed at each other and in the other is Geoff going gabble gabble bang bang and looking googy-eyed at me!"

"I get the picture," she said, trying not to laugh. What did he usually do on holidays after the regulation trip to Lawrie's? Last year the house had been full of other kids most days, flashing around with zinc cream on their noses, in and out of pools, on and off skate-boards. But this year most of his friends had become serious joiners of teams or Scouts, or, like Bobby, they had been involved in a school production that was now over. Endless days of swimming were not enough anymore now that pre-adolescence was setting in.

"Why don't you get some of your mates to come and play with your computer games? James?"

"In Adelaide with his gran and the whole family."

"Scott then?"

"Yeah? How do I invite him? Send a letter by courier?"

"I'll get my taxi to drop you at his house on the way to work. How's that?"

"What if he's out?"

"Then you walk back. And read a book for a change. Or tidy your blasted room. Or run a load of washing through the machine. Or think of someone else to visit. I don't know. Just don't be so . . . so negative!"

Bobby simply looked more crushed and dreary than before. Rosemary glanced at her watch—she was going to be late for work at this rate—and sat down beside him.

"Come on. Tell me. What is it really?"

"What is it really?" he mimicked. "You lose your house. Your dad doesn't even send you a . . . Christmas card . . ." His lips trembled and he sprang away from her. "Isn't that enough, Mum?"

"Yeah. That's enough. That really is enough, darling. You're right. In fact, it's a hell of a lot too much. I suppose I've spent so much time just trying to deal with it all myself that I haven't really thought you were so . . . you looked as though you were having a good time over Christmas."

"Oh, I'm OK."

"The house is just a house, you know. A place to live. We'll get another one. Lawrie's given us the one in Darlinghurst, and we'll soon fix that up—we'll make it really cosy. It will be much nearer the centre of things, and you'll go to school near there, too, and meet new kids. It's got no pool, though; you should take advantage of this one as long as you can!"

Bobby gave her a brave smile and decided to stay at home, perhaps to go out later. He had not finished taking pictures of the house, having run out of film at the last session, so she left him money to get more film later when he felt like a walk or could hitch a ride from a neighbour.

"Get two. Three even—I want you to take some 'before' shots of Lawrie's house in Darlinghurst. Tomorrow? I've got no script conference tomorrow."

.   .   .

Ten minutes late she rushed through the building to the offices the script-writers had been using, to find no one there. The coffee dripolator was empty and clean, its cord wrapped around it. Typewriters were shrouded. There were no scattered papers.

She checked her diary—yes, there it was—Tuesday, January 3. Nine A.M. And today was definitely Tuesday. She'd gone through the motions of a street party on New Year's Eve, which was Saturday night: conical hats, kisses from neighbours whose names she didn't even know, "Auld Lang Syne," and lots of cask wine.

And New Years' Day—Sunday—Andy had made a special trip to tell her that Patrick wouldn't be coming over after all; Geoff had a cold and he had some work to do, fixing up some of the cages that needed re-meshing. Andy had been asked to pick her up if she wanted to help, but Rosemary had elected to spend the day sleeping, reading, and sleeping some more. There hadn't been enough of that lately.

Yesterday—Monday—there had been planning what to take from the house when the time came and where it would fit in the little house. So today was definitely Tuesday.

Rosemary picked up the phone and dialled the switchboard.

"Hello, I'm Rosemary Quilty and I'm . . ."

"Oh Mrs. Quilty, there you are! I've been battling to get you—been away? Just a sec. I'll put you through to Mr. Morgan." Which she did. Rosemary had never heard of Mr. Morgan, but it turned out that he was in a nearby office on the same floor because he had been put in charge of wrapping up the project, and he was glad she'd popped in because he had a note for her.

"Wrapping up?"

"Oh, didn't you know? You must have known! A decision was made not to proceed with the new series of 'The Mount Victorians.' "

"When was it made?"

"Well, by the board in the week before Christmas. I believe Kim Haymes and his team were told on Friday afternoon. This is the first you've heard of it?"

"Yes," she said, sitting heavily on the edge of the table. Her wonderful job!

"Look, it's silly to be talking on the phone. I presume you're in the building?"

"Yes," she said faintly. "In the script-writers' office."

"I've got it in writing for you here, from head office. I'll pop over and give it to you, right?" He did, a genial man with the air of one who could now tick another item off his list.

Rosemary put the envelope in her handbag and smiled politely over the yelling in her head: What now? What now? No job! How will we eat? That pre-Christmas cheque that she'd queried, that apparent overpayment—that must have been simply a payment up to date, plus notice pay.

"I've got a Cab-Charge card here," she said. "Should I give it to you?"

"Oh, well, that's not strictly my department. Did you use it to get here?"

"Yes."

"Then you'll need it to get back again, won't you?" He looked as glad as if he'd solved a difficult puzzle. "Pop it in the post when you're ready," he said.

And so ended Rosemary's second new career in two months.

. . .

She was relieved that the cab driver was surly—she could not have borne a discourse on the weather. Between two pop songs on his radio a political commentator brightly wrapped up the whole year, and Rosemary gathered, without feeling relief or even much interest, that most of the people who had been the subjects of royal commissions and official inquiries for so much of the year had been forgiven or excused. Matters of spying, corruption, influencing judges, and other things which had leaked like slow blood into the public consciousness and which had whipped the media sharks into a shriek of blood-lust were healed now, as though they had indeed been nothing more than small wounds. Nearly all of those who had been the focus of bright, flesh-ripping interest were free again now that the sharks were fed, and most of them were back in their old jobs or into new, better ones with their brave, new scars. Daniel, Robert Talbot, and Rosemary herself were lucky that it was now January and most of the more important and active media press sharks were away on holiday. Despite the gossip Lucy had told her about, Rosemary had got off lightly.

"Drop me here, please," she said when they neared the shops. She would see if Jim Begg was in—he'd probably needed to be in touch in the last few days. And she'd walk home—three brisk miles up the long hill was easy for her now. Rosemary acknowledged that the real reason for the detour to Jim's was because at home, alone with Bobby whose mood was just as low as hers, there was a risk that she'd give way to despair, and that would be the worst thing.

"I've lost my job, Jim."

"What on earth did you do?"

"Nothing. They just axed it."

"But surely you get some sort of compensation? How long were you there?"

"A month. Well, five weeks. But we didn't work last week."

Jim looked at her with a mixture of pity, pain, and irritation. She was sure he deeply regretted having postponed his tennis that long-ago Saturday to take on her hopeless case.

"Geez, I can't help you, Rosie. Only bloke I know in that line of work's on the ABC, and they're talking about cutting back staff, not taking people on."

"I'll find something," she said bravely, thinking of the employment agency's range of job offers. Living in the quaint, wittily restored house in Darlinghurst would have been fine if she'd had her marvellous job to counter it and to offer hope of graduating from it. But if she got a job that only required competence and which rewarded accordingly, she'd probably be stuck there for life. The ladder she'd leapt onto had turned into a footstool.

She thought this while Jim phoned Telecom again to urge them to hurry up and re-connect Rosemary's phone. They said they'd see what they could do and that someone would call him back but that she would not get the same number, as it had been allocated to someone else.

"Pity the poor person who gets it," Rosemary said, thinking in terms of the dozens of people she knew from the schools or the courses or the neighbourhood who would start ringing as soon as they saw the first "mortgagee sale" advertisement appear. Most would offer solace, of course, but all would be curious.

"How long do you think we can stay in the house?"

"You should be right for three months. But don't forget that while you're still there, life won't be quite as private as before; there'll be 'open for inspection' days once the real estate people start advertising the auction. And plenty of stickybeaks in between—no intention of buying, just want to take a look at a house on a mortgagee sale and say 'There but for the grace . . .' Not nice."

Among Rosemary's final duties as a director of Patchwork were documents she had to sign for the Corporate Affairs office and the taxation department. "Damn," Jim said, looking at the date. "These have to be in by tomorrow. And the post can't be trusted."

"I've got to go through the city tomorrow," she said. "I'll take them."

.   .   .

On the way home, Rosemary allowed herself to feel the pain. She was too vain to cry in the street, supposing there was still the energy and the juice for tears after the last . . . how long had it been? Almost a year, now.

What had been happening to her, she felt, had all the awesome power of birth: her marriage squeezing, squeezing her out, her house shrinking around her, impelling her forward. Into what?

Every handle she'd tried to grasp on the way had turned slippery and elusive. There was no control—none for her, anyway. Control was in the forces around her, and there was nothing to do but go with the spasms.

There's one more thing I can try, she thought, rounding the corner to her house: getting the Sandford movie made. It's mine, it's my story, and it's good. All I have to do is find the right people and make it happen.

It was a brave, defiant idea with no roots into reality. She knew that. But at least it gave her hope, which, to Rosemary, was like oxygen on a high-climbed peak.

Gwen's station-wagon was there, straddling two spaces as though trying not to make the three-car garage look so empty. She was playing Scrabble with Bobby, obviously not having got enough of it on her holidays.

"It's been explained to me that the reason I could not get through was because Telecom gave you a lovely Christmas present. I'd have thought someone would have given me a ring from a call-box. I even thought of phoning that old goat Lawrie to see if he'd kidnapped you!"

"No, we were rescued in a golden coach." Rosemary was determinedly bright—she didn't want Bobby to have any more bad news. "Bob, did you tell Auntie Gwen about Lawrie's house that he's giving us?" He had not. Gwen was agog. She produced a street directory from her huge string shopping bag and demanded to be shown where it was and then she did not approve.

"Right in the heart of whoresville. Knife in the back there soon as look at you. Still, beggars can't be choosers."

"Did you buy the film, Bobby?" Rosemary asked in a desperate bid to lighten the subject—his face was set and drawn again, whereas he'd looked quite lively when she'd first come home.

"Nah. Couldn't find the bicycle pump. Anyway, what's the rush?" But Gwen got the hint.

"Tell you what, in my boot is a tin with a chocolate-and-walnut cake I brought and some other goodies. You go and get it, there's the boy." Bobby moved grudgingly as one being disposed of, but he moved. "Then we'll have a slice, hey? With a cup of coffee. You do that for us," said Gwen. Then, as soon as he was out of earshot, "Spit it out," she said to Rosemary. "What's wrong with it."

"With what?"

"The house in Darlinghurst. What tragic complication now? It's written all over your face."

"It's not the house. I've lost my job."

"Oh, my good gawd," Gwen said and slapped her forehead, flashing the encrustation of old-fashioned marcasite rings on her strong, plump hand. "When's it going to end? Has someone put a curse on you?"

"That'd be a nice, simple explanation."

"Well, go on. Tell me what happened—what you did wrong. I can bear it."

"Far as I know, I did nothing wrong, Gwen. They axed the show, that's all. Everyone got the sack, not just me."

"And no explanation? No reason?"

"No. Oh, hang on—they gave me a letter."

It was simply a formal version of what she'd already been told—that the board had taken the decision to halt pre-production on the second series of "The Mount Victorians," that the first series would be scheduled later in the year, probably during the May ratings period, and that they thanked her for her input and co-operation. A cheque would be posted to her within a few days and she was wished luck by the signator, a person she'd never heard of.

"What's the date of the letter?"

"December twenty-third."

"So your cheque is on its way. Could even be here today. At least that's something."

"No. They've already paid me out in full. That's why it was so much."

But they hadn't. On his way back from the car, Bobby had collected the post, and, heading for the kitchen with the cake tin and two supermarket bags, he dropped it in her lap. There were five envelopes: three with windows, one from American Express suggesting she apply for a credit card, and one with the corporation's familiar TV logo. And inside that was a cheque for just over thirty-three thousand dollars.

There was a letter, too, but they were both too stunned to pick it up.

Gwen recovered first. "I'm not hallucinatin'? You can see it, too? That lottery figure?"

"Yes," Rosemary croaked, cleared her throat and tried again. "Yes."

"So, ah. So what did you actually do for Robert Talbot—in a month—to deserve this? I mean . . ."

Rosemary's fingers had begun working again, so she opened the letter.

"It's lots of things, the main one is six-month's pay. Bits for holiday pay, a bonus, a special allowance . . ."

"So it's real?"

"It's real."

"The others would have got the same?"

"Six-months pay? Yes, I suppose . . ."

"They all would have been on sixty grand a year, too? Do you suppose that, too?"

"No, I . . . I think Debby mentioned she was getting thirty-three . . .

Hey! Get off my back! This has happened—I didn't ask for it. God knows I didn't expect it. But . . ." Rosemary snatched the cheque and kissed its back, leaving a clear, pink lipstick mark.

"But . . . !"

Bobby came in with coffee and cake and observed his mother in tears again.

"Well," he said when Gwen had explained, "you lose one, you win one!"

"One door closes, another one opens," said Gwen.

"A stitch in time saves nine," said Rosemary giggling through tears. "Now is the time for all good men to come to the aid of the party. Shut up and let's eat cake!"

.   .   .

Later, propped up by a pile of lacy pillows on her bed, Rosemary did some sums. Insurance from the crashed Volvo would be about twenty thousand dollars, so, with her kissed cheque, there would be more than fifty thousand and a rent-free house. Phyl could go back to her school and Rosemary need only get a part-time job.

A job in film production! She had the contacts now. She knew the foundations, and her stage-managing experience would surely help. She could start humbly and learn the steps. Maybe I'll finish the communications course part-time if they'll let me, she thought. There won't be time to go to university, but I can read history on my own—I don't have to stop doing research.

She'd learn and think and plan and look for gaps and opportunities. She dropped the pen on her stomach and leaned back on the pillows, smiling at her life. It had been a ladder after all, not a footstool. A lovely, tall one that she'd leapt to over that abyss of pain and loss. In fact, it was more like a tree than a ladder, with lots of strong branches from what she could now see was a well-rooted main trunk. It was hard to see what all the branches offered, but the main one, she was sure, would take her into film making.

She sighed contentedly as the Sandford movie's first scenes played themselves in her mind as though she were already watching it on the big screen. *The Wrought-Iron Rose,* she'd call it. The credits would roll over Clarice, sad-eyed, sweet-mouthed, sitting just as she was in the portrait. When the camera tracked back, it would reveal that the chair she was sitting on was at a dining-room table piled with all her father's papers. She'd pick one up and read it, voice-over, and start telling the story of what had happened all those years before.

The images were so clear that they hardly seemed like a product of

Rosemary's own imagination, and quickly, in case she lost them just as easily, she snatched up a pen and started making notes. She felt reborn— a vulnerable feeling but wonderfully exciting. And, despite the fact that Gwen had pointed out that the money Talbot had given her—which of course he had—was only ten percent of the value of the house he'd caused her to lose, she also felt rich. No money had ever actually been hers before.

"Blood money," Auntie Gwen had said.

"Ah, yes. But not my blood."

She wished the phone was working so she could phone Phyl at Patrick's house instead of waiting for Andy to bring her home. Patrick would be pleased.

Later, when Rosemary was taking her lenses out, her blurred reflection said, You've been bought.

Well, she answered boldly, this is the twentieth century.

.   .   .

Gwen had not planned to stay the night, but when she heard that Rosemary was taking Bobby to photograph the Darlinghurst house she said she'd drive them there in the morning, no problem. She wanted to see it, too.

On the way in the car Rosemary talked enthusiastically about how the house was going to be. Ideas had been percolating since her last visit and she was eager to see it again—to see if, for instance, by moving the staircase at right angles, the pokey little livingroom could be extended.

"If it can go past where the kitchen is now, we can build a nice, bright little dining room and a decent kitchen and laundry beyond that. Or perhaps I can turn it around so that the living room is at the back and opens up into the back garden."

"No point telling us until we've seen what you're talking about. But who's got the money for that sort of wall-bashing, rebuilding, folderol? Not Lawrie Stewart! Anything he's got's pinched from the social security is my bet. You just plan something reasonable and sensible, that's if you're determined to go ahead with this silliness; you could rent a perfectly nice house somewhere on a bus route and give yourself some peace."

"But it wouldn't be hard to do, and then the bathroom could . . ."

"Listen, Mrs. Rockefeller, I know this nice young architect chappie whose mother used to be a customer at the shop. He's a sensible bloke, not full of yuppie hogwash. I'll send him over to have a word, OK? That is, if the area is habitable!"

Nevertheless, Rosemary must have managed to generate a lot of positive images about the house, otherwise Bobby would not have been so appalled by the reality. He swore, he whined, he had to be yelled at to come inside. He refused to take pictures.

"It's like a horror movie," he said. "We can't live here! We can't!" Rosemary tried to be kind, but he determinedly shook off her cuddles as well as her reasonableness until she felt her temper start, at which point she removed herself from his self-pity.

Gwen was politely speechless about the house, and Rosemary realised that her memory had glossed over the worst of it. It was indeed, as she'd told Lawrie on the phone, a sow's ear.

"You're out of your mind," Gwen said finally, peering into a kitchen cupboard and then slamming it quickly.

"I still think the back garden's going to be the best part of it," Rosemary said, desperately clinging to her positive feelings. "Gardenias, an umbrella, let's have a look—I haven't been out there yet. The puppy Patrick's giving Bobby would be happy here."

Bobby went out first. Then he jerked with horror, screamed, and pushed past them in a struggling, grey-faced rush out of the house. There was a dead cat, black, its abdomen bloated, its legs stiff. A froth of maggots poured out of its eyes and open mouth.

Bobby was vomiting in the front, holding the fence with one hand and his stomach with the other. Tears and snot trickled down his face. Two passing youths with safety pins through their ears and slashed leather jerkins over their bare chests grinned and made remarks about adding some water to it—this was an area where few people would be surprised to find an eleven-year-old drunk in the middle of the morning.

Gwen was disgusted with him and made no bones about it, and Rosemary was glad when Gwen left them with promises to "launder the lottery money" and instructions to keep in touch daily at least 'til there was a bloomin' phone.

"Rotten bastards!" Gwen said, revving up the street, and Rosemary was not sure whether she meant Telecom or the punks.

.   .   .

Rosemary took Bobby, cleaned up and subdued, to a nearby natural food restaurant for a restorative glass of freshly squeezed carrot juice and a whole wheat bun. He said he'd die rather than live in that terrible house and that he was sick of being pushed around and that the world sucked plus a whole lot more, to all of which Rosemary replied as nicely as she could. But her niceness seemed to make him behave even more badly; at one stage he nudged her quite hard—and, she was sure, deliberately—on her still-tender arm.

"Look," she said—they were on the sidewalk, hoping for a taxi—"I've had just about enough of you!" And she gave his shoulder a shake. He yelled and semi-swooned as though it was still newly sunburnt there.

"Belt up!" she hissed. "You ruddy little ham!"

They maintained a chill silence in the car which she had directed to Wynyard station. Then, "Here," she said, and gave Bobby a ten dollar note, the smallest in her purse. "I've got to go to the tax office and Corporate Affairs. You hop on a train here to Circular Quay—or walk there, it's only a few blocks. Catch the ferry to Mosman and the bus home. And I sincerely hope that by the time I get back you'll have snapped out of this rude, spoiled-brat behaviour. Because, though everything that's happened isn't your fault, it isn't mine either!"

Bobby took the money without a word.

.　　　.　　　.

It was hot and humid in the city and full of mums pushing strollers, flanked by school-age kids who were now on their long school holidays. Rosemary wondered why they didn't all go to the beach on such a day instead of struggling on and off buses and trying to keep five-year-olds from darting into the traffic. Then she realised the attraction: the big department stores were full of sales and Hyde Park was full of Festival of Sydney events especially for kids. The mothers had come as a force, eager as ants to the sugar bowl. They seemed to outnumber the light-suited men and bright-cotton-dressed women who worked in offices and to whom the city belonged for most of the rest of the year.

Poor Bobby, she thought. I could have taken him there for an hour and then had lunch with him in the Botanic Gardens. I'm not much of a mother.

.　　　.　　　.

It had taken Rosemary ages to find the right office at Corporate Affairs and then it turned out that one of the documents was not quite right: something else had to be signed, so she had to wait while a slow clerk prepared yet another official form with a title she could not distinguish from any of the multitude she'd signed in the past weeks.

All these people who worked here, dealing in bankruptcies and takeovers and the other results of living experimentally, looked very secure, she thought. Probably no one in this office had ever been fired. But she would not have swapped places, she told herself, despite their pitying glances. It had begun to feel good to be Rosemary Quilty, back to the wall.

When she got home at four she headed straight for the bathroom, calling Bobby while she turned on the taps. She checked his room in case he'd fallen asleep reading, but he was not there, so she decided he'd probably gone to visit Scott or one of his other friends, and she lay back in the bath to soak.

At six, when Andy brought Phyl home, Rosemary had just tested the phone again, hoping it had been magically restored. "I wanted to phone around—see where Bobby's visiting. He was supposed to come straight here, but we had the snarls in the city, so I guess he's cooling off with a friend."

"I'd drive Phyl around to see but . . ."

"No, no, Andy. I know you've got to work. Thanks anyway—he'll be back." But he wasn't by seven.

By eight Rosemary had relived the entire quarrel from the time of the dead cat. Then from the previous day. Then from Boxing Day. Bobby had been building up to something and she hadn't recognised the seriousness of the signs.

At nine-thirty she went to Tom and Eve's to phone Patrick because it suddenly occurred to Phyl that that's where he'd be. But he wasn't, and Patrick hadn't heard from him.

"I'd come over but I can't leave Geoff—he's still not sleeping well since his cold, and it's too late to get anyone to sit now. But we'll come in the morning, first thing," Patrick said. "Bobby will be back by then, you'll see." But he sounded neither convinced nor convincing.

She phoned Gwen, who was already in bed, but who said she'd come over right away no worries and to let the police know just in case. Rosemary refused to think of "just in case" or of the way the cat looked. Or of how little Bobby was, really, despite his sturdy build. Or of the thousands of people who'd been pushing their way through the lunch time city. Who'd know if there was one less?

The desk sergeant to whom she spoke from Tom's phone was sympathetic but not overly concerned. "He had ten dollars? Probably in George Street, playing pin-ball in one of the parlours. They get like that at that age." All the same he suggested she bring a photograph of Bobby around to the station and give all the information she could about what he was wearing when last seen and so on.

Tom drove her to the police station. She answered questions and talked fluently in a state of calm that bordered on catatonic, while all the time her mind writhed like the maggots in the cat's eye: Where? Where? What? Why? With whom? Where? Oh, Bobby, she begged. Be safe! Anything, anything else I can bear.

"Makes it difficult, no phone. Still we'll get in touch with Mr. Everingham if we hear anything. And we've got the address. You go home and get some sleep now, Mrs. Quilty."

Sleep?

Gwen had obviously broken all speed limits and was there, with every house light on, when Rosemary got home. She made Phyl take a sleeping pill and made a half-hearted attempt at offering Rosemary one, too.

"He said he'd rather die than live in that house," she told Gwen when Phyl at last succumbed.

"You didn't believe him then, so don't believe him now."

"It's Daniel, of course. That's what it's about."

"Mainly, I grant you."

"He sent him an unfeeling thing for his birthday, as you know— money, nothing personal, with a note Shirley must have written. And nothing at all, not even a phone call, at Christmas. It's hard to convince a kid that his father cares!" And suddenly they looked at each other, having come to the same conclusion at the same instant.

"Kirribilli!" said Gwen. "Come on, I'll take you."

"No, you can't. I don't know where she—they—live. Bobby does, though—he's been there a few times. Oh, and Phyl does!"

They struggled to wake her, but when they did she was too groggy to remember the street name. "Quite near the Harbour Bridge," she said and fell peacefully asleep again, believing they'd said they'd definitely located him. Actually, they both felt they had, too, and so both had some fractured sleep.

"I've got Shirley Coote's home number—I'll get Daniel's address from her," Rosemary said at six in the morning. "This is an emergency— she'll have to give it to me." So Gwen drove her to a public telephone, it being too early to disturb Tom and Eve again. Rosemary wished she'd thought of asking them for Lucy's key the night before—that would have given easy access to a phone.

There was a recorded message machine on Shirley's phone. How could anyone have left for work so early? Rosemary thought in amazement, waiting for the tone.

"This is Rosemary Quilty," she said. "This is urgent, so please listen. My son, Bobby, did not come home last night and I am sure he is at Daniel's place. I don't know the address and my telephone has been cut off. Please get him to phone Eve Everingham or the desk sergeant— either of them will get a message to me." She gave the numbers.

"Did you eat last night?" Gwen asked.

"Probably not. I'm not hungry."

"Rubbish! You'll burn yourself out," she said and drove home for scrambled eggs and muffins, which Rosemary chewed and swallowed in anger, thinking about what she'd say to Bobby when Daniel brought him through the door. But after breakfast she became anxious again— it was just a guess, after all. Daniel might not even be there. Or Shirley Coote might be away on holiday, in which case he would never get the message. Anyway, why would Daniel need a message? He should know— should have known last night—how worried she'd be. He'd have phoned the Everinghams then, or brought Bobby home.

But then Bobby might have lied and said Rosemary knew where he was. He might have laid it on and said Rosemary had thrown him out. Or Bobby may never even have gone there at all.

Calm down. Calm down, she told herself.

"I can't bear this! I've got to do something," she said, pushing away the coffee Gwen offered.

"Well, take my car and go and see whether the police have any news. If they do, it'll be good—they wouldn't have minded waking Tom and Eve for bad."

The station-wagon was jerky and bulky. Rosemary didn't like the brakes, but at least it was automatic.

"Nope," said the desk sergeant, a different person. "No news. We'd have let you know, Mrs. Quilty, good or bad, believe me." From there Rosemary drove through the heavy early morning traffic to the houses of three of Bobby's friends. James's family was still away, but Scott's and Tristan's offered useless help and solace which detained her. She used Tristan's mother's phone to check with Eve for messages and was unreasonably angry when there was no reply. A block away from Tristan's family's sympathy, she parked the car under a tree—at ten o' clock it was hot already—and lay her head on her arms on the steering wheel.

This is something you will have to face, she told herself. It can happen. It has happened to other families.

No! It was unfaceable.

It was while scrabbling in her bag for a Kleenex that she found Daniel's keys. They had lived in the bottom of her bag since Bobby dived and retrieved them, one by one, from the pool. And instantly she set off for the North Sydney building where Patchwork PR had had its offices.

Daniel's Magic Button key still operated the electric gate to the underground parking bay though their four reserved spots now had other names on them. But she used one, anyway—the place was half-empty.

A handwritten note was stuck over the Patchwork name and logo on the office door, referring callers to the liquidators offices. She knocked loudly, just in case, and then let herself in to what looked like a struck film set.

It was a shock, even though, logically, it was hardly a surprise. Files, books, and documents were piled in heaps and were obviously being packed into cardboard boxes, a huge flattened stack of which lay in a corner waiting to be assembled. The furniture was higgledy-piggledy and nearly everything bore a string-tied label, like Paddington Bear. Only one desk still stood, with a phone on it, a lamp, and a stack of letters with crossed-out addresses. Someone was redirecting the post that arrived, obviously in no hurry since nearly all of these were bills, lawyers' letters, or other trouble.

Most of the envelopes had been re-addressed to the liquidator, but one—and her belly wrenched in the shock of recognition—was Bobby's Christmas card. And it had been re-addressed to the flat in Kirribilli by whoever had started the job and then got bored or had been called away. Of course Bobby would send it to the office! He knew how to get to Angela's place, having been taken there. But, like Phyl, he wouldn't have noted the address. Rosemary snatched the envelope and ran.

.   .   .

It was an old grey-stone building in a tree-lined avenue off Carabella Street. Once a mansion, it had been tastefully converted into three flats of which number three was approached down a neatly raked side path to its own little garden.

Angela opened the door. Angela pale and dishevelled in a white towelling dressing-gown much too big for her, hardly recognisable as the elegantly intoxicated beauty who had collapsed in Daniel's arms and taken him away from his wife. And hardly recognisable as Sybil, the lovely, energy-charged heroine of "The Mount Victorians." She looked like a white rabbit. With high cheek-bones.

But this was just a fleeting impression for Rosemary, who pushed past her into the flat calling wildly, "Bobby! Bobby! Where are you?" It was only when there was no reply that she turned to look at Angela, who had backed away, obviously afraid of her. A glance in the mirror tiled wall showed her why—she was frenzied, dishevelled, crazed. With worry—but it's hard to tell that from the other kind. So Rosemary made herself calm down.

"He's not here. Daniel got your message an hour ago and left immediately."

"Where to?"

"To look for him. Your house. I don't know—he just ran out."

They stared at each other in wonder, these two women who had figured, by default, so prominently in each other's lives. Rosemary suddenly had no idea what to do.

"Oh, oh, excuse me!" Angela covered her mouth with her hand, and as she lurched past on the way to the bathroom, her body was silhouetted against the light of the open front and Rosemary saw that she was pregnant. And saw, in her frantic distraction about Bobby, the shape, in that rounded belly, of the answer to all the questions about Daniel.

The poor bastard! she thought. He's done it again!

Angela was quite big already—she shouldn't still be throwing up, Rosemary thought. When had Daniel come and yelled about Rosemary trapping him into marriage? July? August? How ironic. He hadn't got very far with his oats-sowing.

These were all fleeting impressions, ideas that filled the tiny spaces between the waves of her terror for Bobby—terror that made her hands shake, which made it difficult to dial Eve's number. It was the obvious thing to do while Angela was in the bathroom, but Eve's phone rang and rang.

I must go, she thought urgently. Must go! I must be there! Bugger Eve—no one knows where I am! She picked up her bag. "I'm going back to my house," she called out to Angela, who had been in too much of a hurry to close the bathroom door and who could now be seen leaning, wilted, over the basin, wiping her face. "When you hear from Daniel, please get him to come around immediately—my phone doesn't work."

And then she heard footsteps—Daniel's?—crunching on the gravel. And then, as Angela, suddenly wild-eyed with anxiety, a towel still at her mouth, made for the door, Robert Talbot came in.

He flinched in shock when he saw Rosemary. Then, smooth as a poker player, he said, "Well, Mrs. Quilty!"

But he couldn't bluff Rosemary—she understood it all. She was soaked in a sudden tidal wave of understanding that left her gasping, unable to speak.

"Her child is lost. She thought he was here," Angela said, sounding apologetic.

Rosemary found her breath. "Poor bloody Daniel!" she sneered. "No wonder you killed his company. It's a wonder you didn't pay someone to kill him! What do you do, Mr. Robert Talbot, hover around in your car, waiting for an all-clear phone call?"

They didn't look guilty at all or even uncomfortable but simply puzzled, looking at Rosemary's furious face. Then Robert Talbot laughed, but it was surprise rather than humour.

"She thinks I'm your lover," he said. He and Angela looked at each other: she tense, steadying herself on a chair back, he frowning deeply as though hypnotising her, or transferring a message. In fact he was simply making an inevitable decision.

"I'm Angela's father," he said to Rosemary, and then crossed over and took his limp child's arm. "It's not widely known."

.   .   .

It was the main piece in the giant jigsaw puzzle—one Rosemary had not even been aware she was doing. Actually, it was more like a section than a piece—a section constructed at another part of the jigsaw table, full of bits she'd been searching for, and suddenly, click, click, it fitted in to her part, joining earth and sky and making sense of the scenery. There were more pieces to fit, but it was obvious, now, where they would go. It was not important anymore. All there was now was Bobby, and dread.

She had not stayed any longer than it took to try Eve's number again and phone the police for news. Robert Talbot had tried to talk to her, to urge her to keep her discovery confidential. People could be hurt, he said, it was important.

"Yes, yes," she'd said, going for the door. "Can I phone you later? I can't think of anything now except Bobby." She didn't have time to say that people had already been hurt—she was one of them. He knew that, anyway.

He held her arm as she hurried to the car and gave her a private number that could find him anywhere, any time. He squeezed her shoulders with one big arm. He looked as though he'd like to say a whole lot more than, "You really mustn't worry—you'd have heard by now if the news was bad."

"But nobody knows where I am!"

"No. You go then. Drive carefully!" he said.

I should have thanked him for the money, she thought as she drove away, and was glad he'd given her his phone number.

There was odd, unwelcome knowledge which intruded into her concentration on Bobby. Robert Talbot's secret had simultaneously given her power and made her vulnerable in a particular way. But this was something to deal with later.

Bobby. There was something she could do, surely? Something obvious, something that had to be done, now, to save him. But what? She had the helpless knowledge that valuable time was being lost while she fumbled around in wrong directions. Oh, Lord! she thought. I haven't phoned the hospitals!

There was a new fear, lurking like the first thunder-clouds on the horizon—it was the knowledge of her own real boundaries. All the events that had pushed and stretched her in the past year had been painful but ultimately bearable. Only two days ago she had been rejoicing, believing that they'd been necessary. But now, she knew, the fabric of her self was very thin. Her elasticity had gone beyond the stretch point, so that if Bobby . . . no, she could not say it. She simply understood that the loss of her child would be what she could not bear.

Twenty-four hours gone and not a word! Every week there were stories about children of his age in Kings Cross: runaways, sick with the heroin habit, prostituting themselves to pederasts with twenty dollars to spare. Of course Bobby wouldn't be hooked so quickly but . . . Sydney's beautiful, beautiful face could never hide its very ugly streak. Rosemary had to keep pushing images of the dead cat from her mind's screen. She'd heard about child hitch-hikers picked up by friendly looking drivers who later turned out to have been escaped killers. Bobby! Bobby! She said his name like a litany to kill thoughts like this. She blotted out the visions of his hurt or lifeless body with images of him as a baby, earnestly catching sunbeams with his pink, sea-creature fingers. Her baby!

It took twenty minutes to drive home. If she had not needed her eyes for driving she'd have buried her head in her lap to blot out the necessary distance.

It was eleven-thirty when she got home and the door was locked.

"Gwen! Phyl!" she called, banging with her fist, jangling the bell. How could they not be there? They must be at the police station or a hospital or . . . or . . .

She was fumbling for her key, starting to cry in fear and frustration, when the golden bus rolled up, and—Patrick blew the horn to alert her—there Bobby was in the front seat. He opened the door and jumped out before Patrick had quite stopped. And then Rosemary simply went limp, half fell against the door, and ended up sitting on the step. He was alive. And whole. Nothing else mattered.

Alone and ashamed, Bobby walked to her and stood a little way off. "I'm sorry, Mum," he said, almost too quietly to hear, then he half dived, half tumbled into her arms and she hugged him and hugged him, and rocked and sobbed with relief and gratitude.

"Hey, don't suffocate the kid now that you've got him back safe." Gwen laughed and helped Bobby to extricate himself. Patrick helped Rosemary up.

"Where . . . where were you?" she asked Bobby. It was difficult to talk.

"Where did you find him?" she asked Patrick. She had begun to tremble; he had not let go her hand.

"At Lawrie's." Patrick looked surprised. "Gwen told you in the note."

"The note?"

He and Gwen looked at each other. "You've just got back? You didn't know he was OK until now?"

"No. I've been all over . . ."

"My word, Rosemary!" Gwen said, as though in anger, opening the door as she spoke. "You've tortured yourself half the day for nothing!"

The good-news note was stuck on the hall mirror.

"I phoned Lawrie early this morning on the off-chance," said Patrick. "His number was on one of the pamphlets he lent me. Bobby had caught the train to Gosford—didn't you, you dummy?" Bobby looked ashamed, though it was well-worn shame now: between Lawrie, Phyl, Gwen, and Patrick he'd obviously had a night and a day of haranguing.

"He phoned Lawrie from Gosford station to pick him up," Patrick continued. "Lawrie couldn't phone you, but he planned to do something this morning through Daniel. He didn't think of the police."

"I'd say he'd rather not think of the police," Gwen murmured for Rosemary's benefit, but her eyes twinkled. It was obvious that she'd survived the trip in good spirits.

Patrick continued talking to Rosemary as though they were the only people there. "As soon as I'd spoken to Lawrie, I came straight here, but you had just gone," he said.

On a wild-goose chase, she thought. And I trapped the golden goose. What she said was, "I was looking for Daniel."

"Well, that hunt's over now, too, by the look," said Gwen.

Rosemary didn't recognise the car, but Bobby had already hurtled down the drive and into his father's arms.

Twenty

Had the Hermanns not been skiing at Aspen they would have observed part of the closing scene in Rosemary Quilty's marriage to Daniel. Like all melodrama it could have ended on a serious note, but the ending remained true to the beginning by containing some of the elements of farce.

They'd have seen Geoff hurl himself, fully dressed, into the simmy poo'. He was immediately followed by Andy and then Phyl—would-be rescuers who soon found that swimming in denim jeans made them more of a liability than an aid. So Patrick had taken off his watch, removed his wallet from the pocket of his shorts, and dived in, too, to help all three of them pull their outer garments off under the water.

Bobby, who had achieved his ambition to see his father, was shivering, as he always did in the presence of strong emotion, and Daniel, who had followed the fuss to the side of the pool, stood him close to his side.

"Who's he?" Daniel asked, tipping his chin towards the tall man in the water who was at that moment lessening the danger of Phyl's drowning by courteously peeling her heavy, water-logged denims off while she giggled shyly, hanging on tightly to the side with one hand and very tightly to her knickers with the other.

"Patrick. Friend of ours. He's got his own zoo," said Bobby.

"I'm not surprised."

Rosemary sat on the patio swing, still too shaken to talk. Daniel looked mauled. His face was blotchy and his eyes smaller, as though partially lost in puffed tissue. Bobby looked like Bobby—awkward in the transition from boy to youth, his newly muscled limbs not fully under his control. He looked alive, tentatively cheeky, and most of all happy that he'd succeeded in getting what he wanted, which was his father's undivided, volunteered attention. He'd got it, despite the cost. Already Rosemary could feel the first percolations of anger at Bobby for making her suffer so.

Now she simply watched them, these two whose visible similarities were accentuated by certain distinct differences in gesture, stance, hairstyle and skin texture, and observed them talk to each other. Not the words—she didn't hear the words. But through the haze of her settling emotions she watched the process of body language. First Bobby's arms unfolded, then his eyes stopped avoiding Daniel's, then both of them half turned and leaned slightly towards each other. She saw Bobby smile—a quick, head ducking smile, but enough for Daniel to look relieved and to stroke his son's hair and neck and pull him closer to his side. The whole process took three minutes.

"But Dad, why didn't you come at Christmas? Or phone?" Rosemary heard Bobby say.

"I did phone, twice at Christmas. Nobody answered. I guessed you were all out gallivanting. Then Lawrie said you'd be there so I went to MacMasters to see you on Boxing Day and you'd left. With the zoo keeper."

"You haven't met Dr. Price yet," Rosemary said coolly, surprised to find herself quite ready to deal with Daniel and Patrick in the same frame. "In my bag," she said to Bobby, "is the Christmas card you sent your Dad. He never got it—it was in still in his office."

This was intended as a comforting explanation and so she was a little surprised when Bobby gasped and dashed off to the front of the house where her handbag still lay. Bobby's dash meant, though, that he did not hear his father's equally surprised gasp.

"The office?"

"I was looking for you. I thought Bobby was with you. I've still got your keys—the ones that . . ." She indicated the pool, where Patrick, having finished his life-saving program, was creating other noisy diversions with a large, coloured ball. Geoff, she could see, was like a porpoise in the water, more agile, more graceful than he ever could be when defying dry gravity. "Come and meet Patrick and the boys. Then we'll go inside and have some tea or something—we can't talk here."

"I don't want to go inside," said Daniel. In his position she would have felt the same way. "I'll take you to the village—we'll have some coffee there," he said, walking to the pool edge.

Patrick saw them coming and heaved himself out of the pool. His hair had made a gutter over his eyes which were already red and half blinded by the chlorine, but he didn't seem to mind the disadvantage up, and I should have been out of the shit before Christmas. But that bastard Talbot got to him, too, in some way. Hell, the whole thing was a game to him."

Tears of pity for Daniel followed the as yet invisible but very definite tracks down Rosemary's cheeks—tracks made by a year of crying.

"Ah, God, don't do that," Daniel said, grasping both her hands.

She shook her head and sniffed. "It's OK." She freed one hand to wipe her face and after a moment freed the other one, too: the one on the arm that had been broken and which still ached a little if held at a bad angle.

"How far is Angela?" she asked, to change the subject. It was strange to think that her children would soon have a relative unconnected with herself.

"Nearly six months. I must phone her—she'll be worried sick," he said, and looked at his watch again and started the car. Was what she felt jealousy? Rosemary didn't think so. Perhaps it was envy for the depth of loyalty Daniel obviously had for Angela. He had never been so protective of Rosemary. But then, their relationship had never been exposed to such intense heat and pressure. She glanced at Daniel, this familiar person, this stranger beside her. He and Angela were probably indivisible now, their relationship smelted like steel. Surely even Robert Talbot could see that.

Just a few hundred years ago, she thought, for a king to have a bastard child would have been a comparatively casual matter—perhaps even a matter of pride. But people like Robert Talbot—kings of the twentieth-century business world—would have to appear to be saints—matrimonially, anyway. However, it would be impossible, in a close, gossip-based city like Sydney, to keep a fact like the existence of a love-child entirely secret. Angela's mother, whoever she was, would almost certainly have had at least one confidante.

Angela herself would hardly have been able to keep such a secret from other children, so it was more likely that she'd found out about it when she was grown up. Perhaps hers was a childhood like the little girl's in *Daddy Long Legs*—an anonymous benefactor providing the best schooling, best clothing, best trips, and elocution lessons—her mother bribed by largesse into silence.

Perhaps, when Angela finally met her father, he asked her what she wanted to do with her life. Rosemary imagined the scene. "I'd like to be an actress," she'd have said. "Right, I'll put you in a mini-series," he'd have replied and bullied his way past his producers and directors.

of being wet and shirtless. He smiled widely while scraping his face with one wet hand and shook Daniel's dry hand with the other as though this was any ordinary poolside meeting. Daniel, in his natty weekend gear that made him look like a yachtsman, smiled more formally.

"I've been hearing a lot about you," Daniel said. It was a provocative, dishonest remark and Rosemary tensed. But Patrick simply raised an eyebrow and looked cheerful.

"All I know about you is that you've got great kids," he said.

The secret language of men, Rosemary thought, fascinated. Daniel thought I've been telling Patrick all about him and Patrick has lyingly reassured him.

"Daniel is taking me for a cup of coffee," Rosemary explained, loudly enough for Phyl and Gwen as well as Patrick to hear. "I won't be long."

Phyl turned in the pool and looked steadily first at Rosemary and then at Daniel, who, apart from a quick hug and kiss, had not spoken to her yet.

"You get dry and dressed while we're gone, darling," Rosemary said. "I'm sure Dad wants to talk to you, too." She noticed Daniel glance at his watch. Bugger you! she thought.

Gwen, standing on the porch with a tea-towel in her hand and a look of loathing on her face said, "Just you be careful with that woman, Daniel Quilty!"

He hunched his shoulders and pretended not to hear.

·   ·   ·

"Seems like a nice enough bloke, that Patrick," Daniel said as they reached the car—Angela's sleek, sporty white Honda Prelude.

"You approve of your children's admirer, then?"

Don't give me that, his look said.

"You broke my arm, you know," she said.

"Yes. Angela phoned the hospital."

"Aren't you going to say 'sorry'?"

"Oh, God," he said, and sighed. "Sorry is all I seem to be able to say nowadays." They were driving slowly in no special direction, since Daniel had decided he didn't want coffee after all. After a while he pulled up under a tree in a quiet street and switched off the engine, which was OK—it was near enough to walk home if necessary, she observed.

"It's been worse than the worst nightmare for the kids and me. I don't know how we'd have got through the last six or seven weeks without Gwen. But part of the worst of it was not being able to understand why you were behaving so terribly . . ."

"You were the one who wouldn't communicate," Daniel interrupted.

"Yes, in the beginning. I was too mad with you. And—hurt. But it suited you, didn't it? You wouldn't have been able to keep it all secret."

"What do you mean?" Daniel tried to keep his face expressionless, but she knew him well enough to see through the careful mask.

"What I mean is I know, now, that Robert Talbot is Angela's father."

He looked frightening for the long moment that he glared at her, cross-examining her with his eyes. Then suddenly he relaxed as though a torturer had switched off an electric current, and dropped back to the head-rest behind him.

"He told you?"

"Well, yes. But only because he had to. He walked in while I was at Angela's place."

Daniel sat up again.

"What the hell were you doing there?"

"Looking for Bobby, of course. I thought he'd gone there. Gwen would have taken me last night, but I didn't have the address. I found it this morning, at Patchwork; someone had half re-addressed a pile of post, including the Christmas card from Bobby, and I got the address from that."

"I hope you didn't go upsetting Angela. She's been very sick."

"I probably did a bit. I don't think she knew who I was at first. But she's in good hands.

"You'd know, wouldn't you?"

"From observation only, Daniel. Please don't start that nonsense again—there has been no collusion between Robert Talbot and me. I felt terribly guilty for a while because I'd blathered to him about the casino. But afterwards I realised he'd known anyway."

Then suddenly, from somewhere deep, Rosemary remembered an important detail from that dramatic Friday night when Robert's Talbot's tiny kiss had sent her crashing into the rock garden—a memory that had been obliterated by shock, confusion, pain. Or was it by the simple desire not to know? She had got up—the children were right. She'd brushed her teeth and taken her lenses out and heard Daniel yelling into the phone to Angela. Now, here it was, the dirty little pile of words: "Why the fuck," Daniel had yelled, "did you tell him about the casino?"

I've known all along, Rosemary thought, and shivered. I needn't have felt so guilty. But she knew she sounded quite calm as she said, "And had Angela told him about the casino?"

"I guess not. They weren't having anything to do with each other. But he was trying to break me, so there'd have been people reporting back to him from all over the place. I probably didn't mak[…] didn't know about during the whole of last year, but it too[…] time to catch on to what he was doing. It seemed insane!" D[…] exhausted.

"It's been even worse for you," she murmured, shaken […] insight.

He nodded briefly. "Yeah, probably."

If Daniel had been free to marry Angela, Robert Talbot […] stopped trying to ruin him. He would have had to accept his […] choice, and accept that Daniel was serious about her. Daniel […] been under pressure from Angela, too, to speed up a divo[…] divorce was not possible without a property settlement, and […] settlement was not possible while Talbot was bankrupting P[…] Daniel had been faced with the intolerable options of fighting […] battle against Talbot while Angela, pregnant, became increa[…] secure, or of giving in and handing Patchwork over, which w[…] have felt, to him, like selling his own child.

Poor, pressured Daniel. There would have been strong, su[…] sure, from Angela, who was undoubtedly unused to having t[…] get her own way. And there would have been pressure ot[…] mishandled and which had backfired into more pressure—the c[…] company, for instance, which had grabbed the house. Worst o[…] the pressure of being publicly humiliated by his rich, powerful[…] And everything, all the pressure, had magnified quickly, becaus[…] don't wait.

His clients were deserting him, one after the other. He wo[…] have known whom to trust. She could understand, now, why he[…] crazy when he saw her kissing Robert Talbot and crazier still wl[…] red roses arrived—perhaps she was lucky that he only broke he[…]

"What I want to know is where the hell did you go? After you[…] broke my arm you just vanished. Shirley only ever told me as l[…] possible. That's one person who's still loyal to you."

"Yeah. She's a good kid." Daniel sighed as one who knew […] weren't many. "To Melbourne, mainly, then other places."

"To raise capital, Shirley said. But you were away for weeks[…] meantime the newspapers were speculating that you'd taken mone[…] run out."

"There's a bloke I know in Melbourne with a nice-sized ad ag[…] who'd been talking to me about a merger, and that would have […] everything, I thought. We'd got it together—the contracts were d[…]

No wonder Michael Stoner was angry when Rosemary arrived at Lithgow to audition for a part—yet another inexperienced, unknown female of Talbot's choosing!

But Angela had turned out to be good at it. So why had she stopped acting? Perhaps they'd quarrelled, she and the new dad who'd played so small a role in her life when she was a needy little child and who, now that she'd survived into independence, was trying to control her. So perhaps she simply went and found a more secure job in the supposedly glamorous world of public relations and thumbed her nose at her father.

It made sense—he would have been trying to woo her back, wean her away from Daniel, by pressing on into the next series of "The Mount Victorians." "You'll have to come back," his actions would have been saying. "You're vital to the plot. And anyway, that man, that married man, is going to be poor and powerless—I'm seeing to that!"

Poor bloody Daniel! she thought. You sowed your oats in a nest of spiders.

"When did you find out Robert Talbot was Angela's father?" she asked.

"In January. Actually, on the day of that bloody anniversary party, which was why she was so stirred up. She'd told me at lunch-time."

They were silent for a while and Rosemary wondered if it had occurred to him that it would soon be their seventeenth anniversary. But he was thinking of other things: "Of course, from the moment I moved in with her the war was on between Talbot and me, though there was a time, in about May, when he offered to buy me."

"What would that have achieved?"

"Nothing much for me, I thought. The computer equipment had just arrived, and I was expecting it to be installed and running within the month, and I thought that would give me the edge. I figured that if he took over Patchwork I'd probably have been put out to pasture. I didn't trust him—he was too pissed off about me and Angela."

"It would have saved a lot of trouble if you'd joined him."

"Maybe. But I got out of the corporation mould when I was a kid!"

Stubborn bastard, she thought. You wanted everything! But she said, hoping it didn't sound sarcastic, "A clash of titans, hey?"

Daniel did not reply.

"And when did Robert Talbot find out that Angela was pregnant?"

"November, probably, I forget. Anyway, too bloody late to make any difference—about the company and the house, I mean, Angela hadn't had anything to do with him for months—to us he just meant trouble—but he kept on trying to find ways to get at us. I suppose that's why he latched on to you when he knew who you were."

"Yes," she said. "But that's not what you thought at the time!"

"No. Things weren't exactly rational then."

Meaning, you weren't exactly rational then. But neither was I, thought Rosemary. "So what happened next? How is it that you're . . . friendly now? Him popping in to see his future grandchild, having a cup of coffee. . . ."

"I don't know what went on in his head, Ro. Truly I don't. Maybe he just got sick of playing war games. But he dropped in one day on Angela, quite unexpectedly, and was nice to her. So she told him about the baby. He could see, anyway."

They turned into the driveway and stopped behind Patrick's bus.

"I must go," Daniel said. "Talbot's probably left by now and I don't like Angela to be alone. She's had a terrible time." None of your women have peaceful pregnancies, Rosemary thought. "This morning was supposed to have been a . . . a sort of peacemaking meeting: her, Talbot, and me. Then Shirley, who'd spent the night away from her flat, got back and your message was on the answering machine. And as soon as she phoned I left, to look for Bobby."

"Where did you go?"

"The boat club. He's been there a few times with me. I don't know why, but I thought he might have tried to find Angela's flat, forgotten where it was, and gone there instead, and fallen asleep in the old covered lifeboat the kids play in. When I got there I made a lot of phone calls—friends, police—you'd done all that. First I tried to phone you, of course. Then I finally reached Lawrie."

Rosemary understood things Daniel had not said: for the first time in months he'd put his son's safety before his own, and that was good. But he'd kept his concern private from Angela and made his anxious phone calls from the nearby club instead of from her flat.

Daniel made no move to get out of the car despite his expressed intention to phone Angela, and it occurred to Rosemary that it was some relief for him to be able to talk about the things that had obsessed him all year.

"What's going to happen to you now?" she asked, and was surprised by her own detachment—this was the man she'd been married to for nearly half her life, the man from whom she was not yet divorced and with whom there might still be a settlement fight in the courts. Yet she could ask him this quite politely.

"That's exactly what we were going to talk about this morning. We'll probably raise Patchwork from the ashes. Don't get your hopes up too high, but Talbot will probably take what's left of it over for a decent price—enough to pay the creditors and get it going again. He could get it for nothing now, of course—there's nothing of value there now."

"Except you."

"For what that's worth," he said, and covered his eyes with one hand. When he looked at her again they were red-rimmed. "God, I'm sorry, Ro. I've—I've fucked it up. Really fucked it up." It was true, and there was nothing she could say about that. She could not even focus on the hint he'd made that the house might yet be saved.

"So, now?" she asked.

He shrugged. "I've learned to know Robert Talbot better. He's not a bad bloke." Don't make me spell it out, his face implored. Don't make me tell you that of course I'll join him now. I'll be the son-in-law. In a gilded cage in the corridors of power. "I won't bother phoning," he said. "I'll just go." And he started the ignition, but Rosemary put out her hand.

"You can't possibly go without first talking to the kids—they're confused and hurt and if you just go off now it'll be the last straw, especially for Phyl."

"Phyl looks as though she's getting on fine with that boy-friend of yours. Bobby, too," he said. "They don't need me." But there was no conviction under the muttering, and he switched off the car and followed her to the front door.

"Jesus! What's happened here?" he asked, peering into the hall. "Where are all the paintings? You haven't sold them, have you?"

"Nope. They were dramatically rescued from the clutches of the liquidator. Ask Bobby to tell you—it'll brighten your day!"

He stood, like a museum visitor, staring around his former home. It made Rosemary feel uncomfortable. "Why don't you go over to Tom and Eve's to phone Angela?" she said. "And I'll go and fetch Phyl and Bobby."

.   .   .

All the swimmers except Geoff were sitting together having cool drinks on the back patio. He was jumping up and down flapping his elbows and imitating the magpies, though not in a way that sincerely threatened their calling pattern.

"Here's some more juice, you lot. And I've made chicken sandwiches," Gwen said from the kitchen door.

"Grab one each," said Rosemary, touching Phyl and Bobby with two hands like a papal blessing. "Daniel's gone next door to make a phone call, then its your turn for a drive in the jazzy car."

Bobby shot off immediately; Phyl held back. "I'm not hungry," she said.

"He's OK," Rosemary murmured for her only. "And I'm OK. And he really wants to talk to you. He's got some rather interesting news for you." So Phyl went, but slowly and without food reinforcements.

Geoff, having messily eaten two or three large sandwiches, was getting restless. He wanted to swing on the patio railing, which would have been all right if his body had been a four-year-old's, but he was at risk of damaging it and falling off. Rosemary didn't pay much attention—her head was still too full of the converstion with Daniel. It was Gwen who suggested that Andy take him to the rumpus room. "There's an exercise bike there, and some games. Come, I'll show you."

Patrick, shirtless, his shorts still damp, his skin cool, sat down next to Rosemary on the patio swing.

"Are you all right? You were away for nearly an hour."

"That long?" Lucy had once said that if you can talk peacefully for more than twenty minutes to someone you were once married to, you've recovered. "I'm perfectly fine, thanks. Perfectly!" Her smile incorporated relief, celebration, and good manners. "I haven't thanked you for fetching Bobby. You are the kindest man!"

"Don't thank me," Patrick said, trying to look at her face, but she turned away slightly.

"I do. I must. Fetching him was such a terrific thing to do! I was going crazy."

"It was a nice drive," he said, matching her light, social tone. "Nicer than the last one. But I just wish we hadn't rushed off this morning until you got back."

"But then Bobby would still be at MacMasters," she said reasonably, "And you would also have wasted the morning." Why do I hold so much back from him? she wondered. I found out about Robert Talbot and Angela. I came to terms with Daniel. It was one of the least-wasted mornings of my life!

He towelled his hair, which made the muscles on his chest and arms re-arrange themselves in ripples and bulges. He was too close again and she started to rise. But he held her back, one strong hand on her shoulder—"Don't go."

So she sat back, breathing lightly, controlling the desire to struggle free from the strong, long-fingered hand which stayed lightly on her arm.

"Gwen told me you've lost your job. She told me lots of things on the way to MacMasters."

"About the money?"

"Money?"

"My payout? For being axed."

"We didn't talk about money. It was mainly about that house in Darlinghurst. She doesn't like the idea of you living there with the kids— it's pretty rough, she says."

"She's a snob!" Rosemary laughed. "Someone threw a dead cat over the back fence, that's all. Do you think we're any safer here?"

"Of course you are. Even the burglars are friendly."

"You're as bad as Gwen!"

"She said that last night when you were talking to Phyl about the place she was full of bravado but that she's nervous about it, too."

"Gwen saw a few oddly dressed characters there, that's all. I'm convinced she's got a vision of night street scenes in Darlinghurst like something out of 'Miami Vice,' only with real blood. Little old ladies live there, for Pete's sake!"

"With barred windows!"

"Everyone's got barred windows in this world! One way or the other!" she said quickly. "Listen, do you know what Phyl really said? She said, I've got to learn to deal with guys, even weirdos. If anyone starts anything with me, I'll say, 'Sir, you've made a mistake. I am a Catholic aide at the Hospice over there. My job is laying out the dead.' I think that's terrific." She glared at Patrick. "Don't you think that's terrific?"

Why am I always losing my temper with this man? she asked herself, then didn't give herself enough time to answer because the next anger-backed accusation had already bubbled through: "Do you know what amazes me most? That you splashed around in the pool for all that time while I was talking to my former husband and you didn't even . . ." And then she dashed into the kitchen. What the hell was I going to say? she asked herself. Her hands were shaking.

It was bad luck for Bobby that he happened to walk in just then in search of a sandwich, looking pleased about whatever Daniel had said to him in the car. Bad luck because he was home again. Safe. Alive, cocky, greedy, and human.

"How dare you do that to me!" Rosemary demanded. "How dare you go away like that?" she shouted. She grabbed him and, though he was strong and though he struggled, she shook him until his head rattled.

"Hey, hey!" It was Patrick, who divided them with a forearm. "Hey!"

"Don't you ever again! You hear?" Rosemary said, still yelling at Bobby, while squirming in Patrick's grasp and breathing hard.

White-faced, Bobby nodded and backed into the interested group who had stuck their heads in from the rumpus room to watch. Gwen was one of them. She glanced at Rosemary and Patrick, grabbed Bobby with one hand, the plate of sandwiches with the other, shooed everybody out, and closed the door.

"That was a shitty thing to do," said Patrick. She had never seen him angry before—not in real life. The power he'd brought to the role of Big Daddy was there now—it seemed to enlarge him and solidify something about him that she'd always taken for diffidence. There was nothing diffident about this tall, firm-chinned, big-handed man whose voice had deepened with feeling. "You were mad with me and you took it out on Bobby!" he boomed.

So Rosemary yelled back. She told him to mind his own business and that she wanted to be free to find out what the real world was like and that she was sick of people—men—telling her how to run her life, sitting, watching and waiting, like trappers. And that she wanted to be a film producer and that she hated men who wore socks with sandals, and green pants with red shirts. And that he was not to look at her like that with his bloody finger on his lips. So he took his finger off his lips and kissed her and she hit him. So he grabbed her hands and after awhile she kissed him back.

"I wanted to offer you a job, that's all," he lied. It was a lie because she could feel, by the way that he was standing, that it wasn't all he had to offer. But talk was a way of restoring them to safer ground than the narrow, sharp-edged kitchen.

"A job. Assistant hydrologist?" She had to control her breathing.

"Decorator. Of my house."

"Your house?"

"I'd like to go up a storey and get more benefit from the view. Expand." He touched her face with delicate finger tips. "I want to make room for you and Phyl and Bobby"—she jerked away—"If you should ever decide to give suburbia another try. After you've conquered Darlinghurst."

"You don't take me seriously!"

"Aren't you glad?"

"Why glad?"

"Because if I took your bullshit seriously, we'd fight all the time."

"Bullshit?"

"About fifty per cent is bullshit. The other fifty percent I take very seriously." He kissed her again. "I must go," he said with some difficulty. "I've got some shopping I must do. Andy has agreed to stay with Geoff, but he's only got until six. Tomorrow night, have dinner with me? Then you can tell me whether you want the job." She cooled her hot face with her palms and hid the smile that struggled to reveal itself.

A little later, while scraping chicken bones into the kitchen bin, she saw the Christmas card to Daniel. Bobby had torn it up. "Merry Christmas, Dad," the pieces said. "Just a tip! If you want to make it up with Mum you'd better move fast because there's a guy called Dr. Patrick Price who I think will marry her if you don't come soon. Missing you! Love, Bobby."

She felt the way cattle must feel when their random grazing is organised into a direction by blue heelers nipping efficiently at their ankles.

.   .   .

She went over to Eve's house after lunch was cleared away, having seen her car pull into the drive. Ben and Mattie, noisy, happy, and lively, rushed in ahead to get to the fridge, since they hadn't eaten a thing for half an hour.

"What a fright you must have had with Bobby!" Eve said. "Little devil! I was so relieved when Phyl came over at breakfast time to tell me he was OK."

"I didn't know until nearly lunch time," said Rosemary. "It was a terrible morning. God, I'll never forget last night and today!"

"But why did it take so long for you to find out? They left you a note, didn't they?"

"Yes, but I only saw it after I saw Bobby. I'd been out, hunting for him. I kept trying to phone you."

"Oh, my goodness, I am sorry. When I heard he was safe, I took the monsters to the zoo. I didn't know . . ."

"Never mind. It's all fine now."

"Lucy's coming back sooner, did you know? Sunday—day after tomorrow, flying back instead of sailing. I think she's missing Mattie."

"No, that's great. Do you want me to meet her? I could take the station-wagon . . ."

"No, no thanks—Mattie wants to be at the airport at dawn in case the plane's early!"

"How has it been with Mattie—she's not a burden?"

"No more than usual." Eve smiled. "I shouldn't say that. She's a sweet little kid underneath some nonsense. And I suppose that applies to most

of us." Her eyes laughed, and Rosemary, for the first time since knowing
her neighbour, felt that she liked her. The spiteful edge had gone from
both of them.

"Do you want to lend me the kids for a swim before dinner? Or
tomorrow? I'm home now, so're Gwen and Phyl and Bobby, so they'll
be safe in the pool."

"Thanks. I'll keep it in mind if they start getting each other down—
or me. But there's a cooking session planned for this afternoon: we
bought biscuit cutters, chocolate drops, hundreds and thousands . . ."

Bobby, who had been avoiding Rosemary, ran over to say that the
telephone had rung—it was reconnected and they had a new number.
They walked back home together, both stiff at first, then Rosemary put
her arm around Bobby's shoulder and squeezed him.

"It was the worst time," she said. "It was terrible!"

"I know, Mum. I'm sorry. I made it OK to Lawrie's house— I wasn't
in any danger—so I just didn't think about how worried you'd be."

She rubbed his ear as they walked. "I thought you might have
been . . . dead. It really was the worst thing that has ever happened to
me."

"Worse than Dad going? And losing the house?"

"Much worse. There's nothing you can do about death."

"I . . . didn't think you'd even miss me," Bobby said, struggling to
keep the conversation light.

"Well, now you know. Now you know for sure, so you can make up
your mind never to do anything like that again, OK? You're my darling
child and I couldn't bear to lose you!"

"Ouch," he said, wriggling away from the intensity of her grip, but
she took hold of him again and there, in the middle of their street,
hugged the boy who had come to believe he was too big for that sort
of thing.

"If the damn phone had been connected yesterday . . ." she said, her
voice unevened by emotion.

"If it was, do you know what I'd have done? Phoned from Lawrie's
and asked if I could stay there for a week or so. He said it would be
OK with him—we'd Windsurf and fish . . ."

"Then you wouldn't have seen your dad."

"No, I s'pose not. And it was great. Great, talking to Dad. He told
us about how maybe he's going to start Patchwork up again and how,
from now on, he won't be so . . ." Distant. Unfriendly. Mysterious. All
these words applied but none, Rosemary guessed, would bridge the gap

between truth and disloyalty. "We'll go out together more and everything."

"Did he tell you about Angela?"

"What about her?" Bobby asked, suddenly awkward, turning away from looking at his mother as they reached the front door.

"That, when he and I are divorced, he'll marry her."

"Yeah."

"And"—Had he told Phyl and Bobby about the pregnancy? Well, they'd know sooner or later—"that she's going to have a baby."

"Yeah," he said again, looking relieved. Obviously he had not been sure if Rosemary knew. Good on you, Daniel, she thought. You've faced up to something!

"So you'll be a half-brother. Just the right age for baby-sitting, too, and with loads of good references." They smiled at each other like friends. "Come on," she said. "Let's go and phone Lawrie on our brand-new phone and see if he meant it. Then, since you're such an independent world traveller, you can catch the train tomorrow. With luggage, this time!"

"And you, Mum," he said shyly. "Are you going to marry Patrick?"

Her quick laugh sounded forced—even she could hear that. "Good heaven's no! He's a friend, a very nice friend, that's all."

.   .   .

Lawrie was full of apologies. He should have tried harder to reach her last night, but he really had not guessed how worried she would be. He had thought of phoning Tom and Eve but could not remember their surname and Bobby had not been able to either—or that's what he had said.

"But I gave the little tiger hell. Surprised he wants to come back!"

"Perhaps because a little touch of hell is what he needs," she said.

"Hmm. Gwen says if we go ahead and do up my house we'll be throwing good money after bad," he said. "And who would argue with that lady? I believe you are in no immediate danger of eviction; you will be OK where you are for a bit, is that right? I've been thinking, we could sell that Darlinghurst dump and use the money towards somethin' better. What do ya say?"

"I don't know, Lawrie." She sighed. There'd be new plans, new compromises, and, worst of all, obligations. "I can't think. Too much has happened to me today and my brain's gone numb."

"No rush," he said. "Think about it. And ring me when you put my fishing companion on the train, huh, so I can be sure to meet him. Why don't you come, too? We've got some unfinished business to attend to, you and I."

She was furious. Until now there had been no mention of that embarrassing, somewhat drunken scene, and she had believed he would do what she had almost succeeded in doing—forget it ever happened. She felt herself go hot with anger and embarrassment.

"Lawrie, if you ever say another word on that subject, I promise I'll never speak to you again!"

"Just testin'," he said cheerfully. "I can see some other feller's moved faster than I did."

This made her even angrier. "That's not true, and the subject is closed. Permanently. OK? I mean, if we're going to be friends—deal with the house, have visits, all that—I want your guarantee that you won't . . . that you'll never again . . ."

"OK, OK, OK," he said, interrupting her angry spluttering. "I get the drift. Honest. From what you've said it is possible to work out that you're not a consenting adult." There was laughter in his voice and this added to her fury. He knew as well as she did how close she'd come.

.   .   .

She was tired through to her bones, but she'd promised she would ring Robert Talbot. Best to get it over with, she thought as she dialled his secret, private number.

He answered on the first ring and she guessed he was in the Porsche.

"Your boy, he's all right?"

"Yes, thank heaven."

"Where did he get to?"

"He went to Daniel's stepfather's place at MacMasters Beach. He's home now, and fine."

"Does Daniel know?"

"Yes."

"Good. Good. So that's all right then. I'm very glad of that." She was surprised by how concerned he sounded. "I'd like to talk to you," he said. "Can I pick you up in half an hour?"

"Oh no, please not, if you don't mind. It's been an incredible day and I didn't sleep last night . . ."

"Yes, of course. I understand that. But I won't take much of your time."

"But not tonight," she said firmly. There was a silence while she tried to think of something reassuring to add. Then she gave up because she was too tired to find appropriate words. Why should I reassure him, anyway? she asked in justification. Then she remembered her manners and prepared to thank him for the cheque, but there were no words for that either—certainly no words that would not sound humble, which she was not, or hypocritical, which she feared she might be. Of course he was feeling uncomfortable about the fact that she knew Angela was his daughter—not that his voice revealed any signs of discomfort. And of course he would want her allegiance. But he could wait. "Can we make it tomorrow morning? she asked. "I'd rather go straight to bed right now than even try to think."

He said he'd pick her up at ten, which was fine because by then Gwen would have taken Bobby to the station and not too many people would see her drive off in the Porsche.

She got up tiredly from the chair and turned to find Gwen standing in the archway from the stairwell holding two cups of tea.

"Was that who I think it was or am I hallucinatin'?" she asked. Rosemary's face did the answering. "You've had the lot of them today then, haven't you?" Rosemary's face pretended to be bewildered while she tried to work out how long Gwen had been standing there. Had she heard that revealing little exchange with Lawrie? The tea was still steaming—good.

"It's time you settled down, in my opinion," said Gwen. "You'll drop that cup. Here, give it to me and get yourself into bed. I'll follow you up." Of course you will, thought Rosemary. I can escape from my own head but not yours.

Washing her face revived a little corner of her brain. By the time she'd taken out her lenses and got into her pyjamas, Gwen had brought a plate of cheese toast upstairs as well as the cup of tea, steaming again from a short burst of microwaves. Gwen was expecting to run this conversation, Rosemary could see that, so she started first. "What did you mean exactly by 'settle down.' "

"I mean stop being a wrestling mat for all the world to have their sweaty fights on!" Rosemary had a quick vision of Lawrie's near seduction on Christmas Day and hoped her face was impassive. But Gwen was hardly looking at her—she was counting her fingers. "First it's Bobby fighting with his dad. Then it's Daniel fighting with Robert Talbot. Now it's Talbot himself. What does he want from you? And, what's more to the point, what do you want from him?"

The lie came so smoothly that Rosemary observed it in amazement as though it was a silver snake that slithered confidently from her toast-crumbed lips. "This morning, when I was desperate, I phoned him. He's been trying to buy Patchwork, so I thought he might have Daniel's home phone number. He did, and he gave it to me. And he asked me to phone him this afternoon, to let him know what happened about Bobby. He was very concerned," she added, and hoped that single pat of truth was enough to coat the whole lie.

Flicking her focus from one eye to the other in a way that made Rosemary think of police interrogation, Gwen stared at Rosemary's face. "And?"

"And what?"

"What do you want from him?"

The snake-lie's mate slithered out with equal ease: "I want him to put up the money so that I can make a film about William and Clarice Sandford," she said. But as soon as it emerged, it stopped looking like a lie.

"Hah! You've flipped! You've lost your marbles!" Gwen said, as though she'd won a bet.

"Yes, of course I have," Rosemary answered weakly. Yes, of course I have, she thought fearfully.

"Well, never mind about him. I'm interested in the one who really matters."

Oh, my God, thought Rosemary. Lawrie must have said something. He must believe—be hoping—that he and I . . . that . . . "He doesn't matter at all!" she said, shocked and furious.

"He certainly does, Rosemary Quilty. He's in love with you!"

Rosemary sat straight up, knocking the plate of toast crusts one way and the cup and saucer the other. "What did he say?" she demanded.

"Nothing, in so many words." Gwen had half stood up, too, also shocked. "Though he never stops talking about you. But I've seen him look at you." Then she got cross, too. "Damn it all, Rosemary. What are you playing at? I saw the pair of you together in the kitchen. I'm not blind!"

Oh, you mean Patrick! Rosemary nearly said. She pretended, instead, to choke on a crumb. The patting and sips of water helped them both settle down. "Sorry," said Rosemary. "I'm a bit—overwrought."

"I'll say! I admire that man's persistence. Ten thousand others would have been knocked back by the sheer dramatic content of your life in these past months. What I want to know is how you feel about his kid?"

Rosemary gazed tiredly at Gwen. We've fought before, she thought. You mustn't come too close. Then, What the hell, she thought. She's not just stickybeaking—she's on my side.

"You haven't thought about it, have you? Typical, Rosemary! Typical!"

"What's there to think about?" she retorted, wishing she didn't sound angry. "What's the big deal? I'm not in love with Patrick!"

"No?" Gwen dismissed that. "Patrick's life revolves around Geoff. That won't change."

"Why should it? Mine revolves around Phyl and Bobby."

"But Patrick likes Phyl and Bobby."

"Well, I like Geoff. I get on well with him. He responds to me."

Gwen smiled and nodded with satisfaction that carried with it an annoying hint of smugness. "What I've never been able to understand about you is the way you hone in on people like Daniel and Talbot, who you should be able to see a mile off. Ask yourself, what attracts you to those bastards?" Rosemary blinked. "Money? You can earn your own. You know how. You're smart enough. Power? You've seen how much that kind of power is worth when the money goes."

"But . . ." said Rosemary. However she was still not required to answer.

"Patrick now. He's got real power—the power of integrity. Oh, he may not be flash, he may not have style, I grant you that. But those are things that can be learned or bought—they're easy!"

I wish you hadn't said all that, thought Rosemary.

"Well?" demanded Gwen. "What is it with you?"

"I've always been like that," Rosemary said miserably. "You should know. I only know how to make the wrong choices."

"Now that's nonsense," said Gwen in the conciliatory voice of one who knows she's gone too far. "Look at your work. And the way you bring up the kids and run things . . ."

"I mean men."

"Well, granted. I think it is because you're too trusting—you believe everyone is going to turn out as decent as you are."

"Decent?"

"Decent." Gwen would not be budged. "It occurs to me that since Daniel was virtually the first bloke you ever met, your problem is simply lack of experience. I mean, most girls your age will have had half a dozen fairly serious love affairs and at least a handful of one-night stands, wouldn't they? I've read *Cosmopolitan!* But, far's I know, you're only one step away from total purity!"

"Gwen, I'm very tired . . ."

"Yes, I'm sorry. We all are; the kids both crashed while you were on the phone and my eyes are like wet sandbags. But I heard you make a date with that ruddy Talbot tomorrow and I just want to make sure you're thinking straight. He's only after your body, make no mistake!" No he's not! thought Rosemary. "Just ask yourself, before you go flirting around with heartless tycoons, what you really want." If Rosemary had any intention of doing that, Gwen didn't give her a chance. "I know what you want," she said, her face mottled with effort and concern. "Sweetness and kindness and someone who's not in competition with you. Think about that!"

"Yes, I will," said Rosemary sweetly and kindly. "Thanks, Gwen."

Satisfied, Gwen pushed down on her knees in order to raise her large bum from the armchair and left with the pile of plates and cups.

Twenty-One

Early next morning, Rosemary persuaded her hairdresser to squeeze her in for a quick trim and blow dry. "I've got to be back here by ten at the latest. Are you sure I'll be done?"

"If you're here within the half hour, yes," he said.

She was tempted to phone Robert Talbot and get him to pick her up there, three miles from the eyes of wakeful neighbours, but decided against imposing on familiarity for the sake of convenience. Besides, she thought, who knows who might be listening at his end of the line? Instead she imposed on Gwen, who still had flour on her apron—the legacy of a baking session from which Bobby and Lawrie would be the main beneficiaries.

"And how are you going to get back, may I ask?" Gwen asked, twiddling the knobs on the television.

"I'll walk," said Rosemary, who intended to take a cab and pay the fare in cash, and intended, also, not to have any more arguments with Gwen. "Are you sure it's all right for you to put Bobby on the train? I'll cancel the hair if you like . . ."

"No, no. Got to go home anyway . . . my plants. Nothing on this stupid box 'til February," she said and clicked it off.

"Not true. Lucy's program starts in about ten days. That'll be good."

"Not good, I shouldn't think. Just worth watching, as part of a fan club. We can check to see if her earrings are on straight and make notes of her mistakes. I'll be back, never fear, in good time."

"In good time for what?"

Gwen registered Rosemary's uncomprehending expression. "To stay with Phyl. While you go out with Patrick."

"Good grief, Gwen, Phyl's okay. She's spent evenings alone here often." Rosemary hoped she didn't sound ungracious but Gwen seemed to be looming too large again. "Its lovely of you, but Phyl really doesn't need baby-sitting."

"Maybe I do," said Gwen, grinning.

.   .   .

The girl who washed her hair and the boy who cut it were both too busy for small talk, so Rosemary was free to think about power.

Before meeting Robert Talbot, she had never questioned its attractiveness. Gwen was right—her instinctive choice of Daniel had been based on the early signs of it in his character.

Power had suggested safety, glamour, opportunity, and the possibility of vast freedom; and power, or rather its product, influence, had certainly had its excitements. Those ear-to-the-ground days were thrilling when Daniel knew what the news reports really meant. He knew, before anyone—except the people actually involved and his friends the journalists—who the suspect judges or magistrates or politicians were and what it was that they were suspected of and what the real names were of rich, shady characters the papers referred to as Prominent Racing Identities. The rest of the world had had to content itself with printed or spoken words bland enough to ensure against comprehensibility and writs.

But in the end, what had all Daniel's contacts and all his hard work achieved? Had it made him happy? Rosemary had actually asked him this once, when he was working around the clock again on some major launch and she and the children had visited him at the office with a chicken dinner and clean underwear.

"Happiness is irrelevant," he'd replied with his mouth full.

"Irrelevant to what?"

"Just irrelevant."

"Then what matters?"

"What do you mean what matters? You sound like someone on social security benefits, in search of a guru! This matters!" he'd said, waving a half-chewed drumstick around the office. "This, because of what it can buy for us. Do you think we'd be living where we're living if I was still on the *Herald?*"

But Daniel's kind of power was too limited to be safe, this she could see clearly now. He had put too much value on something that could—and had been—taken away from him. Now, she guessed, he would believe that it was even more important to insulate himself against it ever happening again.

Robert Talbot could afford to make terrible mistakes in the belief that he could buy himself out of their effects. In his business, people got hired for his wonderful new ventures and then fired when the ventures failed or ceased to interest him. But he would always attract new people and start new ventures, with a wealthy gambler's confidence that some of them would pay off. He did it with his love affairs, too, no doubt. Who had Angela's mother been? And how many women had there been between her and his current mistress in St Ives? And how long would this one last before, once again, he felt obliged to try and cover some huge pain or guilt with money? Rosemary shuddered with relief at the thought that she might have been flattered into being one of those women if she hadn't brought with her the absurd complication of being Daniel's wife.

That attraction, that flickering, flowering lust she had felt on the journey back from Lithgow and again on the night she'd seen "The Mount Victorians"—it had been reciprocated. Her instincts had been absolutely right. But Robert Talbot had controlled himself in the interests of enmity. And what had seemed like a mortal wound to her confidence was, she could see now, a fairly shallow dent—and a small price to pay for a lucky escape.

Her hair, trimmed a little and softly curled, gleamed under the polish of hot air. I look okay, Rosemary thought. And she set off to find a taxi.

.   .   .

"Phylly, how do you really feel about living in Darlinghurst?" Rosemary asked. They were in the yellow living room, peacefully together for the first time in weeks.

"Don't forget I'm the only one who hasn't seen it yet. But it doesn't sound exactly like a palace—Auntie Gwen and Bobby won't even talk about it."

"I never thought you wanted to live in a palace."

"In a way we already do," she said, waving her hand around to take in the tall, cool room and those beyond it. "It's what we're used to."

"Yes. We've been spoiled."

"I know. Millions of people live in huts."

"Or park benches," said Rosemary with a that's-my-girl expression.

"I think," Phyl said seriously, "that maybe going to Darlinghurst is our fate."

"Or our doom?"

"Well, if doom is what we've been going through for the past year, Mum, you must admit, it has its moments!"

Rosemary loved that.

.   .   .

"Oh, no! Guess who's here!" Phyl said looking out of the window at the throbbing Porsche.

"Yes, I know. He's picking me up for a cup of coffee."

"Mum! You mustn't get mixed up with him!"

"Don't worry, I won't. I'm perfectly safe now." And she was, because on the way back from the hairdressers Rosemary had realised that the loop of power and terror that held them all, Robert Talbot, Daniel, Angela, and herself, in the grip of its costly secret was a loop that couldn't last; it was inevitably going to be unravelled by nature: the baby would free them all.

And this was what she told Robert Talbot in the car. Unnecessarily, of course—he had already worked that out, as his grim nod showed. For him the repercussions were not over yet. Perhaps people were talking already. Certainly they would when Daniel married Angela, which, because of the slow progress of matters to do with legal settlement, might not even happen until after the baby was born.

Daniel and Angela would take their place in Sydney's business society and the gossip and the speculation and the leaks by some of those in the know would ripple through their world and inevitably settle on the truth. Actually, Rosemary realised, the truth would probably come from Angela herself because by then she would have little or nothing to lose, and she could hardly spend the rest of her life bearing and raising Robert Talbot's grandchildren in secret. But first there would be the pain Robert Talbot's wife would feel, and his embarrassment, and the dinner-table laughter. That would be hard for him to bear. He sighed and she realised there would be no point in telling him how wonderful babies are and how much he was going, in time, to enjoy it.

Rosemary had been searching her handbag, and she and Robert Talbot started talking at once, she about the Cab-Charge card, which she handed him with thanks, and he about her.

"I wanted to make sure you were all right," he said.

"Oh, yes. Yes, perfect, thank you. Good as new. Where are we going? There's a fairly nice coffee shop at Lindfield."

"You really want coffee? I thought we'd drive up north a bit where it's cool and quiet. Have a look at the water. I've been thinking about you a lot."

Oh, no! she thought. Not now. Not another rock!

"Well . . ." she said in a businesslike voice and glanced at her watch. "Perhaps not, if you don't mind. I'm expecting someone for lunch. If you just turn right at these next lights . . ."

The lights were red, which gave him an opportunity to look at her in a way which suggested that there was unfinished business to attend to. It was a look which, a few weeks ago, would have had her glistening inside and reaching into his lap. Instead, she hummed a little tune and examined her finger-nails as though they were what mattered. Bloody Gwen, she thought, how does she know so much?

"Do you know why I came out with you this morning?" she said. "Two things. One, I wanted to thank you for giving me that job, which I loved. I adored it! The other is business."

"Business?" he said in the voice of one who's had experience of blackmail.

"Yes," she said in the voice of one who has been pronounced decent. "When some of this"—she chopped the air to indicate divorce, take-overs, birth, marriage, scandal and humiliation—"has settled down. I want to . . . to produce a film." There, she thought, I've said it. It sounded OK. "I've got a terrific idea for it. Actually, it was your idea. I . . . I thought you might put up the money."

"An idea?" he smiled wryly, and she could see that, to him, she was a pushy woman who pretended to be a professional actress, who had worked briefly for one of his companies in a non-executive position and who had hot pants. "Just an idea? No script?"

"Not yet, no," she said with dignity. "But we're working on that, my . . . associate and I."

"You know, of course, that I don't really get mixed up in the film-making business at all." He did not have to be so polite. She knew that. "The most we usually do is partly finance outside producers to do things we've commissioned. 'The Mount Victorians' was . . . exceptional, for me."

"Of course. But," she said smoothly, bravely, to the man who was not used to hearing the word 'but' from more than a handful of top advisors, and certainly not from women, "I happen to know, from listening to you talk for a couple of hours on the way back from Lithgow, that you loved it." She said it lightly, teasingly, and not at all like a governess, so he could dismiss it if he liked. But she couldn't tell whether his silence meant dismissal. "The coffee shop's in the next block," she added.

"And you really want coffee?" he asked, still hopeful of a secluded country spot somewhere. Perhaps a little guest-house, his red lips seemed to say.

"Oh, yes, please. Coffee!" she said sincerely.

He stopped the car in a No Standing zone that happened to be in the shade, pulled up the hand brake and turned to grin at her. "So you want me to finance you in a film after how much? Three weeks' experience as a research assistant on a mini-series that was never made. You've got more cheek than a sackful of dingo pups."

"You must have thought quite highly of my skills, since you paid me an executive salary," she said coolly. But she grinned, too, and hoped he could read her thanks in her smile. "At least look at the script, please."

"Yes, OK, that's fair. Don't hold out much hope, Mrs. Q. However, if I think it's got a shred of merit, I'll give it to a good script editor to have a look at. But I'm warning you, both he and I will look at it from only one point of view: will it make a buck or not? That's what matters to me."

"Yes," she said demurely. "It's about William Sandford, the man who made the first steel." She could see, as they crossed the road with her arm in his hand, that his eyes were smiling.

"What is interesting about you," he said over coffee and two French pastries in the pink, navy, and white shop, "is why you're not angry."

"With you?"

"Yes. And Daniel."

"I was furious with Daniel. Furious! You can't imagine how awful it has been for most of the year!"

"You didn't show it."

Hah, she thought. You're used to women who make big, ugly scenes! "I told you—I'm an actor," she said. "But I felt it," she said with lowered lashes, like a heroine. Let him not imagine her flinging crystal vases or whining into the phone at three A.M. or wrestling with half-slammed doors.

"You would have had a right to be angry with me when you learned that I'd indirectly caused you to lose your house."

Is this the way you apologise for the pain you cause people? she wondered. But she continued to play his way—more or less: "I was more mystified than angry. I couldn't work things out. Did you know, by the way, that I had met Angela? A year ago? Did you know that when you invited me to see 'The Mount Victorians'?"

"Didn't give it a thought," he said with his mouth full of éclair.

No? she thought. You're a good liar, too. You were checking to see how much I knew. No wonder you didn't make a real pass at me—you thought I might be Daniel's spy!

She was struck by the irony: now that he knew she had been innocent, indeed naive, he was eager to take up the offer she'd so clearly made on both previous occasions when they had been alone together. But the offer was now permanently withdrawn.

"The business of your house," he said. "That upset me. As I explained before, it wasn't my doing, but my hands were tied at the time."

"Yes, I suppose they were; if you were still trying to break Daniel, you could hardly give him back his house."

His heavy features with their tendency to submit to gravitational pull made him look naturally stern, but nevertheless she believed she could see a touch of shame in his face. "Anyway," he said, "what I want to tell you is that you don't have to worry now—I'll make bloody sure you don't have any more trouble from the liquidators." He wiped his mouth on the pink linen napkin and looked at her as though he expected more of a reaction than a blank, stunned stare.

Rosemary couldn't open her mouth because the first words pressing to get out, were "And no strings attached?" But she could not ask him that—it would suggest doubt.

As Daniel had said, Robert Talbot was not a bad bloke when you got to know him. First she would surprise him with her professionalism and with the quality of the script—maybe Debby would be interested in working on it, too? And after that, Rosemary thought, smiling gratefully at Robert Talbot over the remains of their cakes, I will simply make sure my business dealings with you are businesslike, friendly, and stringless.

.   .   .

"What will you wear?" Phyl was curled up on the double bed watching Rosemary do her face. Patrick would arrive in half an hour.

"My red dress. I have to try and get my money's worth!"

"Thought so. But he'll just see it as grey. Isn't it sad? Imagine being colour-blind!"

"But if you didn't know . . ."

"Wouldn't it be marvellous to be the person who invents special glasses to cure colour-blindness? Wouldn't you love to be with someone who sees colour for the first time? What a trip! Wow, what a trip!"

"That's something you could do."

"Yeah? And also be a brain surgeon and a musician and a gourmet cook and kind to animals. And a ballet dancer. Why not?"

"You left out prime minister. And portraitist."

"Right. Yeah, OK. I'll do that too, and have seventeen children and a spotless house."

"Doesn't everybody?"

"Only if they're females."

"You'll be OK," said Rosemary, smiling at her child in the mirror. "Whatever you choose, you'll be OK."

"Can I have it in writing?"

"Sure," said Rosemary, selecting a dark green eye pencil. Phyl giggled and squirmed because it tickled as Rosemary wrote on her thigh: "This person is authorised to do whatever she chooses because she is OK."

"It'll wash off."

"Never. I've burned it through to the marrow."

"Then I'll get cancer."

"Then, my darling daughter, you'll find the cure," said Rosemary, and kissed Phyl on her forehead, like a blessing.

Contentedly, Phyl lay back on the bed, idly tapping the words on her leg. Rosemary, carefully applying mascara, glanced at her from time to time.

"You going to marry Patrick?" Phyl asked, perhaps too casually, but it made Rosemary smudge her mascara.

"Not you, too!" she said. "That's what Bobby thinks. And Gwen!"

"Well?"

"Well what? Listen, darling, I hardly know him. And I'm still married to your father and . . ."

"Dad's going to marry Angela. And Patrick's mad about you," Phyl interrupted, not impressed by the outrage. Rosemary decided to change the subject.

"You haven't told me how you and Daniel got on yesterday."

"OK. Not at first—I was still . . . mad, upset, and he was, too, for different reasons. But we talked about it a whole lot. When Dad hurt me, I guess it was like when Geoffy was lashing out in the bus. He didn't mean to hit us. But he's felt really bad about that, and about Bobby needing him. Do you know what he said? That he'd been ashamed. Because of Angela's baby. Isn't that silly?"

"Ashamed?"

"I mean, of telling us—Bobby and me. As though it meant he couldn't be ours anymore—that we'd reject him, or something. I'm really sorry we were so horrible to him."

"But he . . ." Rosemary began hotly, then thought about it. "Yes," she said more calmly, remembering that she had shed tears of pity for him. "I know what you mean. I felt it, too. It's just been such a terrible time for everybody. Everybody!"

"And now, suddenly, everybody's happy," said Phyl. "Especially you. And you still haven't told me about Patrick."

But Patrick was confined to a small, shining place in Rosemary's head, the rest of which was still taken up by more vivid, though less worthy, men. She was not ready to talk about Patrick, and she told Phyl this with her chin, her shoulder, her wrist. Phyl grinned. You think I'm this happy because of Patrick, don't you? Rosemary thought. But it's because, to save your father's face, my new friend Robert Talbot is going to buy Patchwork. And then the liquidators will simply melt away like evil spirits.

But she wouldn't say it yet—not until she had it in writing.

.   .   .

Rosemary was expecting the golden bus and so was surprised when a taxi pulled up. It waited as a new Patrick came up the drive: Patrick transformed. Patrick sartorial. Patrick in a casual, well-cut, cream, cotton jacket suit and new light tan shoes and a snappy haircut. Phyl and Rosemary, still upstairs, gaped at him and then at each other.

"Wow!" said Phyl. Downstairs, Gwen was loudly saying much the same. "Like it?" Rosemary heard him say as she came down the stairs. "I put myself in the hands of a certain Gwynneth at Fletcher Jones."

When he directed the driver to the Regent Hotel, Rosemary smiled. Private joke. She felt extraordinarily shy with him.

"This job," he said, one knee crossed over the other, his elbows up behind him in the corner of the cab. He cleared his throat. "I'm serious. I was going to have the house done up, anyway, but there was no point before Geoff was house-trained. I'd love some more air and light. Like your house—the feeling of your house. If you hire the people and choose things, plan things, I'd give you a fee. Seriously."

"Well, if you think . . ." she said in a bubble of pleased surprise. She'd always thought she was good at decorating, but no one apart from Lucy had ever said anything about her house before. "But I wouldn't take money for it; it would be fun."

"No money, no job."

"Oh, I see." She laughed.

"Now that I've decided to do it, I wouldn't want to wait much longer. It's oppressive—it's always been—but I didn't mind before because, you know, it was just where I slept and ate and where Geoff came for weekends. Now I'd like it to be home."

Rosemary sat pressed in the far corner of the cab. She stroked the silk of her beautiful red dress and, like Phyl, wished Patrick could see its full glory. She did not know what to say. Fifty per cent of what she said was bullshit, he'd told her, but which fifty per cent? It made conversation very difficult and they'd already used up the main topic. She cleared her throat and said she believed Lucy knew a good architect. He said that was good. She asked him whether he'd brought his script— she could read it at dinner—but he said no, with no apology.

At the hotel they got into the lift with about five other elegantly dressed couples, and when it stopped at the second floor where Kables was, like most of the others she stepped towards the door. But he stopped her and the lift took off again. Different restaurant, different floor.

They got out at the thirty-sixth floor, where, she assumed, there was a roof garden restaurant. And so she was utterly unprepared when he produced a key, unlocked a door, and led her into a suite with a view over the harbour with its fingers of headland resting bejewelled on the dark water and pointing north and east to the end of the world. And then he took her in his arms and kissed her and kissed her so that the view, and the flowers, and the small table set with silver and crystal and candles, and the silver-covered platters that undoubtedly concealed their dinner, and the ice bucket with champagne, all became part of the kiss, as did fear and doubt and confusion and courage and pain, which, having become part of it, were neutralised by it. There was even some passion in that kiss. In fact, there was everything in it except bullshit. Even Rosemary knew that.

"I brought you here as part of the job interview program," Patrick said as seriously as possible, "to test your suitability as an eventual house sharer."

The sensual Rosemary took over—the one whom Robert Talbot and then Lawrie had so easily aroused and so nearly let out of the cage of habit and morality. Now there were no bars. Brave, standing tall, she slipped the dress off her shoulders and let it slither-billow to the ground in a liquid-like mass. I can be surprising, too, she said with her eyes. And she loved his response.

.   .   .

They were drinking champagne, her head on his stomach, his knees arched. His long fingers made gentle curls in her hair.

"What time is it?" she asked, almost too langorous to speak.

"Time has stopped."

"That's how it feels. But I suppose we'd better keep half an eye on my watch or we'll be here all night."

"That's the whole idea. I wish we could be here all week—all ever." She looked at him, surprised. She'd had never seen him so light—almost frivolous. "Martha could only manage the one night with Geoff, so we'll have to make the best of it."

"But I can't stay all night!"

"If the reasons are technical, I've solved them. It won't come as any surprise to Gwen if you're not tucked into your little narrow bed before midnight, and I doubt if Phyl will think you've run away to Lawrie's."

Gwen and he set this up! she thought. She opened her mouth to speak, perhaps to protest.

"Uh uh," Patrick said, touching her lips. He gently transferred her head off his body onto a pillow and walked across the room, opened a cupboard, and produced a white cotton one-piece jump suit on a hanger, a small lingerie box which, it transpired, contained a tissue-wrapped pair of white, lace-trimmed panties, and a plastic shopping bag with cold cream, tissues, talcum power, two toothbrushes, paste, and soap. "I discovered after I bought the chemist gear that the hotel supplies much of this anyway," he said, proud of the surprise, spreading the articles around her on the bed. "I hope the clothes fit—the woman who helped me was about the same size as you."

He was so serious that Rosemary, who had watched the whole per-formance with her knees up under her chin, laughed at him. "I've been kidnapped!"

"Yup," he said. "Kidnapped. It was the only way I could make sure of your undivided attention."

"Oh, wow, you've certainly got that!" she said, watching his hand move slowly, seriously along her body as though he were committing her skin to print.

She said she'd left her glasses at home and had no solution for her lenses.

"Then I'll lick them clean," he said.

"Then I'll go blind,"

"Then I'll lead you."

"That's OK then."

There was renewed delight in every touch and with every kiss. With-out words she willed him to know how silly she'd been, avoiding him, delaying this, yet at the same time she knew it could not have been sooner. At times, during that long, wonderful night, they were peace-ful together, and then wild in ways that broke new frontiers for Rose-mary.

·   ·   ·

They had arranged themselves in a comfortable disposition of limbs and hollows. Patrick gently stroked her skin, which made her feel safe and as though she was valuable. He told her about the lonely years with Geoff as an infant and a small child, about the narrowness of his life, and his deep grief and bitterness that his own young manhood should so be thwarted.

"Was there no one? In all those years?" she asked.

"What do you think?" He laughed. "That I've been a monk?" Then, more seriously, "But there was no one really important. Twice, I thought . . . but nothing developed."

In the short silence that followed she speculated about the two women he'd hoped to love. Perhaps they'd not been able to bear Geoff. Fools, she thought. What a man you lost!

Holding her more tightly, he told her about Geoff's terrible illnesses, especially the one in the winter when he was seven when a cold became bronchitis and then pneumonia and no antibiotics helped. He'd nursed him and nursed him, first at home and then in hospital among the sensible, hard-eyed nurses who'd looked curiously at this sleepless, unshaven man trying so hard to save a child everyone else could see would be better off dead. "Once, very late at night, he did die—they thought he'd died—and then he breathed again. I cried when he breathed."

He told her about Martha, his be-wigged aunt, arriving from Melbourne on a holiday two years ago and, he said, "starting to run a strip of colour through my life." Martha had made him go out, first for a night, then a week; he'd gone fishing with two work mates. But during that week Geoff had had three violent rages and then been ill again and both Martha and Patrick had realised it was too much, too soon.

"Boxing Day in the bus, that was the first really bad tantrum Geoff has had for a year. He was overtired, of course. But it was my fault, too. I'd been easing off on the tranquillisers—I don't like dosing him. It's just such a good thing that you were there. I kept thinking about what I'd have done if I'd been alone with him on the freeway; he's perfectly capable of opening a door and jumping out.

"Aaah! He's just a lamb chop under that racket," said Rosemary.

"Yes, that's what Martha says. She calls him the barking bunny."

Martha had found the special school for Geoff and helped both him and Patrick through the hard first months of separation, when Geoff had fought and screamed at being left there. Then there had been slow, wonderful progress. First Geoff had fed himself. Then he'd dried himself after a shower, then dressed himself, then used the toilet. He'd got used to staying at the school for at least five and up to seven nights a week, fifty weeks a year. "It just happens to be close-down period now," Patrick said. "From Monday we're back to normal." He thought for a while, his hands under his head, his elbows up. "I felt so guilty when I could see all the things he could learn to do that I'd never been able to teach him myself. But then I realised that no matter what I did, he probably would not have learned much from me; it was mainly from watching the other kids. He loves it there now."

Rosemary could not easily conceive of the depths of Patrick's loneliness in all those years. She leaned over him, this man she had so long ago filed away under "decent, dull widower." How wrong I am about people, she thought. It's so much better that he did the choosing.

She wanted to tell him that she thought his devotion to his son had developed parts of his personality that may have lain dormant otherwise. It had made him unlike Daniel, who had subverted love and loyalty into competitiveness, or Robert Talbot, who had perverted love and loyalty into guilt and secrecy. But it was too hard to say this without sounding patronising, or without mentioning names that were irrelevant here, or without revealing too much. So she kissed him instead, slowly and tenderly, as though time really wasn't important.

"I was always very rude to you," she said. "I'm sorry. I was afraid, confused. And you always looked so sure and . . . purposeful."

"I was," he said, and began to make it very clear that he accepted her apology.

But she had more to say and held his hands and punctuated talk with little kisses. "When Geoff had that tantrum on the Hawksbury Expressway, I saw, for the first time, that you are . . . can be . . . vulnerable. You were so controlled before, and I was trying so hard to be, so between us there was just too much control. Then when you yelled at me yesterday—about Bobby—I could see you were . . . real."

"I'm real," he said. "Feel."

"Patrick!" she said. "Hey!"

.   .   .

"I think I've been in love with you since you first came bouncing into Jeremy's speech class," Patrick said. "A married lady. Hopeless. But then suddenly you weren't married anymore." He smiled. "I suppose I was the only person at that party of yours who was glad to see Daniel go. And I suppose I did start closing in on you—I wanted to make sure no one else got to you first."

"I had no idea . . ."

"I know that now, though I showed you in every way I could. I did Big Daddy because of you. I heard you say to Jeremy when he was casting that you thought I'd be right for the part."

"You were wonderful. Wonderful! But I didn't know it had anything to do with me," Rosemary said. "You should have given me a sign. . . ."

"I did! Dozens! You ignored them. Sometimes I thought I could have killed Daniel for giving you such a bad time."

"What I don't know is why you want me, since I'm fifty per cent bullshit."

It made him laugh. "I love the bullshit!" he said. "Didn't I tell you? You feel so strongly about everything. Everything, for you, is so vivid." And he smiled and smiled like a colour-blind Cheshire cat.

Oh, no! she thought, when it was much, much too late. Contraception! Damn! I've got no talent for promiscuity! What if . . . ? But, no. She refused to believe that her complicated destiny had that particular card up its sleeve—it would go beyond farce if she and Angela were to push prams together. So she put the whole, horrifying thought right out of her mind.

They ate their dinner—pâté, lobster, prawns, and avocado—at three in the morning, when the edges of the thin-sliced bread had started to curl. And then they went to sleep, warm and safe, holding each other.

Rosemary woke at dawn and watched the light change from silver to salmon to blue. She looked at Patrick's strong, clean-lined face made innocent by sleep. He really is a person to love, she thought. She remembered what he'd said about the birds in his aviary: "All they want is regular meals, the illusion of freedom, and no predators. . . ."

She wondered what he was like as a husband. Was he one of those who walked around constantly armed with a screwdriver, fixing things the moment they loosened, or did he call a man in once the shelves had fallen? Did he get up early, vibrantly expecting orange juice and jogging, or did he prefer coffee and newspapers in bed? Would he enjoy sharing the bathroom, talking to her while she bathed, or would he prefer to lock himself in there with a book? There would be harder things to learn, too—this man, after all, had lived an eccentric, bachelor life-style for many years. But all that, and all the other things like favourite foods and music and books could be learned slowly, while she and the kids lived somewhere else.

Yes, she decided. I'll stay on the outside of his free, safe aviary for a while, until I'm sure that it's right for us all. It will give me time to work towards becoming a film producer. I won't rush it. I'll get a job in the industry first and learn everything I can about it. I'll get my own life into a shape first and never again be too ready to dissolve it—into Patrick's or anyone else's.

Patrick half rolled in his sleep—soon he'd wake up, too. Gently she touched his hair. I'll do everything, slowly and carefully. I'll learn. And I'll work and I'll be just me, fully me, in reality, and not an actor. Maybe, eventually, in Patrick's house full of dogs and ducks, I, Phyl, and Bobby and the yellow sofa and the portrait of Clarice will fit in in a way I can feel sure about.

When her fingers traced Patrick's lips, the tip of his tongue came out to meet them.

"Ah, yes," whispered Rosemary Quilty, gazing at the morning sky. "Doom has its moments."